BIRTHRIGHT

VOLUME TEN
EPILOGUE

IMAGE COMICS, INC.
Todd McFarlane: *President*
Jim Valentino: *Vice President*
Marc Silvestri: *Chief Executive Officer*
Erik Larsen: *Chief Financial Officer*
Robert Kirkman: *Chief Operating Officer*
Eric Stephenson: *Publisher / Chief Creative Officer*
Nicole Lapalme: *Controller*
Leanna Caunter: *Accounting Analyst*
Sue Korpela: *Accounting & HR Manager*
Marla Eizik: *Talent Liaison*
Jeff Boison: *Director of Sales & Publishing Planning*
Dirk Wood: *Director of International Sales & Licensing*
Alex Cox: *Director of Direct Market Sales*

Chloe Ramos: *Book Market & Library Sales Manager*
Emilio Bautista: *Digital Sales Coordinator*
Jon Schlaffman: *Specialty Sales Coordinator*
Kat Salazar: *Director of PR & Marketing*
Drew Fitzgerald: *Marketing Content Associate*
Heather Doornink: *Production Director*
Drew Gill: *Art Director*
Hilary DiLoreto: *Print Manager*
Tricia Ramos: *Traffic Manager*
Melissa Gifford: *Content Manager*
Erika Schnatz: *Senior Production Artist*
Ryan Brewer: *Production Artist*
Deanna Phelps: *Production Artist*

www.imagecomics.com

SKYBOUND

Robert Kirkman *Chairman*
David Alpert *CEO*
Sean Mackiewicz *SVP, Editor-in-Chief*
Shawn Kirkham *SVP, Business Development*
Brian Huntington *VP, Online Content*
Andres Juarez *Art Director*
Arune Singh *Director of Brand, Editorial*
Alex Antone *Senior Editor*
Jon Moisan *Editor*
Amanda LaFranco *Editor*
Carina Taylor *Graphic Designer*
Dan Petersen *Sr. Director, Operations & Events*

Foreign Rights & Licensing Inquiries: *contact@skybound.com*
SKYBOUND.COM

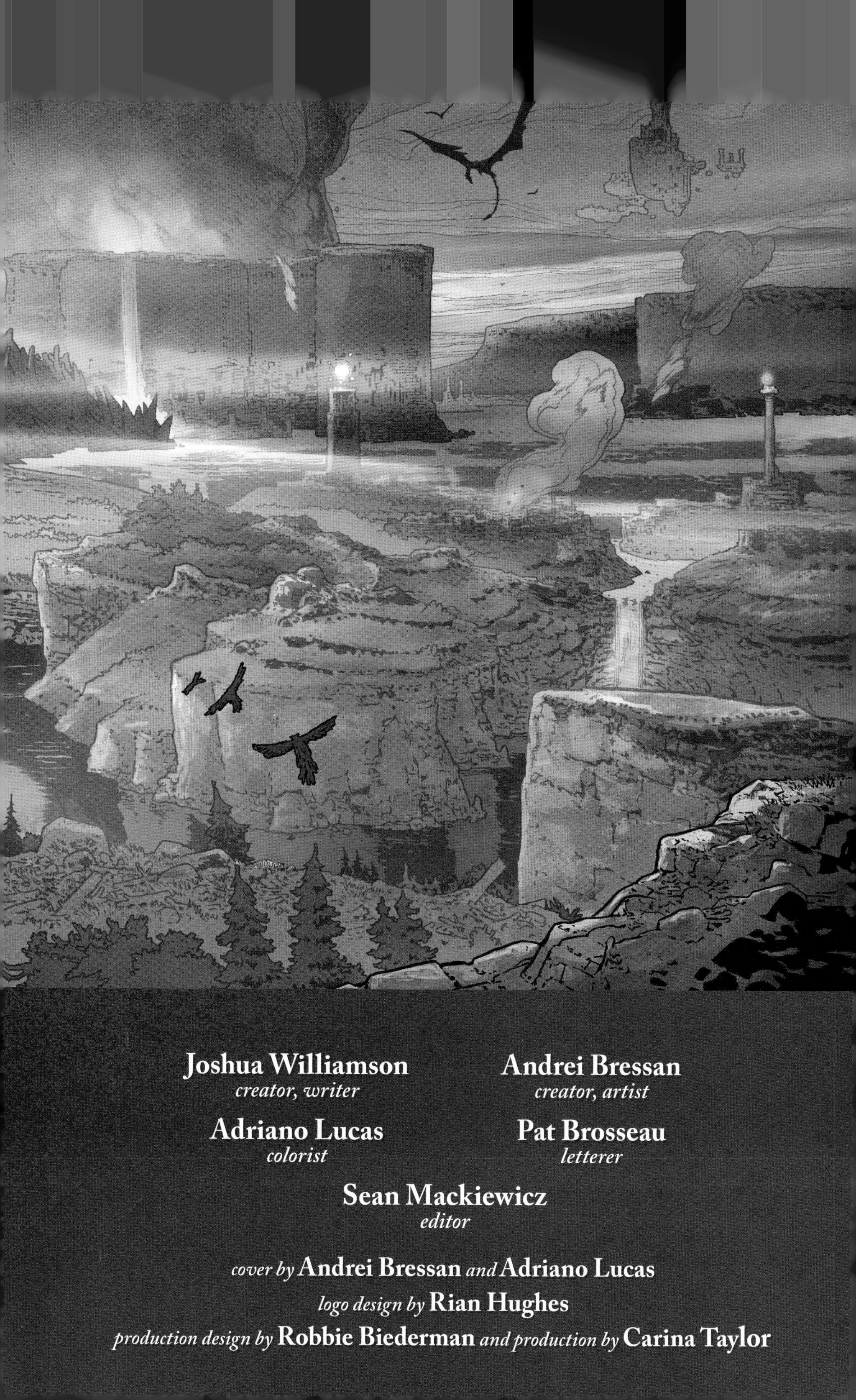

Joshua Williamson
creator, writer

Andrei Bressan
creator, artist

Adriano Lucas
colorist

Pat Brosseau
letterer

Sean Mackiewicz
editor

cover by **Andrei Bressan** *and* **Adriano Lucas**

logo design by **Rian Hughes**

production design by **Robbie Biederman** *and production by* **Carina Taylor**

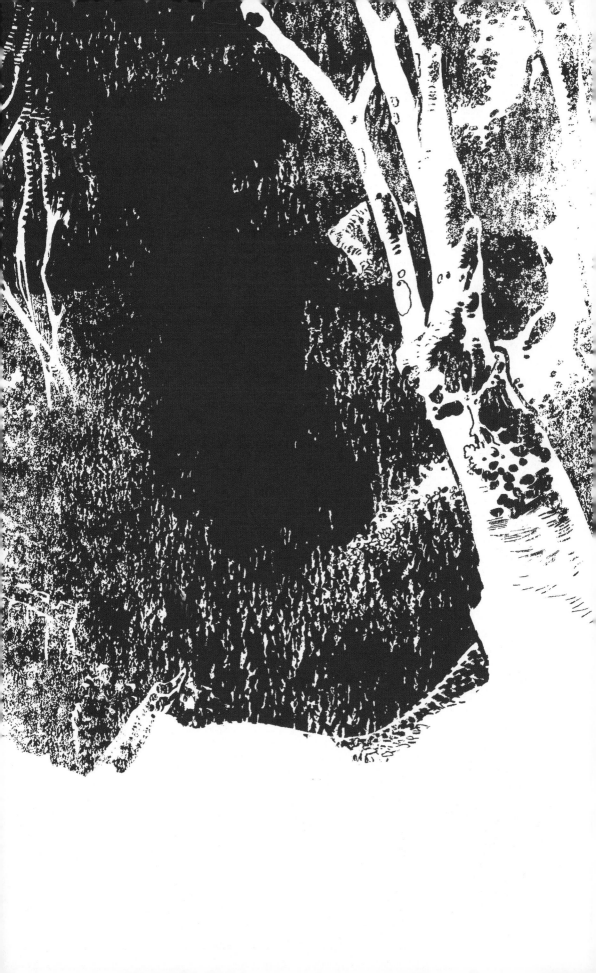

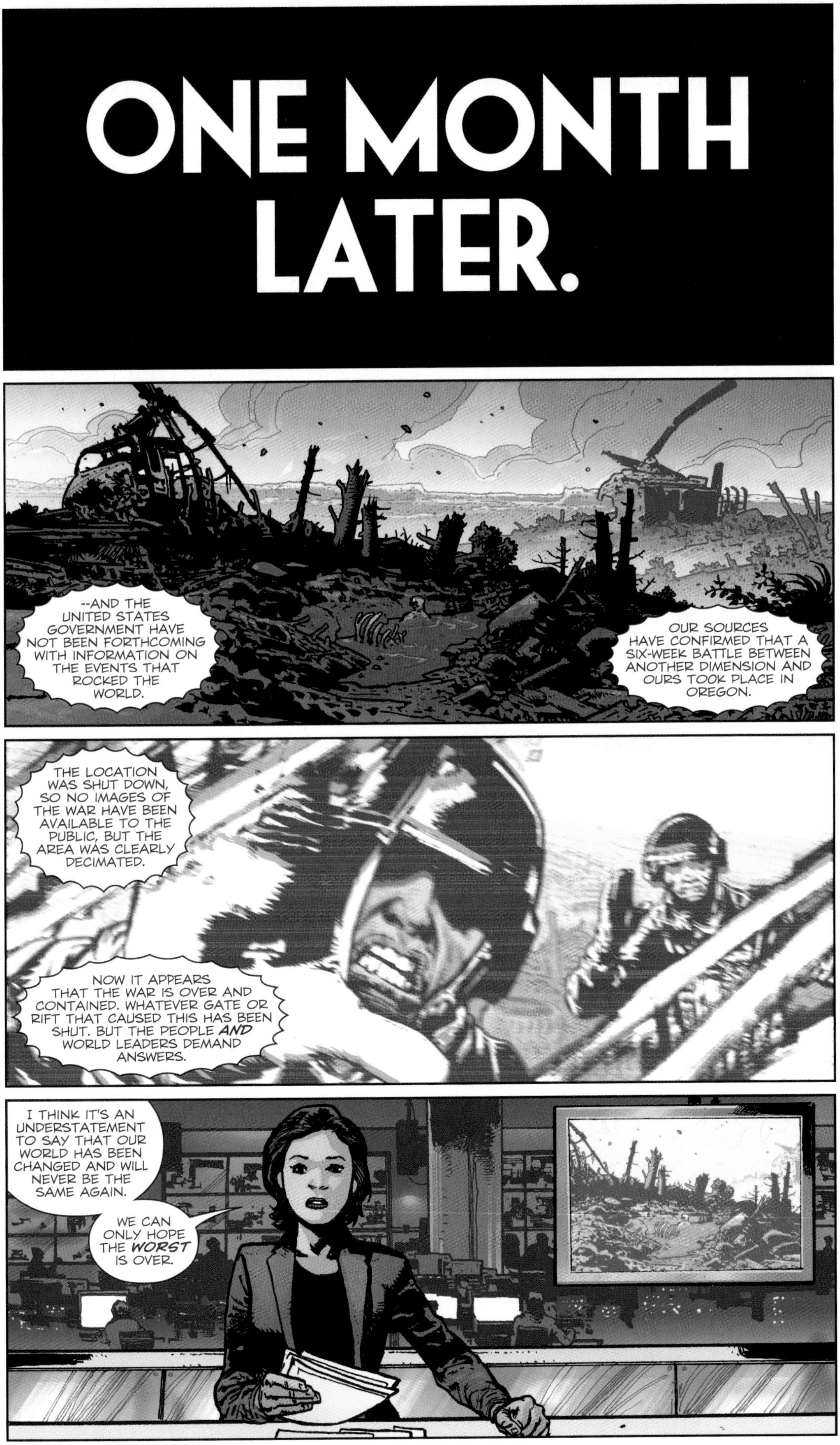
ONE MONTH LATER.
--AND THE UNITED STATES GOVERNMENT HAVE NOT BEEN FORTHCOMING WITH INFORMATION ON THE EVENTS THAT ROCKED THE WORLD.
OUR SOURCES HAVE CONFIRMED THAT A SIX-WEEK BATTLE BETWEEN ANOTHER DIMENSION AND OURS TOOK PLACE IN OREGON.
THE LOCATION WAS SHUT DOWN, SO NO IMAGES OF THE WAR HAVE BEEN AVAILABLE TO THE PUBLIC, BUT THE AREA WAS CLEARLY DECIMATED.
NOW IT APPEARS THAT THE WAR IS OVER AND CONTAINED. WHATEVER GATE OR RIFT THAT CAUSED THIS HAS BEEN SHUT. BUT THE PEOPLE ***AND*** WORLD LEADERS DEMAND ANSWERS.
I THINK IT'S AN UNDERSTATEMENT TO SAY THAT OUR WORLD HAS BEEN CHANGED AND WILL NEVER BE THE SAME AGAIN.
WE CAN ONLY HOPE THE ***WORST*** IS OVER.

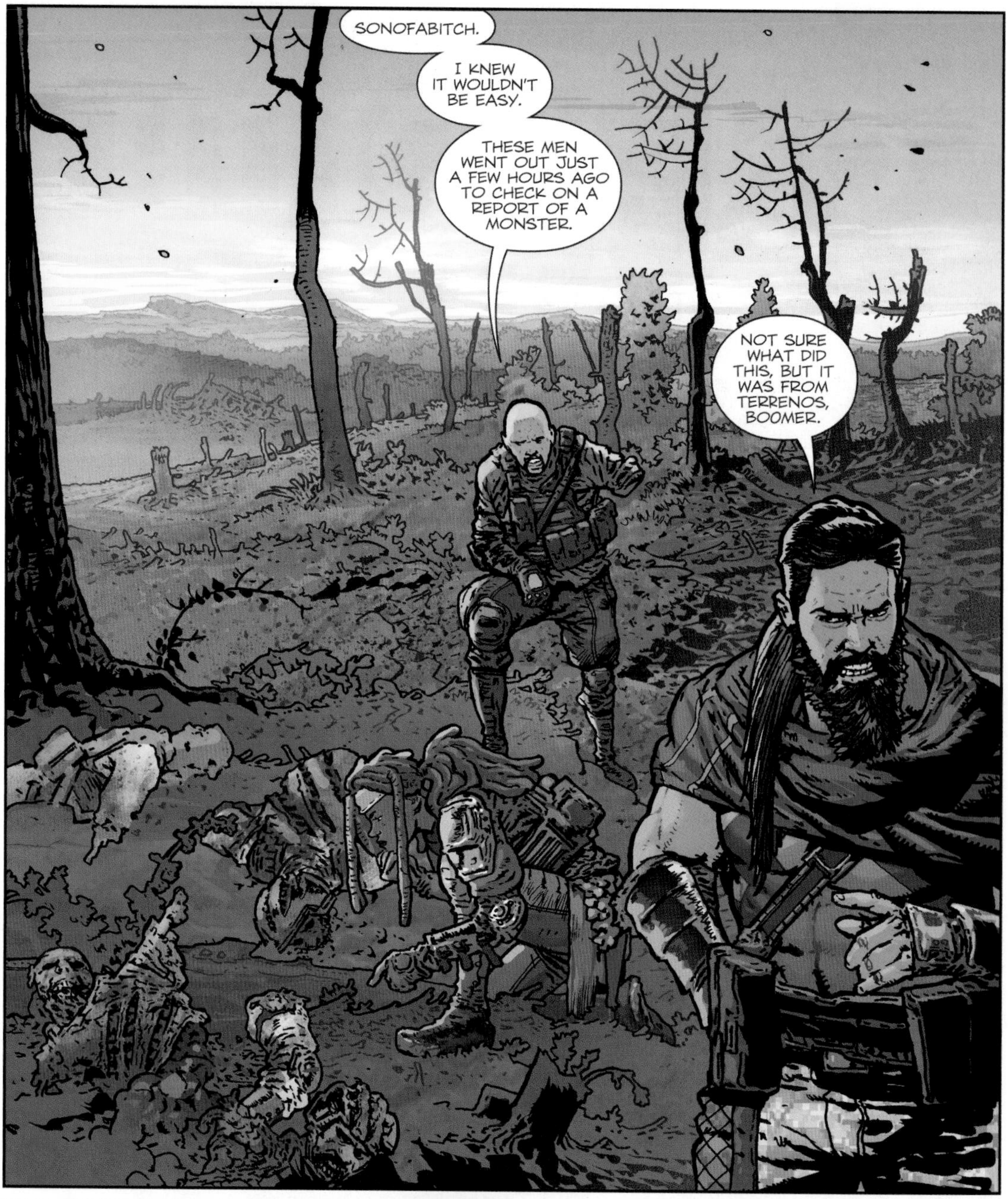
SONOFABITCH.
I KNEW IT WOULDN'T BE EASY.
THESE MEN WENT OUT JUST A FEW HOURS AGO TO CHECK ON A REPORT OF A MONSTER.
NOT SURE WHAT DID THIS, BUT IT WAS FROM TERRENOS, BOOMER.

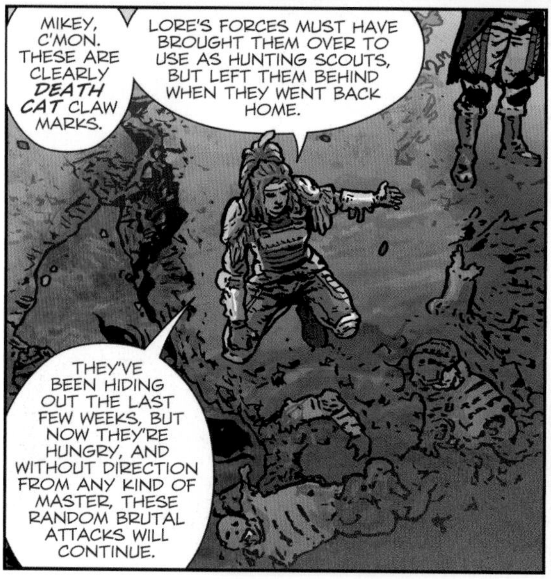
MIKEY, C'MON. THESE ARE CLEARLY ***DEATH CAT*** CLAW MARKS.
LORE'S FORCES MUST HAVE BROUGHT THEM OVER TO USE AS HUNTING SCOUTS, BUT LEFT THEM BEHIND WHEN THEY WENT BACK HOME.
THEY'VE BEEN HIDING OUT THE LAST FEW WEEKS, BUT NOW THEY'RE HUNGRY, AND WITHOUT DIRECTION FROM ANY KIND OF MASTER, THESE RANDOM BRUTAL ATTACKS WILL CONTINUE.

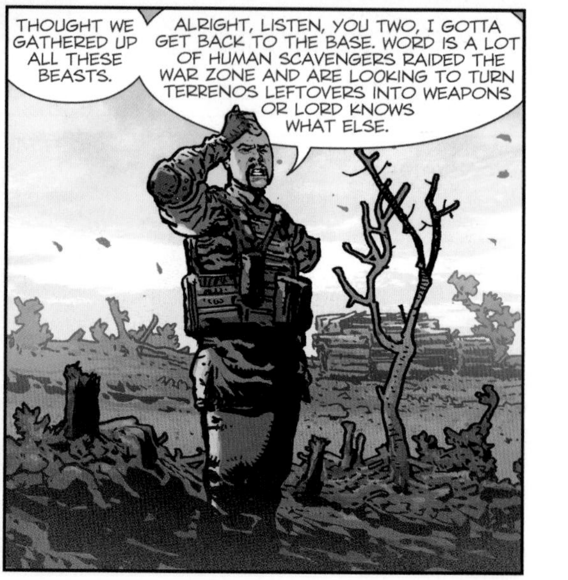
THOUGHT WE GATHERED UP ALL THESE BEASTS.
ALRIGHT, LISTEN, YOU TWO, I GOTTA GET BACK TO THE BASE. WORD IS A LOT OF HUMAN SCAVENGERS RAIDED THE WAR ZONE AND ARE LOOKING TO TURN TERRENOS LEFTOVERS INTO WEAPONS OR LORD KNOWS WHAT ELSE.

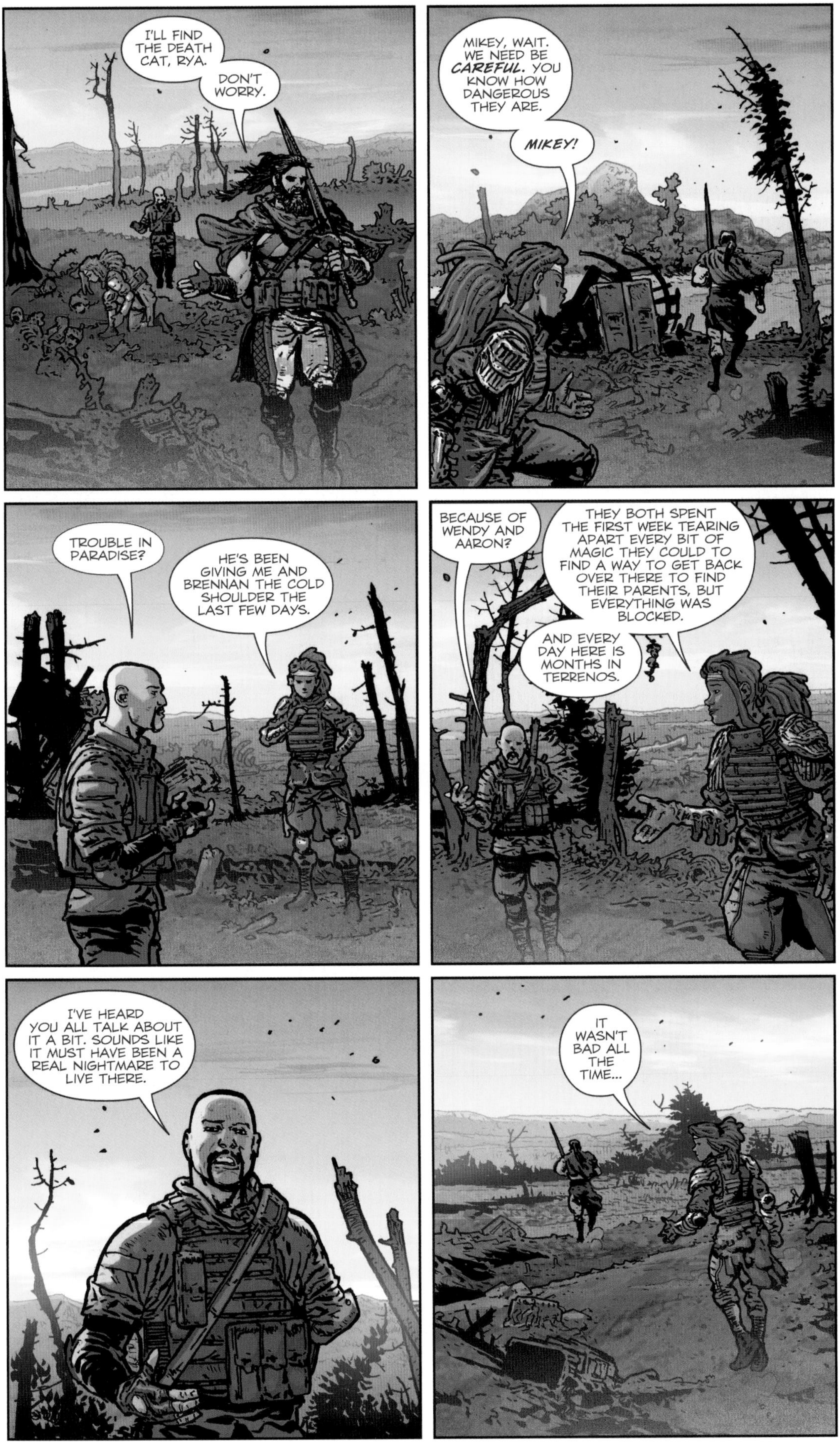
I'LL FIND THE DEATH CAT, RYA.
DON'T WORRY.
MIKEY, WAIT. WE NEED BE **CAREFUL.** YOU KNOW HOW DANGEROUS THEY ARE.
MIKEY!
TROUBLE IN PARADISE?
HE'S BEEN GIVING ME AND BRENNAN THE COLD SHOULDER THE LAST FEW DAYS.
BECAUSE OF WENDY AND AARON?
THEY BOTH SPENT THE FIRST WEEK TEARING APART EVERY BIT OF MAGIC THEY COULD TO FIND A WAY TO GET BACK OVER THERE TO FIND THEIR PARENTS, BUT EVERYTHING WAS BLOCKED.
AND EVERY DAY HERE IS MONTHS IN TERRENOS.
I'VE HEARD YOU ALL TALK ABOUT IT A BIT. SOUNDS LIKE IT MUST HAVE BEEN A REAL NIGHTMARE TO LIVE THERE.
IT WASN'T BAD ALL THE TIME...

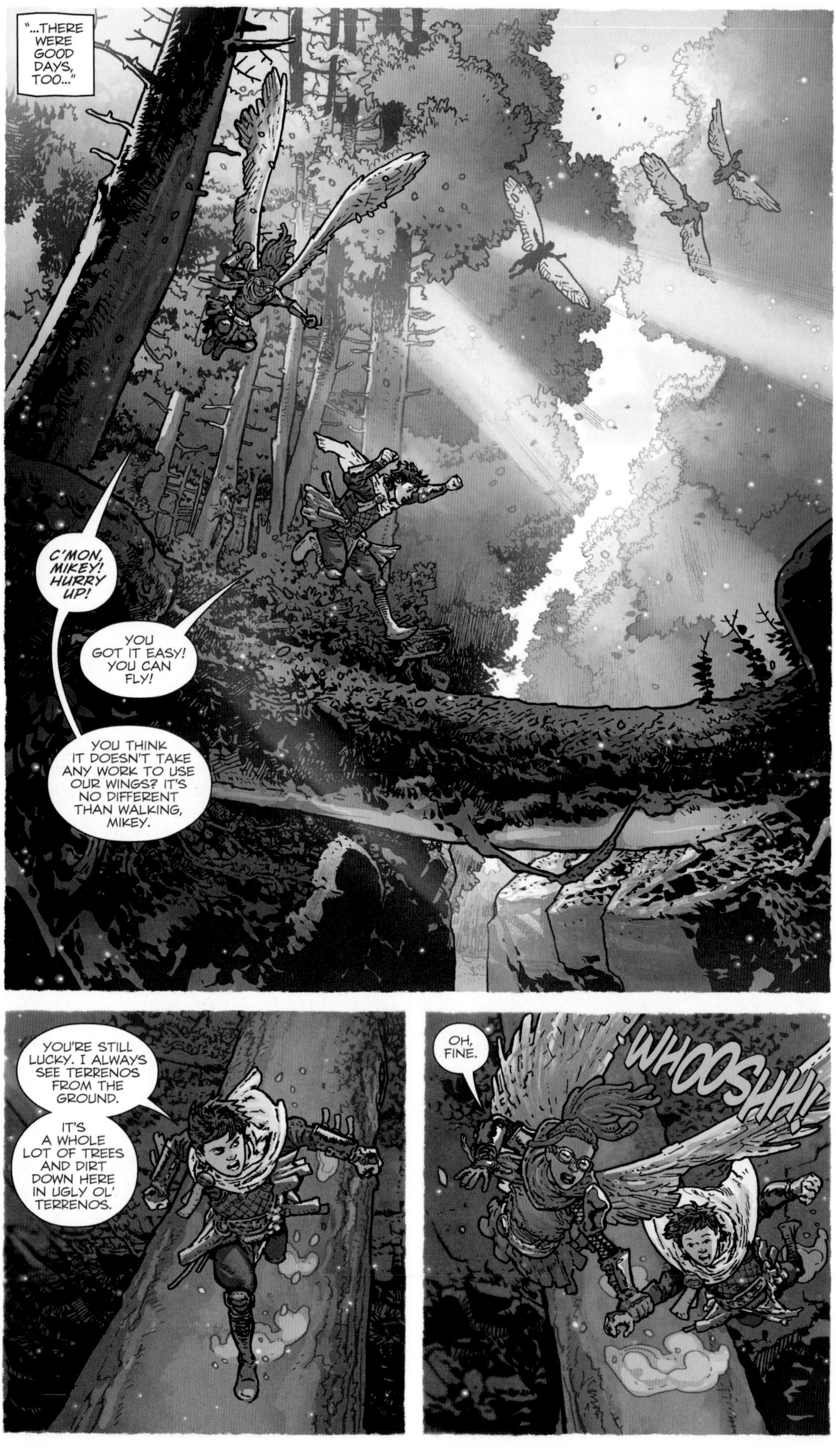
"...THERE WERE GOOD DAYS, TOO..."
C'MON, MIKEY! HURRY UP!
YOU GOT IT EASY! YOU CAN FLY!
YOU THINK IT DOESN'T TAKE ANY WORK TO USE OUR WINGS? IT'S NO DIFFERENT THAN WALKING, MIKEY.
YOU'RE STILL LUCKY. I ALWAYS SEE TERRENOS FROM THE GROUND.
IT'S A WHOLE LOT OF TREES AND DIRT DOWN HERE IN UGLY OL' TERRENOS.
OH, FINE.
WHOOSHH!

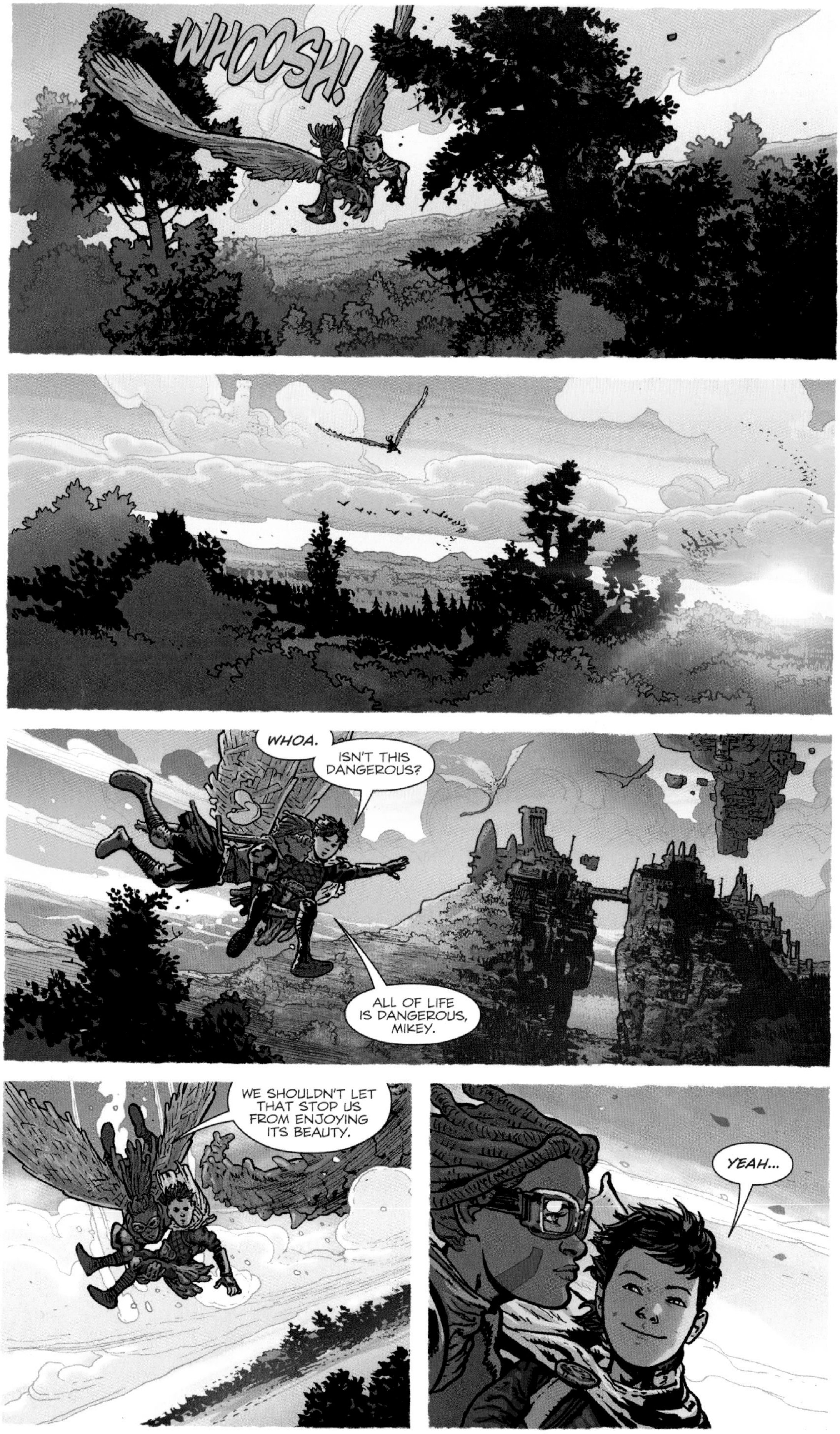
WHOOSH!
WHOA.
ISN'T THIS DANGEROUS?
ALL OF LIFE IS DANGEROUS, MIKEY.
WE SHOULDN'T LET THAT STOP US FROM ENJOYING ITS BEAUTY.
YEAH...

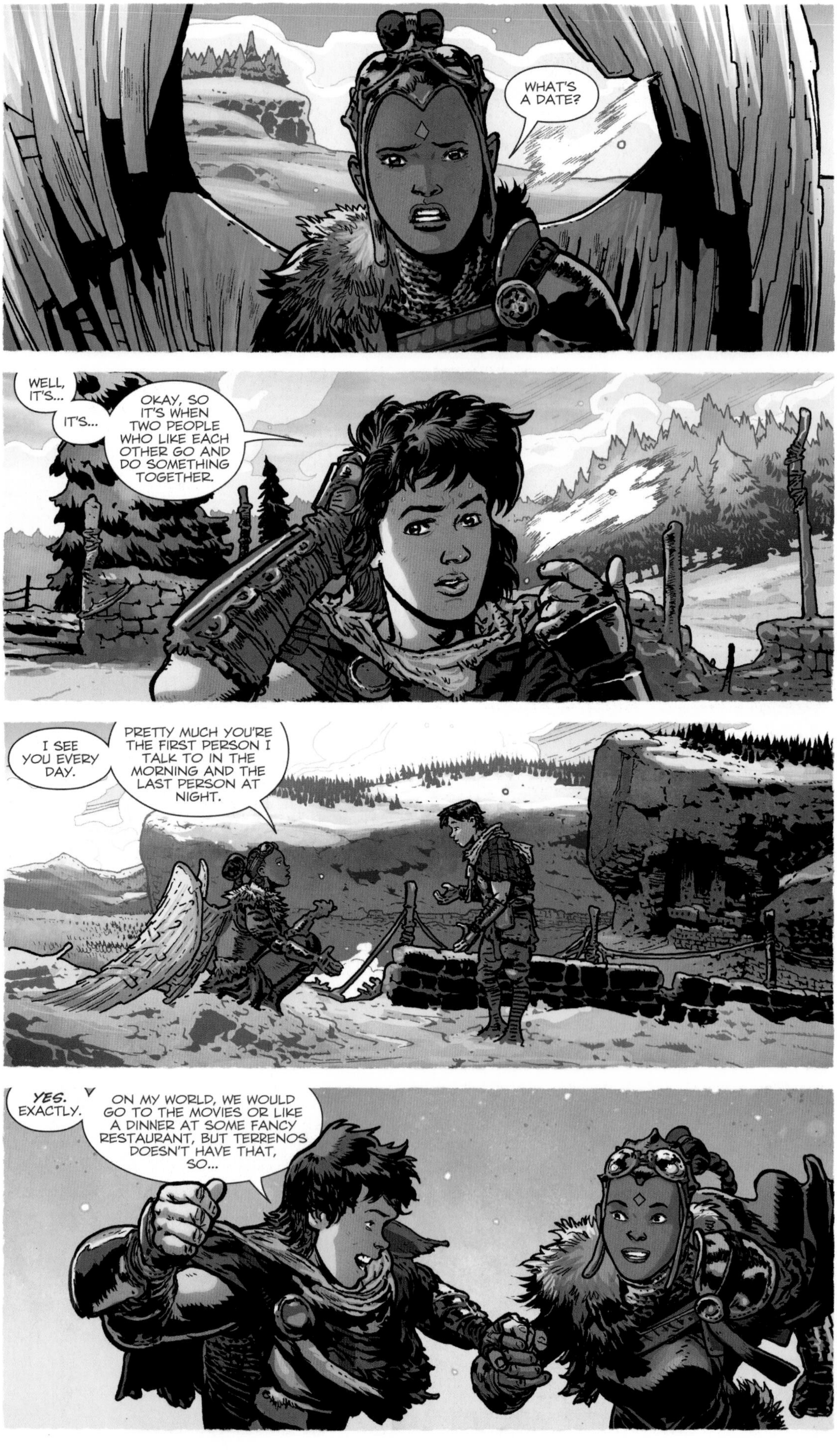
WHAT'S A DATE?
WELL, IT'S...
IT'S...
OKAY, SO IT'S WHEN TWO PEOPLE WHO LIKE EACH OTHER GO AND DO SOMETHING TOGETHER.
I SEE YOU EVERY DAY.
PRETTY MUCH YOU'RE THE FIRST PERSON I TALK TO IN THE MORNING AND THE LAST PERSON AT NIGHT.
YES. EXACTLY.
ON MY WORLD, WE WOULD GO TO THE MOVIES OR LIKE A DINNER AT SOME FANCY RESTAURANT, BUT TERRENOS DOESN'T HAVE THAT, SO...

...I MADE *THIS* INSTEAD.

YOU MADE THIS? *YOU?*

NOT EVERY MINUTE OF MY DAY IS SPENT LEARNING HOW TO KILL *LORE.*

NOT BAD.

SO...ARE YOU SAYING YOU WANT TO *COURT?*

YES. I THINK SO. YES. MAYBE.

MIKEY, WE DON'T REALLY HAVE TIME FOR THIS. YOU NEED TO TRAIN. YOU NEED TO BE READY FOR--

BUT I GOTTA LIVE, TOO. GOTTA KNOW WHAT I'M FIGHTING FOR.

WHAT ABOUT ZOSHANNA?

I KNOW THAT'S PART OF MY DESTINY, BUT...WE'LL ALWAYS BE FRIENDS, AND WE'RE NOT...Y'KNOW...WHAT I'M LOOKING FOR.

WHAT *ARE* YOU LOOKING FOR?

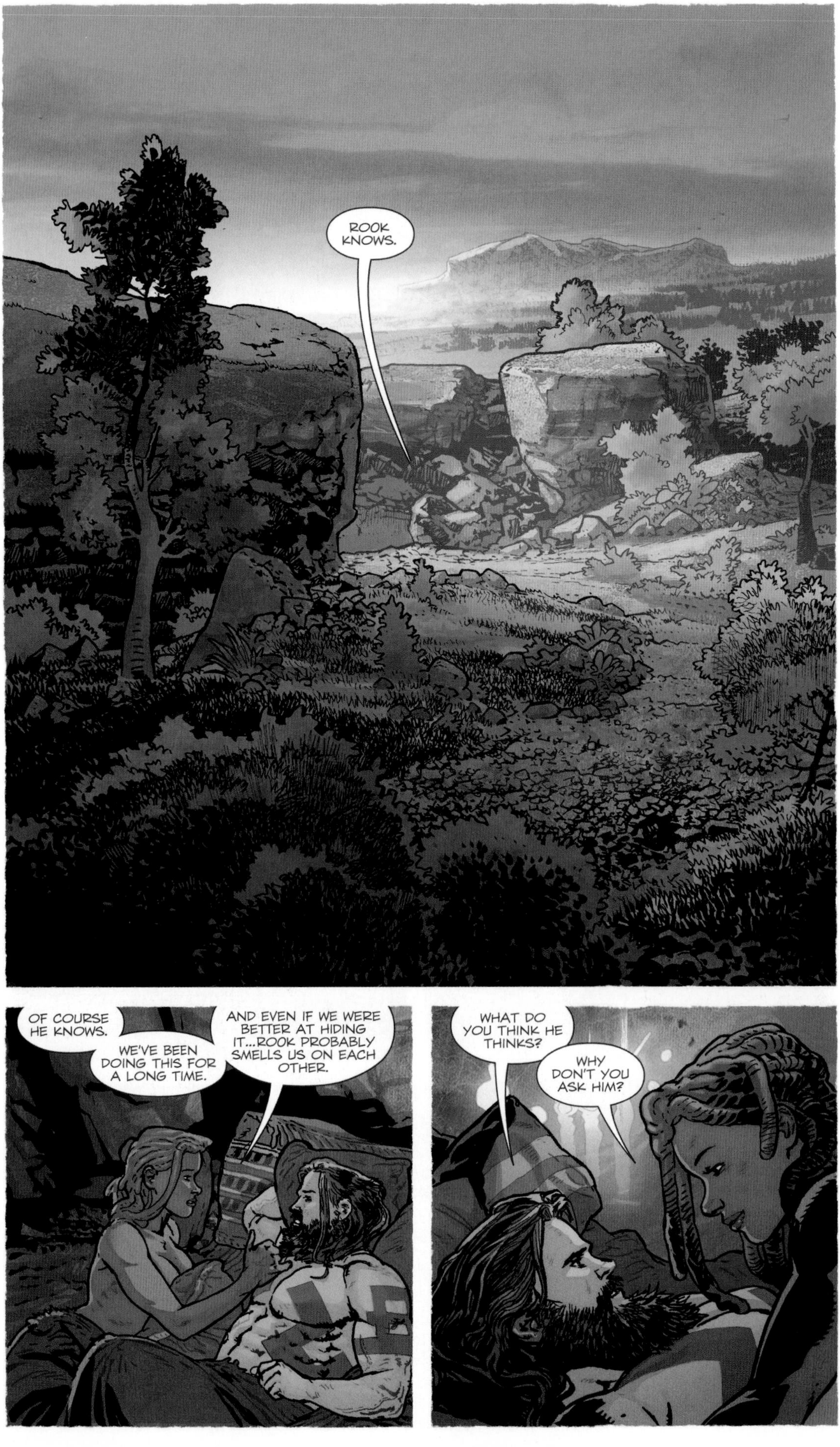
ROOK KNOWS.
OF COURSE HE KNOWS.
WE'VE BEEN DOING THIS FOR A LONG TIME.
AND EVEN IF WE WERE BETTER AT HIDING IT...ROOK PROBABLY SMELLS US ON EACH OTHER.
WHAT DO YOU THINK HE THINKS?
WHY DON'T YOU ASK HIM?

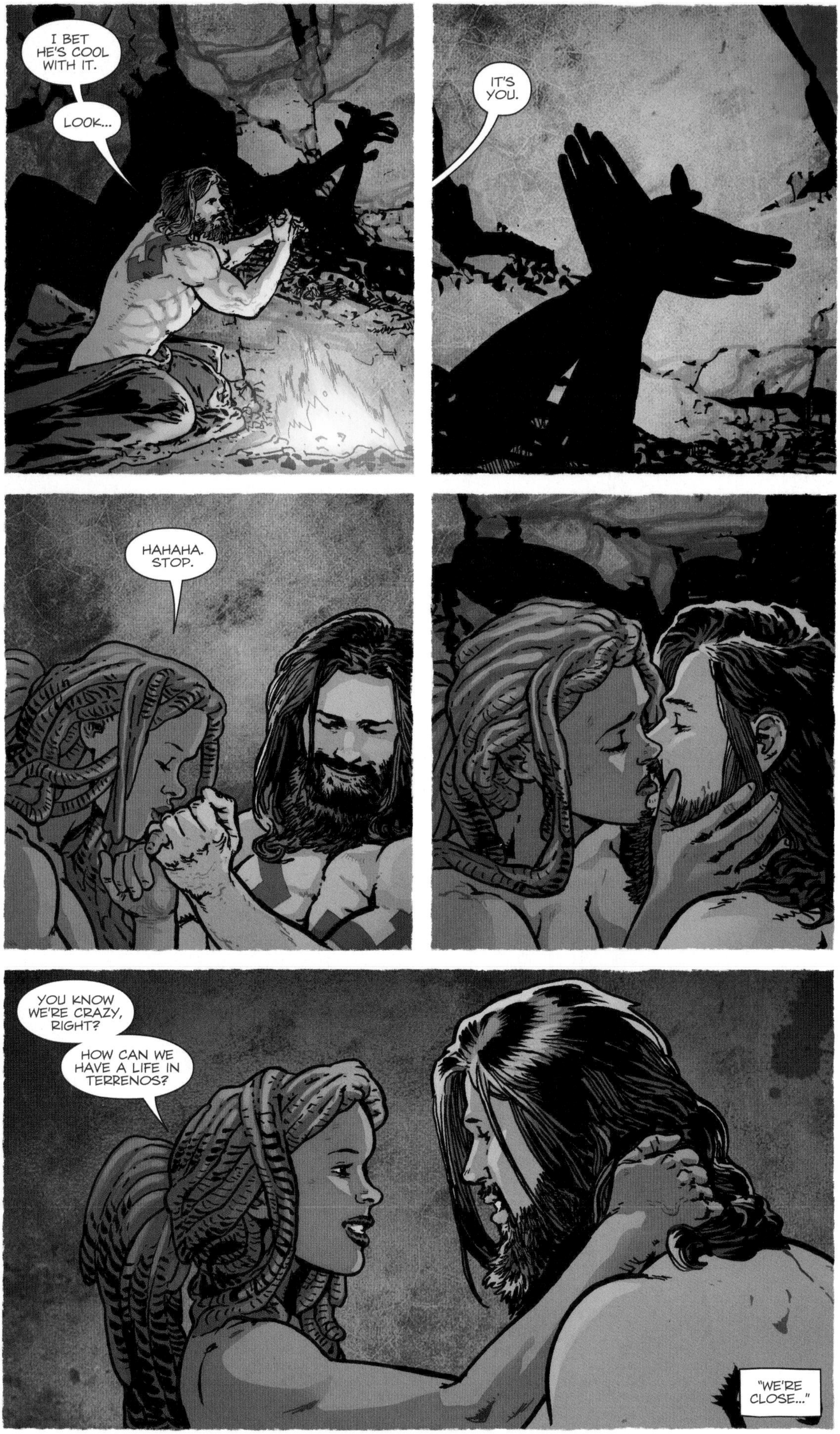
I BET HE'S COOL WITH IT.
LOOK...
IT'S YOU.
HAHAHA. STOP.
YOU KNOW WE'RE CRAZY, RIGHT?
HOW CAN WE HAVE A LIFE IN TERRENOS?
"WE'RE CLOSE..."

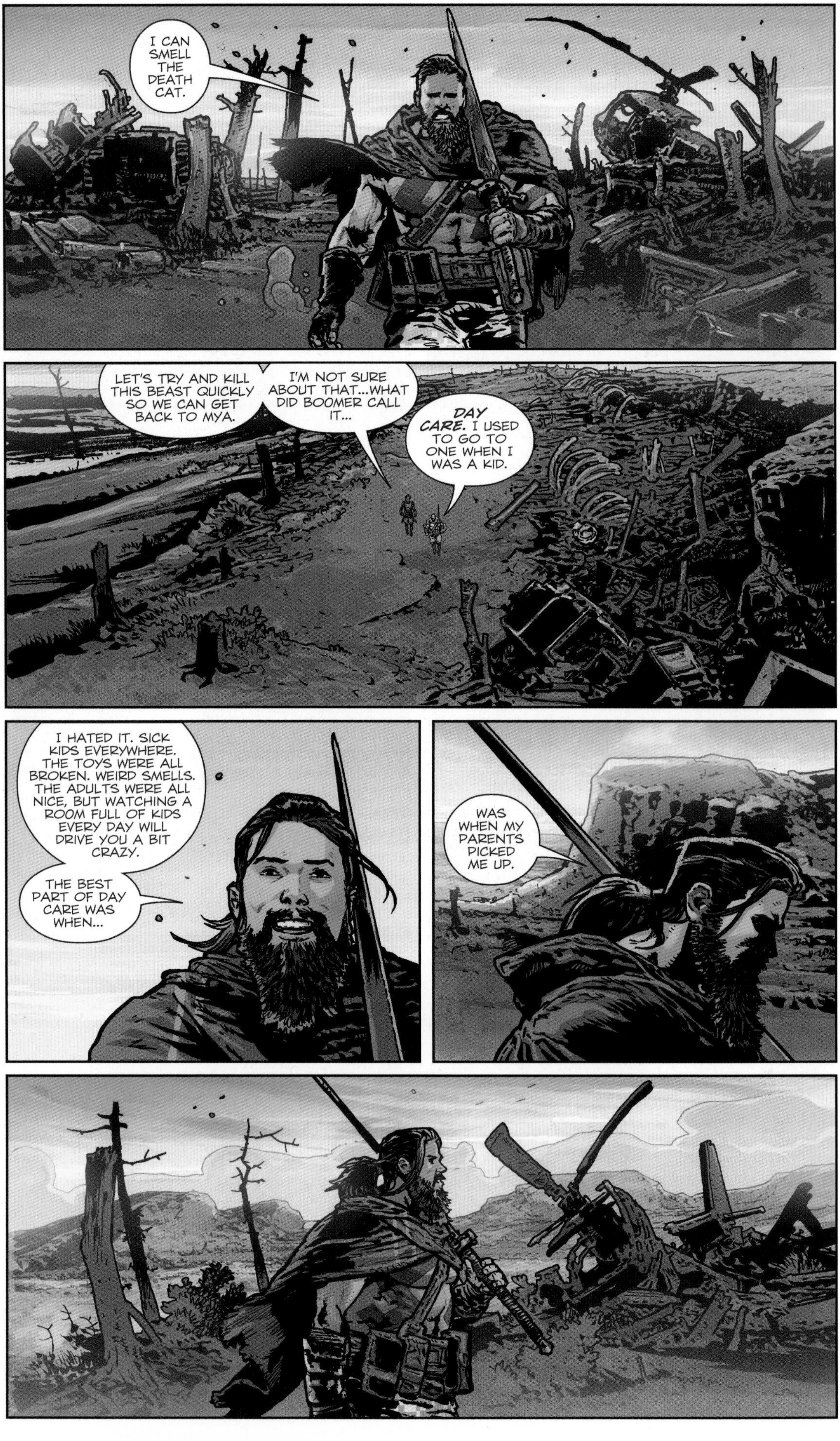
I CAN SMELL THE DEATH CAT.
LET'S TRY AND KILL THIS BEAST QUICKLY SO WE CAN GET BACK TO MYA.
I'M NOT SURE ABOUT THAT...WHAT DID BOOMER CALL IT...
DAY CARE. I USED TO GO TO ONE WHEN I WAS A KID.
I HATED IT. SICK KIDS EVERYWHERE. THE TOYS WERE ALL BROKEN. WEIRD SMELLS. THE ADULTS WERE ALL NICE, BUT WATCHING A ROOM FULL OF KIDS EVERY DAY WILL DRIVE YOU A BIT CRAZY.
THE BEST PART OF DAY CARE WAS WHEN...
WAS WHEN MY PARENTS PICKED ME UP.

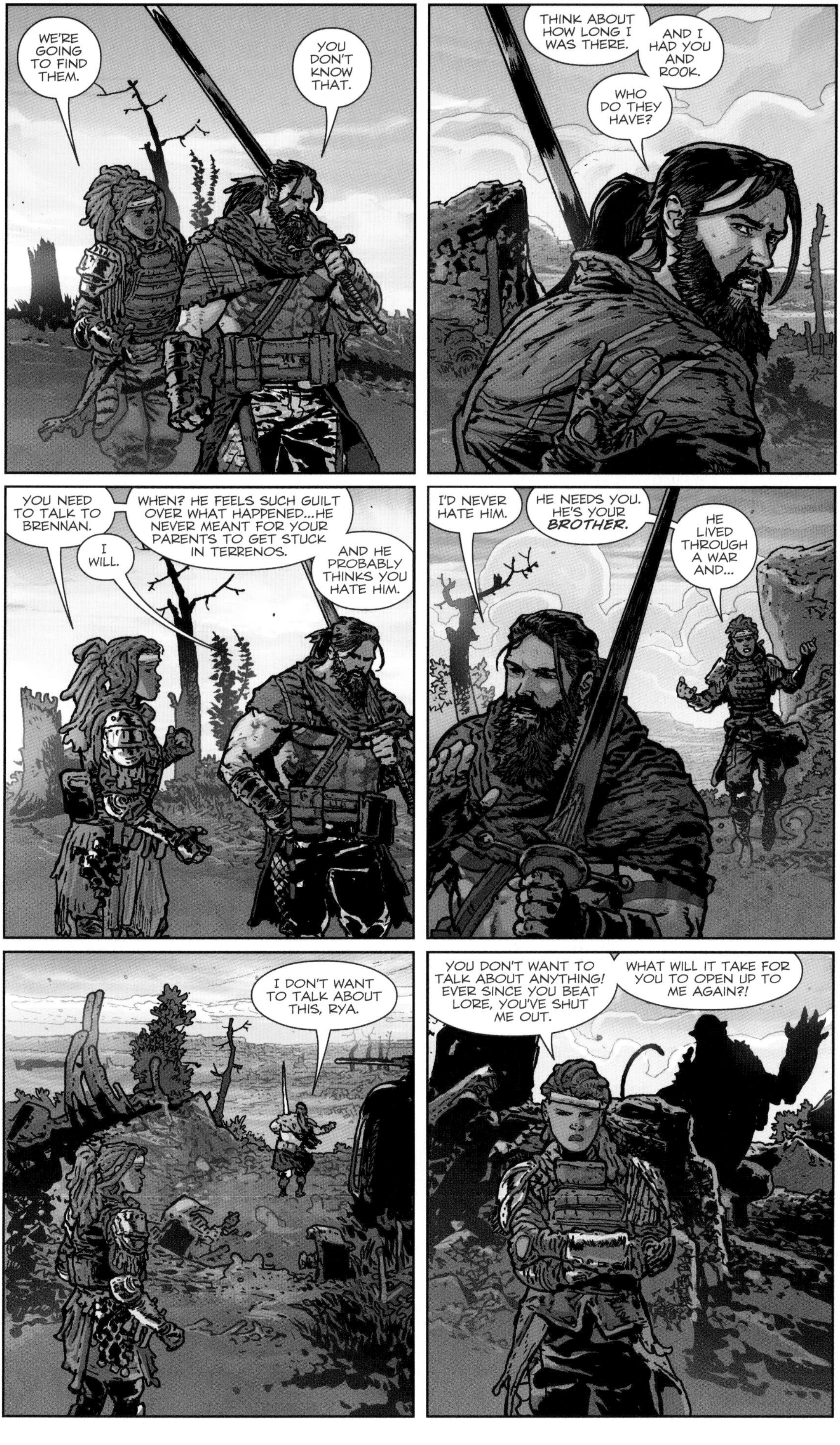
WE'RE GOING TO FIND THEM.
YOU DON'T KNOW THAT.
THINK ABOUT HOW LONG I WAS THERE.
AND I HAD YOU AND ROOK.
WHO DO THEY HAVE?
YOU NEED TO TALK TO BRENNAN.
I WILL.
WHEN? HE FEELS SUCH GUILT OVER WHAT HAPPENED...HE NEVER MEANT FOR YOUR PARENTS TO GET STUCK IN TERRENOS.
AND HE PROBABLY THINKS YOU HATE HIM.
I'D NEVER HATE HIM.
HE NEEDS YOU. HE'S YOUR BROTHER.
HE LIVED THROUGH A WAR AND...
I DON'T WANT TO TALK ABOUT THIS, RYA.
YOU DON'T WANT TO TALK ABOUT ANYTHING! EVER SINCE YOU BEAT LORE, YOU'VE SHUT ME OUT.
WHAT WILL IT TAKE FOR YOU TO OPEN UP TO ME AGAIN?!

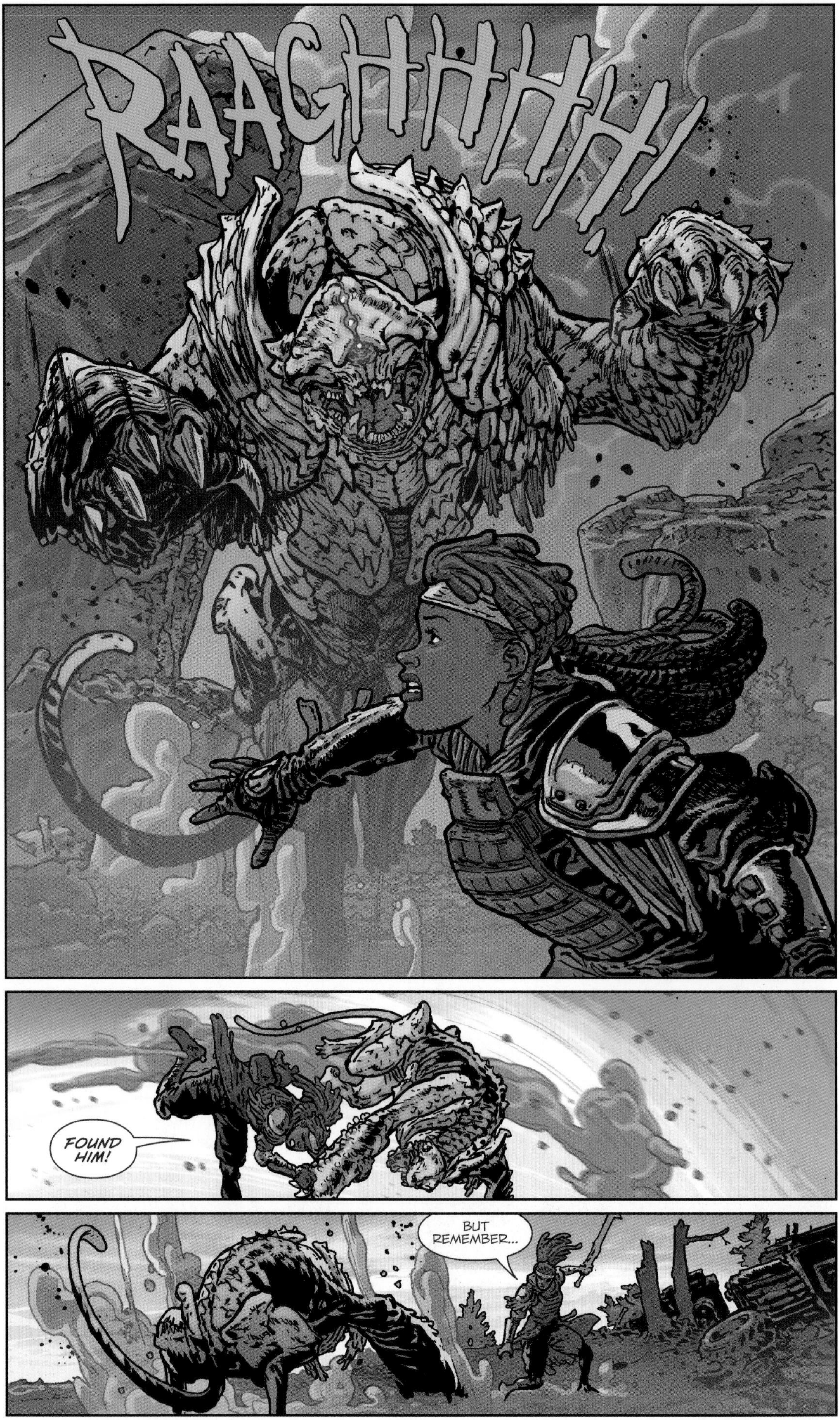
RAAGHHHHH!
FOUND HIM!
BUT REMEMBER...

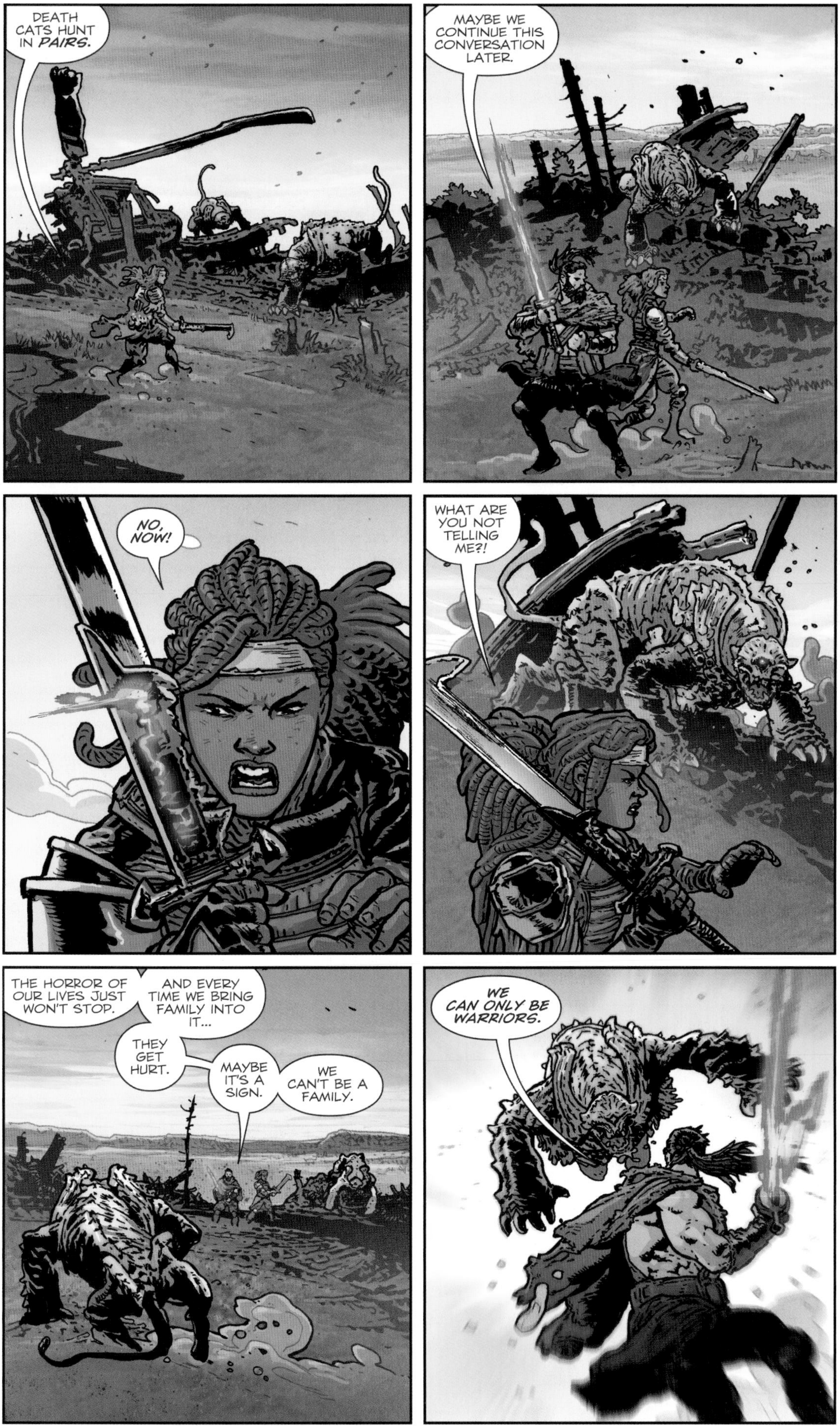
DEATH CATS HUNT IN *PAIRS.*
MAYBE WE CONTINUE THIS CONVERSATION LATER.
NO, NOW!
WHAT ARE YOU NOT TELLING ME?!
THE HORROR OF OUR LIVES JUST WON'T STOP.
AND EVERY TIME WE BRING FAMILY INTO IT...
THEY GET HURT.
MAYBE IT'S A SIGN.
WE CAN'T BE A FAMILY.
WE CAN ONLY BE WARRIORS.

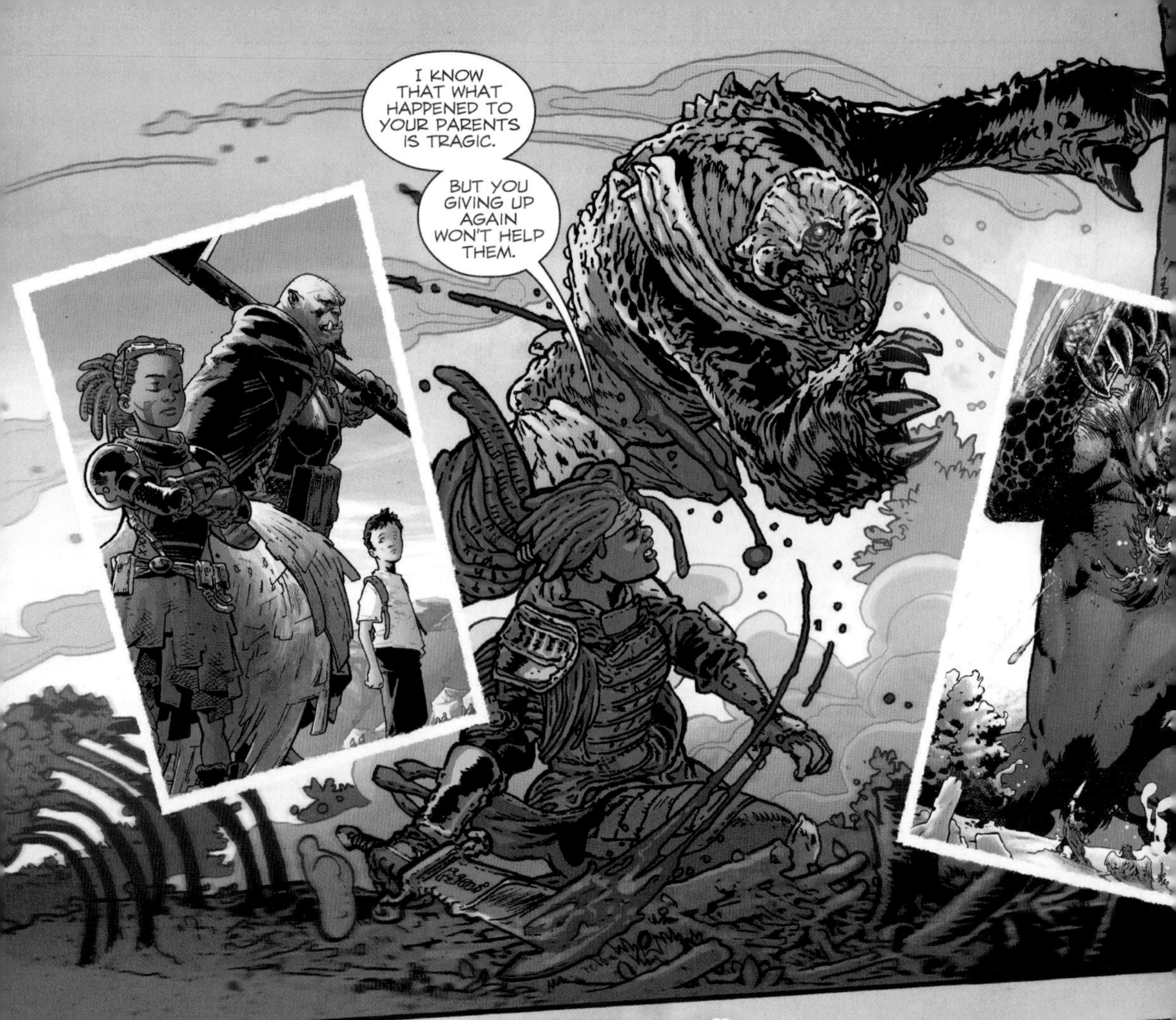
I KNOW THAT WHAT HAPPENED TO YOUR PARENTS IS TRAGIC.
BUT YOU GIVING UP AGAIN WON'T HELP THEM.
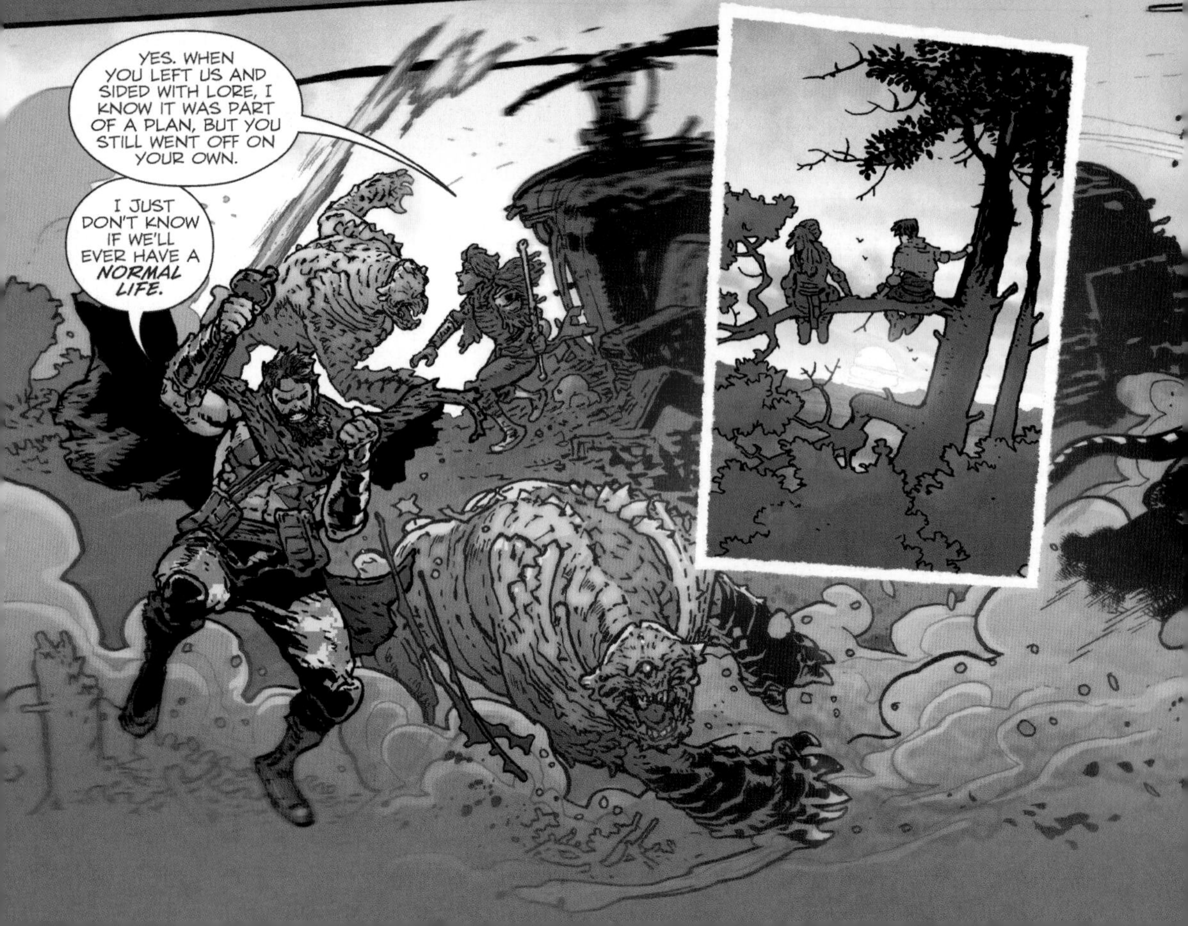
YES. WHEN YOU LEFT US AND SIDED WITH LORE, I KNOW IT WAS PART OF A PLAN, BUT YOU STILL WENT OFF ON YOUR OWN.
I JUST DON'T KNOW IF WE'LL EVER HAVE A ***NORMAL LIFE.***

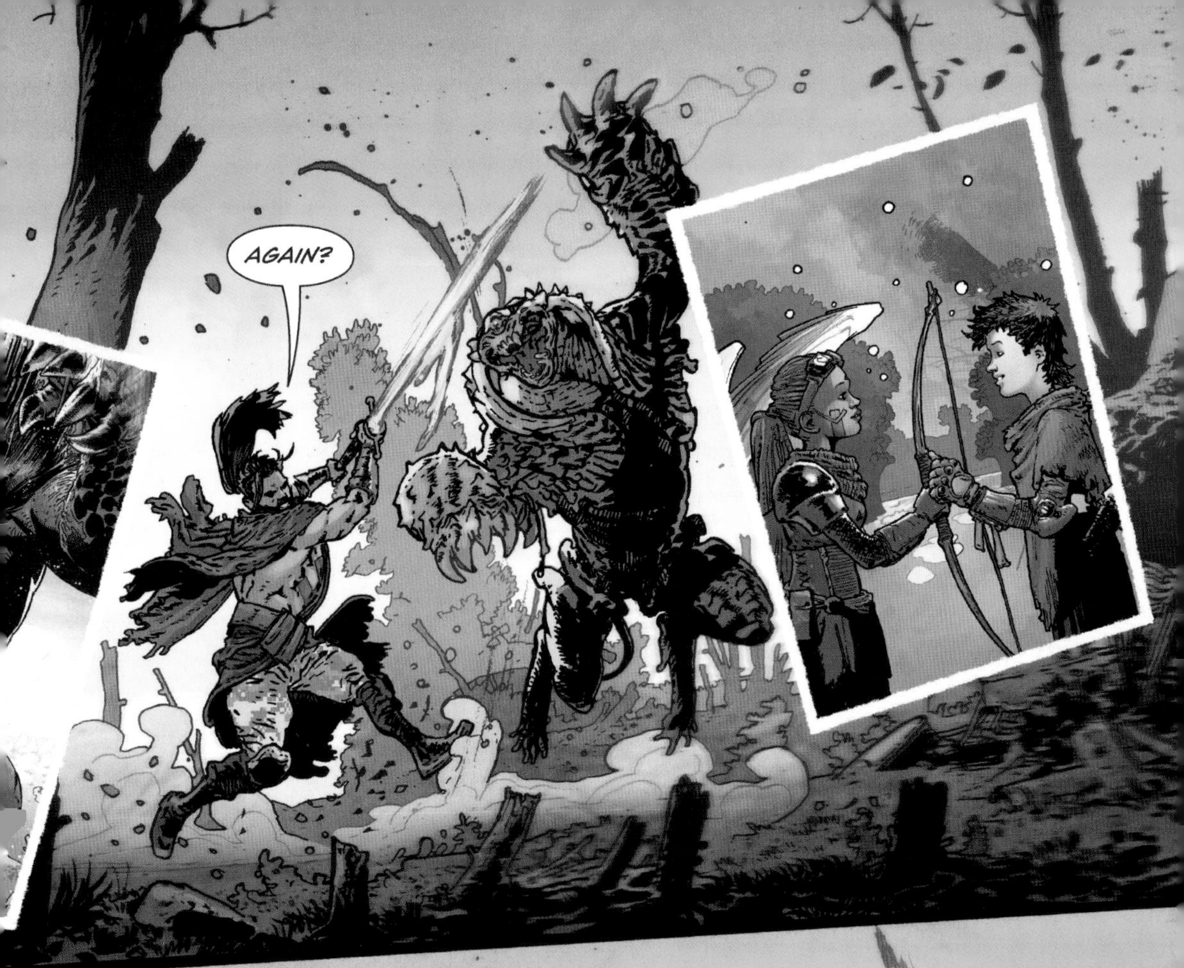
AGAIN?

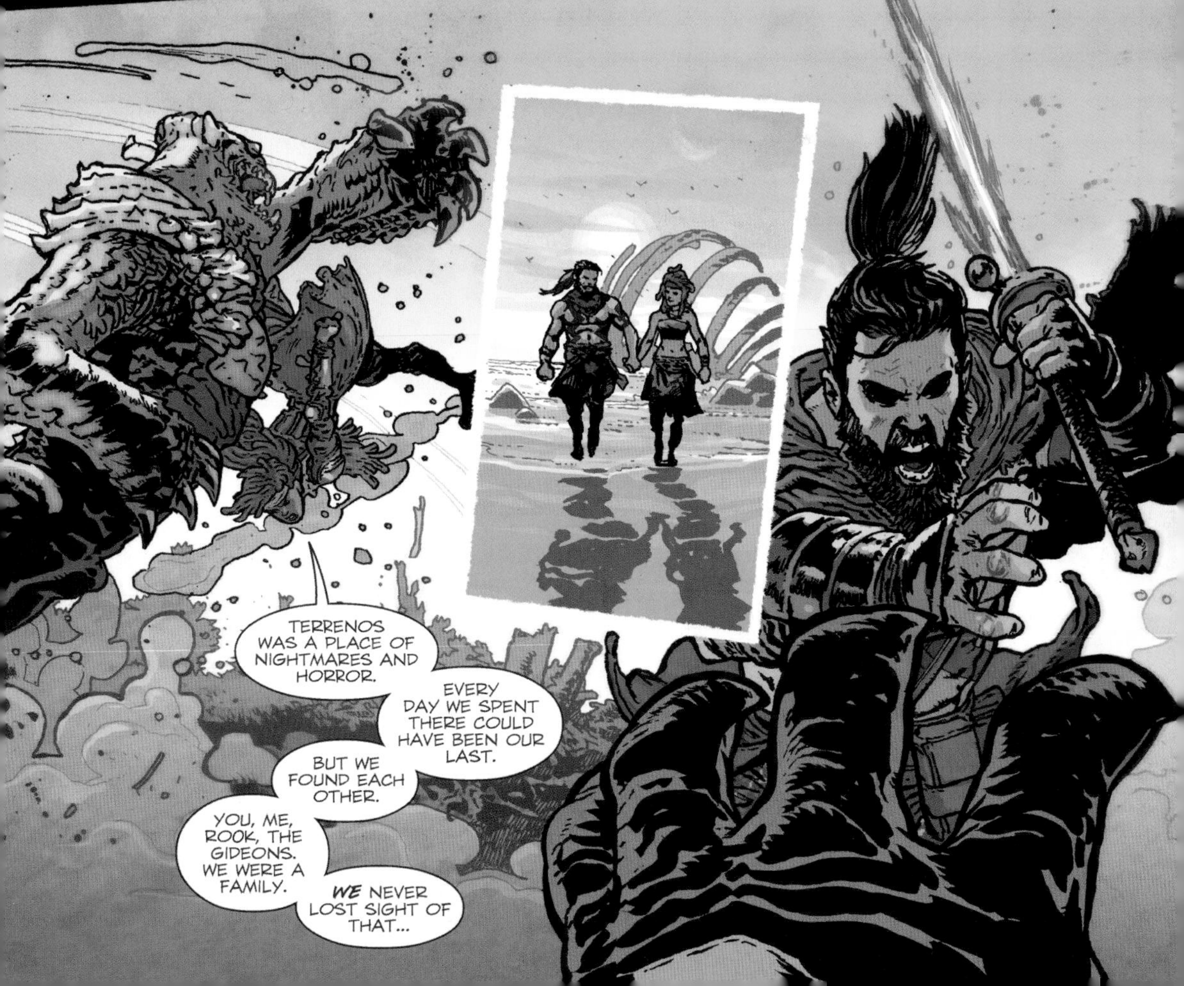
TERRENOS WAS A PLACE OF NIGHTMARES AND HORROR.
EVERY DAY WE SPENT THERE COULD HAVE BEEN OUR LAST.
BUT WE FOUND EACH OTHER.
YOU, ME, ROOK, THE GIDEONS. WE WERE A FAMILY.
WE NEVER LOST SIGHT OF THAT...

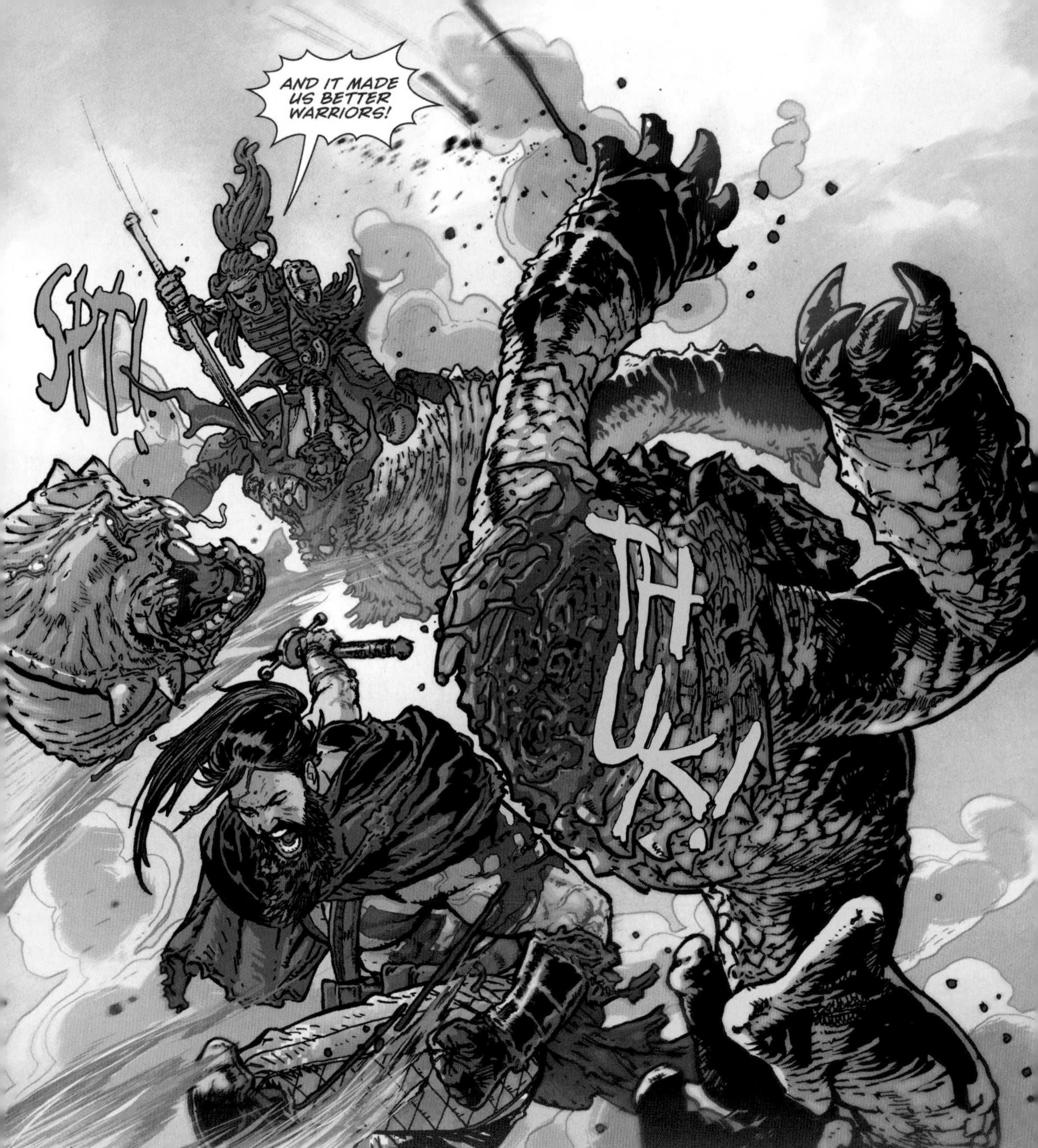
AND IT MADE US BETTER WARRIORS!
SPTT!
THUK!

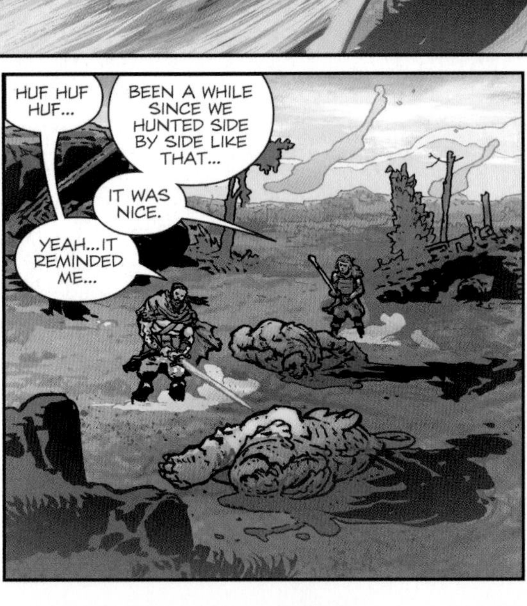
HUF HUF HUF...
BEEN A WHILE SINCE WE HUNTED SIDE BY SIDE LIKE THAT...
IT WAS NICE.
YEAH...IT REMINDED ME...

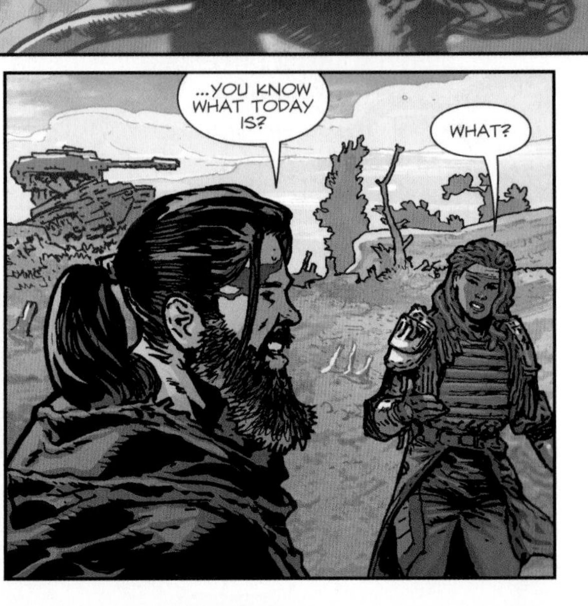
...YOU KNOW WHAT TODAY IS?
WHAT?

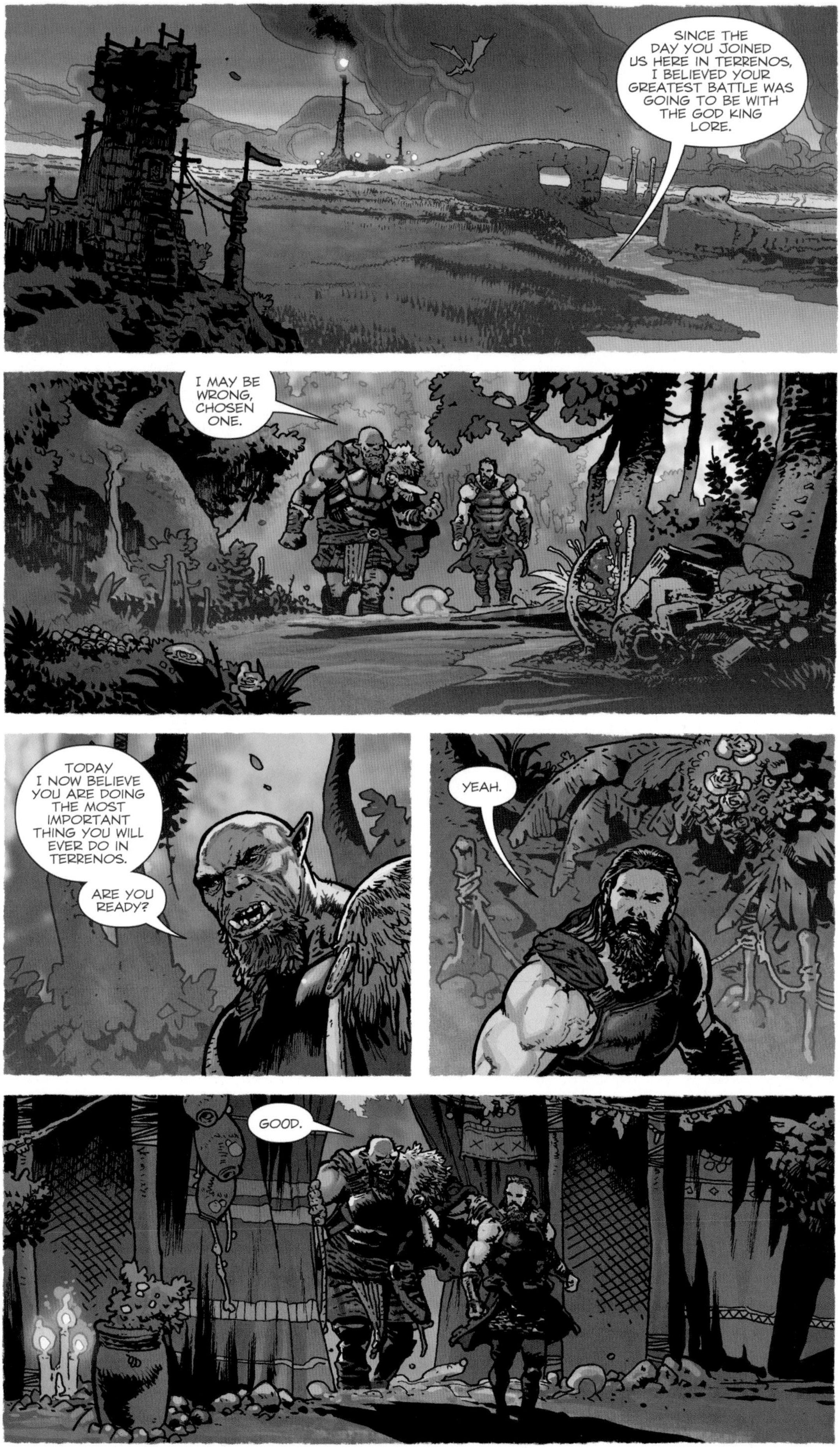
SINCE THE DAY YOU JOINED US HERE IN TERRENOS, I BELIEVED YOUR GREATEST BATTLE WAS GOING TO BE WITH THE GOD KING LORE.
I MAY BE WRONG, CHOSEN ONE.
TODAY I NOW BELIEVE YOU ARE DOING THE MOST IMPORTANT THING YOU WILL EVER DO IN TERRENOS.
ARE YOU READY?
YEAH.
GOOD.

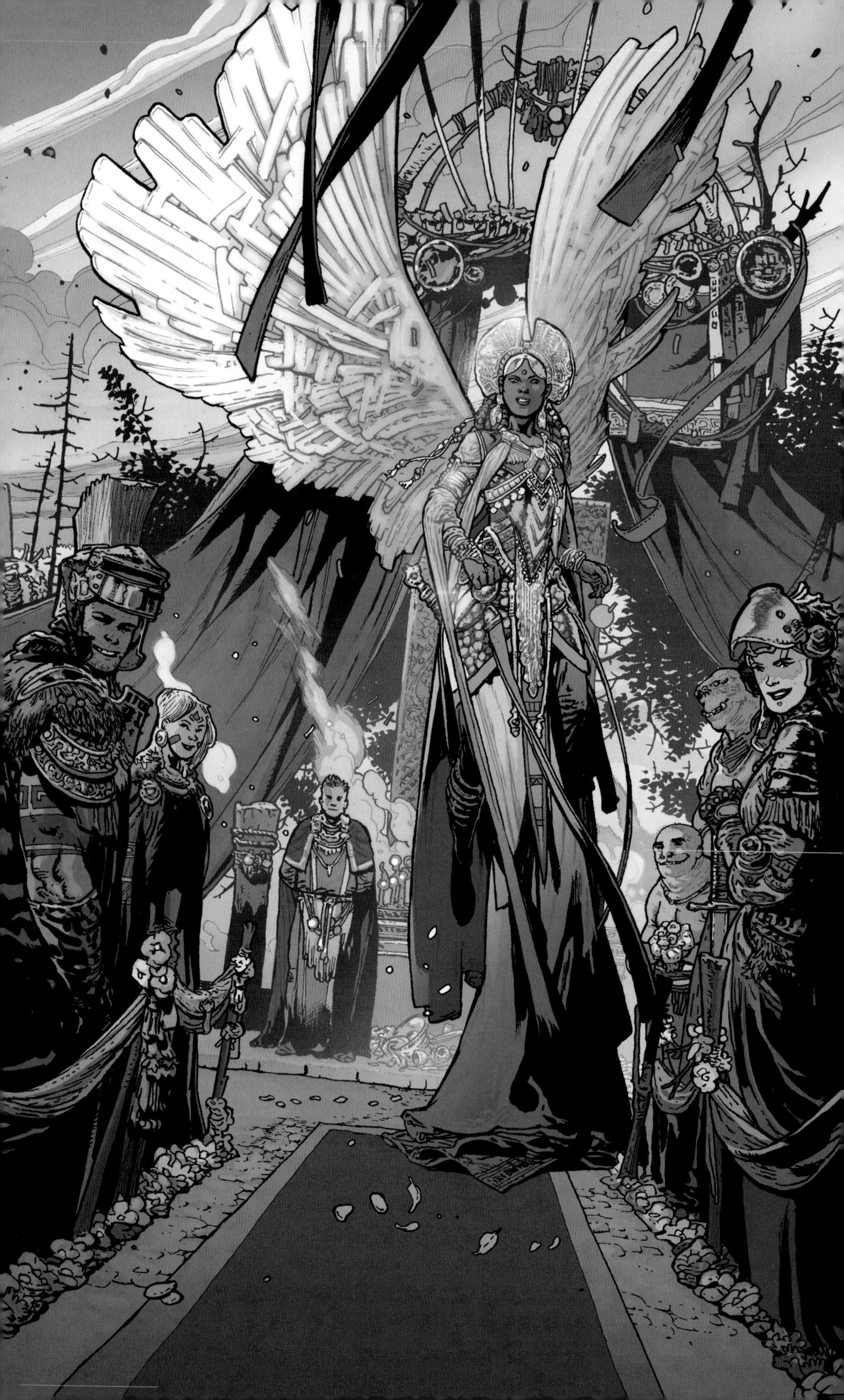

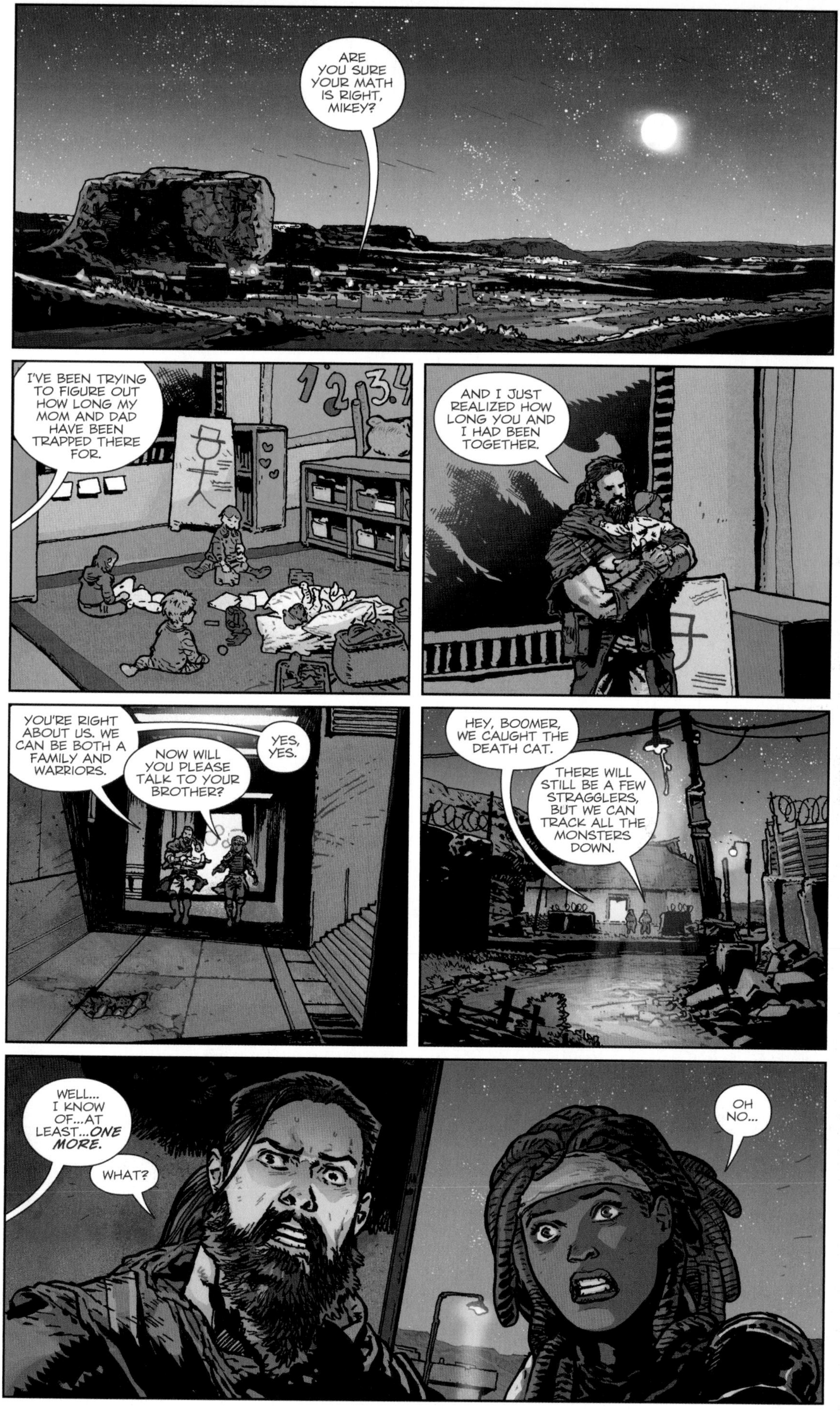
ARE YOU SURE YOUR MATH IS RIGHT, MIKEY?
I'VE BEEN TRYING TO FIGURE OUT HOW LONG MY MOM AND DAD HAVE BEEN TRAPPED THERE FOR.
AND I JUST REALIZED HOW LONG YOU AND I HAD BEEN TOGETHER.
YOU'RE RIGHT ABOUT US. WE CAN BE BOTH A FAMILY AND WARRIORS.
NOW WILL YOU PLEASE TALK TO YOUR BROTHER?
YES, YES.
HEY, BOOMER, WE CAUGHT THE DEATH CAT.
THERE WILL STILL BE A FEW STRAGGLERS, BUT WE CAN TRACK ALL THE MONSTERS DOWN.
WELL... I KNOW OF...AT LEAST...*ONE MORE.*
WHAT?
OH NO...

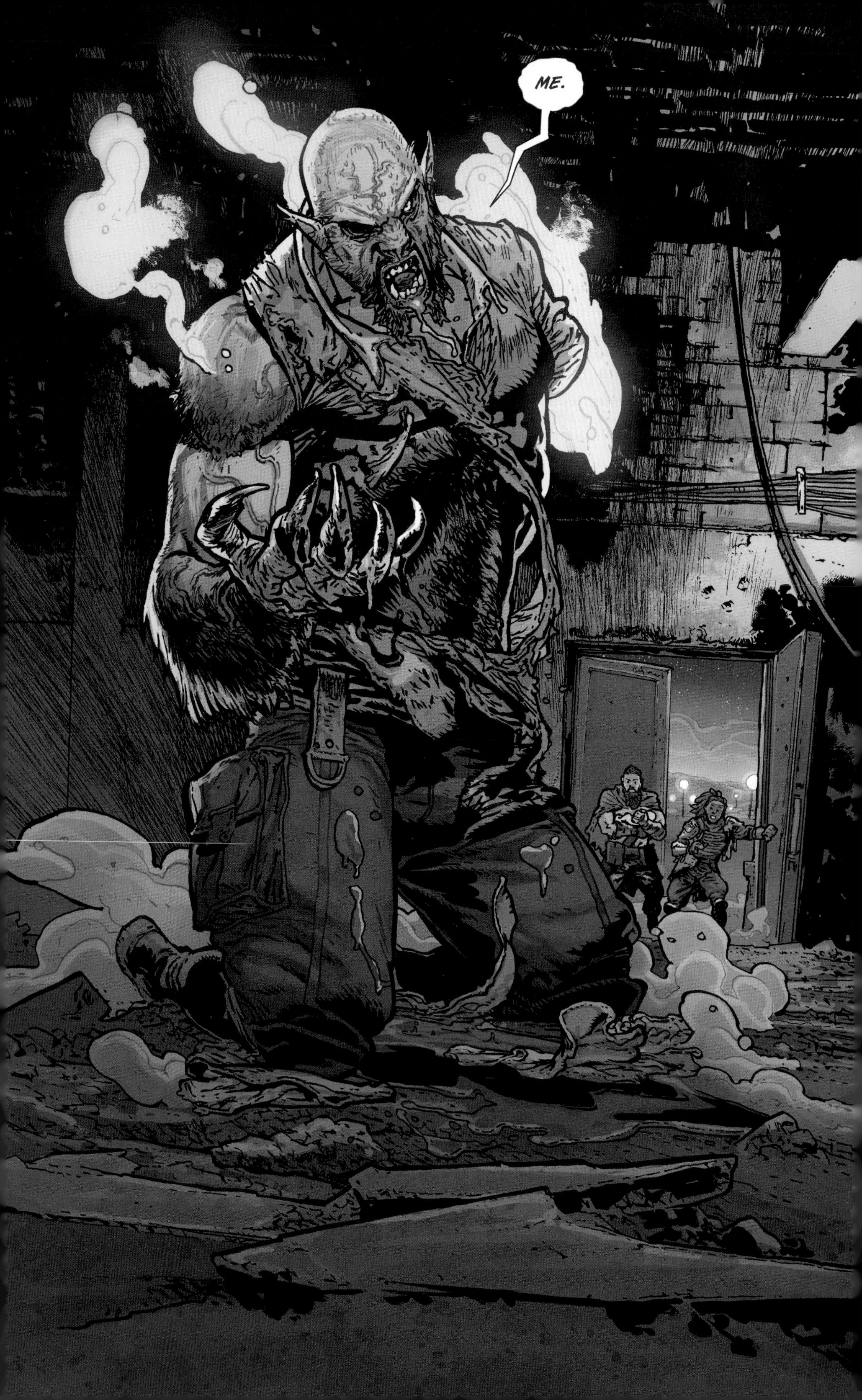
ME.

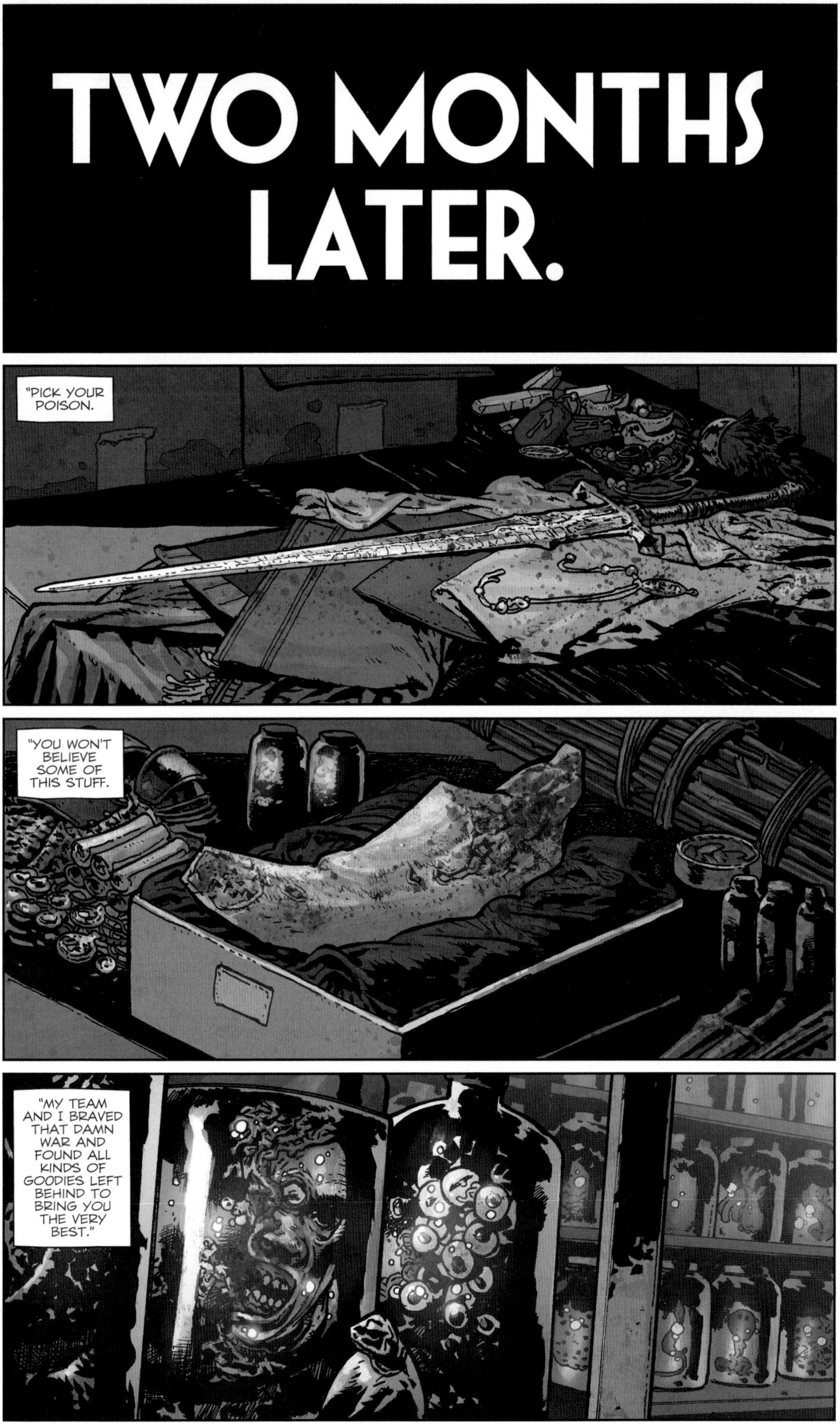
TWO MONTHS LATER.
"PICK YOUR POISON.
"YOU WON'T BELIEVE SOME OF THIS STUFF.
"MY TEAM AND I BRAVED THAT DAMN WAR AND FOUND ALL KINDS OF GOODIES LEFT BEHIND TO BRING YOU THE VERY BEST."

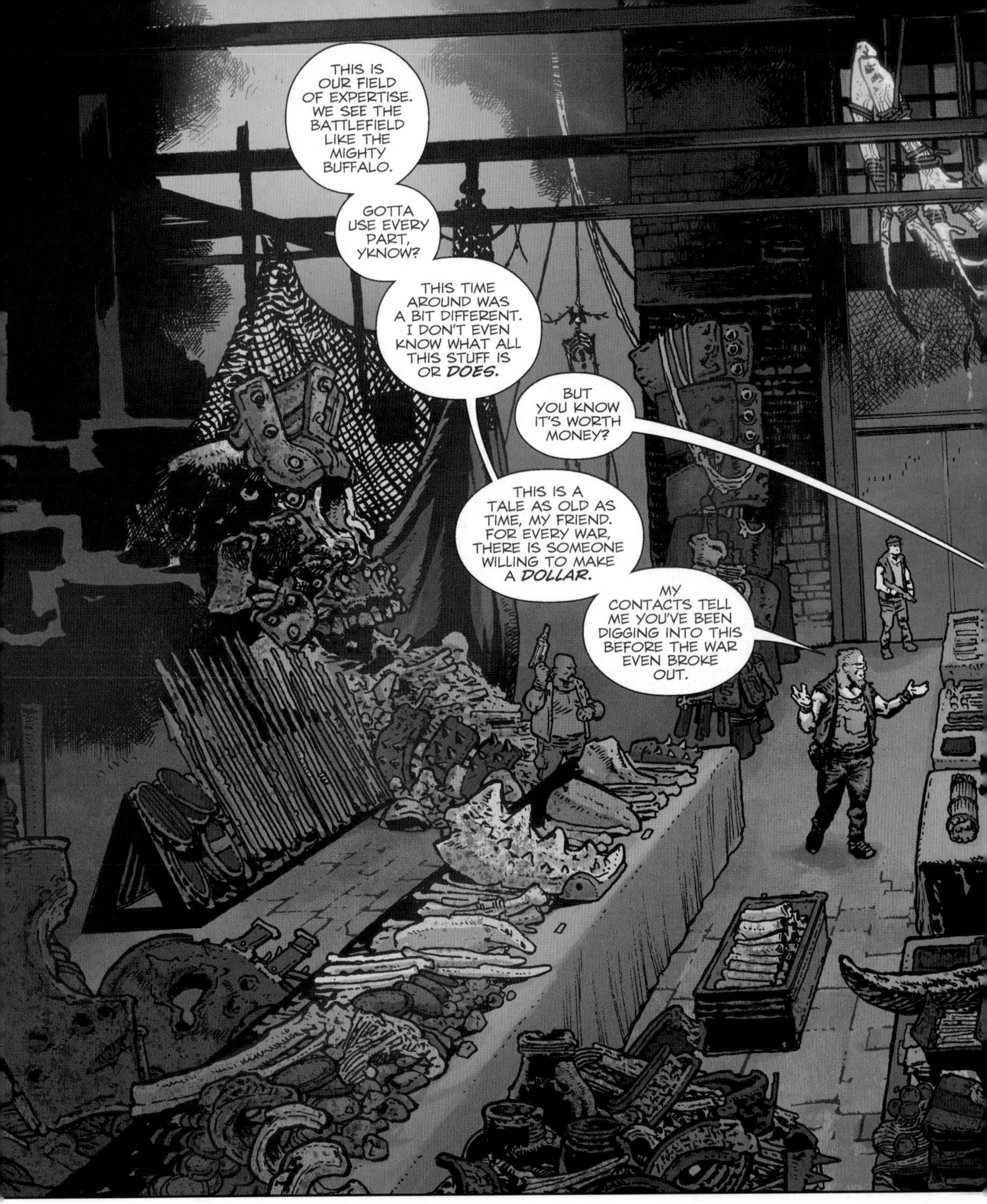
THIS IS OUR FIELD OF EXPERTISE. WE SEE THE BATTLEFIELD LIKE THE MIGHTY BUFFALO.
GOTTA USE EVERY PART, YKNOW?
THIS TIME AROUND WAS A BIT DIFFERENT. I DON'T EVEN KNOW WHAT ALL THIS STUFF IS OR DOES.
BUT YOU KNOW IT'S WORTH MONEY?
THIS IS A TALE AS OLD AS TIME, MY FRIEND. FOR EVERY WAR, THERE IS SOMEONE WILLING TO MAKE A DOLLAR.
MY CONTACTS TELL ME YOU'VE BEEN DIGGING INTO THIS BEFORE THE WAR EVEN BROKE OUT.
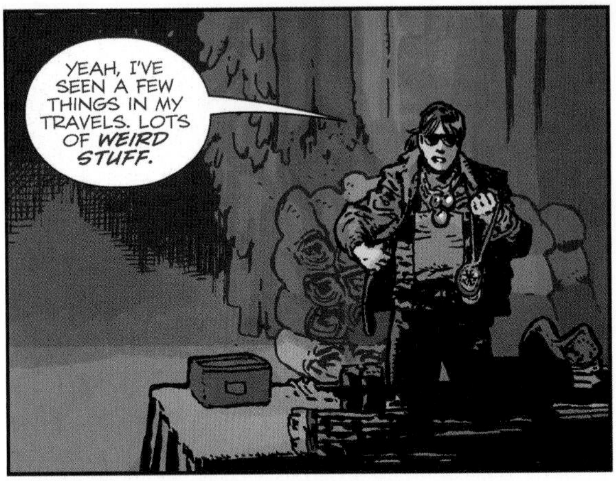
YEAH, I'VE SEEN A FEW THINGS IN MY TRAVELS. LOTS OF WEIRD STUFF.
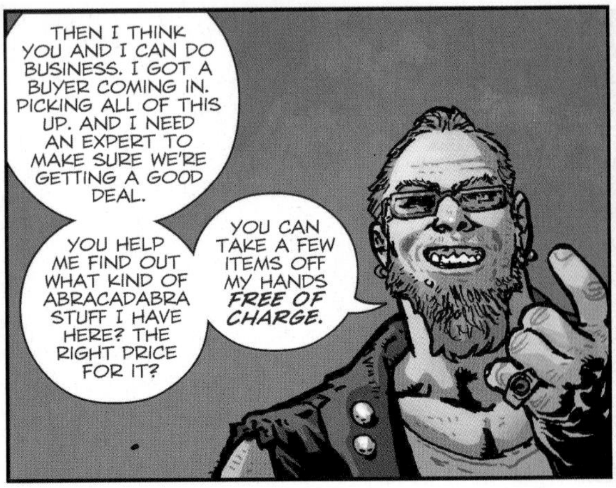
THEN I THINK YOU AND I CAN DO BUSINESS. I GOT A BUYER COMING IN. PICKING ALL OF THIS UP. AND I NEED AN EXPERT TO MAKE SURE WE'RE GETTING A GOOD DEAL.
YOU HELP ME FIND OUT WHAT KIND OF ABRACADABRA STUFF I HAVE HERE? THE RIGHT PRICE FOR IT?
YOU CAN TAKE A FEW ITEMS OFF MY HANDS FREE OF CHARGE.

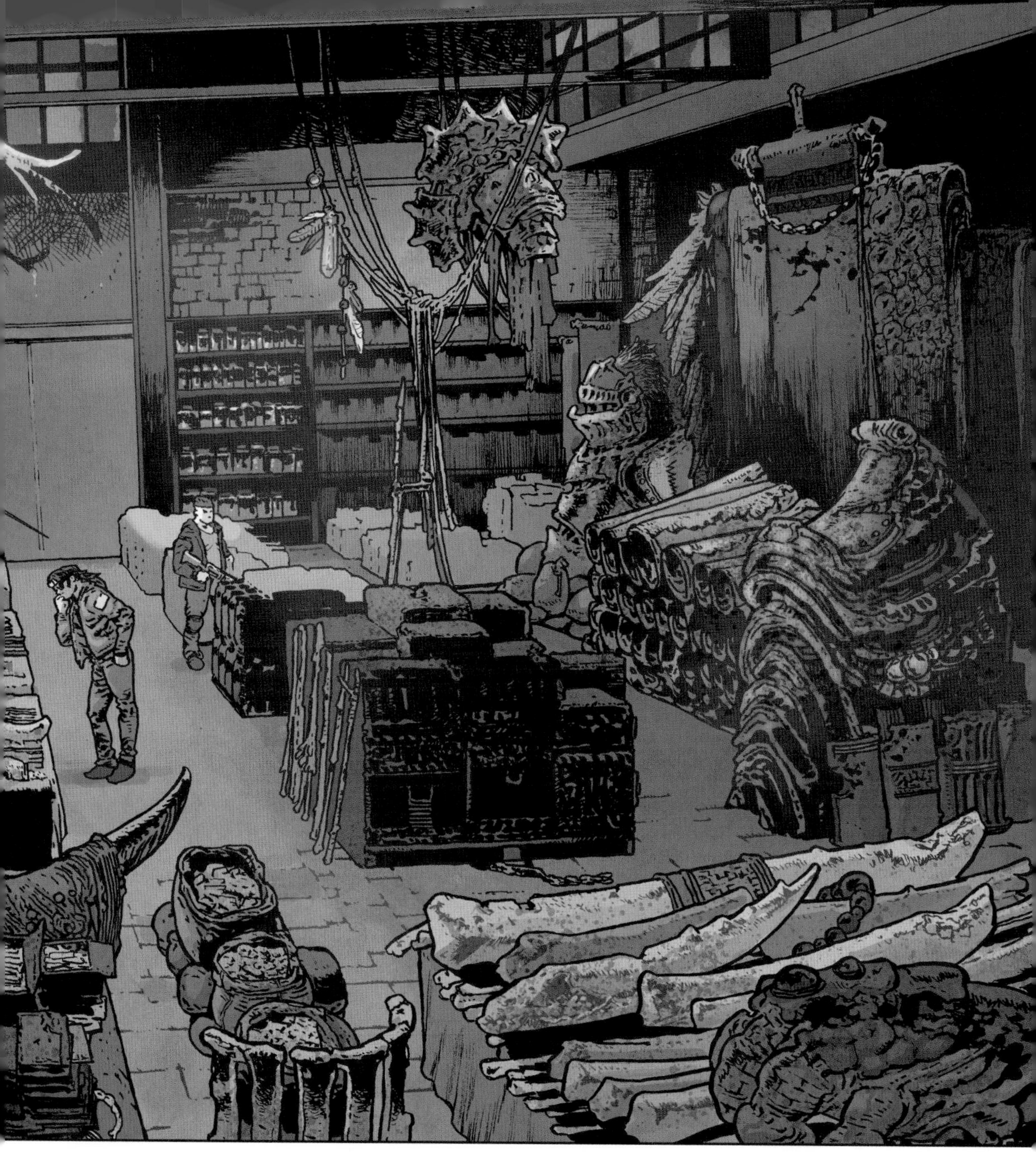
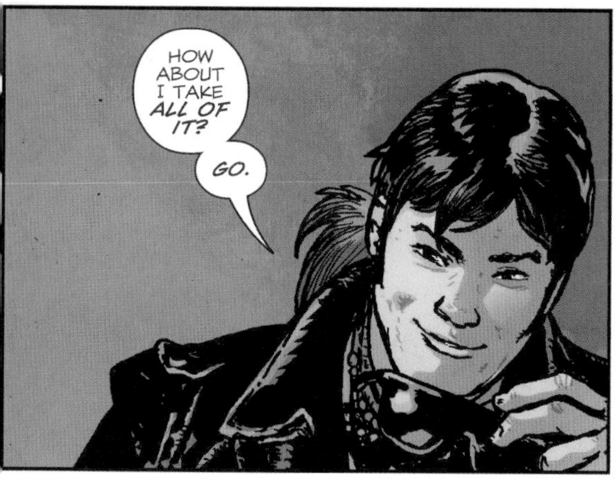
HOW ABOUT I TAKE ALL OF IT?
GO.
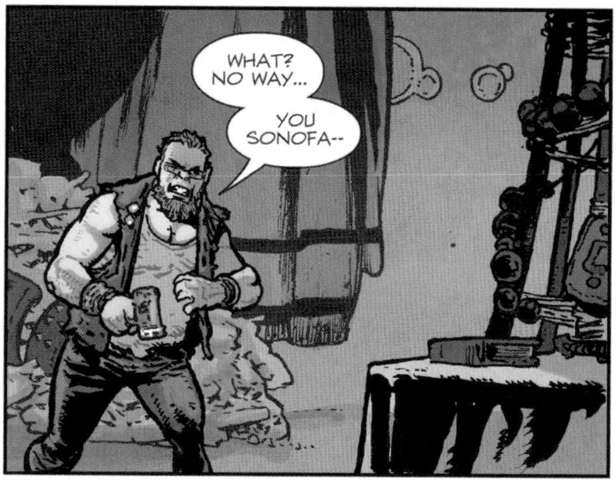
WHAT? NO WAY...
YOU SONOFA--

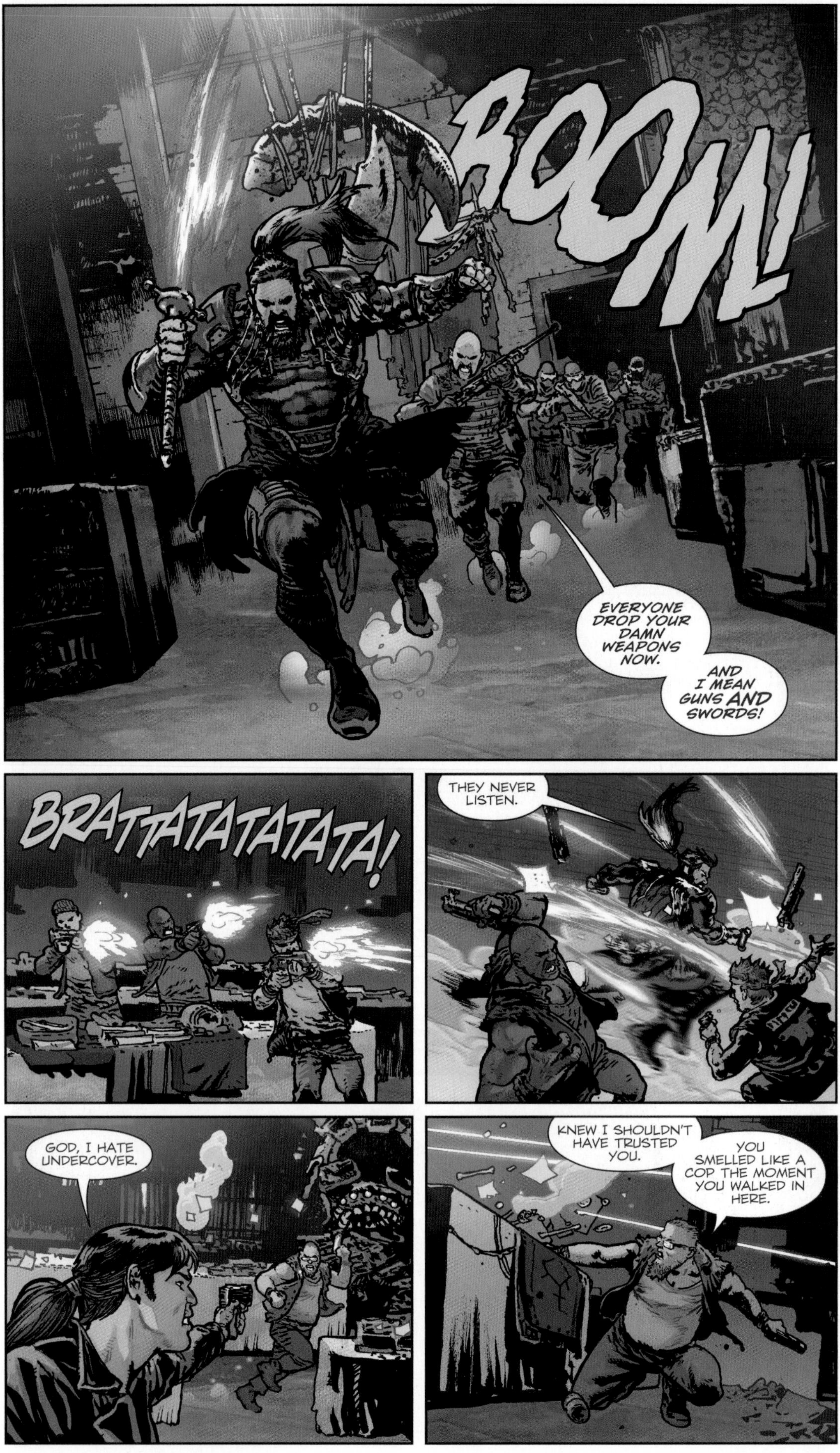
BOOM!
EVERYONE DROP YOUR DAMN WEAPONS NOW.
AND I MEAN GUNS AND SWORDS!
BRATTATATATATATA!
THEY NEVER LISTEN.
GOD, I HATE UNDERCOVER.
KNEW I SHOULDN'T HAVE TRUSTED YOU.
YOU SMELLED LIKE A COP THE MOMENT YOU WALKED IN HERE.

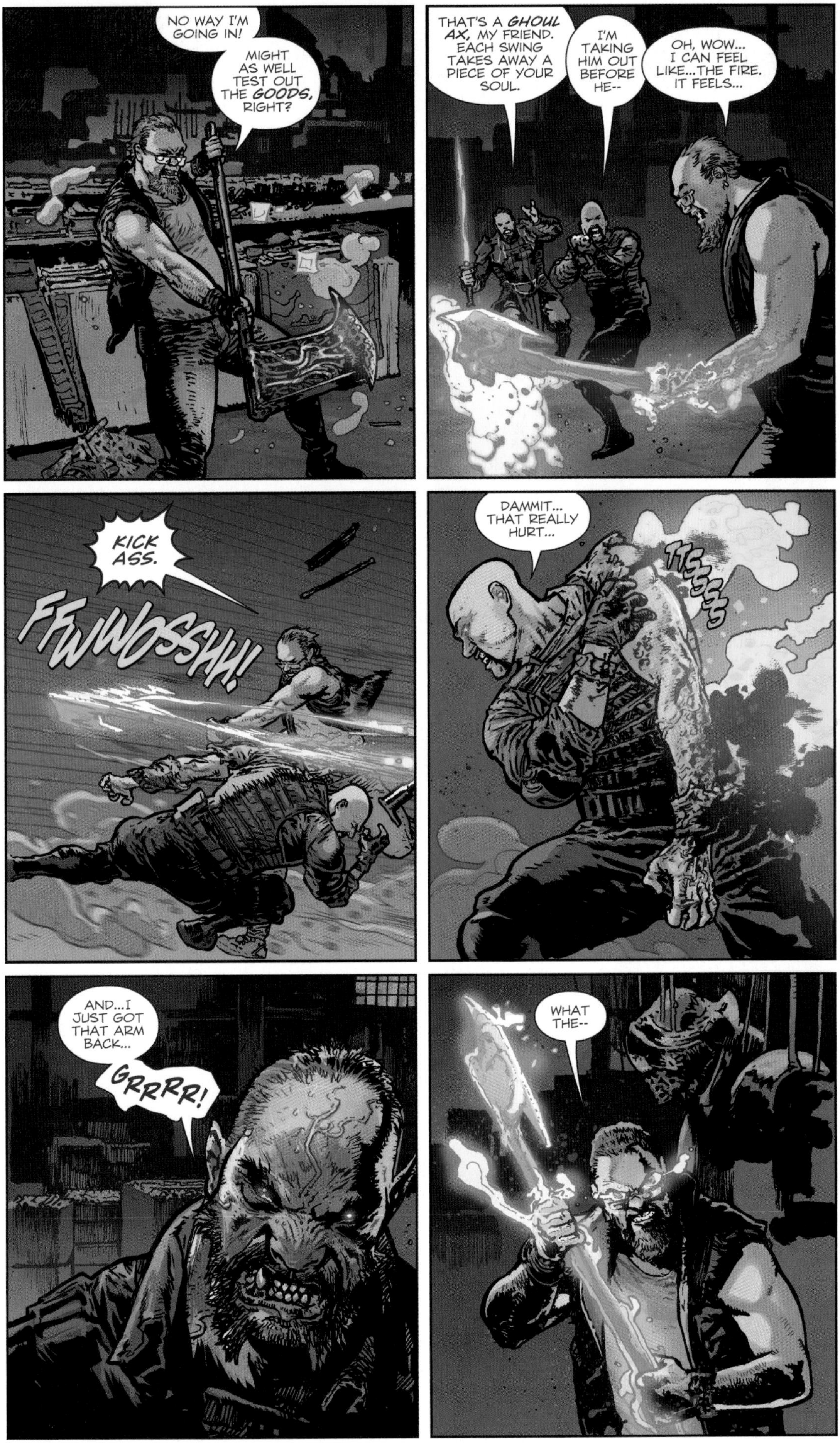
NO WAY I'M GOING IN!
MIGHT AS WELL TEST OUT THE GOODS, RIGHT?
THAT'S A GHOUL AX, MY FRIEND. EACH SWING TAKES AWAY A PIECE OF YOUR SOUL.
I'M TAKING HIM OUT BEFORE HE--
OH, WOW... I CAN FEEL LIKE...THE FIRE. IT FEELS...
KICK ASS.
FFWWOSSHH!
DAMMIT... THAT REALLY HURT...
TSSSS
AND...I JUST GOT THAT ARM BACK...
GRRRR!
WHAT THE--

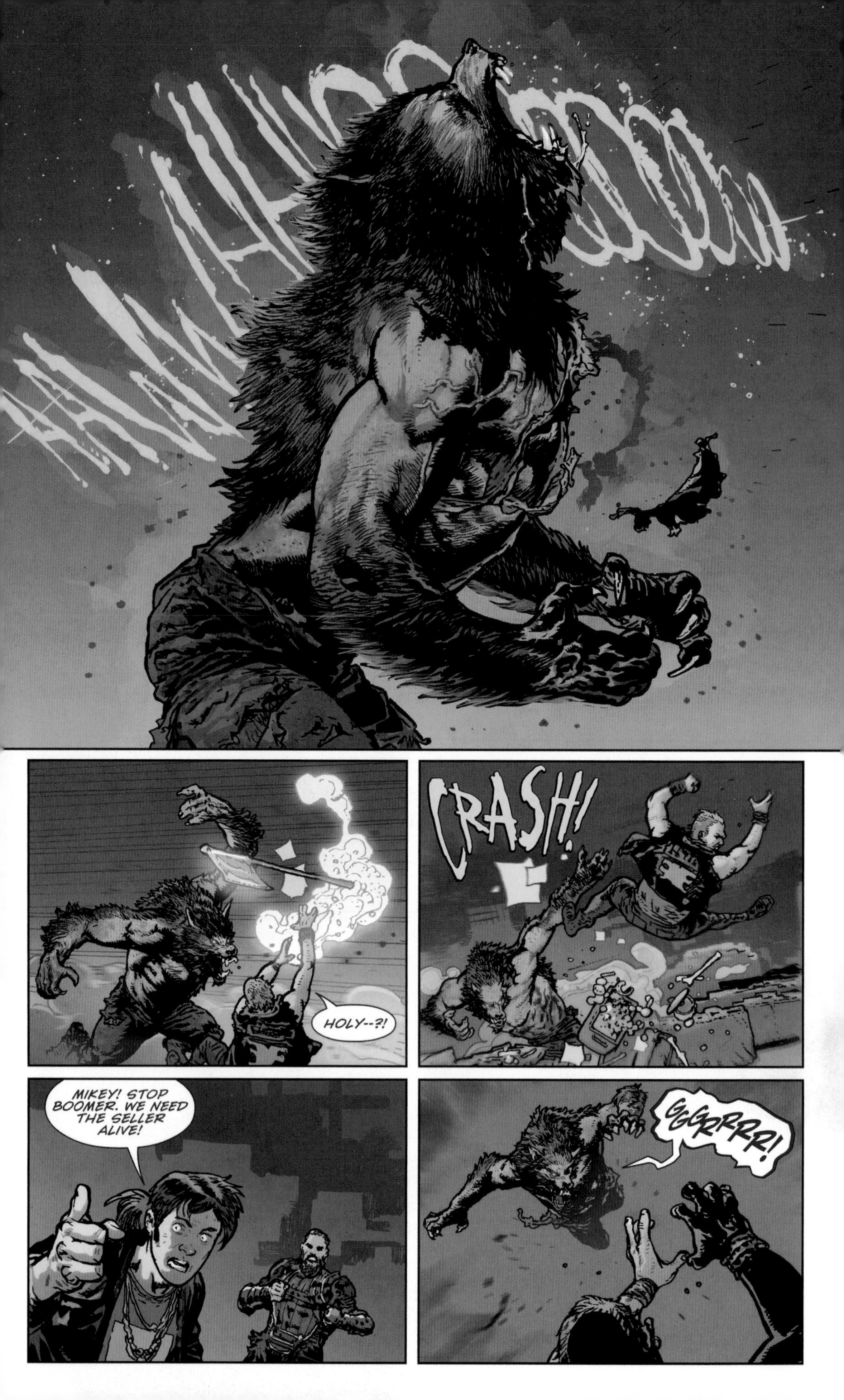
HOLY--?!
CRASH!
MIKEY! STOP BOOMER. WE NEED THE SELLER ALIVE!
GGGRRRR!

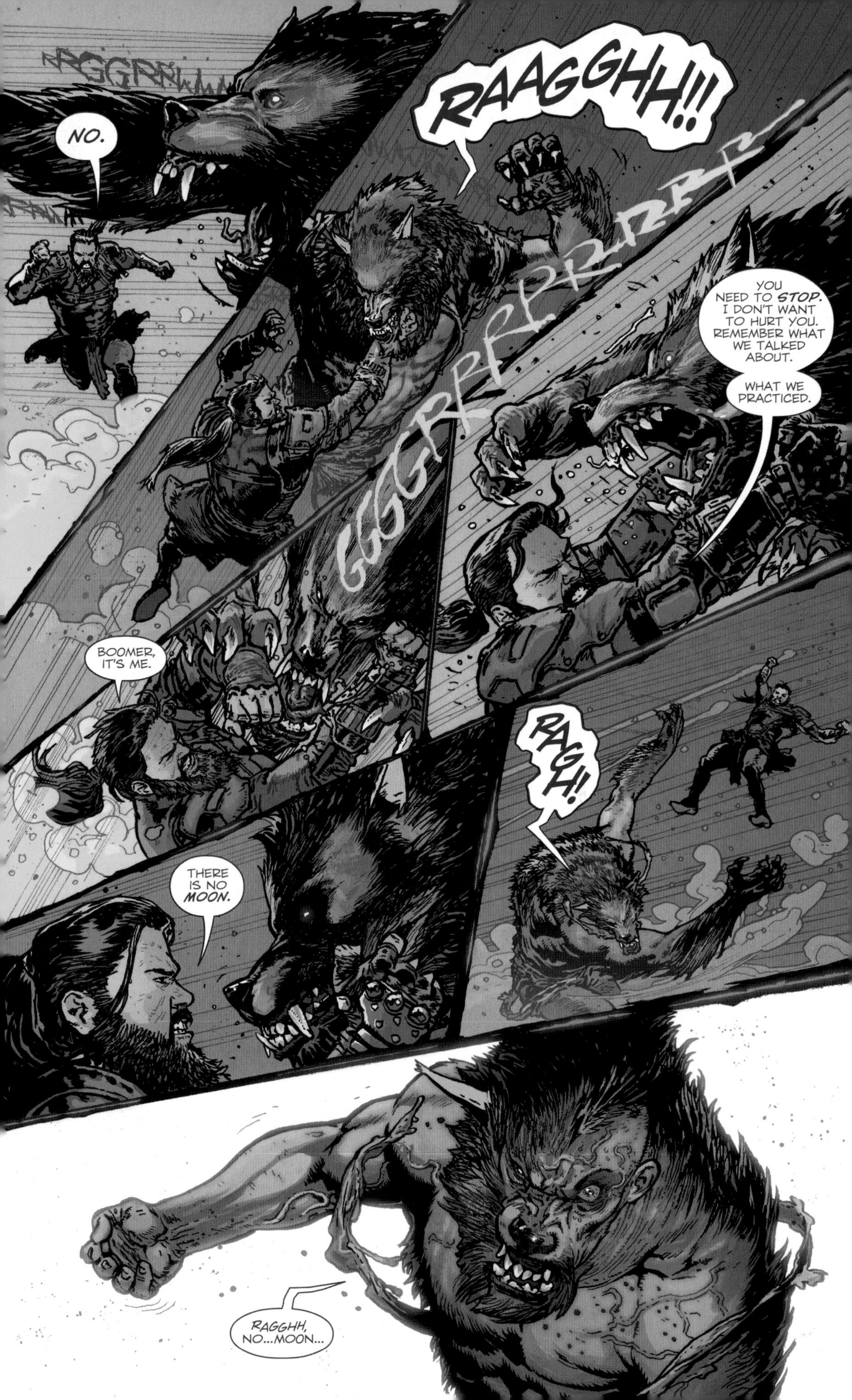
NO.
RAAGGHH!!
BOOMER, IT'S ME.
YOU NEED TO **STOP.** I DON'T WANT TO HURT YOU. REMEMBER WHAT WE TALKED ABOUT.
WHAT WE PRACTICED.
THERE IS NO **MOON.**
RAGH!
RAGGHH, NO...MOON...

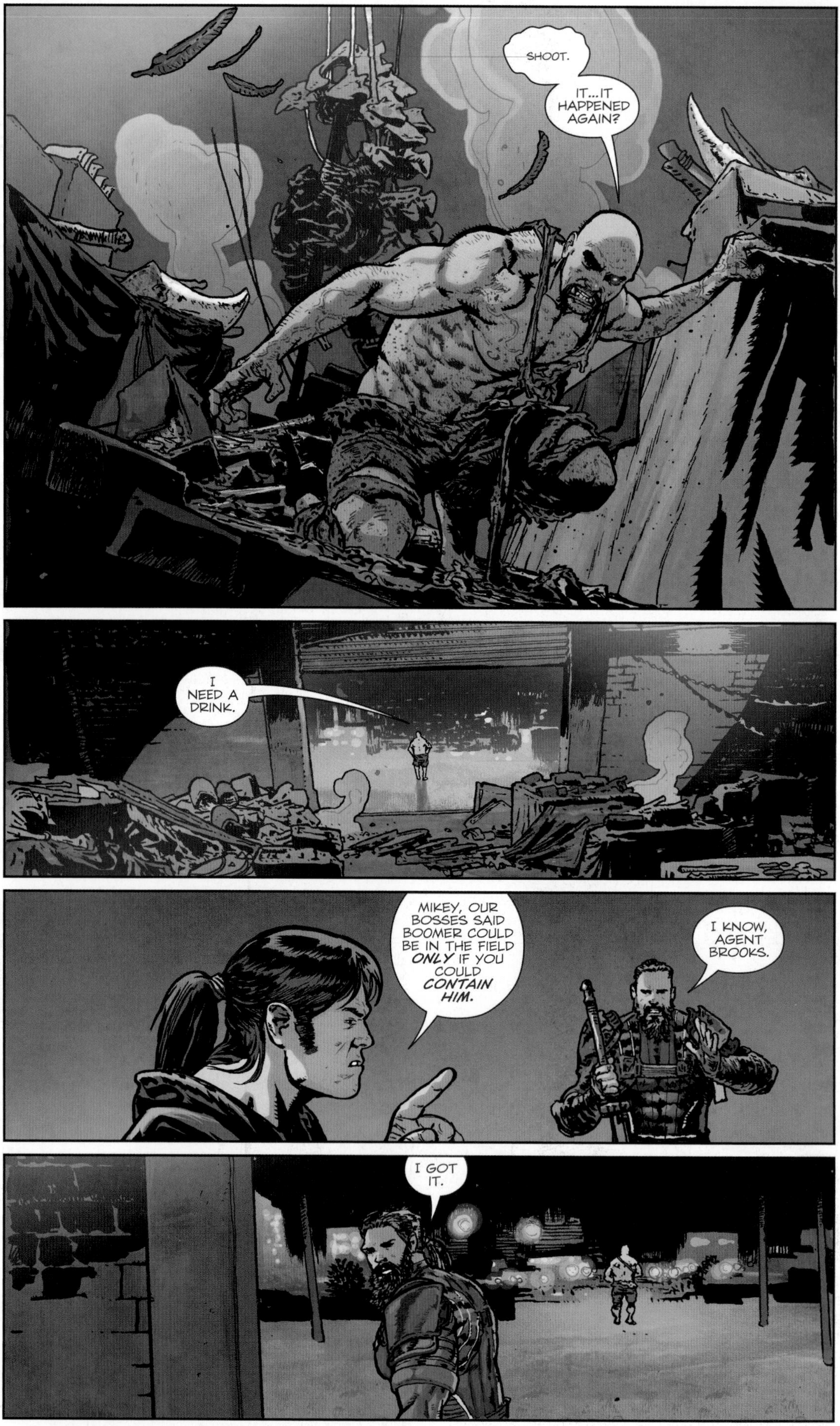
SHOOT.
IT...IT HAPPENED AGAIN?
I NEED A DRINK.
MIKEY, OUR BOSSES SAID BOOMER COULD BE IN THE FIELD ONLY IF YOU COULD CONTAIN HIM.
I KNOW, AGENT BROOKS.
I GOT IT.

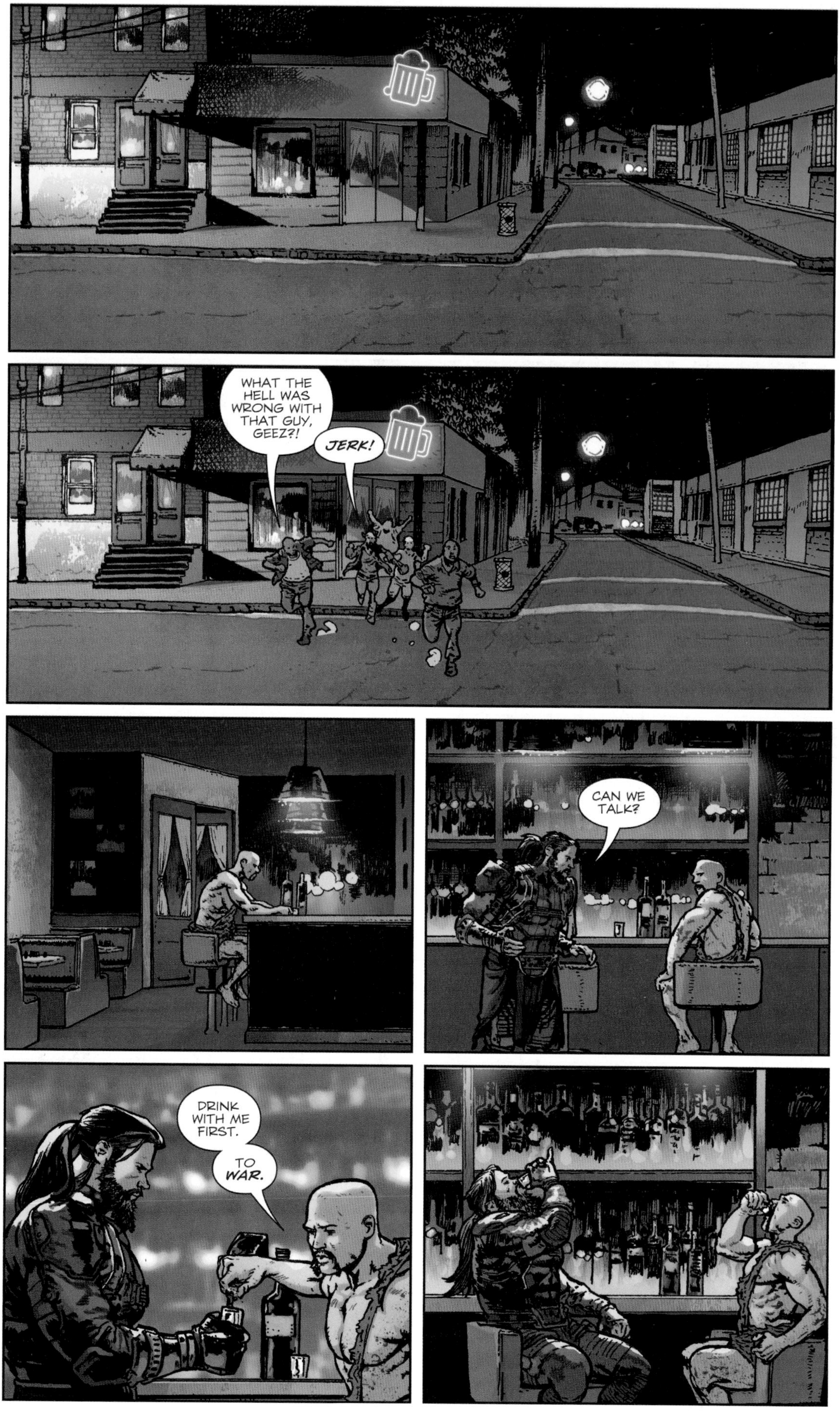

WHAT THE HELL WAS WRONG WITH THAT GUY, GEEZ?!
JERK!
CAN WE TALK?
DRINK WITH ME FIRST.
TO *WAR.*

SPIT!

HA, I SOMETIMES FORGET YOU'RE STILL A *KID* IN SOME WAYS.

THEY DIDN'T HAVE TEQUILA IN TERRENOS?

I THOUGHT YOU HAD IT UNDER CONTROL, BOOMER?

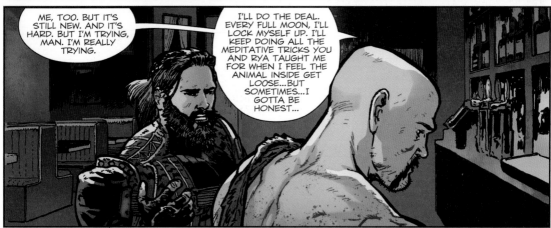

ME, TOO. BUT IT'S STILL NEW. AND IT'S HARD. BUT I'M TRYING, MAN. I'M REALLY TRYING.

I'LL DO THE DEAL. EVERY FULL MOON, I'LL LOCK MYSELF UP. I'LL KEEP DOING ALL THE MEDITATIVE TRICKS YOU AND RYA TAUGHT ME FOR WHEN I FEEL THE ANIMAL INSIDE GET LOOSE...BUT SOMETIMES...I GOTTA BE HONEST...

THERE IS A PIECE OF ME THAT... *LOVES IT.* THE ANGRY PART THAT WILL ALWAYS BE THERE. THE WOLF IN ME...HE LIVES IN THAT PLACE.

AND LET ME TELL YOU...IF IT'S FEEDING ON MY *ANGER,* IT'S GOING TO BE WELL FED.

ONCE BRENNAN GETS BACK, WE'LL HAVE HIM TAKE A LOOK AT YOU.

YOU STILL HAVEN'T HEARD FROM HIM?

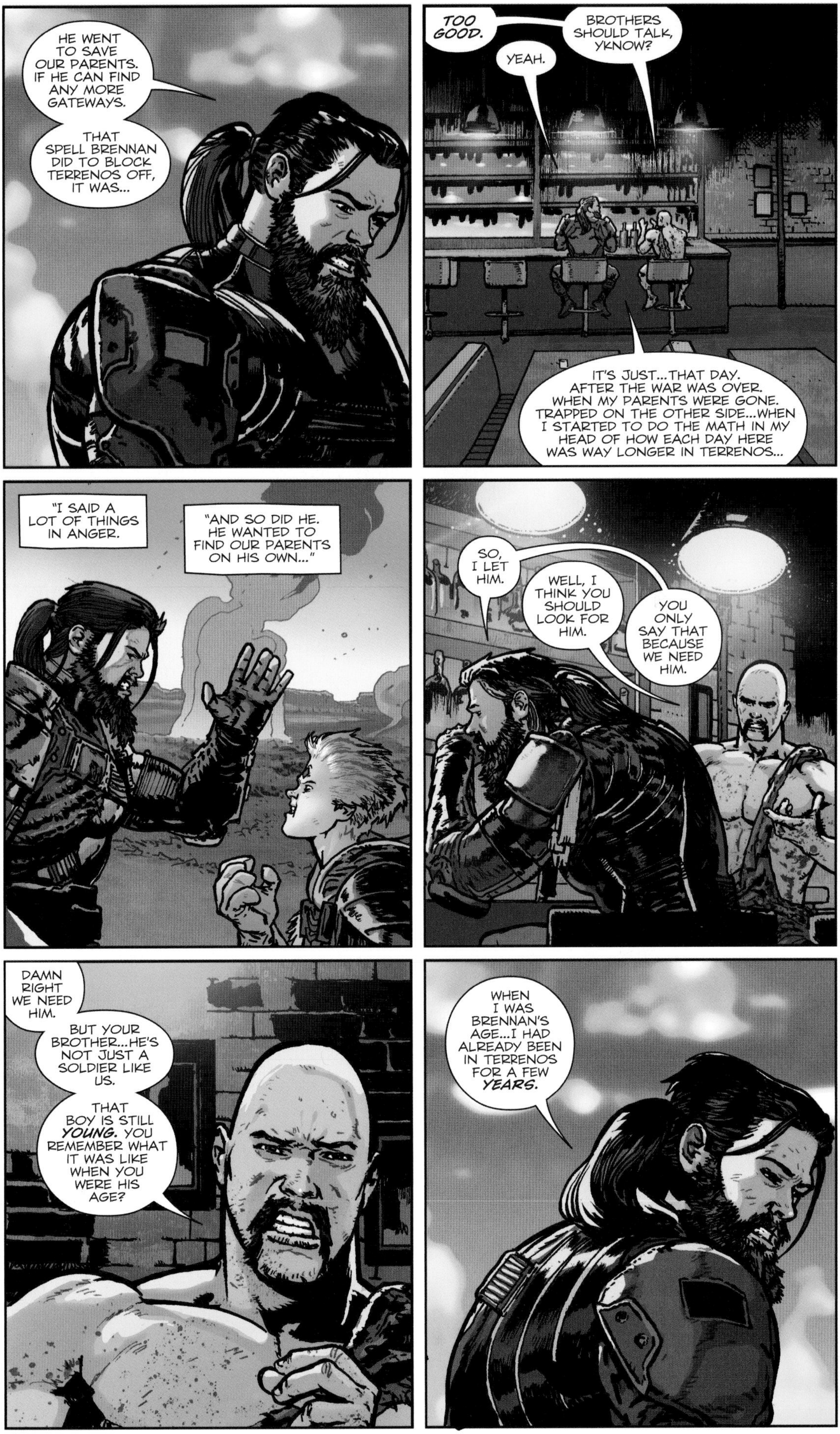
HE WENT TO SAVE OUR PARENTS. IF HE CAN FIND ANY MORE GATEWAYS.
THAT SPELL BRENNAN DID TO BLOCK TERRENOS OFF, IT WAS...
TOO GOOD.
BROTHERS SHOULD TALK, YKNOW?
YEAH.
IT'S JUST...THAT DAY. AFTER THE WAR WAS OVER. WHEN MY PARENTS WERE GONE. TRAPPED ON THE OTHER SIDE...WHEN I STARTED TO DO THE MATH IN MY HEAD OF HOW EACH DAY HERE WAS WAY LONGER IN TERRENOS...
"I SAID A LOT OF THINGS IN ANGER.
"AND SO DID HE. HE WANTED TO FIND OUR PARENTS ON HIS OWN..."
SO, I LET HIM.
WELL, I THINK YOU SHOULD LOOK FOR HIM.
YOU ONLY SAY THAT BECAUSE WE NEED HIM.
DAMN RIGHT WE NEED HIM.
BUT YOUR BROTHER...HE'S NOT JUST A SOLDIER LIKE US.
THAT BOY IS STILL YOUNG. YOU REMEMBER WHAT IT WAS LIKE WHEN YOU WERE HIS AGE?
WHEN I WAS BRENNAN'S AGE...I HAD ALREADY BEEN IN TERRENOS FOR A FEW YEARS.

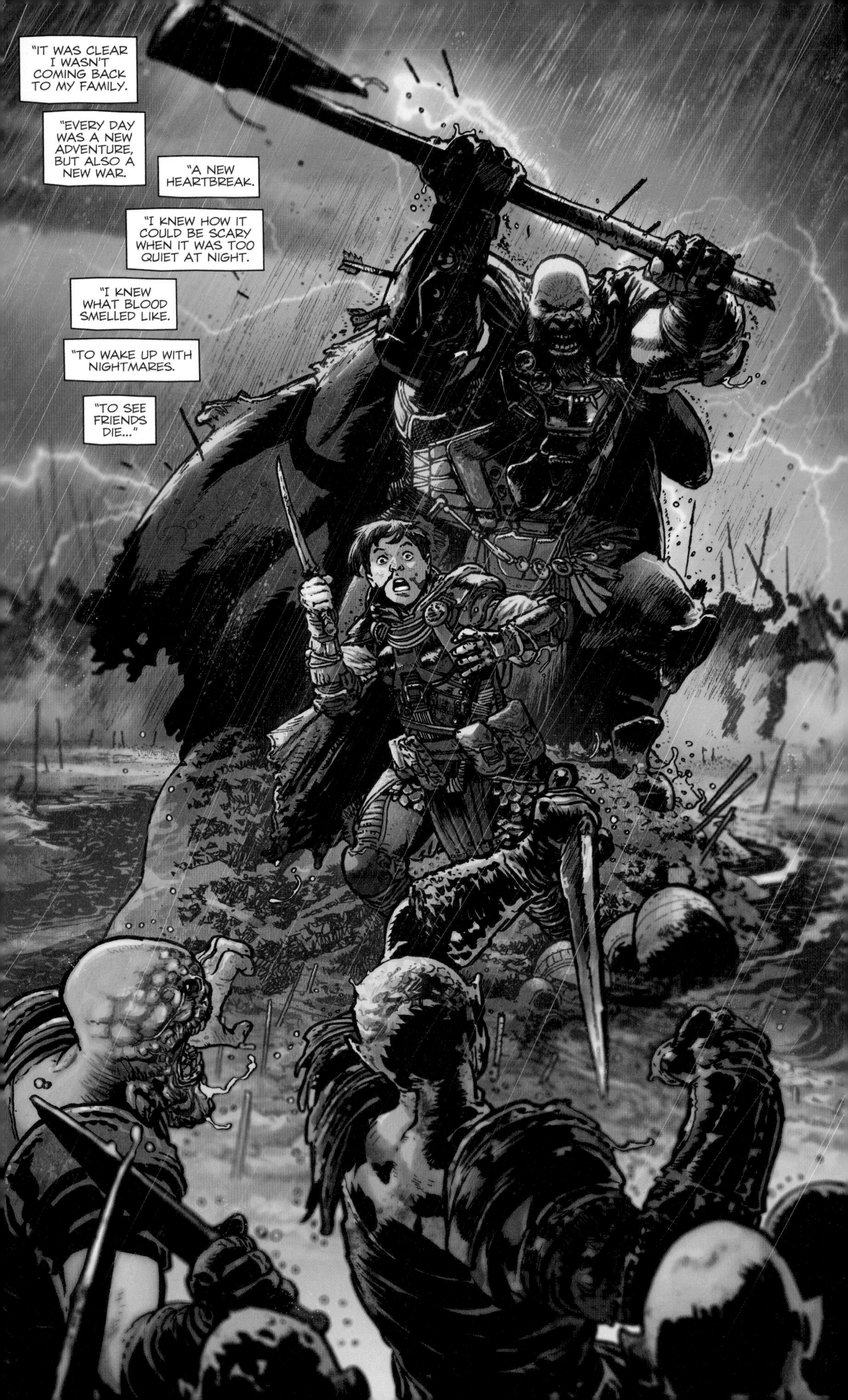
"IT WAS CLEAR I WASN'T COMING BACK TO MY FAMILY.
"EVERY DAY WAS A NEW ADVENTURE, BUT ALSO A NEW WAR.
"A NEW HEARTBREAK.
"I KNEW HOW IT COULD BE SCARY WHEN IT WAS TOO QUIET AT NIGHT.
"I KNEW WHAT BLOOD SMELLED LIKE.
"TO WAKE UP WITH NIGHTMARES.
"TO SEE FRIENDS DIE..."

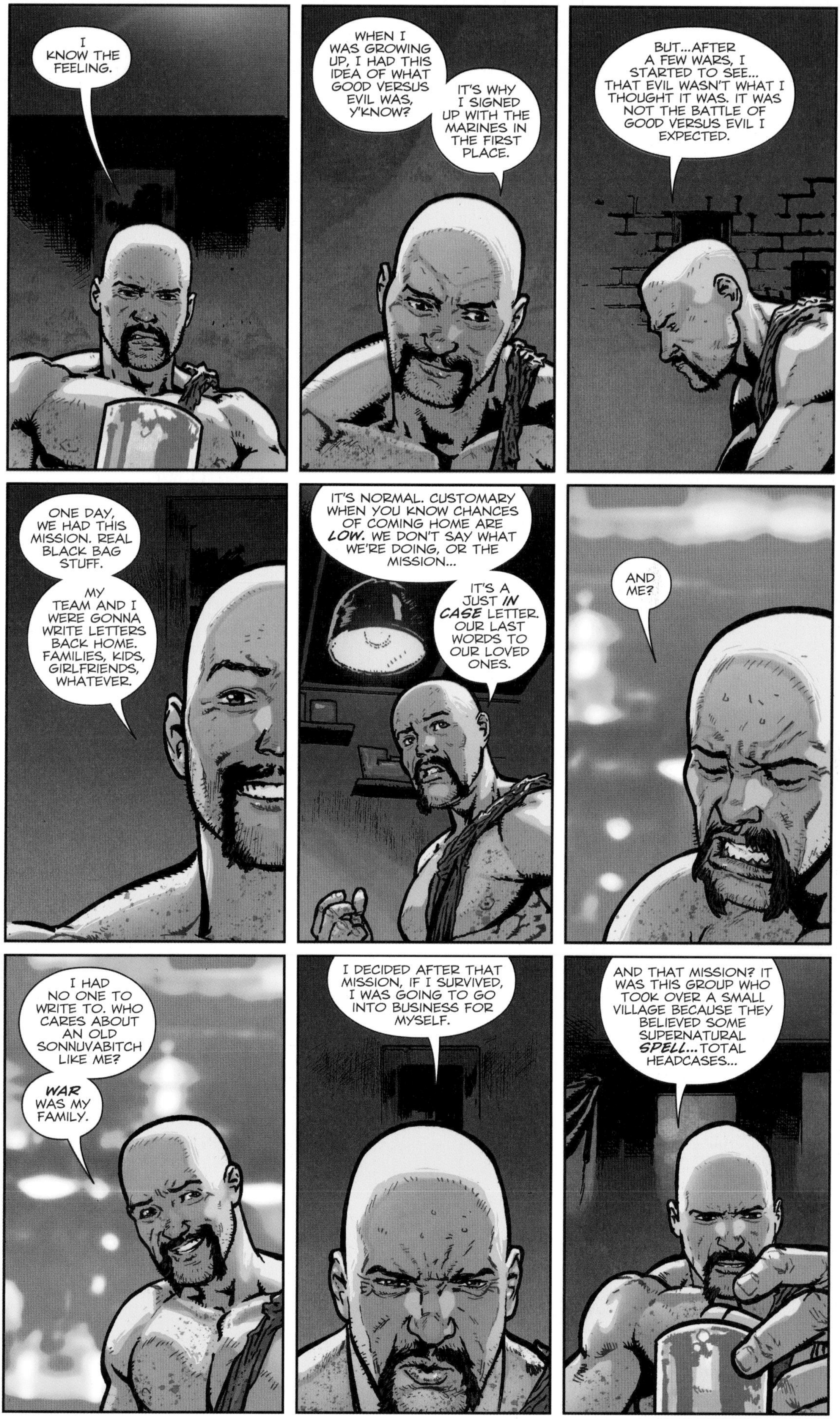
I KNOW THE FEELING.
WHEN I WAS GROWING UP, I HAD THIS IDEA OF WHAT GOOD VERSUS EVIL WAS, Y'KNOW?
IT'S WHY I SIGNED UP WITH THE MARINES IN THE FIRST PLACE.
BUT...AFTER A FEW WARS, I STARTED TO SEE... THAT EVIL WASN'T WHAT I THOUGHT IT WAS. IT WAS NOT THE BATTLE OF GOOD VERSUS EVIL I EXPECTED.
ONE DAY, WE HAD THIS MISSION. REAL BLACK BAG STUFF.
MY TEAM AND I WERE GONNA WRITE LETTERS BACK HOME. FAMILIES, KIDS, GIRLFRIENDS, WHATEVER.
IT'S NORMAL. CUSTOMARY WHEN YOU KNOW CHANCES OF COMING HOME ARE **LOW.** WE DON'T SAY WHAT WE'RE DOING, OR THE MISSION...
IT'S A JUST ***IN CASE*** LETTER. OUR LAST WORDS TO OUR LOVED ONES.
AND ME?
I HAD NO ONE TO WRITE TO. WHO CARES ABOUT AN OLD SONNUVABITCH LIKE ME?
WAR WAS MY FAMILY.
I DECIDED AFTER THAT MISSION, IF I SURVIVED, I WAS GOING TO GO INTO BUSINESS FOR MYSELF.
AND THAT MISSION? IT WAS THIS GROUP WHO TOOK OVER A SMALL VILLAGE BECAUSE THEY BELIEVED SOME SUPERNATURAL ***SPELL...*** TOTAL HEADCASES...

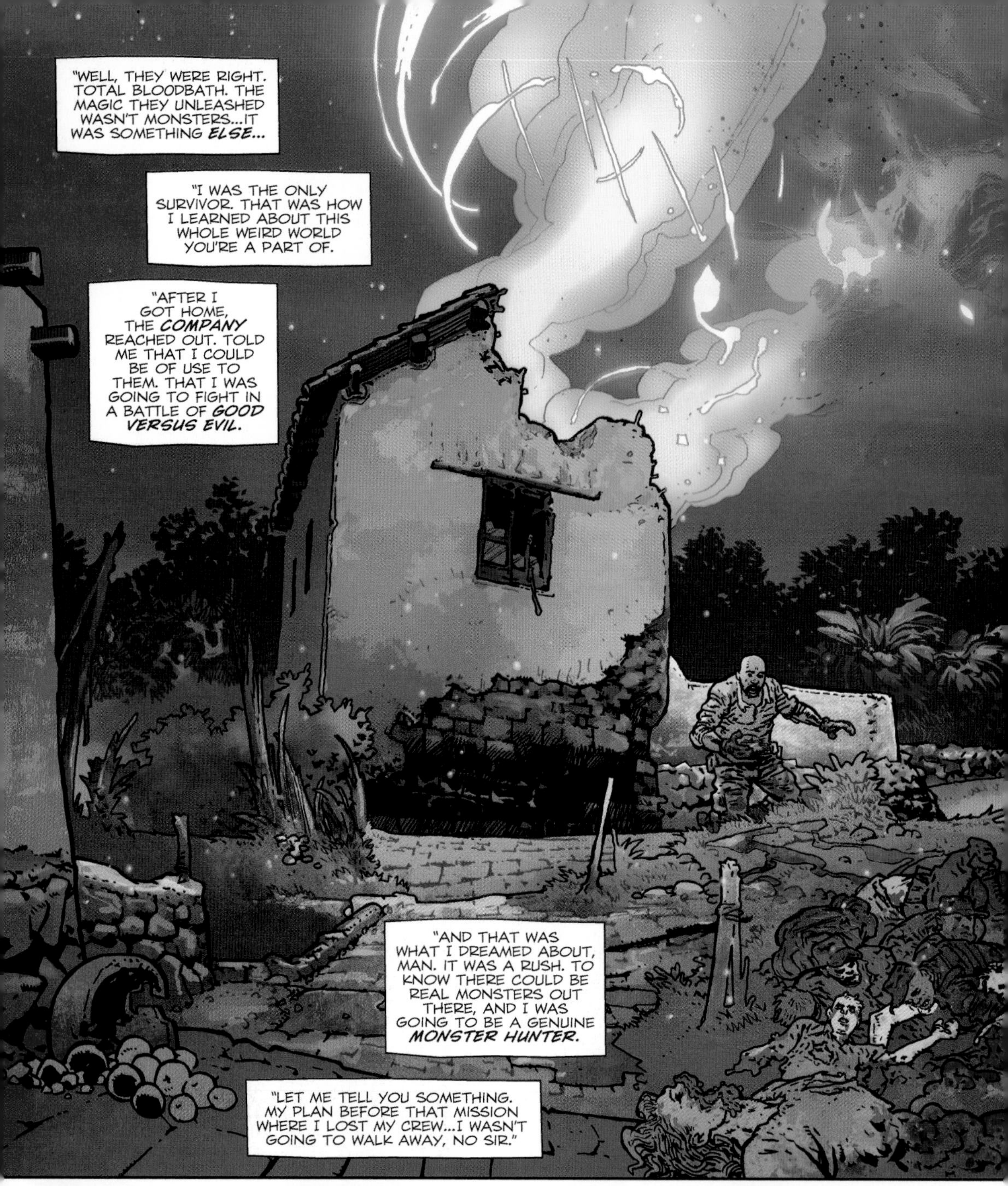
"WELL, THEY WERE RIGHT. TOTAL BLOODBATH. THE MAGIC THEY UNLEASHED WASN'T MONSTERS...IT WAS SOMETHING *ELSE*...
"I WAS THE ONLY SURVIVOR. THAT WAS HOW I LEARNED ABOUT THIS WHOLE WEIRD WORLD YOU'RE A PART OF.
"AFTER I GOT HOME, THE *COMPANY* REACHED OUT. TOLD ME THAT I COULD BE OF USE TO THEM. THAT I WAS GOING TO FIGHT IN A BATTLE OF *GOOD VERSUS EVIL*.
"AND THAT WAS WHAT I DREAMED ABOUT, MAN. IT WAS A RUSH. TO KNOW THERE COULD BE REAL MONSTERS OUT THERE, AND I WAS GOING TO BE A GENUINE *MONSTER HUNTER*.
"LET ME TELL YOU SOMETHING. MY PLAN BEFORE THAT MISSION WHERE I LOST MY CREW...I WASN'T GOING TO WALK AWAY, NO SIR."

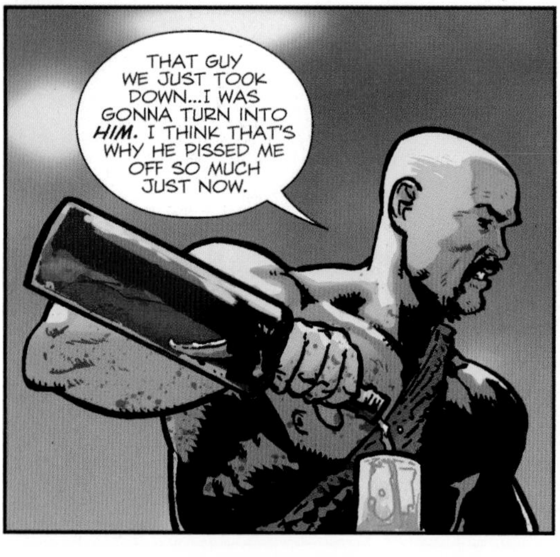
THAT GUY WE JUST TOOK DOWN...I WAS GONNA TURN INTO *HIM*. I THINK THAT'S WHY HE PISSED ME OFF SO MUCH JUST NOW.

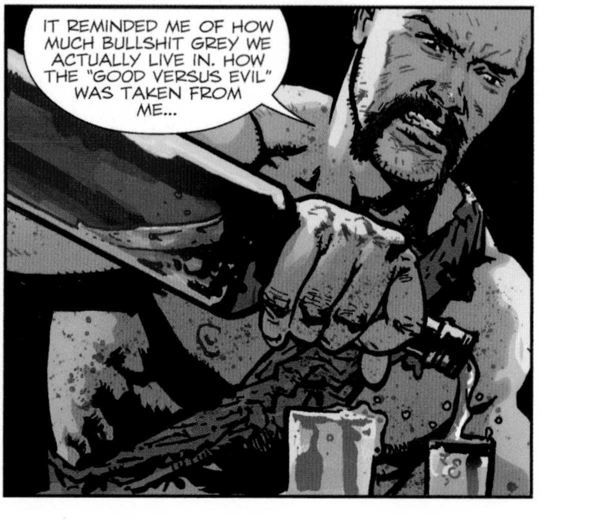
IT REMINDED ME OF HOW MUCH BULLSHIT GREY WE ACTUALLY LIVE IN. HOW THE "GOOD VERSUS EVIL" WAS TAKEN FROM ME...

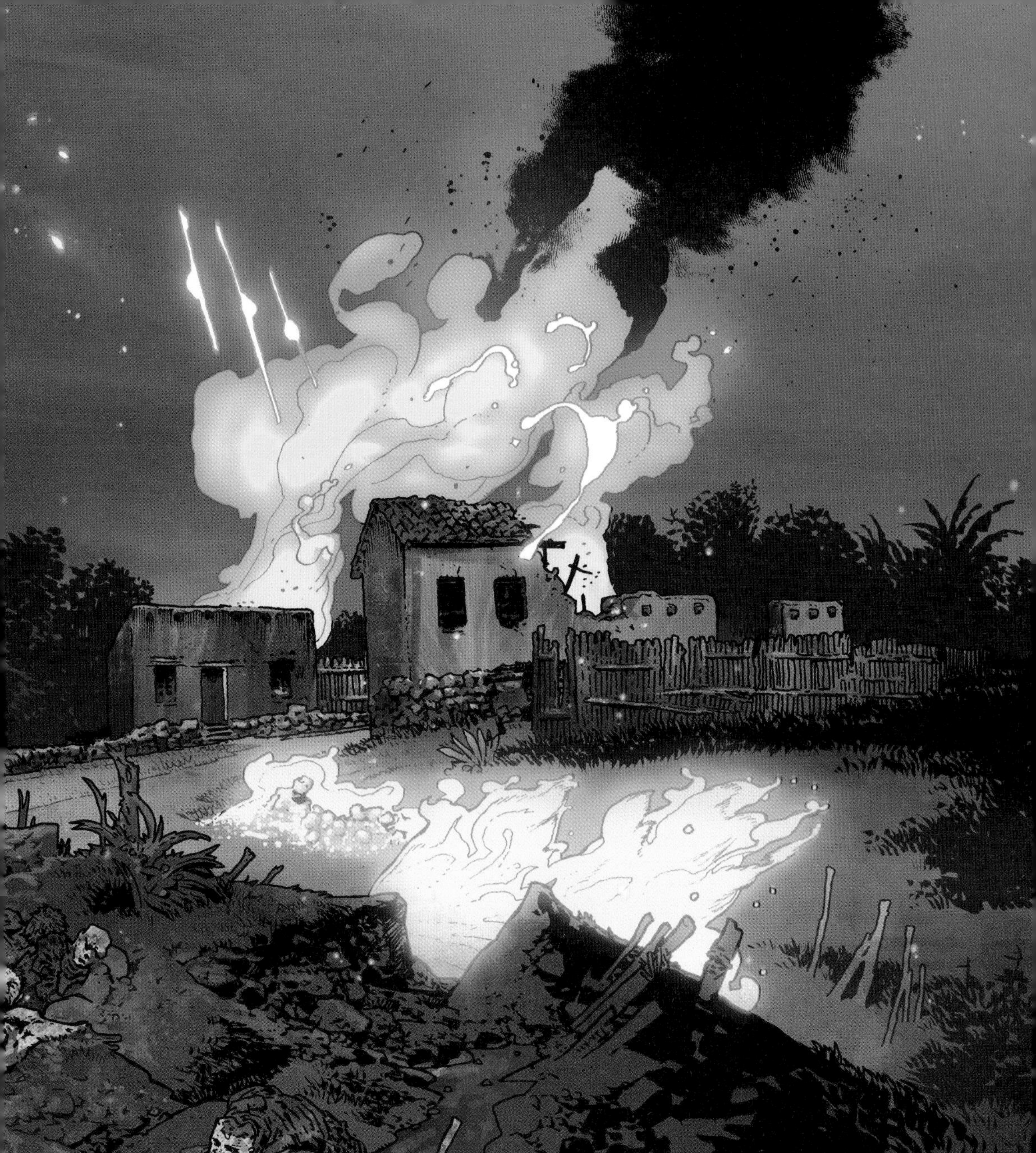

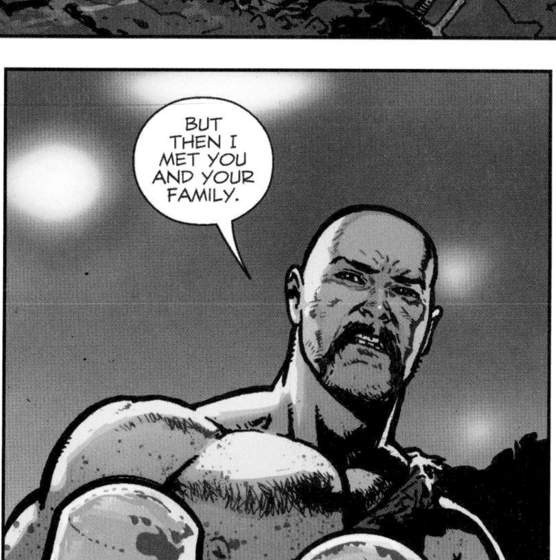
BUT THEN I MET YOU AND YOUR FAMILY.

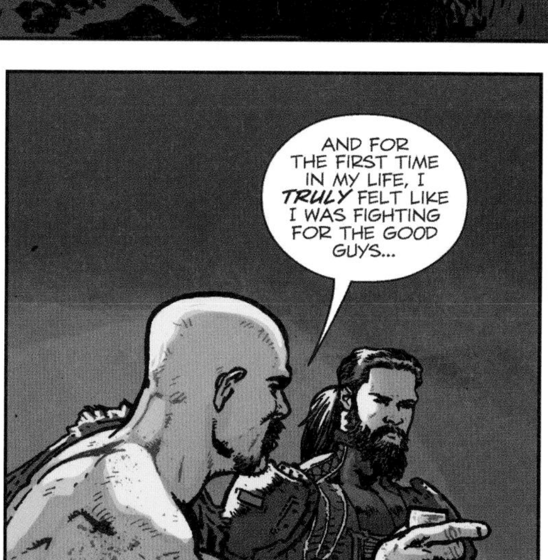
AND FOR THE FIRST TIME IN MY LIFE, I *TRULY* FELT LIKE I WAS FIGHTING FOR THE GOOD GUYS...

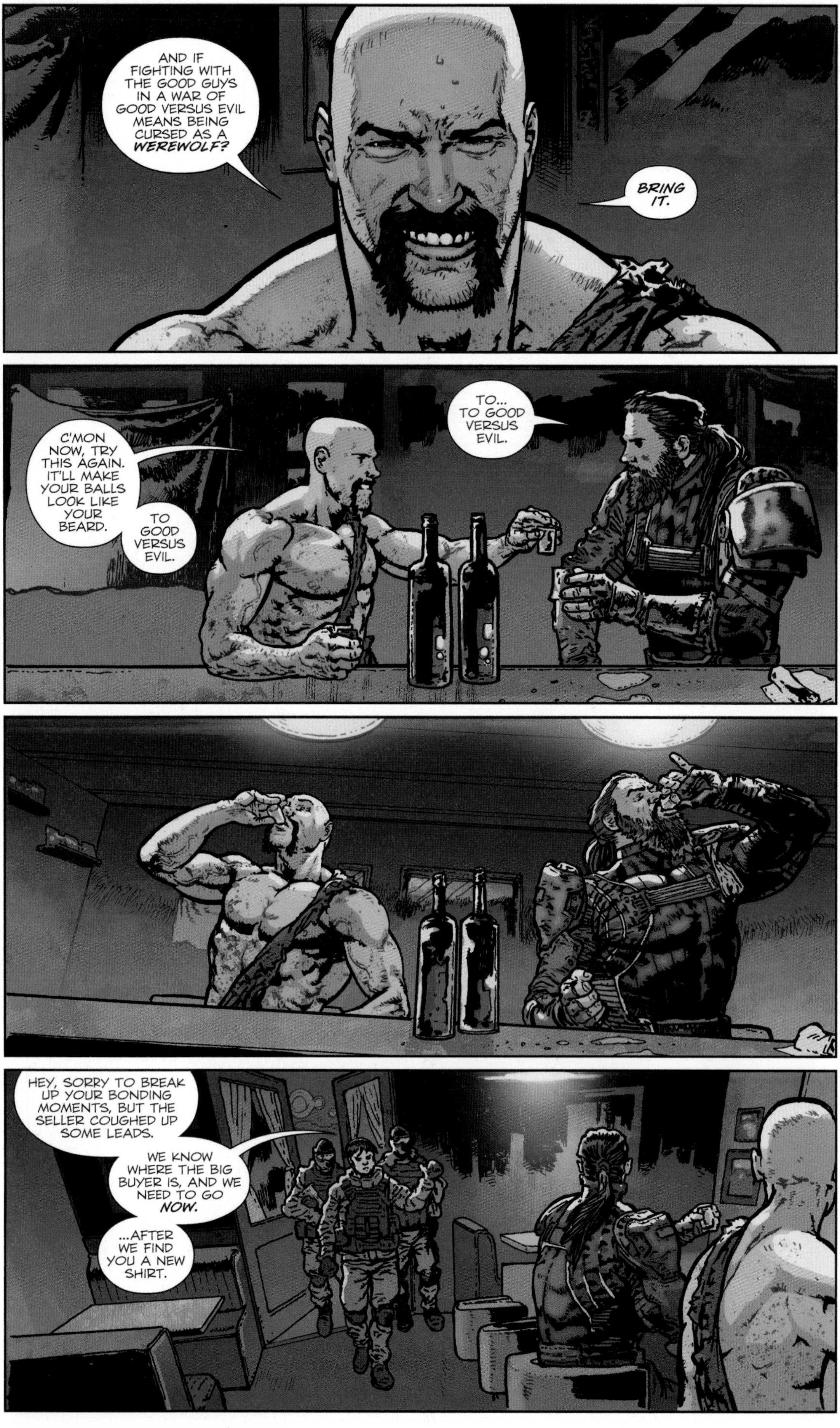
AND IF FIGHTING WITH THE GOOD GUYS IN A WAR OF GOOD VERSUS EVIL MEANS BEING CURSED AS A *WEREWOLF?*
BRING IT.
C'MON NOW, TRY THIS AGAIN. IT'LL MAKE YOUR BALLS LOOK LIKE YOUR BEARD.
TO GOOD VERSUS EVIL.
TO... TO GOOD VERSUS EVIL.
HEY, SORRY TO BREAK UP YOUR BONDING MOMENTS, BUT THE SELLER COUGHED UP SOME LEADS.
WE KNOW WHERE THE BIG BUYER IS, AND WE NEED TO GO *NOW.*
...AFTER WE FIND YOU A NEW SHIRT.

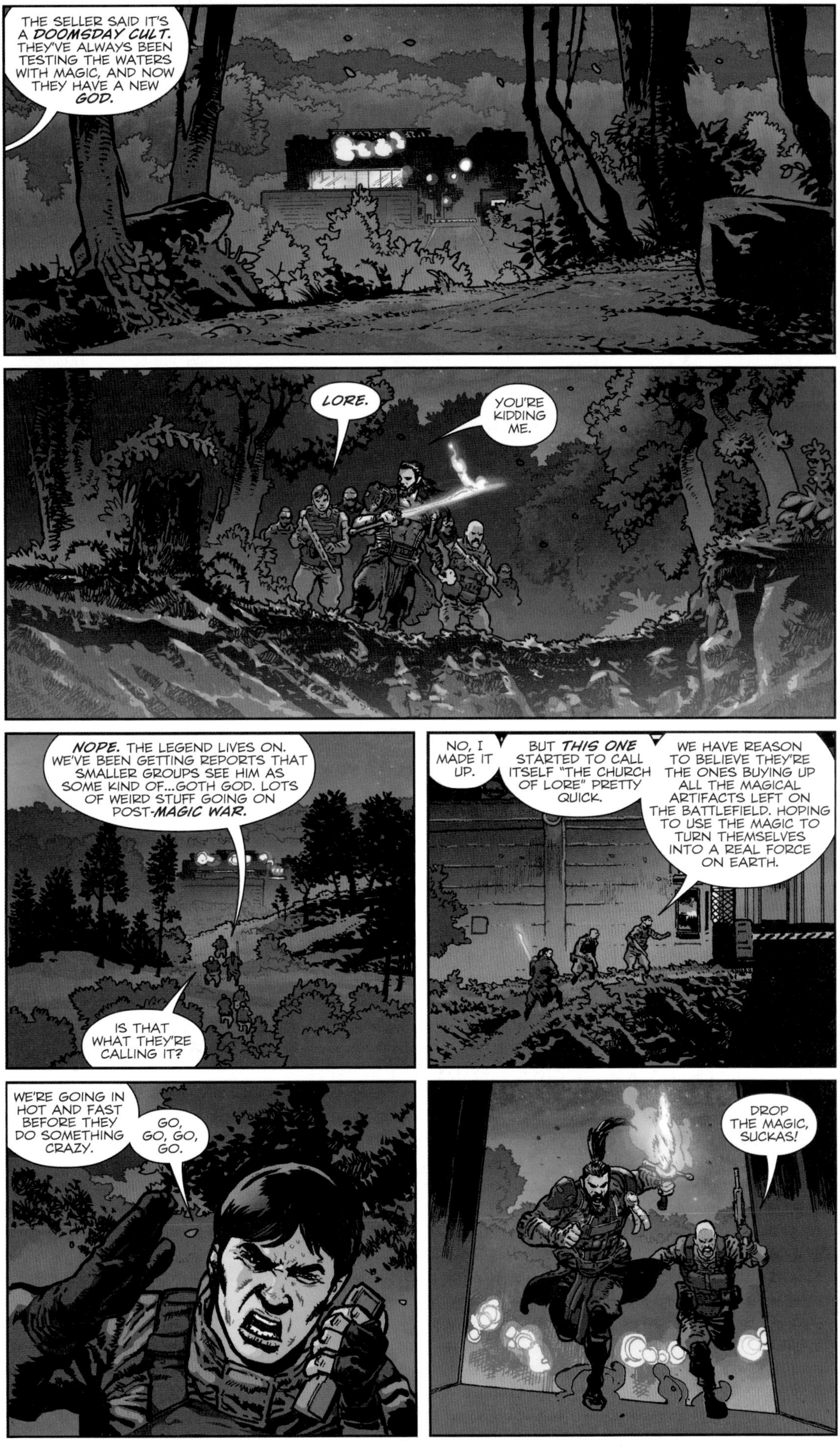
THE SELLER SAID IT'S A DOOMSDAY CULT. THEY'VE ALWAYS BEEN TESTING THE WATERS WITH MAGIC, AND NOW THEY HAVE A NEW GOD.
LORE.
YOU'RE KIDDING ME.
NOPE. THE LEGEND LIVES ON. WE'VE BEEN GETTING REPORTS THAT SMALLER GROUPS SEE HIM AS SOME KIND OF...GOTH GOD. LOTS OF WEIRD STUFF GOING ON POST-MAGIC WAR.
IS THAT WHAT THEY'RE CALLING IT?
NO, I MADE IT UP.
BUT THIS ONE STARTED TO CALL ITSELF "THE CHURCH OF LORE" PRETTY QUICK.
WE HAVE REASON TO BELIEVE THEY'RE THE ONES BUYING UP ALL THE MAGICAL ARTIFACTS LEFT ON THE BATTLEFIELD. HOPING TO USE THE MAGIC TO TURN THEMSELVES INTO A REAL FORCE ON EARTH.
WE'RE GOING IN HOT AND FAST BEFORE THEY DO SOMETHING CRAZY.
GO, GO, GO, GO.
DROP THE MAGIC, SUCKAS!

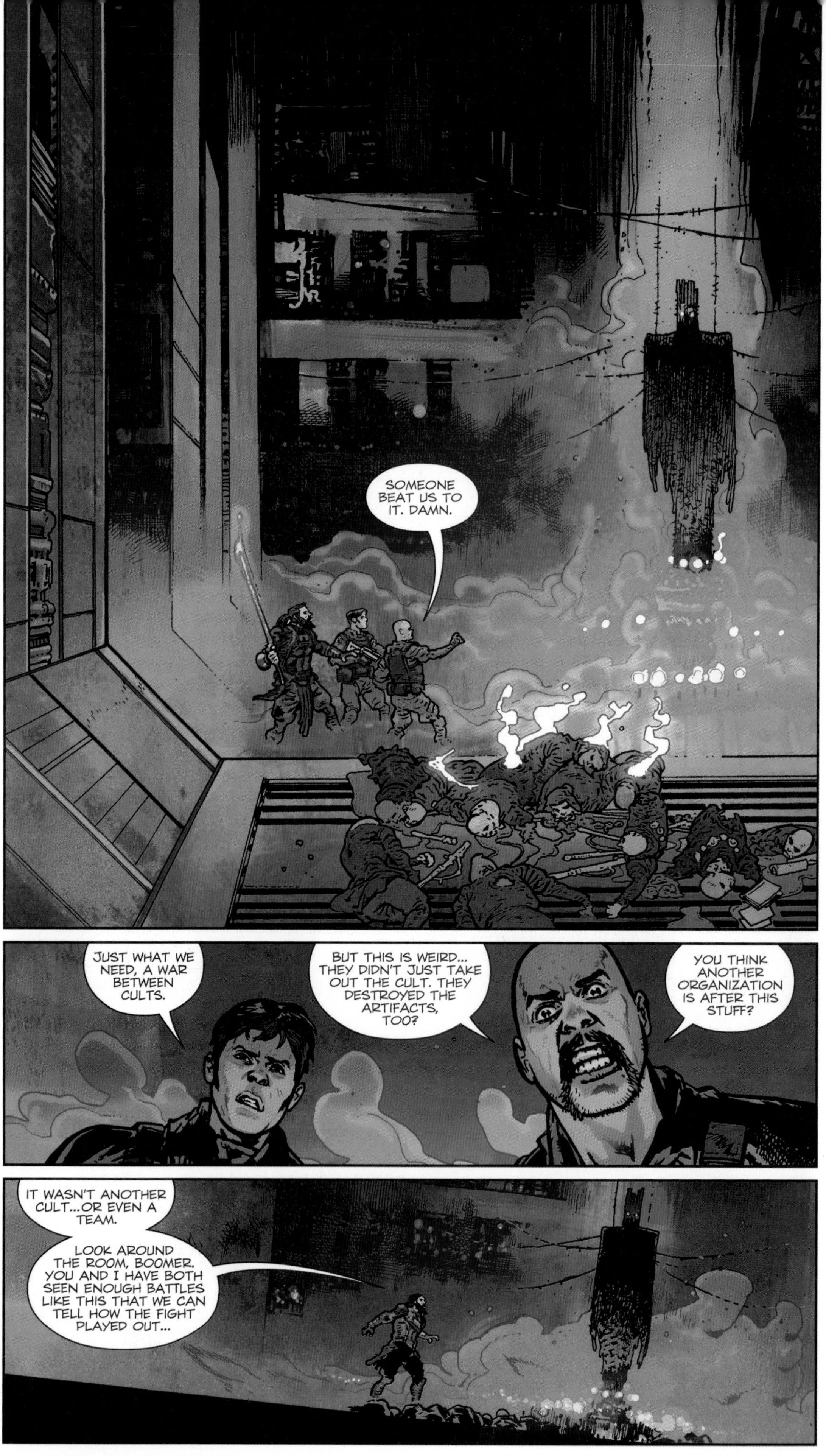
SOMEONE BEAT US TO IT. DAMN.
JUST WHAT WE NEED, A WAR BETWEEN CULTS.
BUT THIS IS WEIRD... THEY DIDN'T JUST TAKE OUT THE CULT. THEY DESTROYED THE ARTIFACTS, TOO?
YOU THINK ANOTHER ORGANIZATION IS AFTER THIS STUFF?
IT WASN'T ANOTHER CULT...OR EVEN A TEAM.
LOOK AROUND THE ROOM, BOOMER. YOU AND I HAVE BOTH SEEN ENOUGH BATTLES LIKE THIS THAT WE CAN TELL HOW THE FIGHT PLAYED OUT...

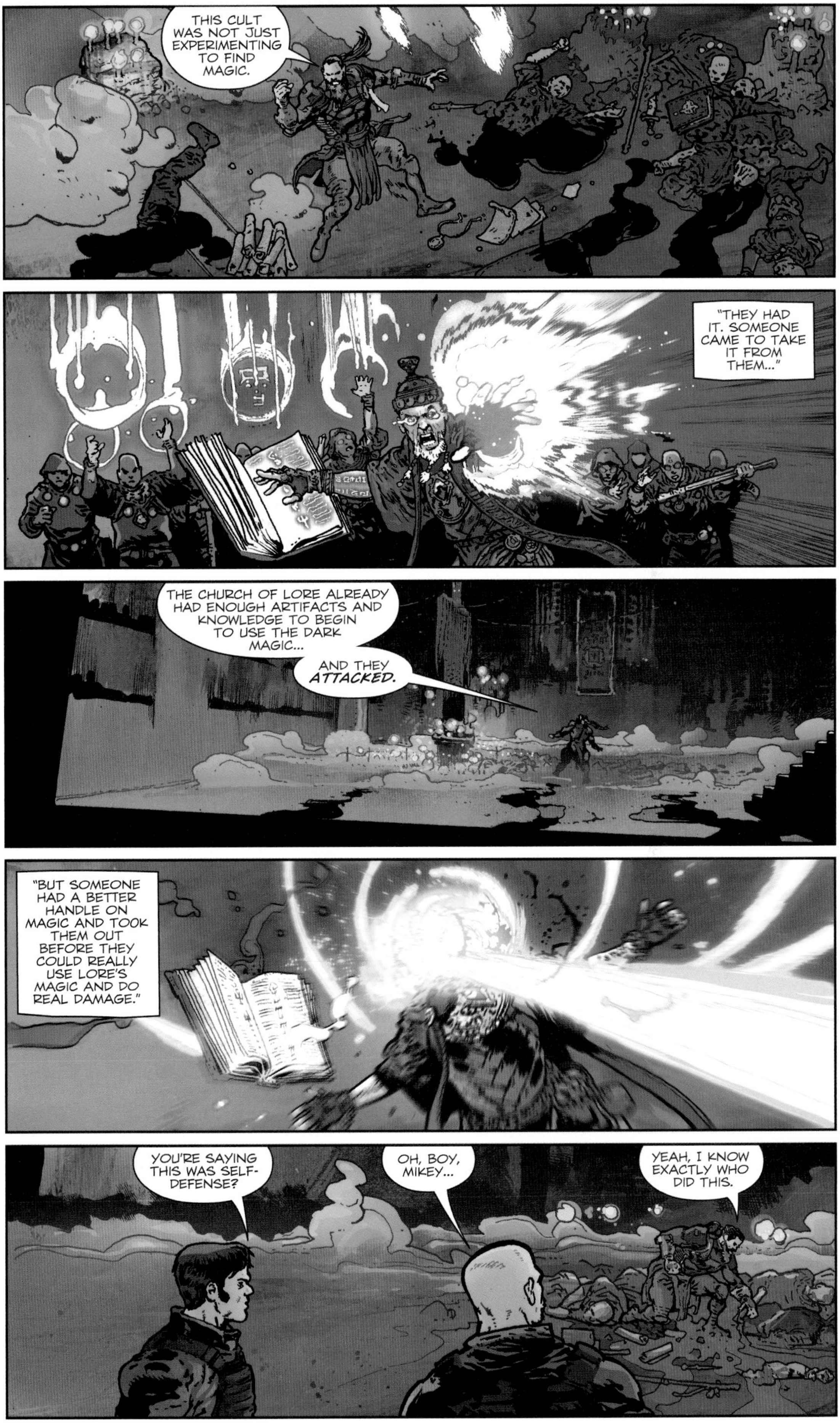
THIS CULT WAS NOT JUST EXPERIMENTING TO FIND MAGIC.
"THEY HAD IT. SOMEONE CAME TO TAKE IT FROM THEM..."
THE CHURCH OF LORE ALREADY HAD ENOUGH ARTIFACTS AND KNOWLEDGE TO BEGIN TO USE THE DARK MAGIC...
AND THEY *ATTACKED.*
"BUT SOMEONE HAD A BETTER HANDLE ON MAGIC AND TOOK THEM OUT BEFORE THEY COULD REALLY USE LORE'S MAGIC AND DO REAL DAMAGE."
YOU'RE SAYING THIS WAS SELF-DEFENSE?
OH, BOY, MIKEY...
YEAH, I KNOW EXACTLY WHO DID THIS.

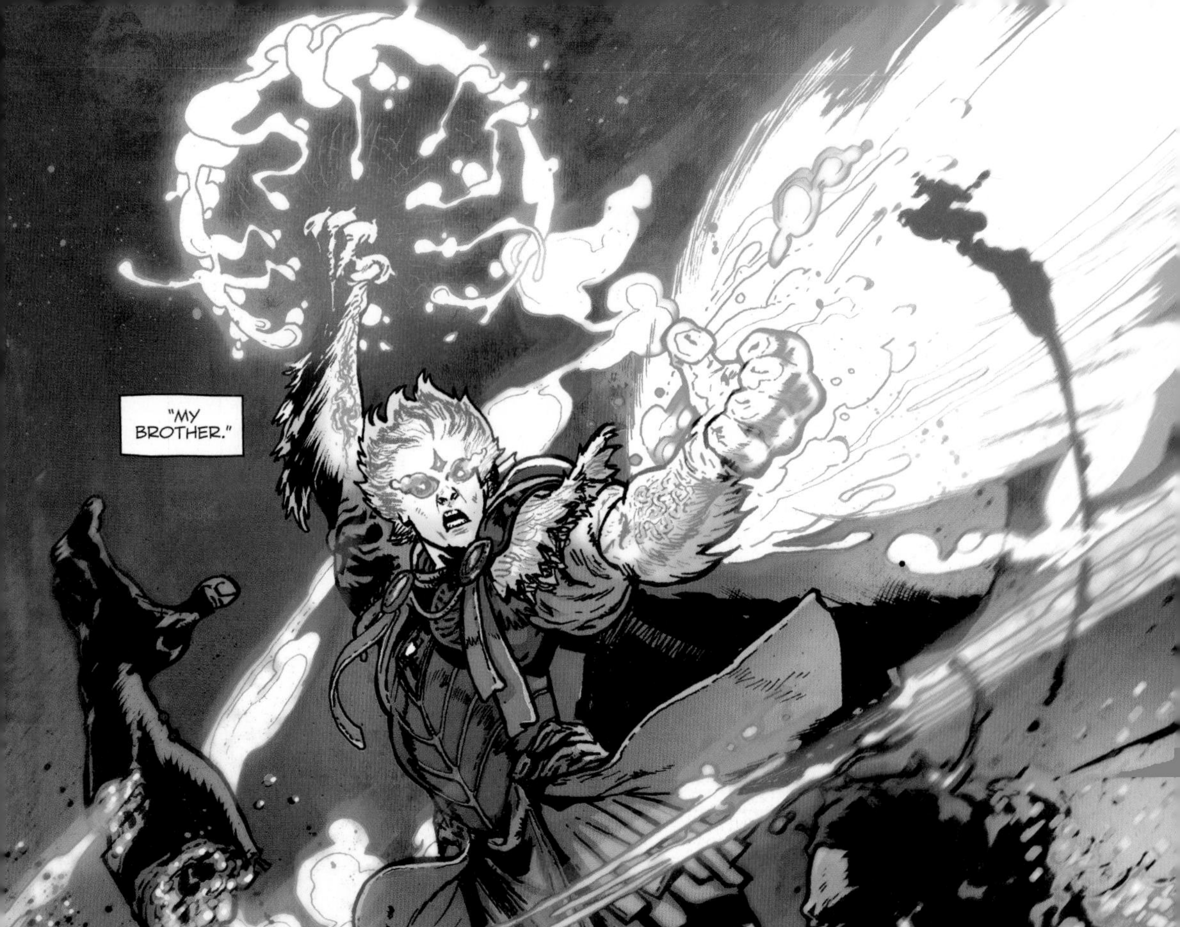
"MY BROTHER."
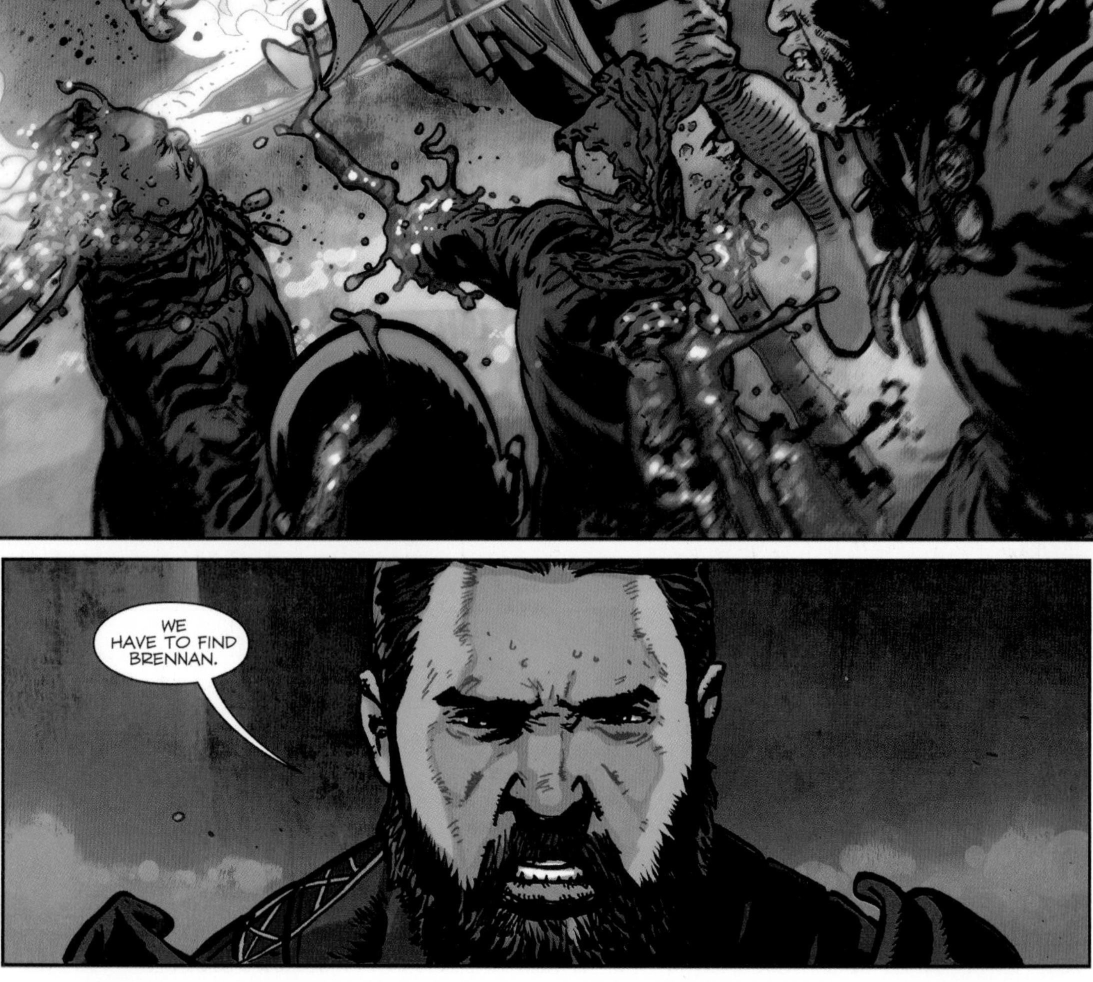
WE HAVE TO FIND BRENNAN.

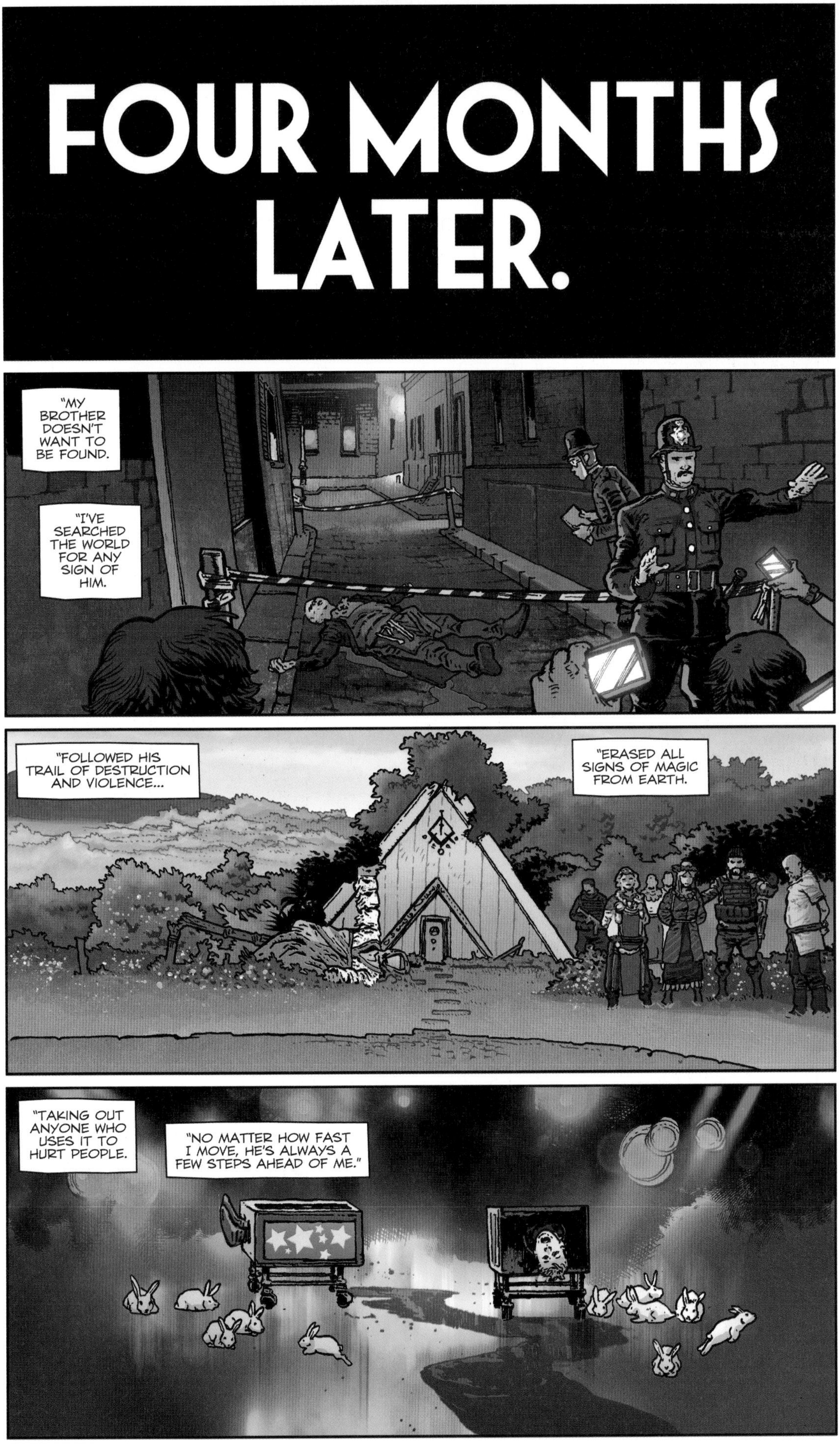
FOUR MONTHS LATER.
"MY BROTHER DOESN'T WANT TO BE FOUND.
"I'VE SEARCHED THE WORLD FOR ANY SIGN OF HIM.
"FOLLOWED HIS TRAIL OF DESTRUCTION AND VIOLENCE...
"ERASED ALL SIGNS OF MAGIC FROM EARTH.
"TAKING OUT ANYONE WHO USES IT TO HURT PEOPLE.
"NO MATTER HOW FAST I MOVE, HE'S ALWAYS A FEW STEPS AHEAD OF ME."

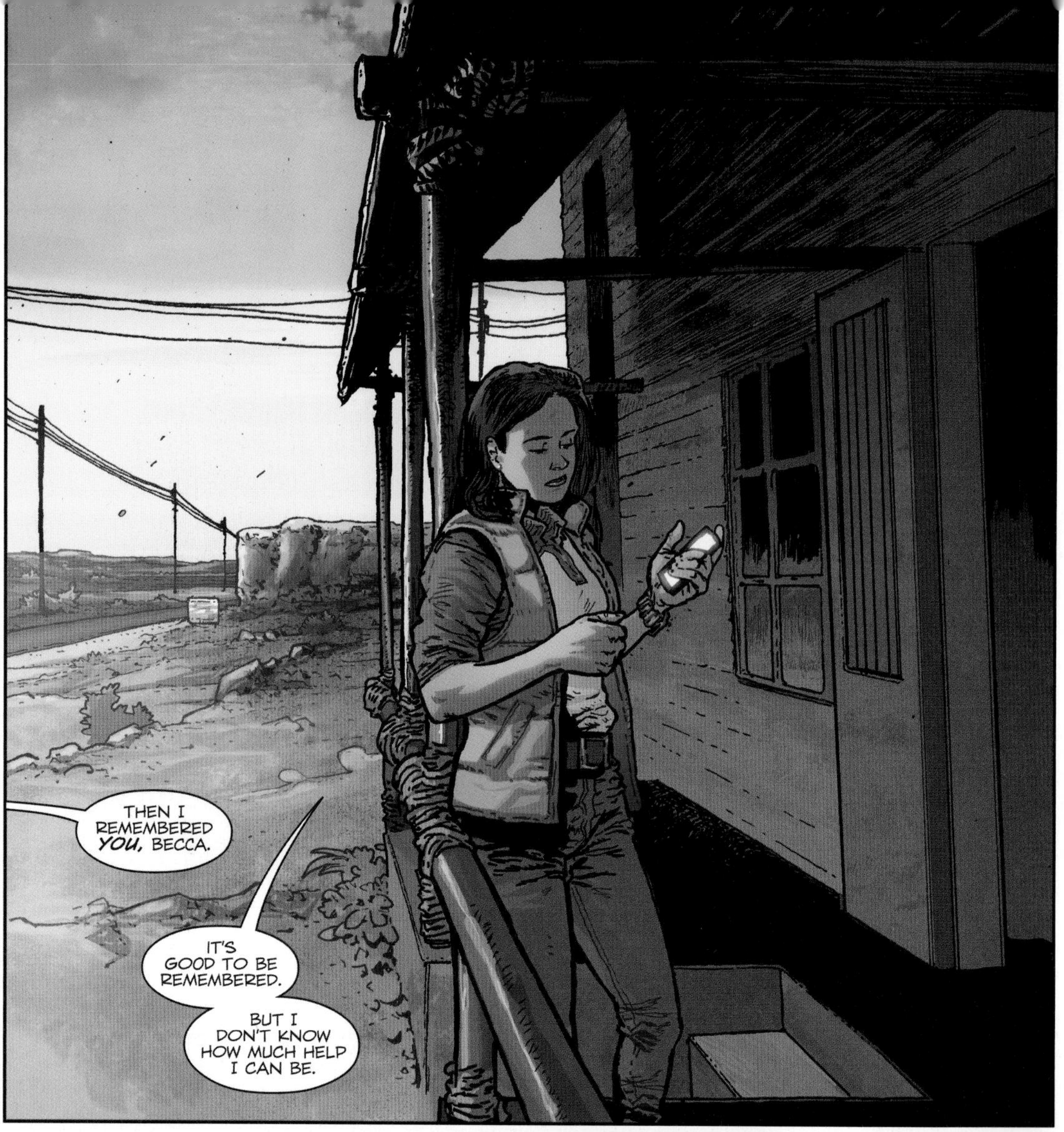
THEN I REMEMBERED *YOU,* BECCA.
IT'S GOOD TO BE REMEMBERED.
BUT I DON'T KNOW HOW MUCH HELP I CAN BE.

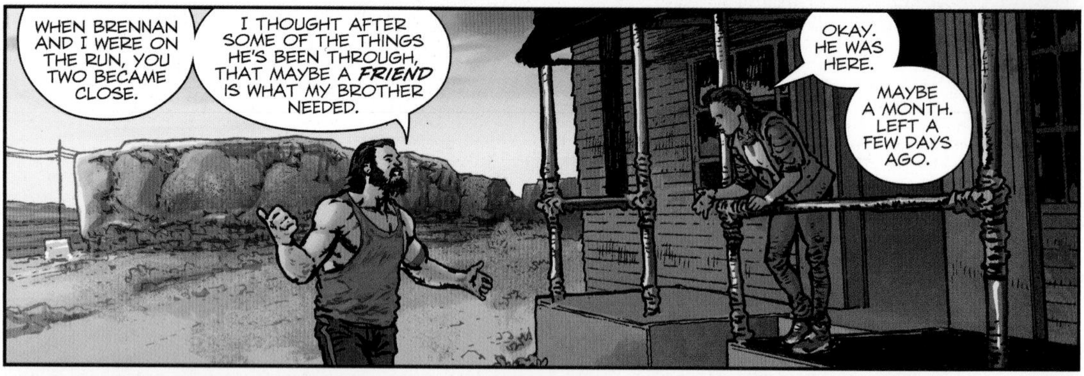
WHEN BRENNAN AND I WERE ON THE RUN, YOU TWO BECAME CLOSE.
I THOUGHT AFTER SOME OF THE THINGS HE'S BEEN THROUGH, THAT MAYBE A *FRIEND* IS WHAT MY BROTHER NEEDED.
OKAY. HE WAS HERE.
MAYBE A MONTH. LEFT A FEW DAYS AGO.

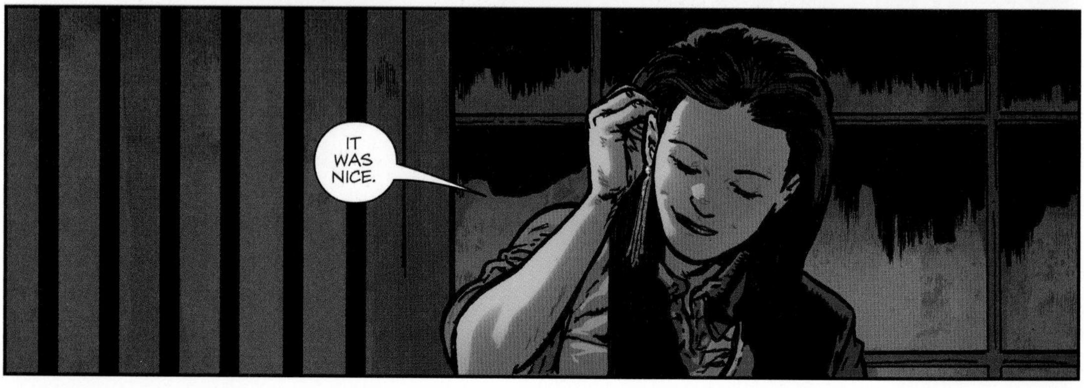
IT WAS NICE.

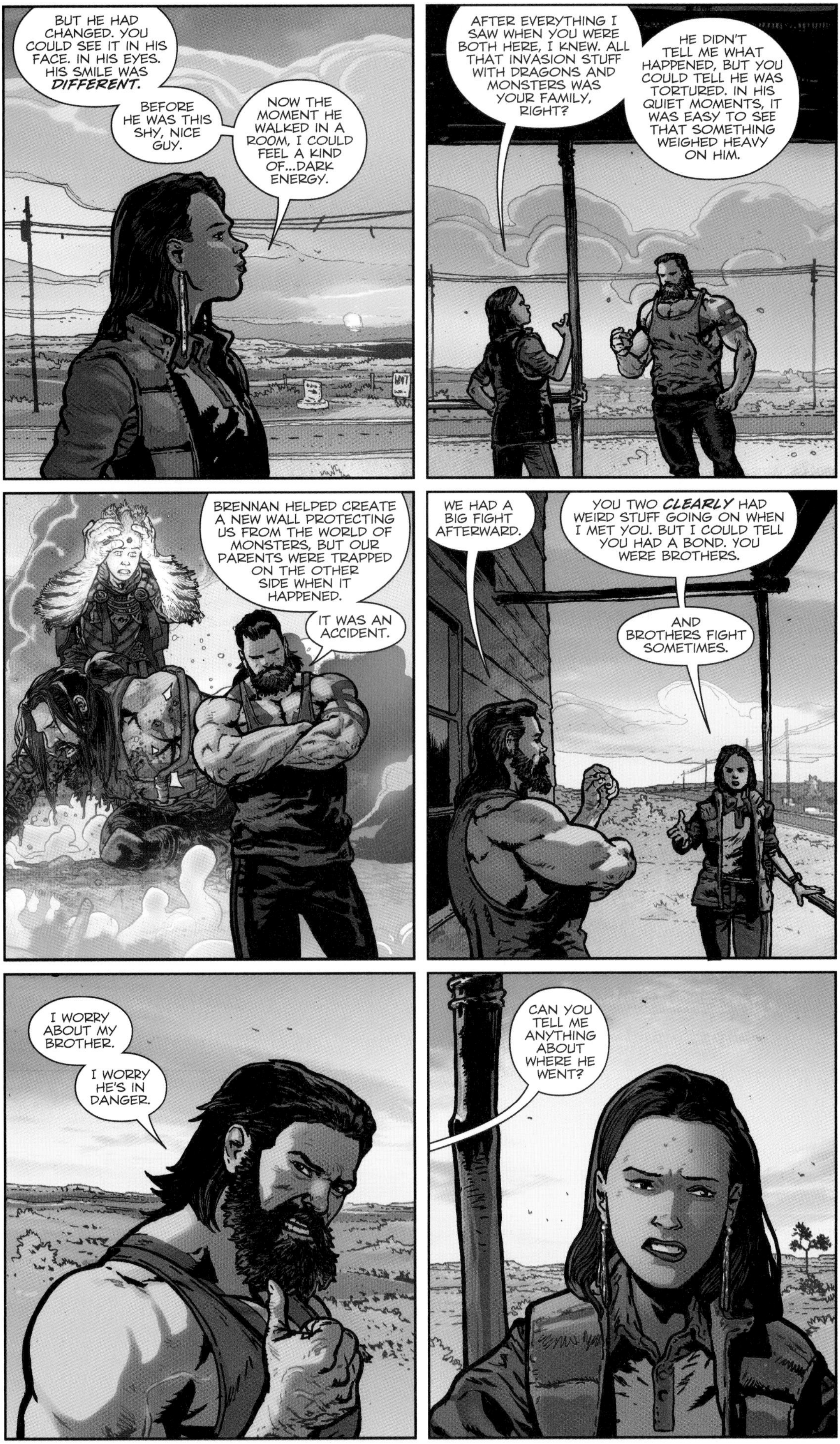
BUT HE HAD CHANGED. YOU COULD SEE IT IN HIS FACE. IN HIS EYES. HIS SMILE WAS *DIFFERENT.*
BEFORE HE WAS THIS SHY, NICE GUY.
NOW THE MOMENT HE WALKED IN A ROOM, I COULD FEEL A KIND OF...DARK ENERGY.
AFTER EVERYTHING I SAW WHEN YOU WERE BOTH HERE, I KNEW. ALL THAT INVASION STUFF WITH DRAGONS AND MONSTERS WAS YOUR FAMILY, RIGHT?
HE DIDN'T TELL ME WHAT HAPPENED, BUT YOU COULD TELL HE WAS TORTURED. IN HIS QUIET MOMENTS, IT WAS EASY TO SEE THAT SOMETHING WEIGHED HEAVY ON HIM.
BRENNAN HELPED CREATE A NEW WALL PROTECTING US FROM THE WORLD OF MONSTERS, BUT OUR PARENTS WERE TRAPPED ON THE OTHER SIDE WHEN IT HAPPENED.
IT WAS AN ACCIDENT.
WE HAD A BIG FIGHT AFTERWARD.
YOU TWO *CLEARLY* HAD WEIRD STUFF GOING ON WHEN I MET YOU. BUT I COULD TELL YOU HAD A BOND. YOU WERE BROTHERS.
AND BROTHERS FIGHT SOMETIMES.
I WORRY ABOUT MY BROTHER.
I WORRY HE'S IN DANGER.
CAN YOU TELL ME ANYTHING ABOUT WHERE HE WENT?

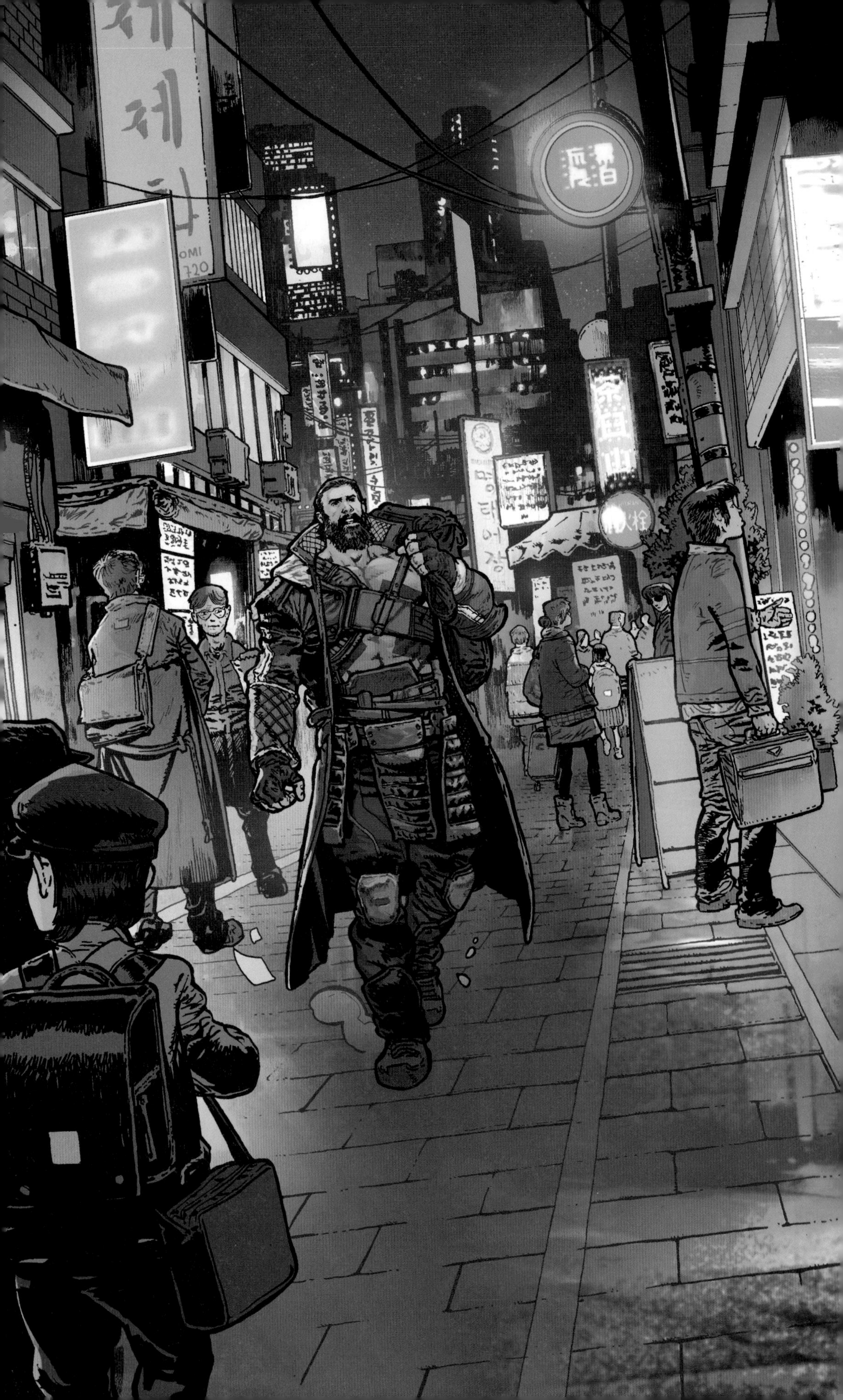

WOW...

⟨HEY, BRO!⟩

⟨GIVE IT BACK.⟩

⟨JUST HOLD ON!⟩

⟨I'M TELLING MOM!⟩

TOY STORE

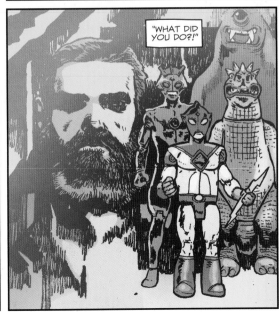

"WHAT DID YOU DO?!"

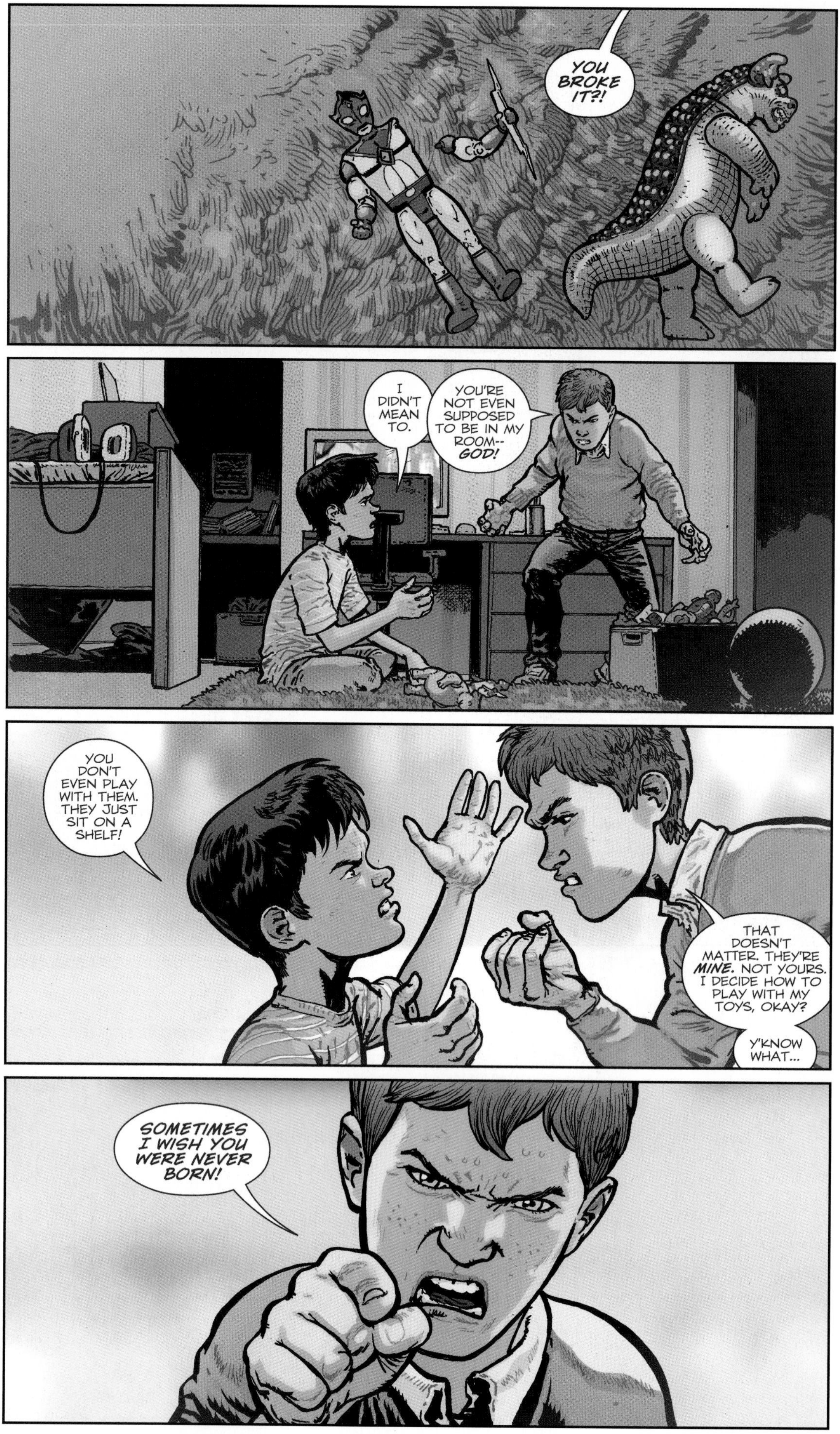

YOU BROKE IT?!
I DIDN'T MEAN TO.
YOU'RE NOT EVEN SUPPOSED TO BE IN MY ROOM-- GOD!
YOU DON'T EVEN PLAY WITH THEM. THEY JUST SIT ON A SHELF!
THAT DOESN'T MATTER. THEY'RE MINE. NOT YOURS. I DECIDE HOW TO PLAY WITH MY TOYS, OKAY?
Y'KNOW WHAT...
SOMETIMES I WISH YOU WERE NEVER BORN!

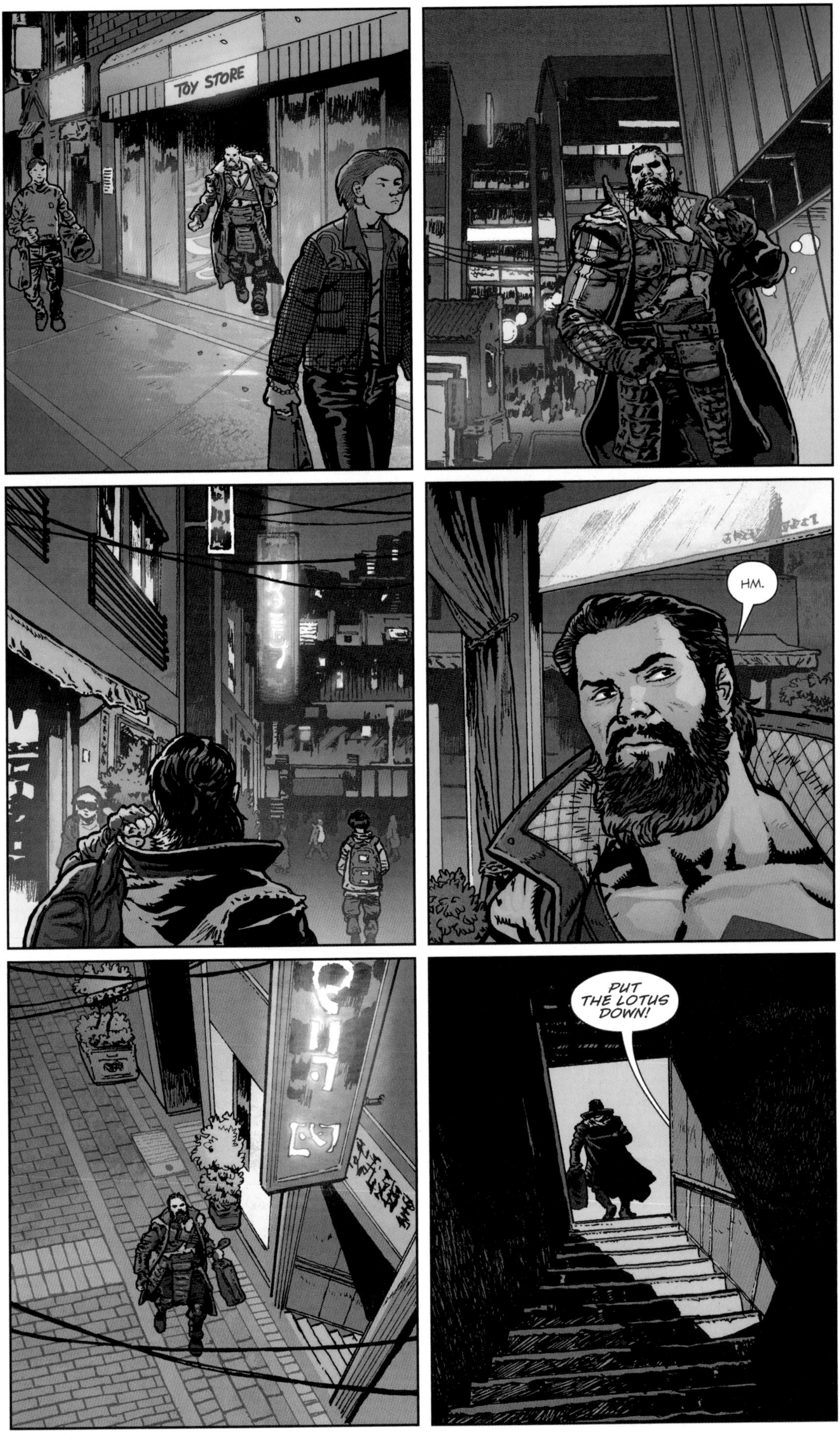
TOY STORE
HM.
PUT THE LOTUS DOWN!

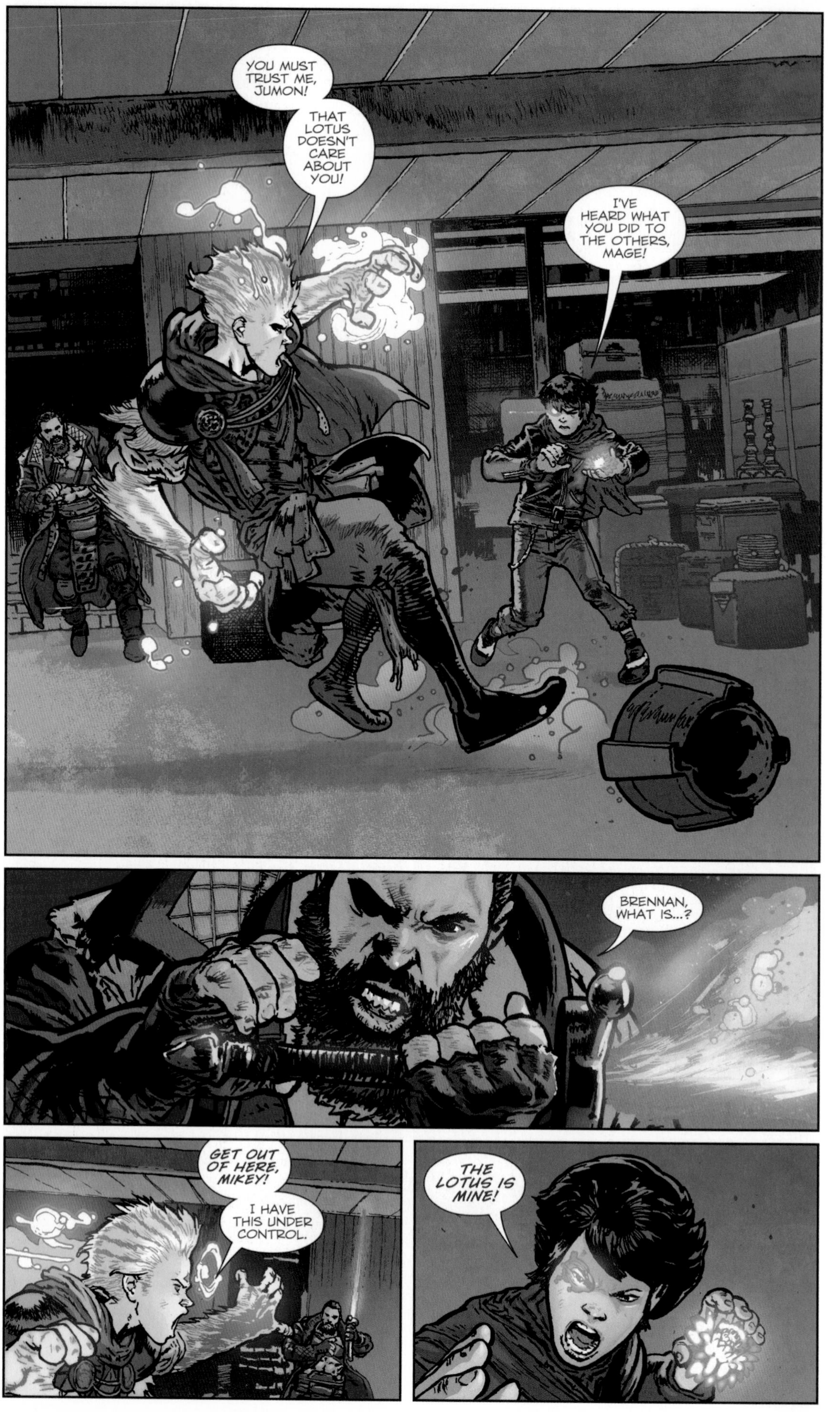
YOU MUST TRUST ME, JUMON!
THAT LOTUS DOESN'T CARE ABOUT YOU!
I'VE HEARD WHAT YOU DID TO THE OTHERS, MAGE!
BRENNAN, WHAT IS...?
GET OUT OF HERE, MIKEY!
I HAVE THIS UNDER CONTROL.
THE LOTUS IS MINE!

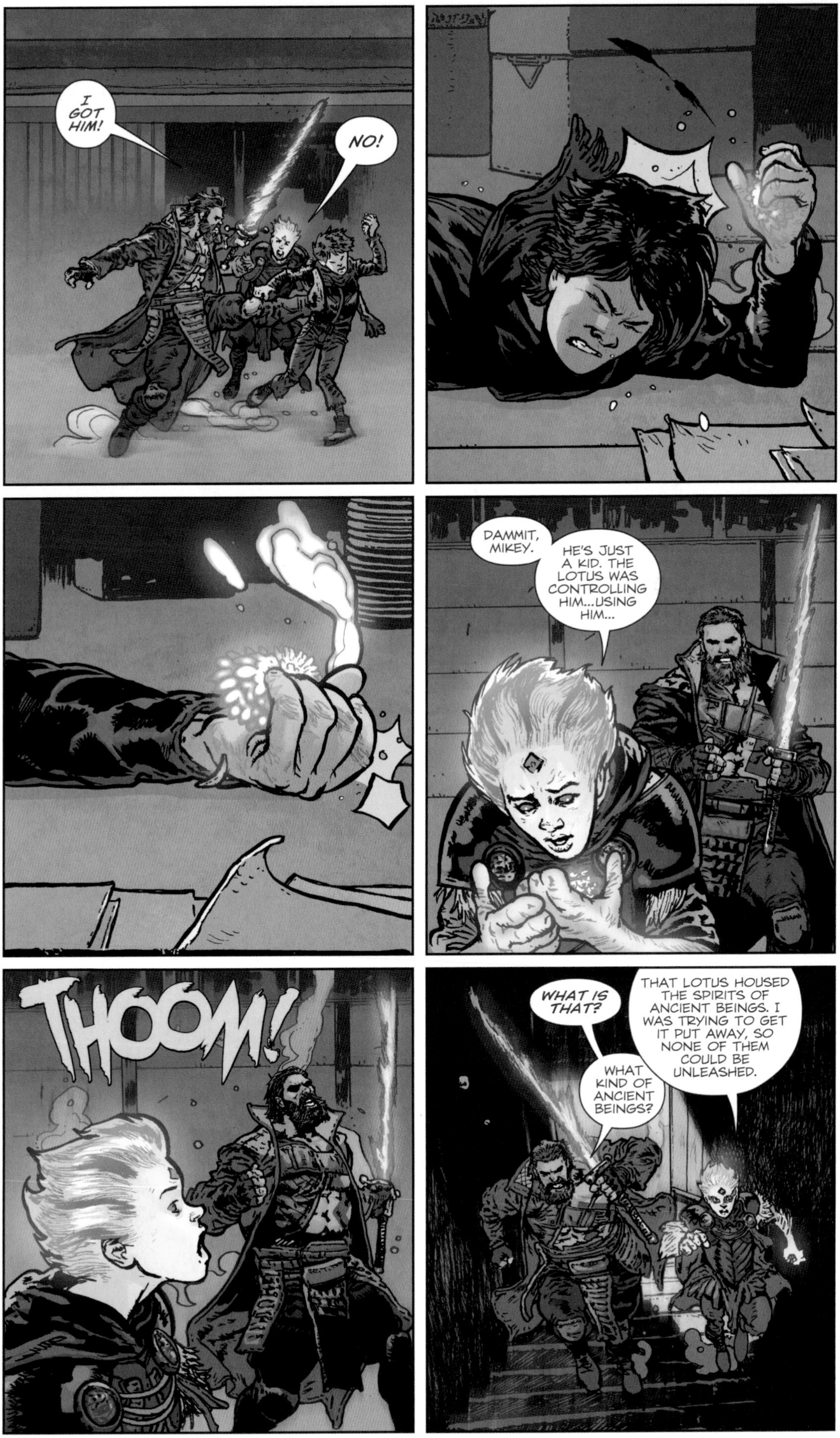
I GOT HIM!
NO!
DAMMIT, MIKEY.
HE'S JUST A KID. THE LOTUS WAS CONTROLLING HIM...USING HIM...
THOOM!
WHAT IS THAT?
WHAT KIND OF ANCIENT BEINGS?
THAT LOTUS HOUSED THE SPIRITS OF ANCIENT BEINGS. I WAS TRYING TO GET IT PUT AWAY, SO NONE OF THEM COULD BE UNLEASHED.

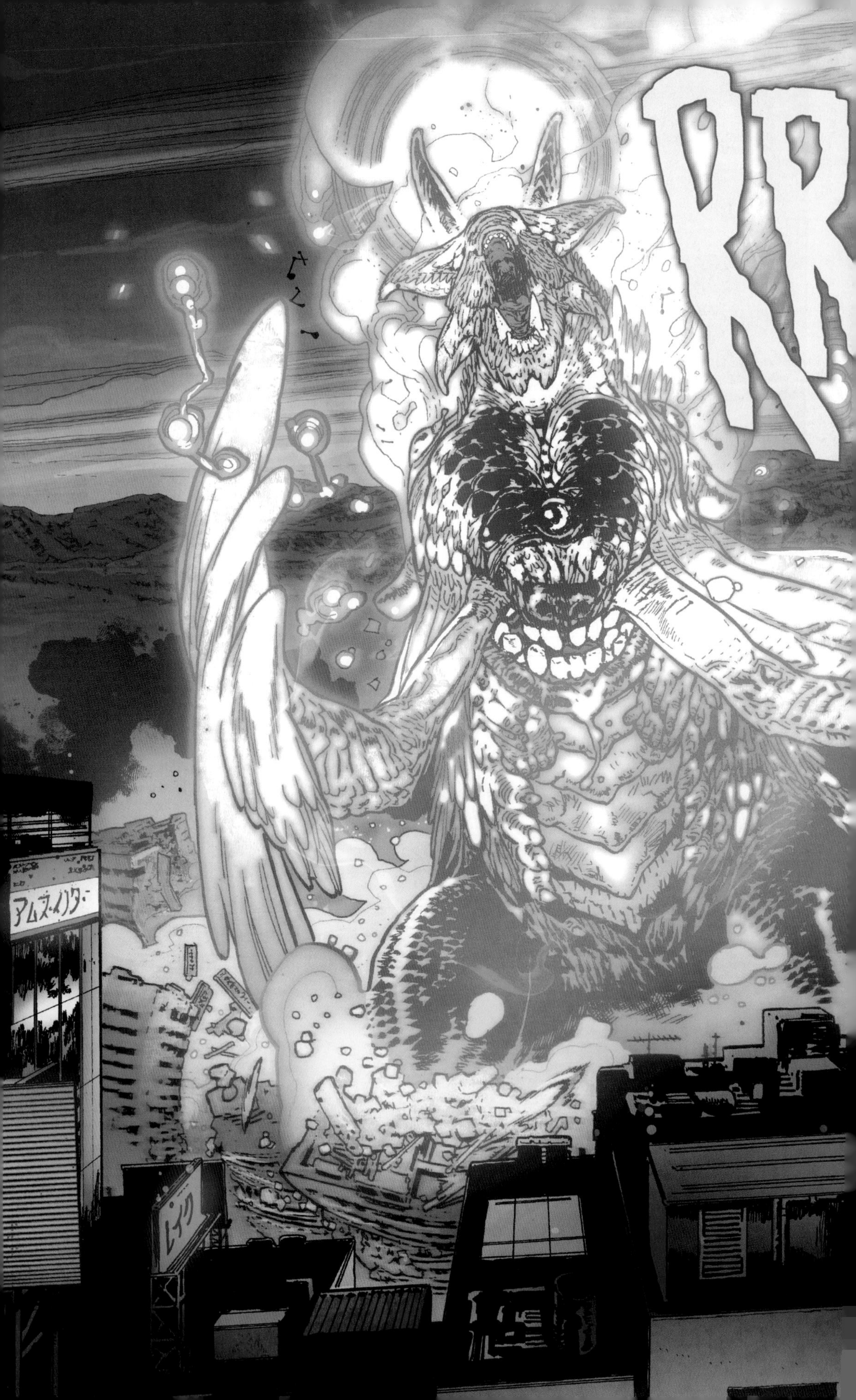
RR
アムズ・インター
レイク

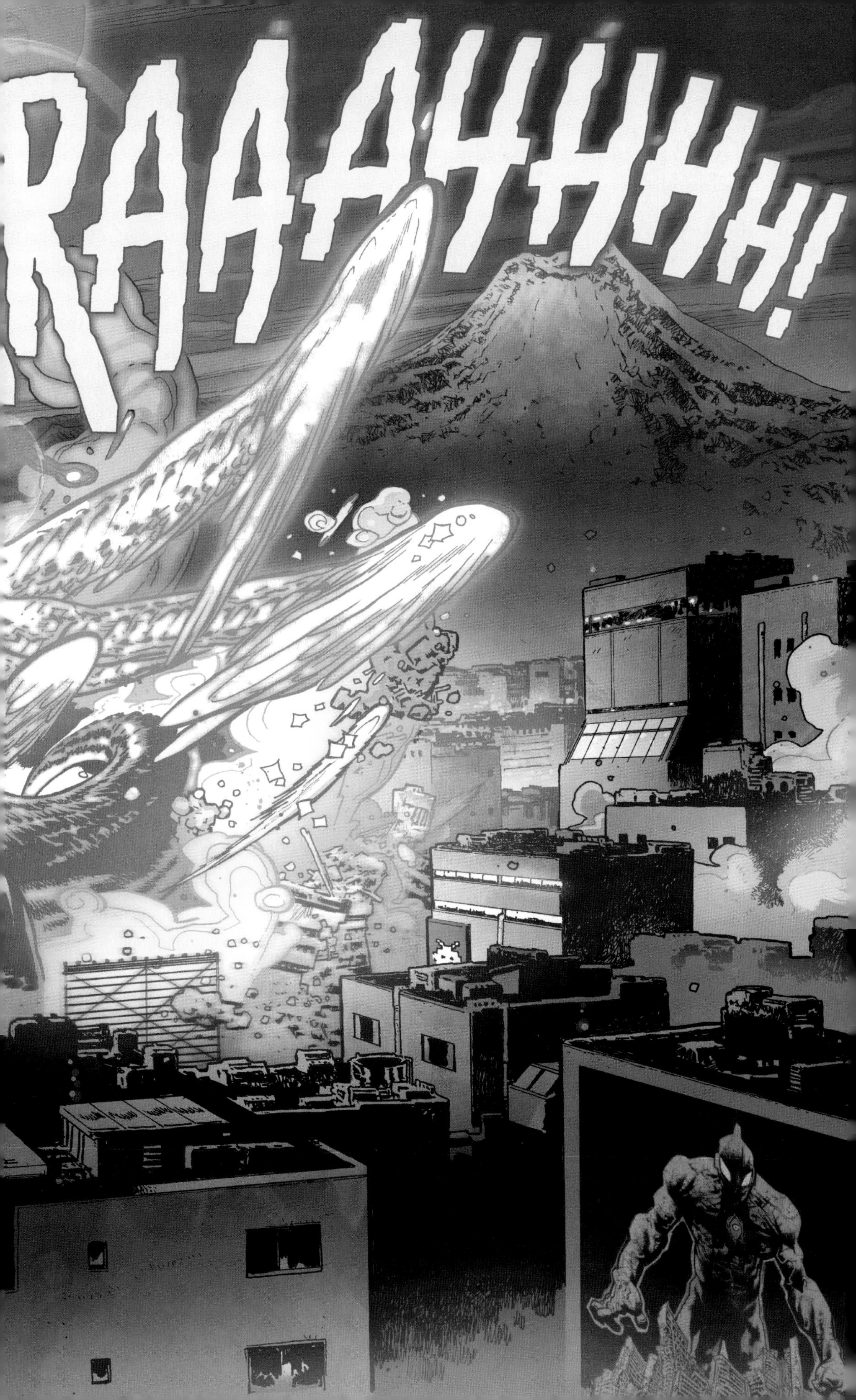
RAAAHHHH!

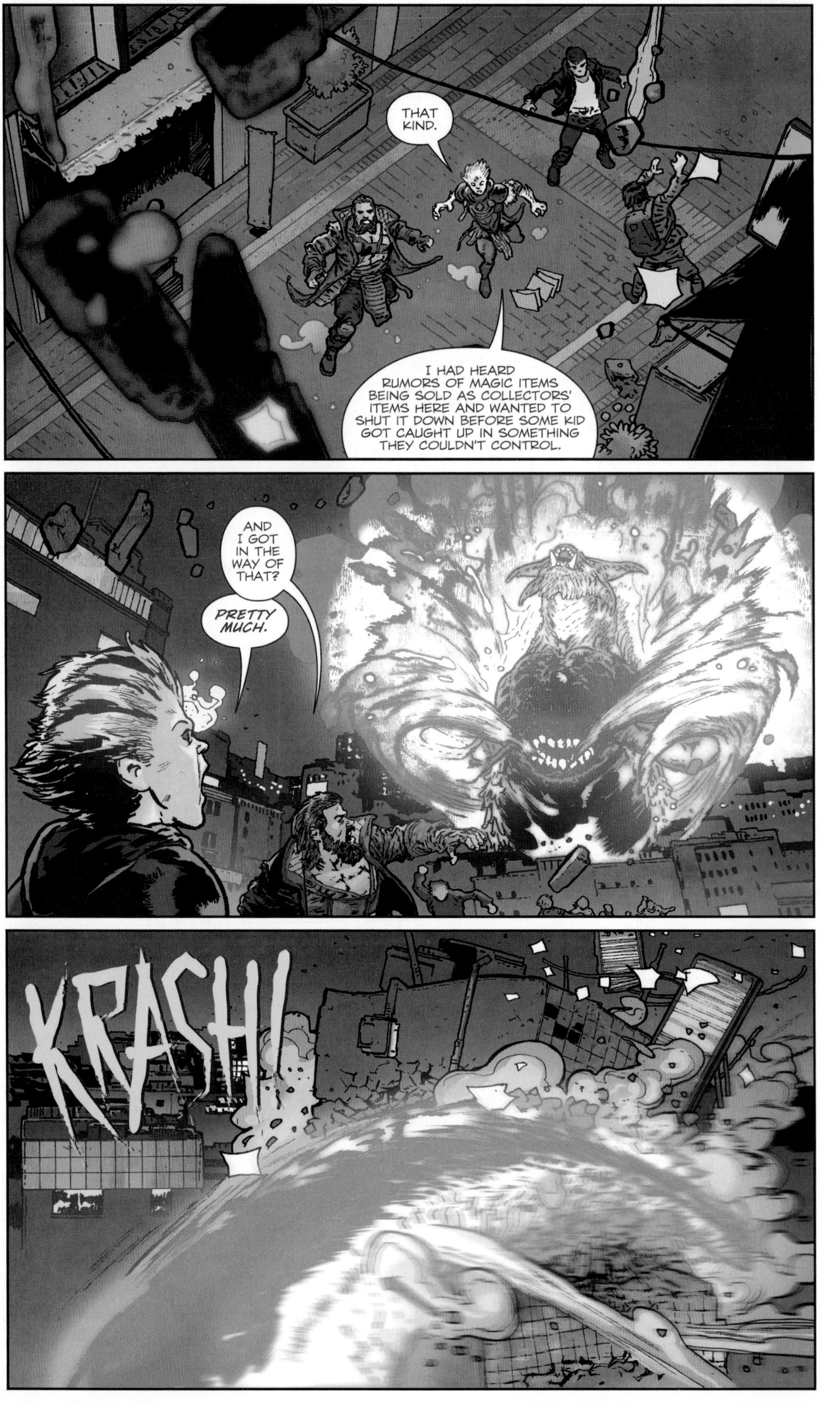
THAT KIND.
I HAD HEARD RUMORS OF MAGIC ITEMS BEING SOLD AS COLLECTORS' ITEMS HERE AND WANTED TO SHUT IT DOWN BEFORE SOME KID GOT CAUGHT UP IN SOMETHING THEY COULDN'T CONTROL.
AND I GOT IN THE WAY OF THAT?
PRETTY MUCH.
KRASH!

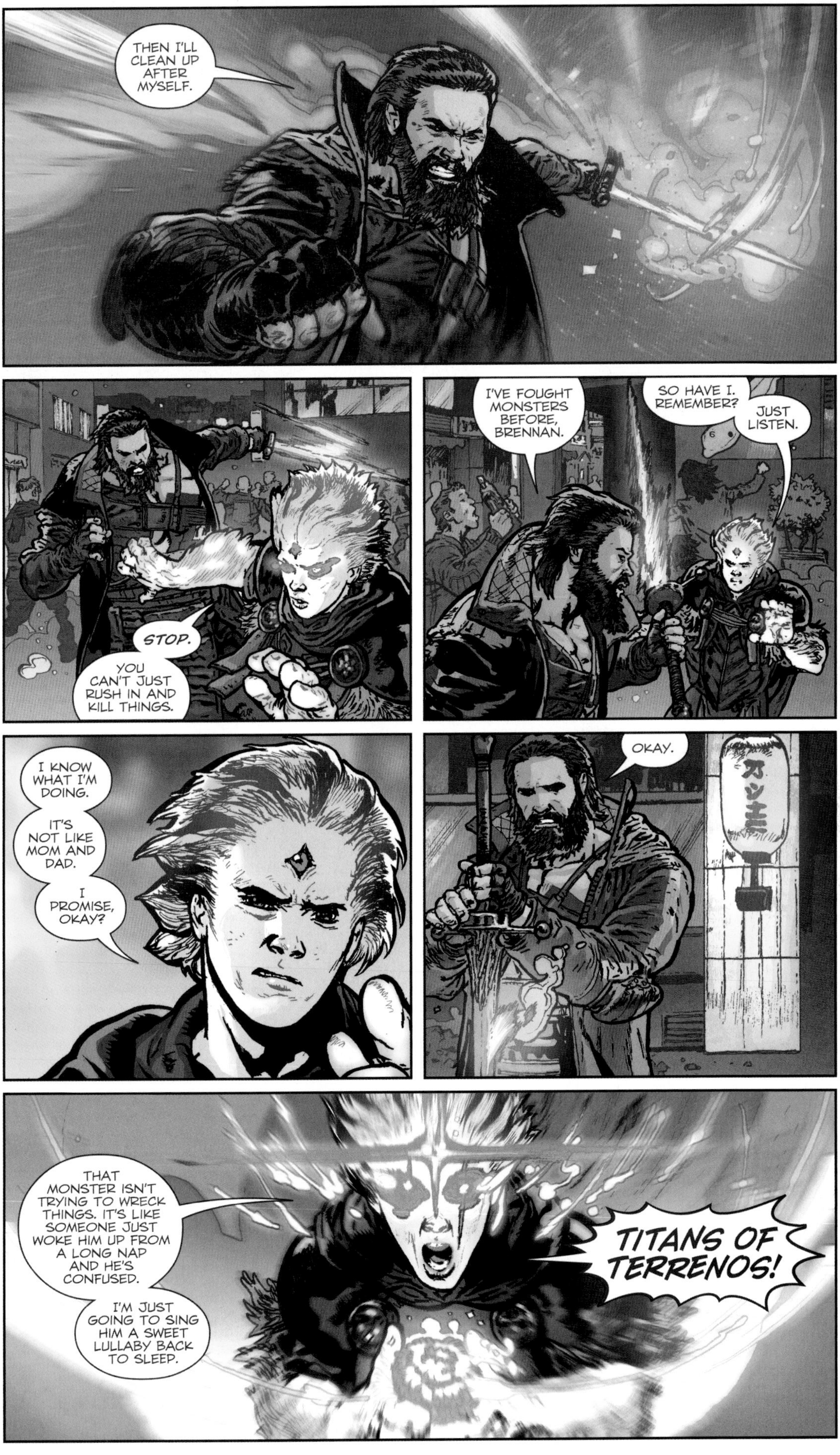
THEN I'LL CLEAN UP AFTER MYSELF.
STOP.
YOU CAN'T JUST RUSH IN AND KILL THINGS.
I'VE FOUGHT MONSTERS BEFORE, BRENNAN.
SO HAVE I. REMEMBER?
JUST LISTEN.
I KNOW WHAT I'M DOING.
IT'S NOT LIKE MOM AND DAD.
I PROMISE, OKAY?
OKAY.
THAT MONSTER ISN'T TRYING TO WRECK THINGS. IT'S LIKE SOMEONE JUST WOKE HIM UP FROM A LONG NAP AND HE'S CONFUSED.
I'M JUST GOING TO SING HIM A SWEET LULLABY BACK TO SLEEP.
TITANS OF TERRENOS!

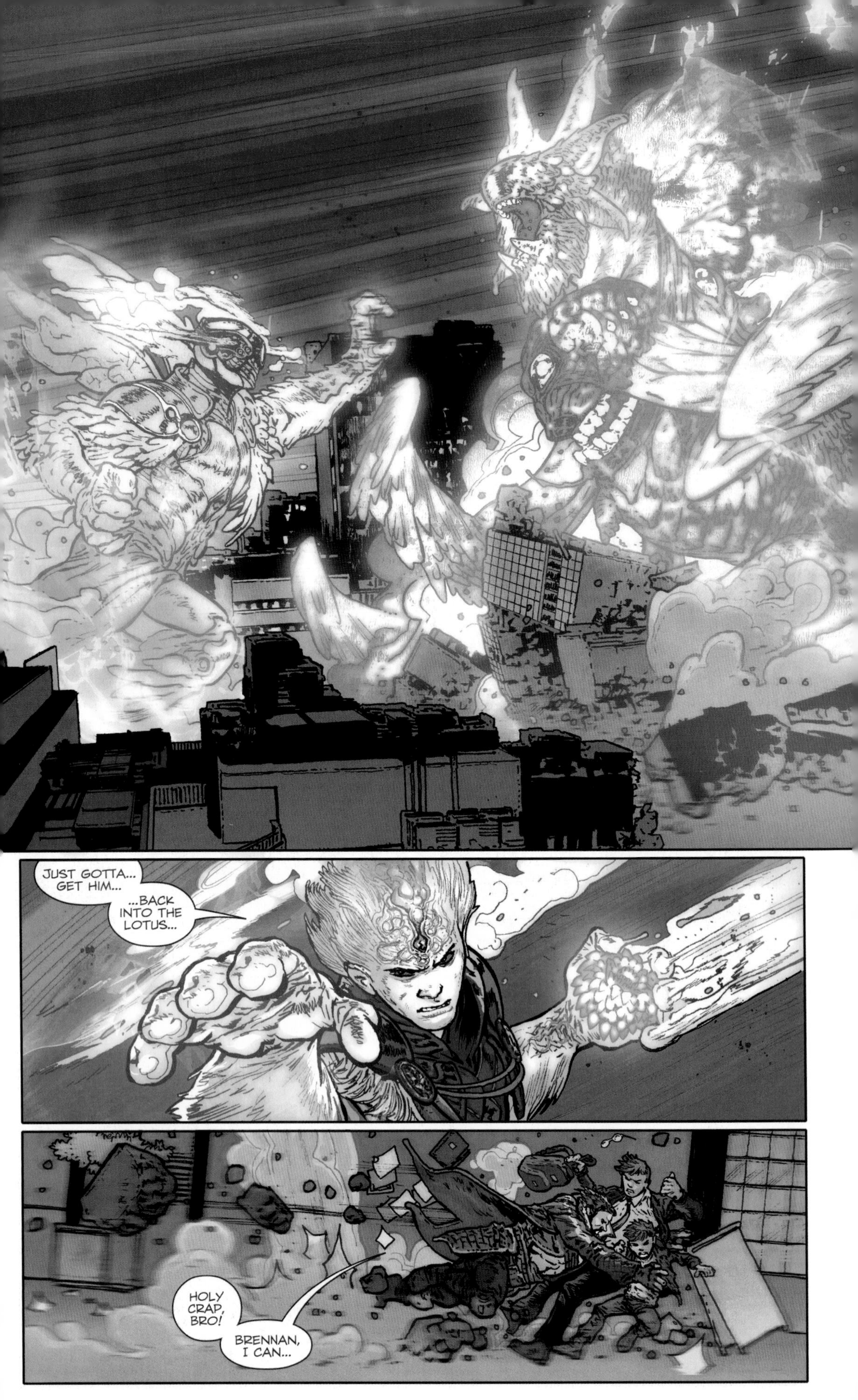
JUST GOTTA... GET HIM...
...BACK INTO THE LOTUS...
HOLY CRAP, BRO!
BRENNAN, I CAN...

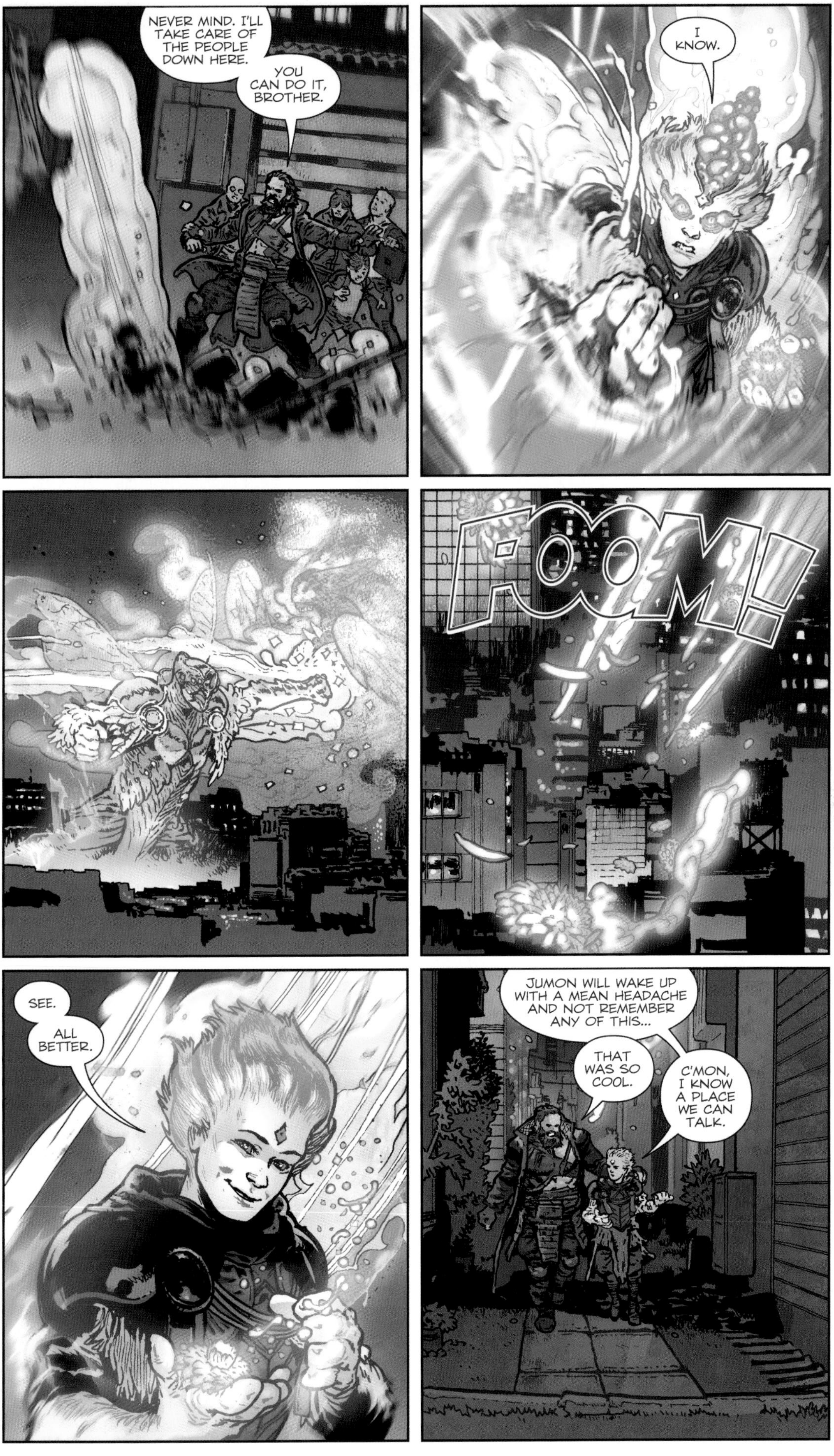
NEVER MIND. I'LL TAKE CARE OF THE PEOPLE DOWN HERE.
YOU CAN DO IT, BROTHER.
I KNOW.
FOOM!
SEE.
ALL BETTER.
JUMON WILL WAKE UP WITH A MEAN HEADACHE AND NOT REMEMBER ANY OF THIS...
THAT WAS SO COOL.
C'MON, I KNOW A PLACE WE CAN TALK.

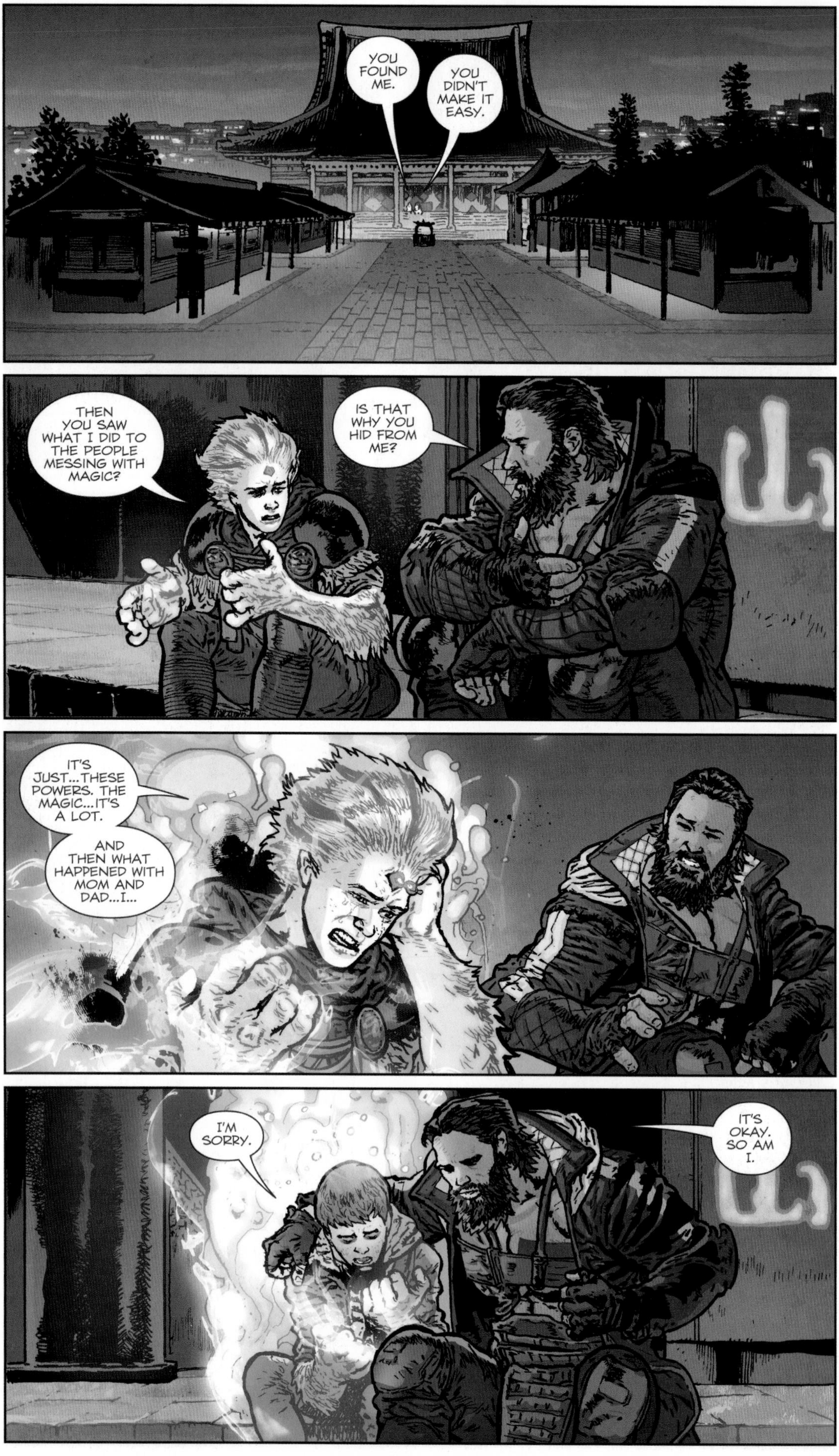
YOU FOUND ME.
YOU DIDN'T MAKE IT EASY.
THEN YOU SAW WHAT I DID TO THE PEOPLE MESSING WITH MAGIC?
IS THAT WHY YOU HID FROM ME?
IT'S JUST...THESE POWERS. THE MAGIC...IT'S A LOT.
AND THEN WHAT HAPPENED WITH MOM AND DAD...I...
I'M SORRY.
IT'S OKAY. SO AM I.

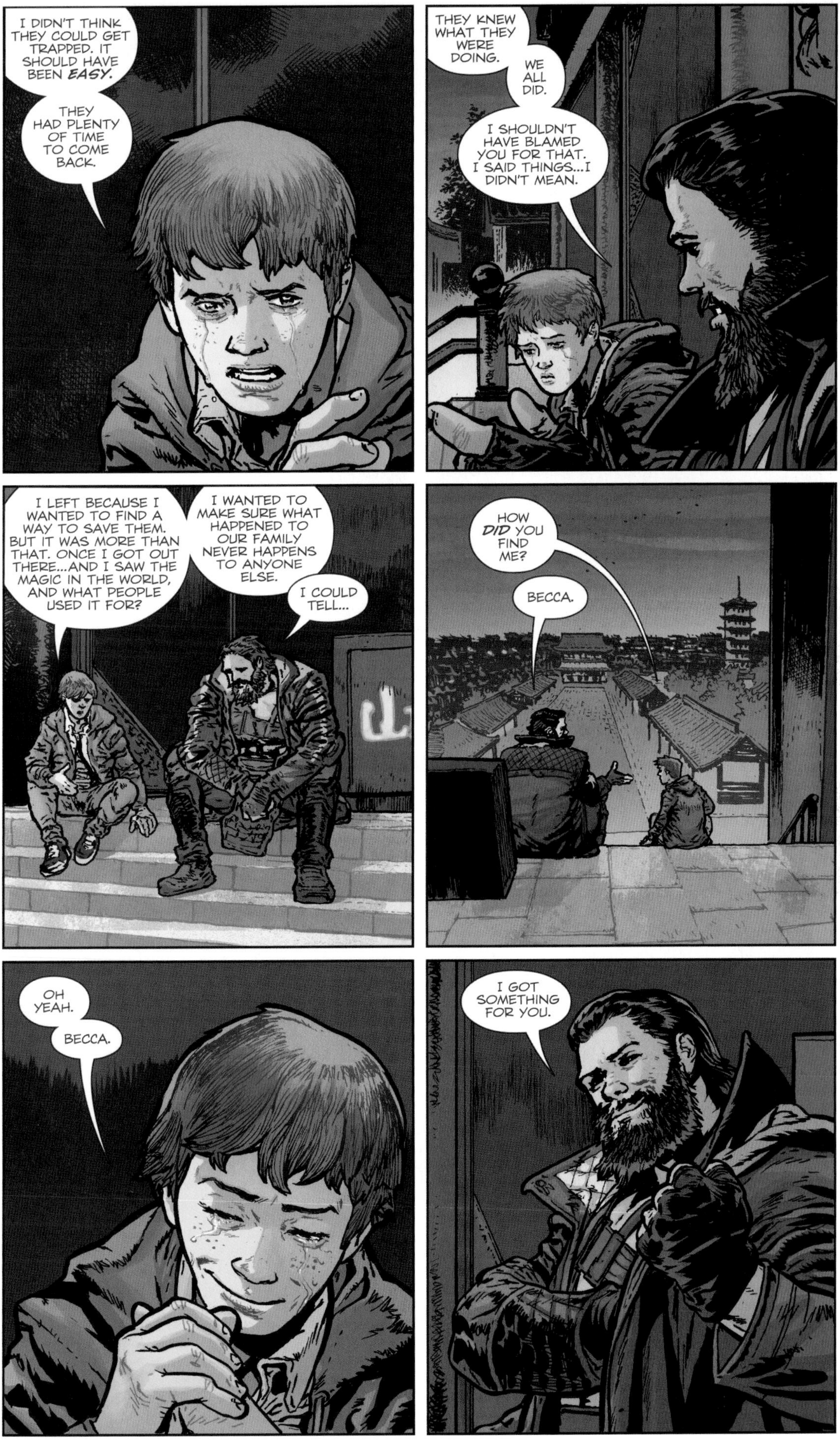
I DIDN'T THINK THEY COULD GET TRAPPED. IT SHOULD HAVE BEEN EASY.
THEY HAD PLENTY OF TIME TO COME BACK.
THEY KNEW WHAT THEY WERE DOING.
WE ALL DID.
I SHOULDN'T HAVE BLAMED YOU FOR THAT. I SAID THINGS...I DIDN'T MEAN.
I LEFT BECAUSE I WANTED TO FIND A WAY TO SAVE THEM. BUT IT WAS MORE THAN THAT. ONCE I GOT OUT THERE...AND I SAW THE MAGIC IN THE WORLD, AND WHAT PEOPLE USED IT FOR?
I WANTED TO MAKE SURE WHAT HAPPENED TO OUR FAMILY NEVER HAPPENS TO ANYONE ELSE.
I COULD TELL...
HOW DID YOU FIND ME?
BECCA.
OH YEAH.
BECCA.
I GOT SOMETHING FOR YOU.

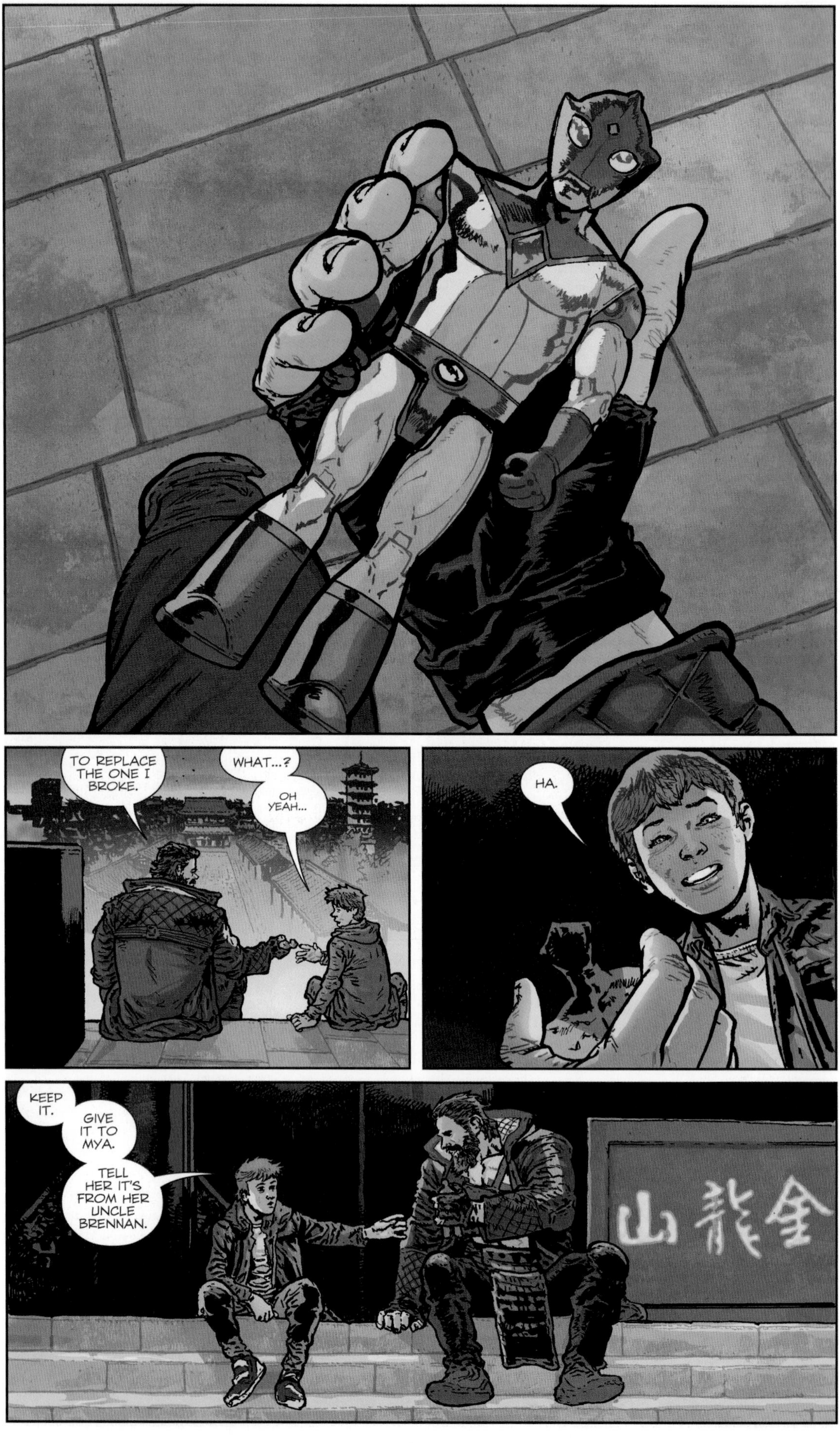
TO REPLACE THE ONE I BROKE.
WHAT...?
OH YEAH...
HA.
KEEP IT.
GIVE IT TO MYA.
TELL HER IT'S FROM HER UNCLE BRENNAN.
金龍山

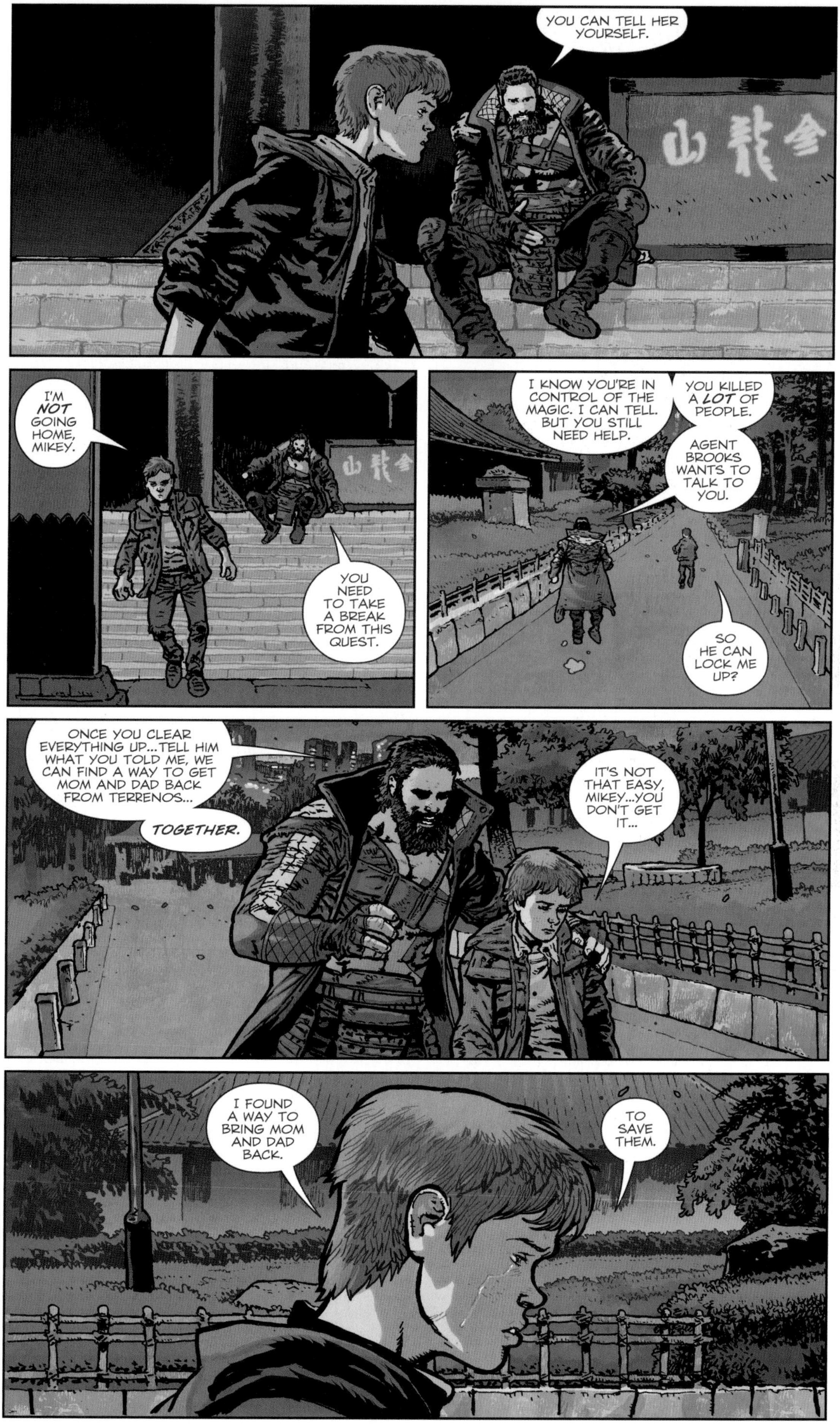
YOU CAN TELL HER YOURSELF.
I'M NOT GOING HOME, MIKEY.
YOU NEED TO TAKE A BREAK FROM THIS QUEST.
I KNOW YOU'RE IN CONTROL OF THE MAGIC. I CAN TELL. BUT YOU STILL NEED HELP.
YOU KILLED A LOT OF PEOPLE.
AGENT BROOKS WANTS TO TALK TO YOU.
SO HE CAN LOCK ME UP?
ONCE YOU CLEAR EVERYTHING UP...TELL HIM WHAT YOU TOLD ME, WE CAN FIND A WAY TO GET MOM AND DAD BACK FROM TERRENOS...
TOGETHER.
IT'S NOT THAT EASY, MIKEY...YOU DON'T GET IT...
I FOUND A WAY TO BRING MOM AND DAD BACK.
TO SAVE THEM.

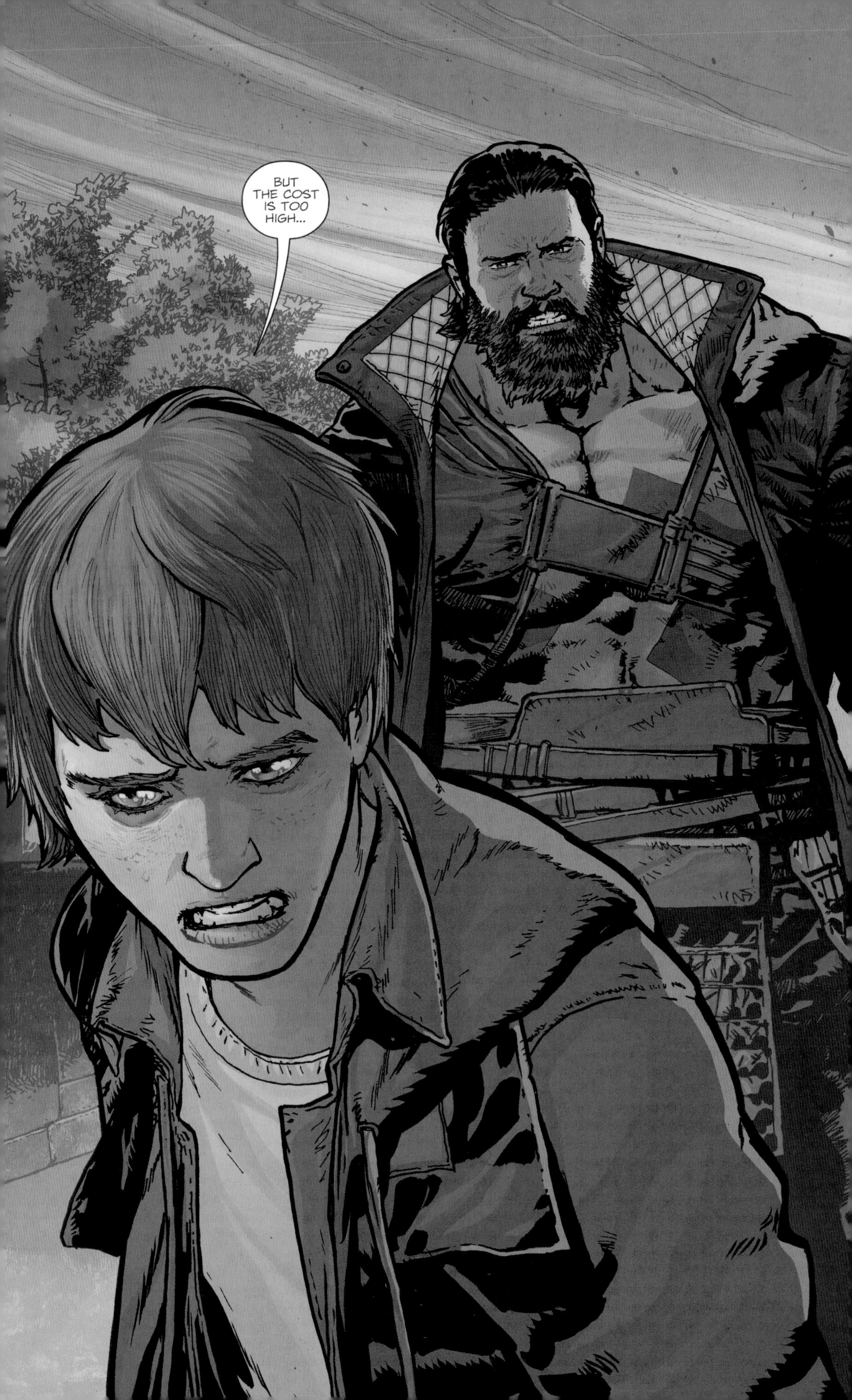
BUT THE COST IS TOO HIGH...

SIX MONTHS LATER.

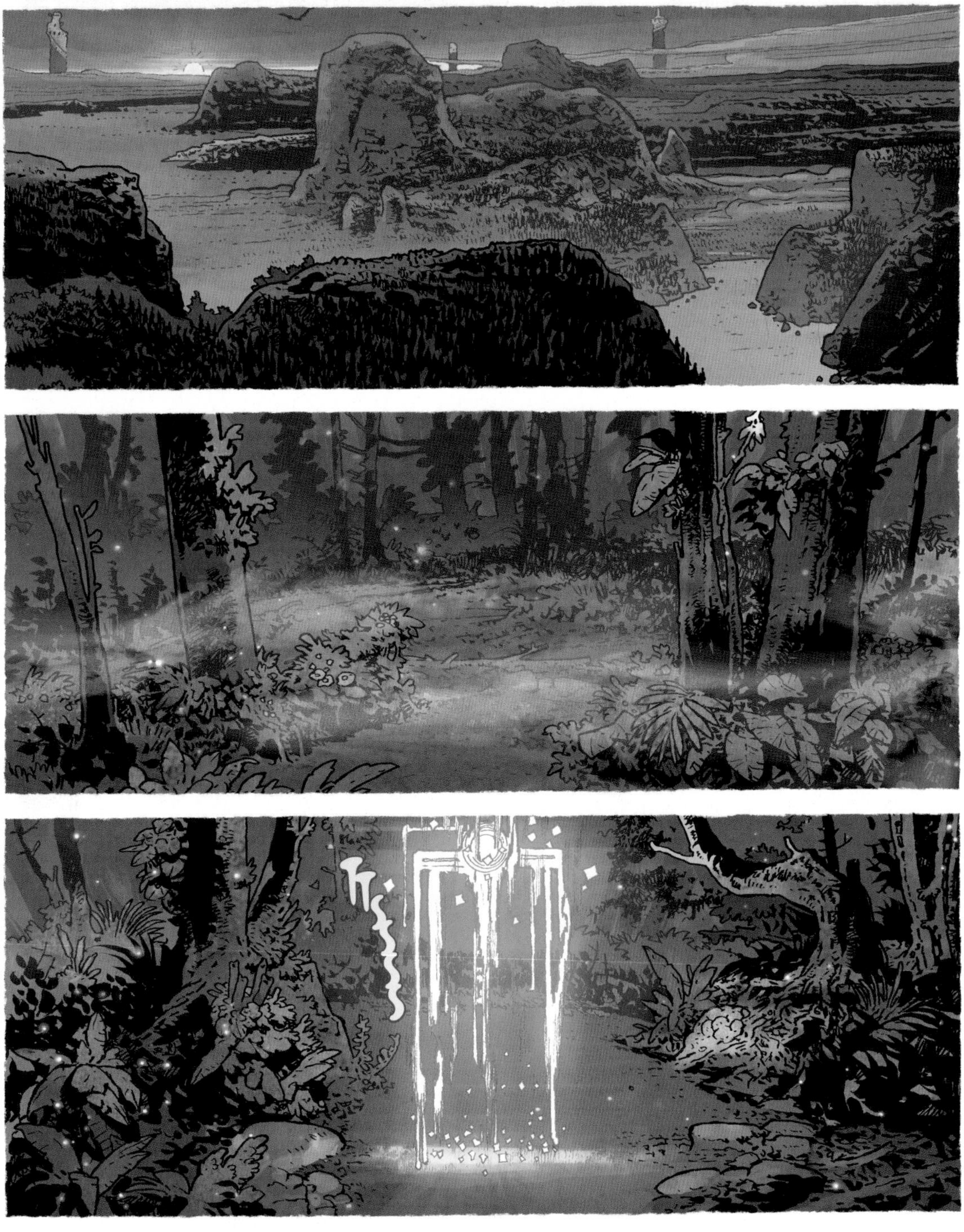

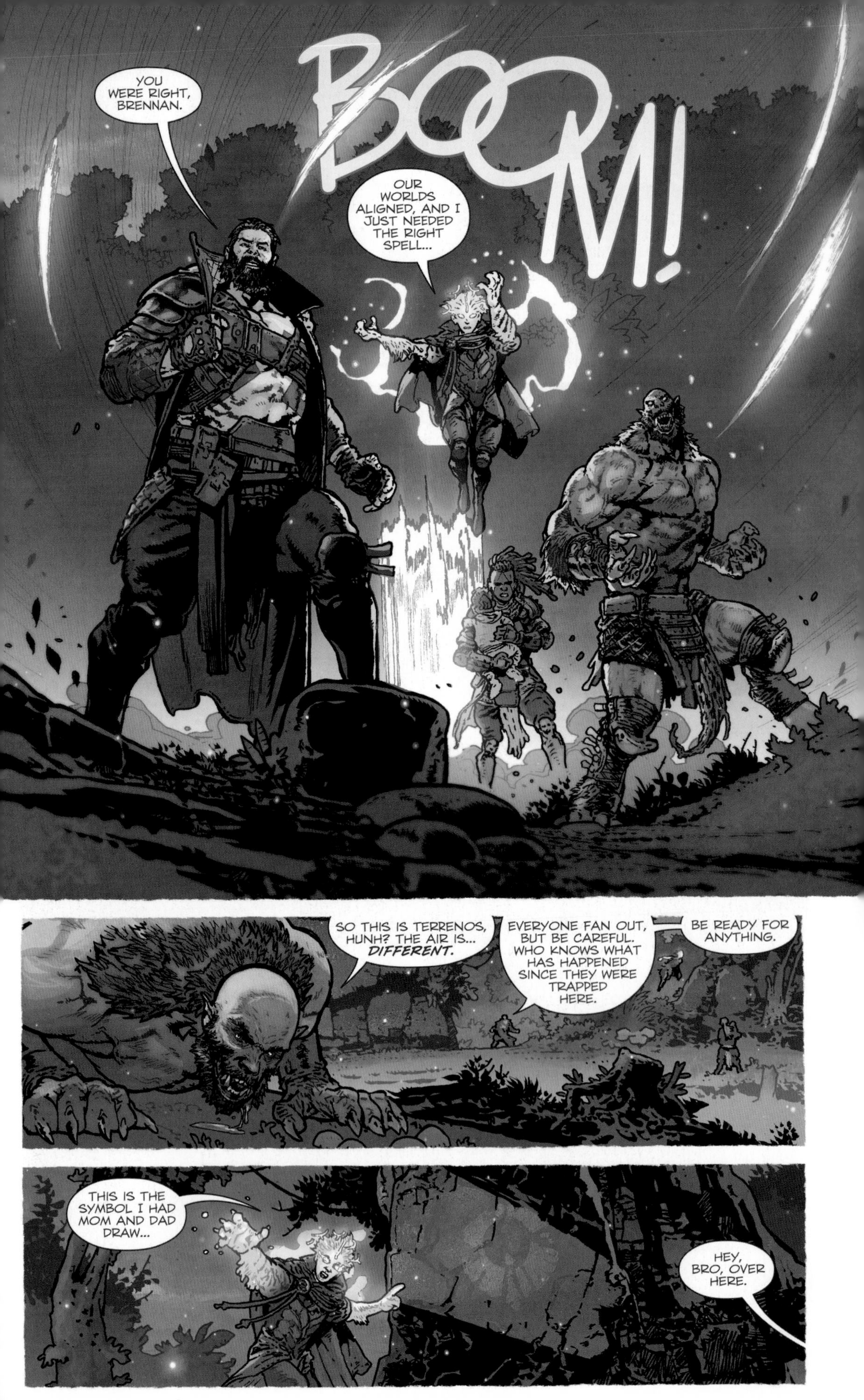
BOOM!
YOU WERE RIGHT, BRENNAN.
OUR WORLDS ALIGNED, AND I JUST NEEDED THE RIGHT SPELL...
SO THIS IS TERRENOS, HUNH? THE AIR IS... *DIFFERENT.*
EVERYONE FAN OUT, BUT BE CAREFUL. WHO KNOWS WHAT HAS HAPPENED SINCE THEY WERE TRAPPED HERE.
BE READY FOR ANYTHING.
THIS IS THE SYMBOL I HAD MOM AND DAD DRAW...
HEY, BRO, OVER HERE.

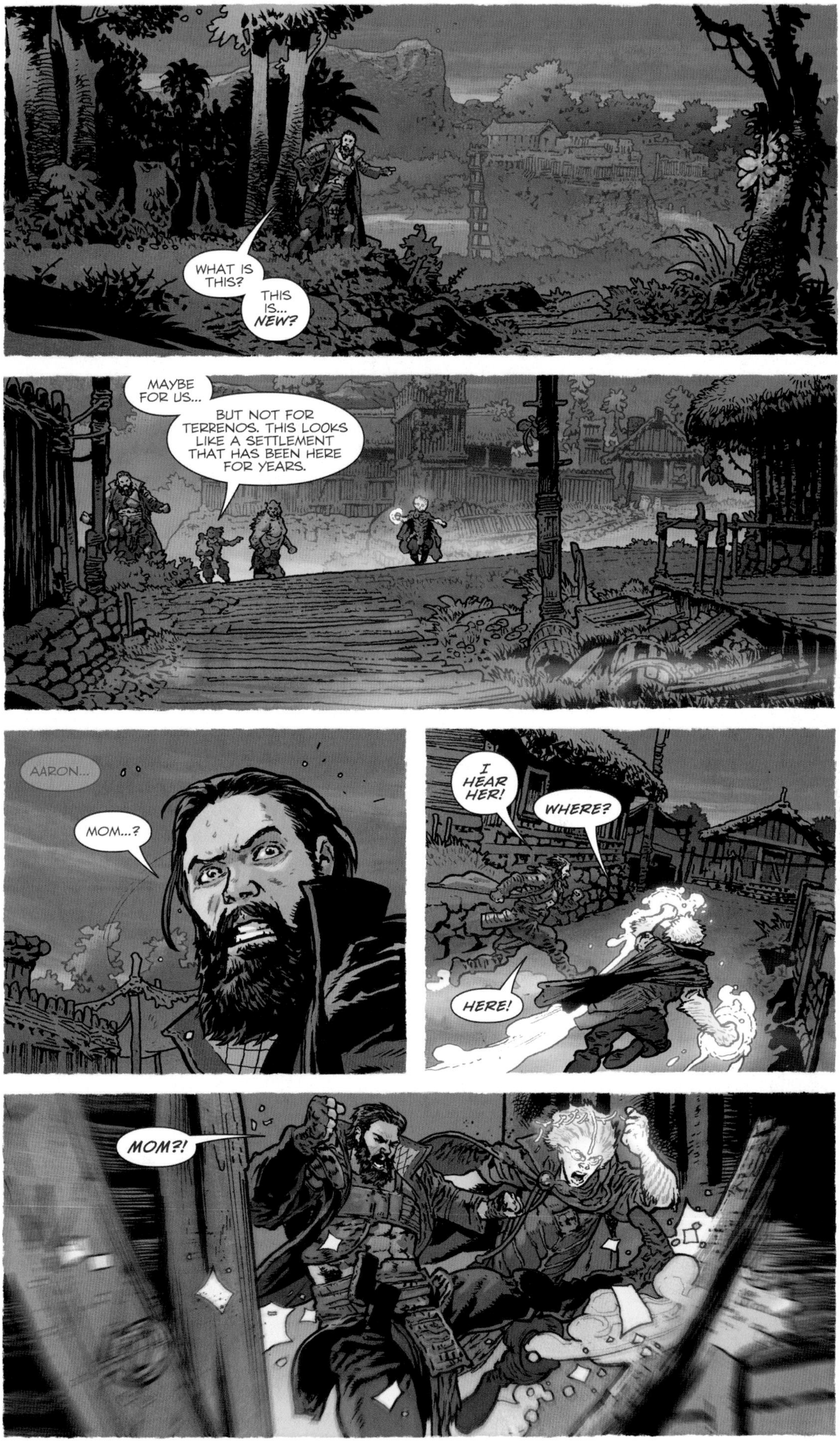
WHAT IS THIS?
THIS IS... NEW?
MAYBE FOR US...
BUT NOT FOR TERRENOS. THIS LOOKS LIKE A SETTLEMENT THAT HAS BEEN HERE FOR YEARS.
AARON...
MOM...?
I HEAR HER!
WHERE?
HERE!
MOM?!

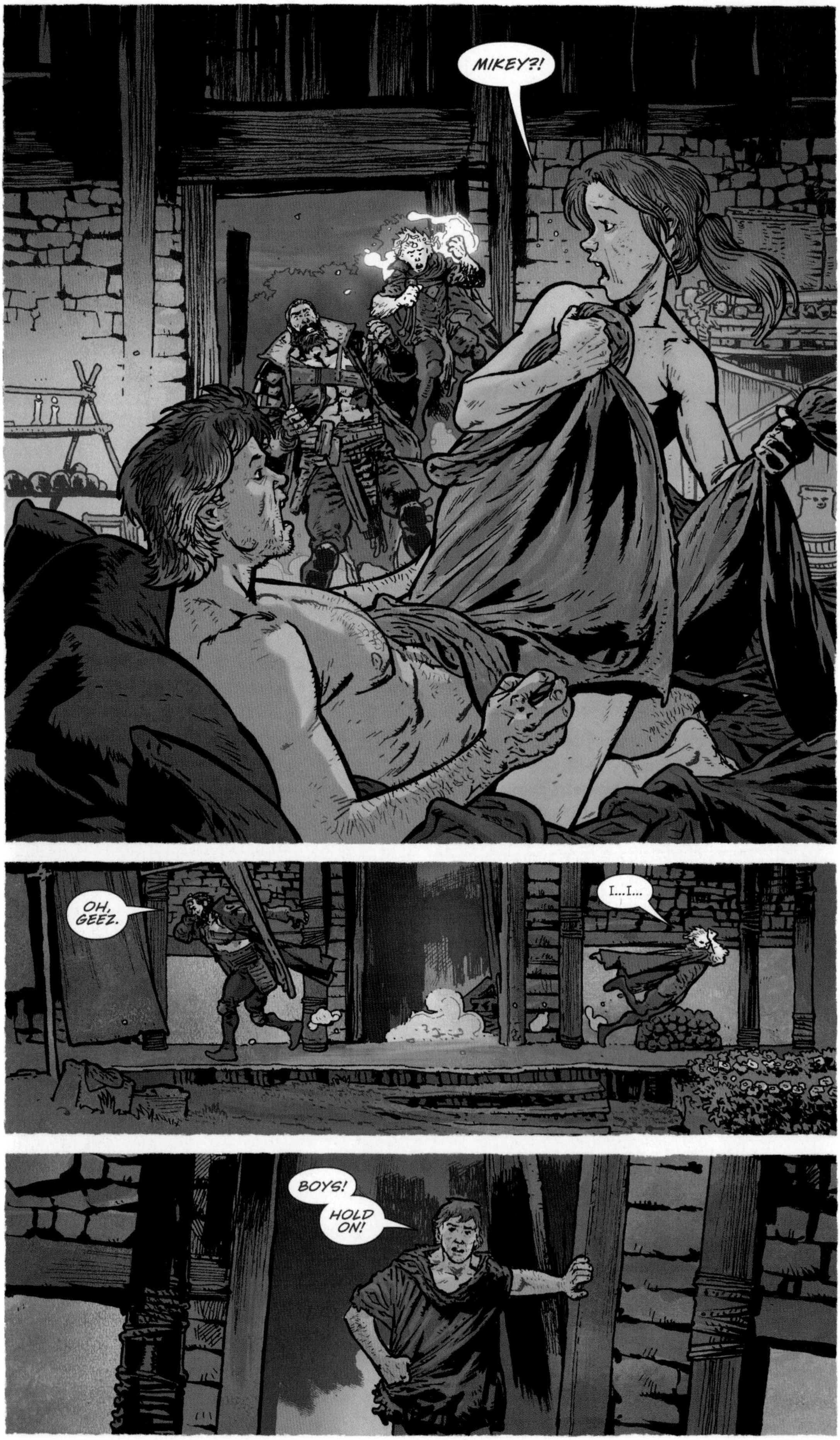
MIKEY?!
OH, GEEZ.
I... I...
BOYS!
HOLD ON!

ㄷㅂㄷㅂ
ㄷㅂㄷㅂㄷㅂ
ㄷㅂㄴㄴㄴㅂ
ㄷㅂ ㄷㅂㄷㅂ、

WHOA,
LOST
BOYS!

IT'S
MIKEY AND
BRENNAN!

OUR
SONS!

YOUR PARENTS
FOUND US
DURING THE
WAR BETWEEN
WORLDS.

THEY SAVED US.
HELPED US FIND
OUR FAMILY.

SO
YOU'RE
OKAY?

I MEAN...
IT TOOK SOME
GETTING USED
TO, BUT YEAH,
WE'RE OKAY.

I'D
KILL FOR
A PIZZA
AND
BEER.

MIKEY...
YOU HAVE
TO SEE
THIS.

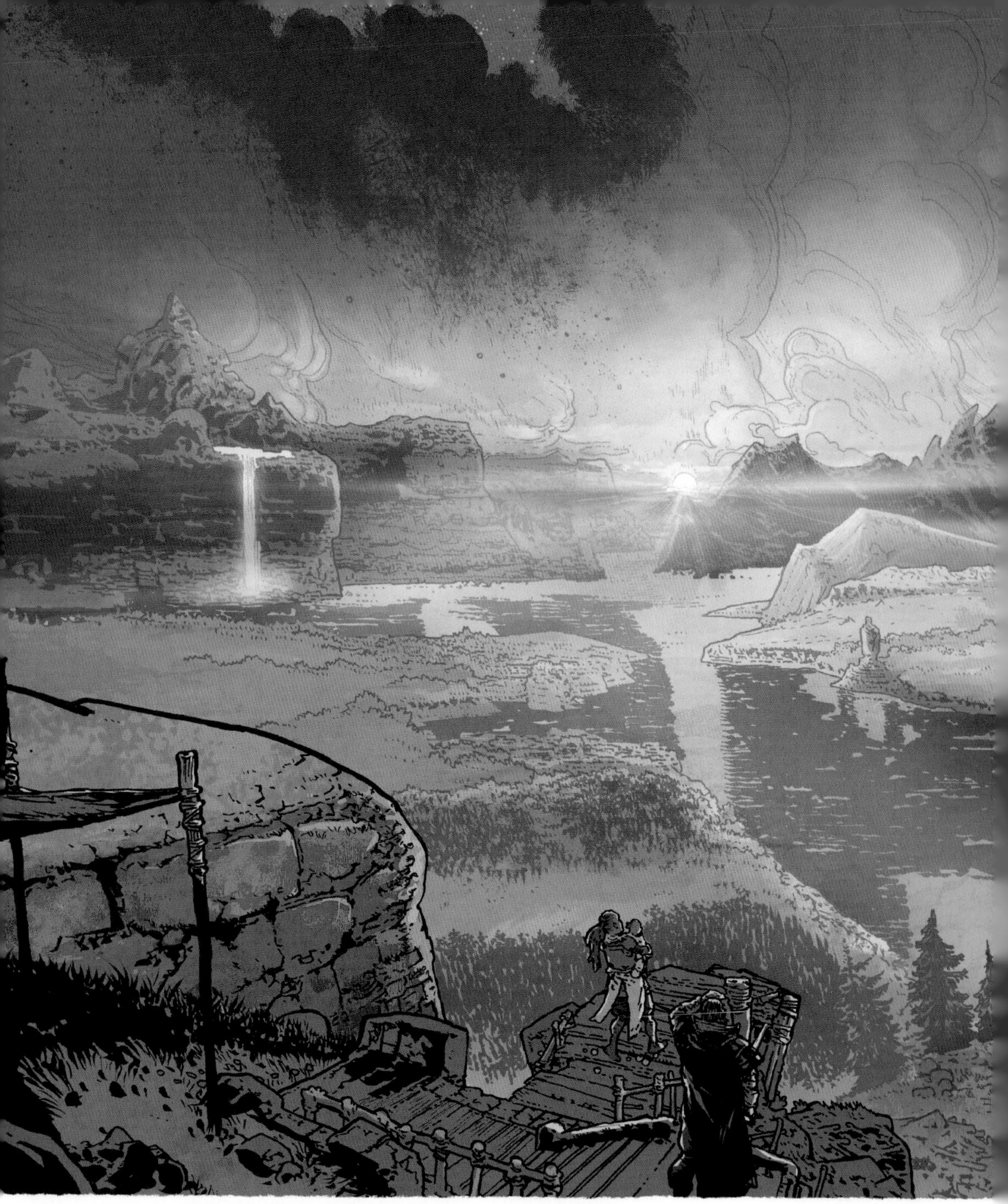

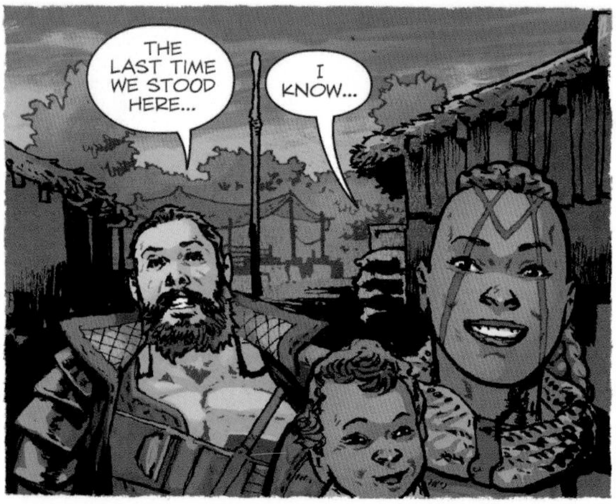
THE LAST TIME WE STOOD HERE...
I KNOW...

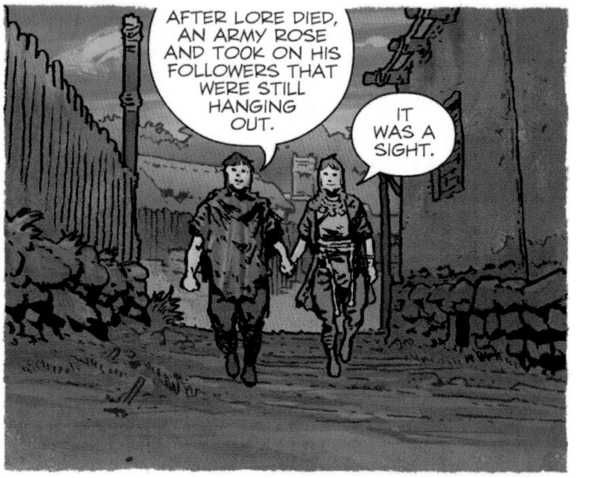
AFTER LORE DIED, AN ARMY ROSE AND TOOK ON HIS FOLLOWERS THAT WERE STILL HANGING OUT.
IT WAS A SIGHT.

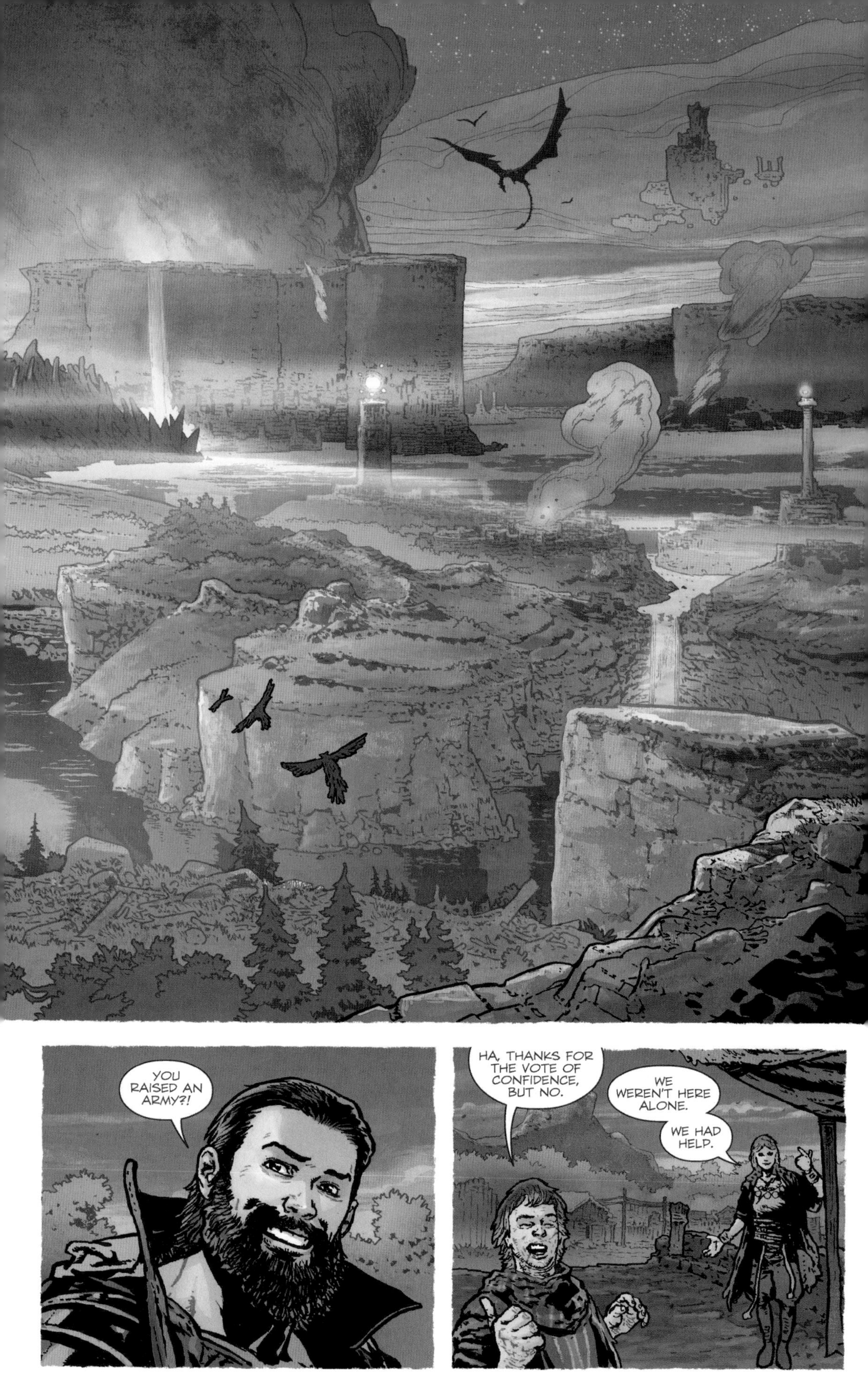
YOU RAISED AN ARMY?!
HA, THANKS FOR THE VOTE OF CONFIDENCE, BUT NO.
WE WEREN'T HERE ALONE.
WE HAD HELP.

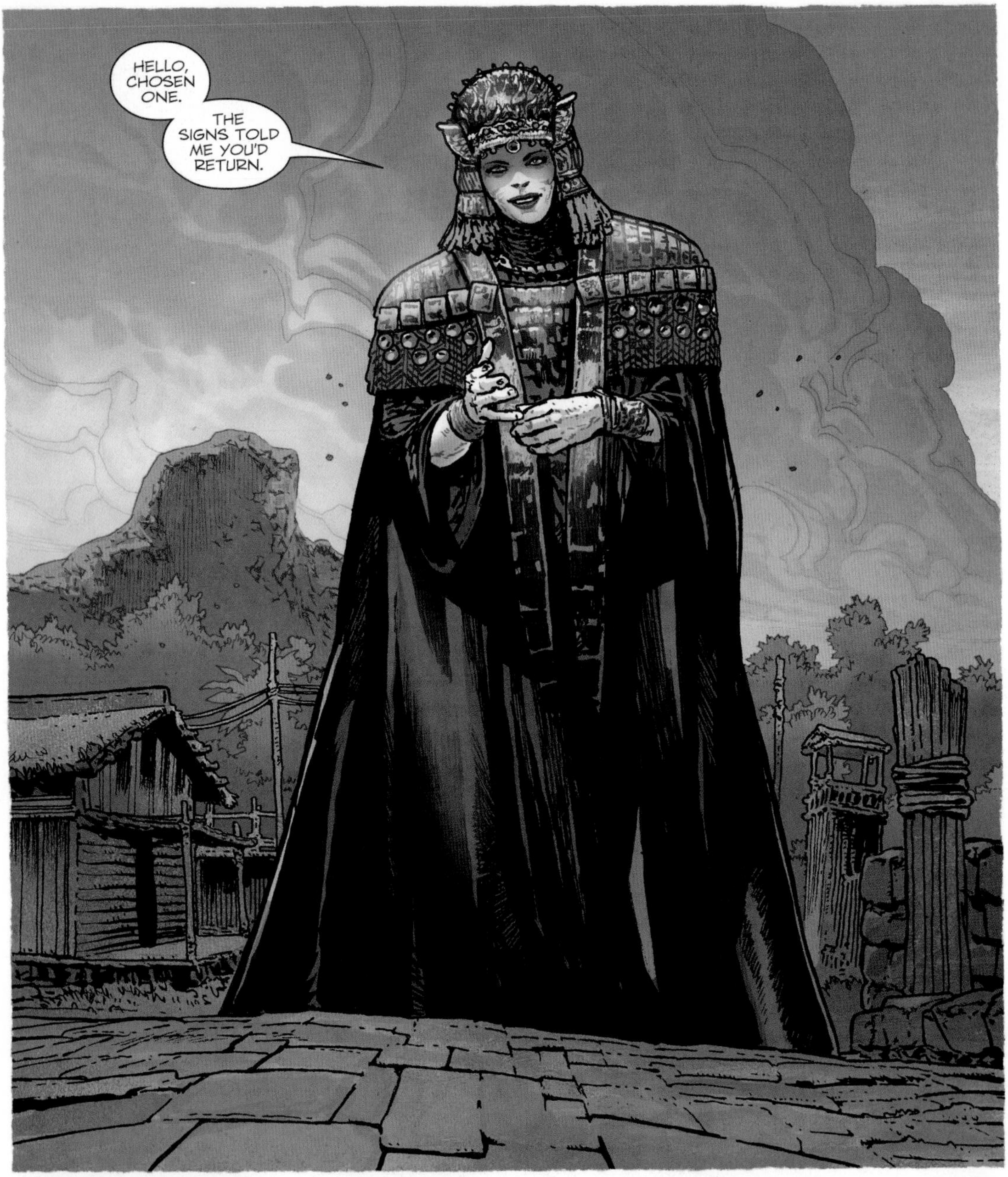
HELLO, CHOSEN ONE.
THE SIGNS TOLD ME YOU'D RETURN.

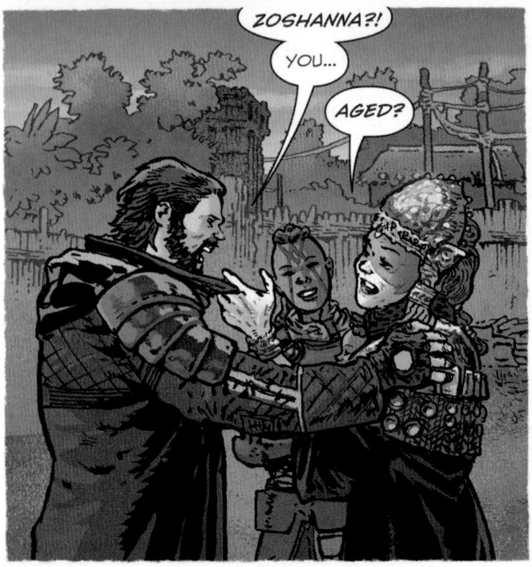
ZOSHANNA?!
YOU...
AGED?

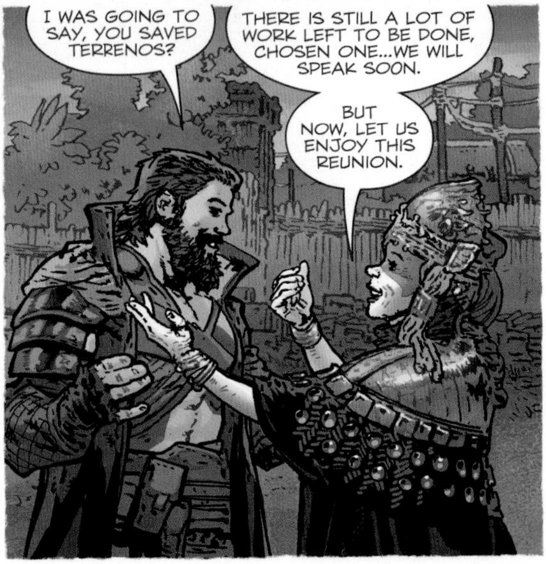
I WAS GOING TO SAY, YOU SAVED TERRENOS?
THERE IS STILL A LOT OF WORK LEFT TO BE DONE, CHOSEN ONE...WE WILL SPEAK SOON.
BUT NOW, LET US ENJOY THIS REUNION.

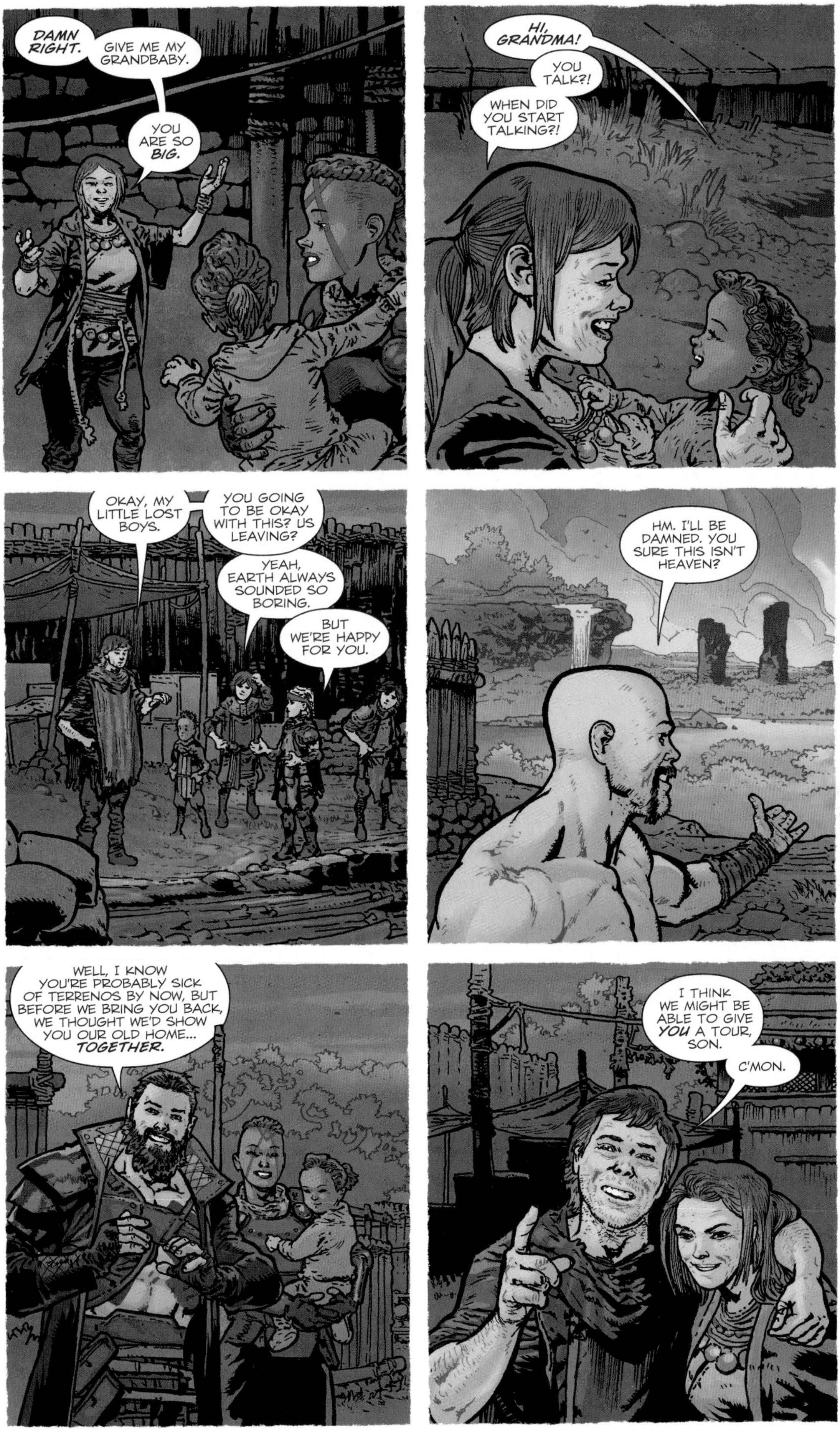
DAMN RIGHT.
GIVE ME MY GRANDBABY.
YOU ARE SO BIG.
HI, GRANDMA!
YOU TALK?!
WHEN DID YOU START TALKING?!
OKAY, MY LITTLE LOST BOYS.
YOU GOING TO BE OKAY WITH THIS? US LEAVING?
YEAH, EARTH ALWAYS SOUNDED SO BORING.
BUT WE'RE HAPPY FOR YOU.
HM. I'LL BE DAMNED. YOU SURE THIS ISN'T HEAVEN?
WELL, I KNOW YOU'RE PROBABLY SICK OF TERRENOS BY NOW, BUT BEFORE WE BRING YOU BACK, WE THOUGHT WE'D SHOW YOU OUR OLD HOME... TOGETHER.
I THINK WE MIGHT BE ABLE TO GIVE YOU A TOUR, SON.
C'MON.

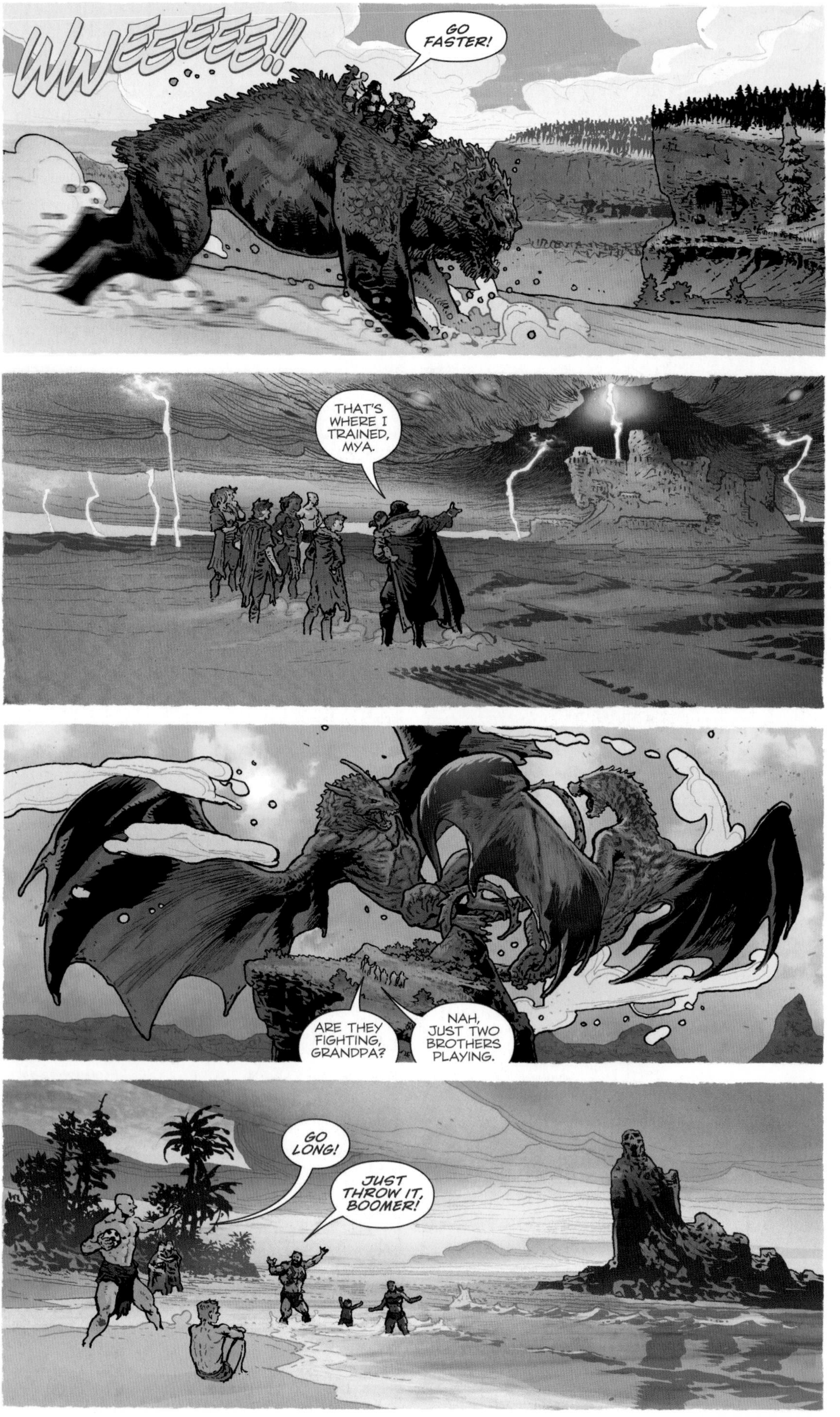
WWEEEEEE!!
GO FASTER!
THAT'S WHERE I TRAINED, MYA.
ARE THEY FIGHTING, GRANDPA?
NAH, JUST TWO BROTHERS PLAYING.
GO LONG!
JUST THROW IT, BOOMER!

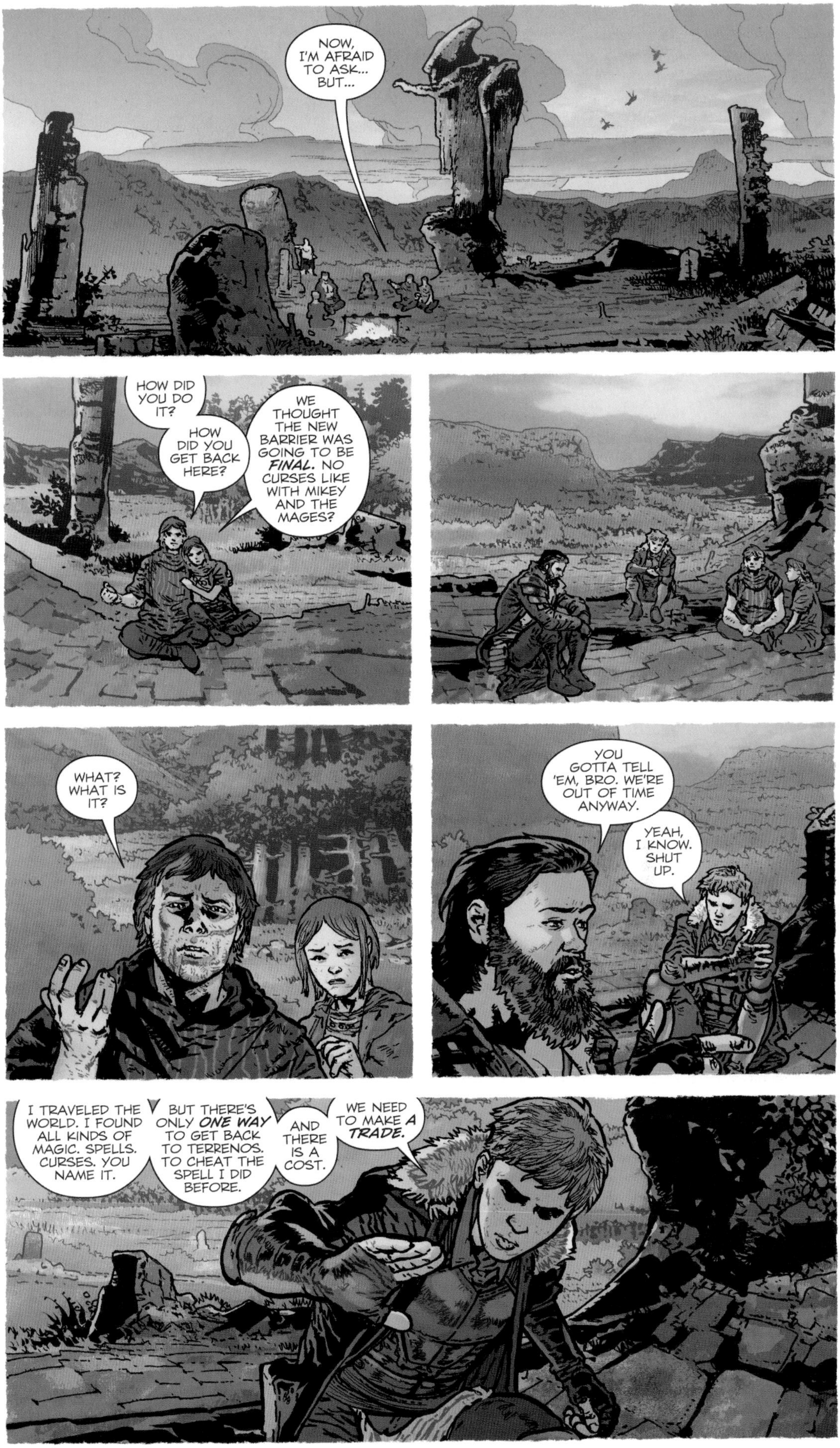
NOW, I'M AFRAID TO ASK... BUT...
HOW DID YOU DO IT?
HOW DID YOU GET BACK HERE?
WE THOUGHT THE NEW BARRIER WAS GOING TO BE FINAL. NO CURSES LIKE WITH MIKEY AND THE MAGES?
WHAT? WHAT IS IT?
YOU GOTTA TELL 'EM, BRO. WE'RE OUT OF TIME ANYWAY.
YEAH, I KNOW. SHUT UP.
I TRAVELED THE WORLD. I FOUND ALL KINDS OF MAGIC. SPELLS. CURSES. YOU NAME IT.
BUT THERE'S ONLY ONE WAY TO GET BACK TO TERRENOS. TO CHEAT THE SPELL I DID BEFORE.
AND THERE IS A COST.
WE NEED TO MAKE A TRADE.

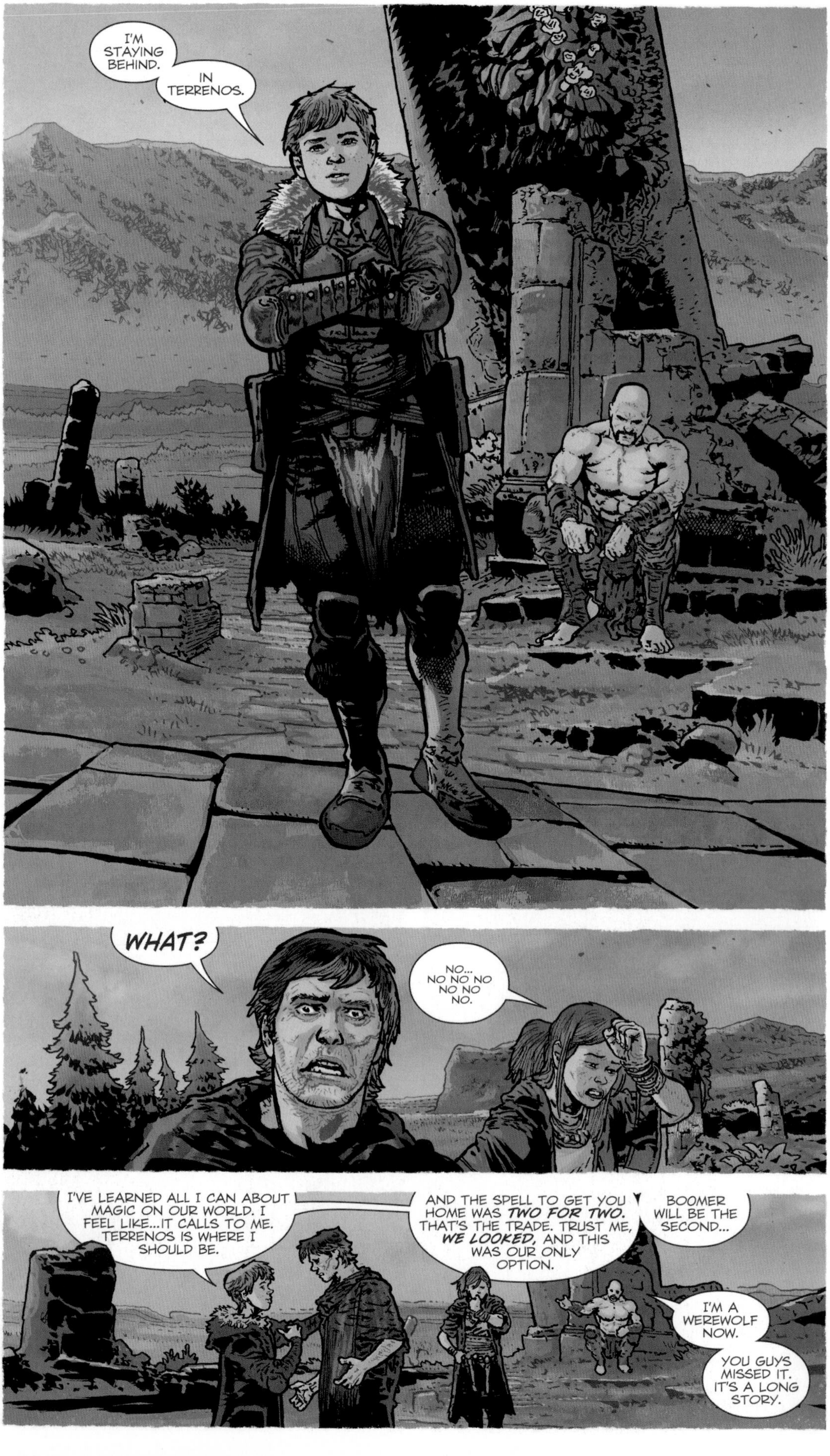
I'M STAYING BEHIND.
IN TERRENOS.
WHAT?
NO... NO NO NO NO NO NO.
I'VE LEARNED ALL I CAN ABOUT MAGIC ON OUR WORLD. I FEEL LIKE...IT CALLS TO ME. TERRENOS IS WHERE I SHOULD BE.
AND THE SPELL TO GET YOU HOME WAS TWO FOR TWO. THAT'S THE TRADE. TRUST ME, WE LOOKED, AND THIS WAS OUR ONLY OPTION.
BOOMER WILL BE THE SECOND...
I'M A WEREWOLF NOW.
YOU GUYS MISSED IT. IT'S A LONG STORY.

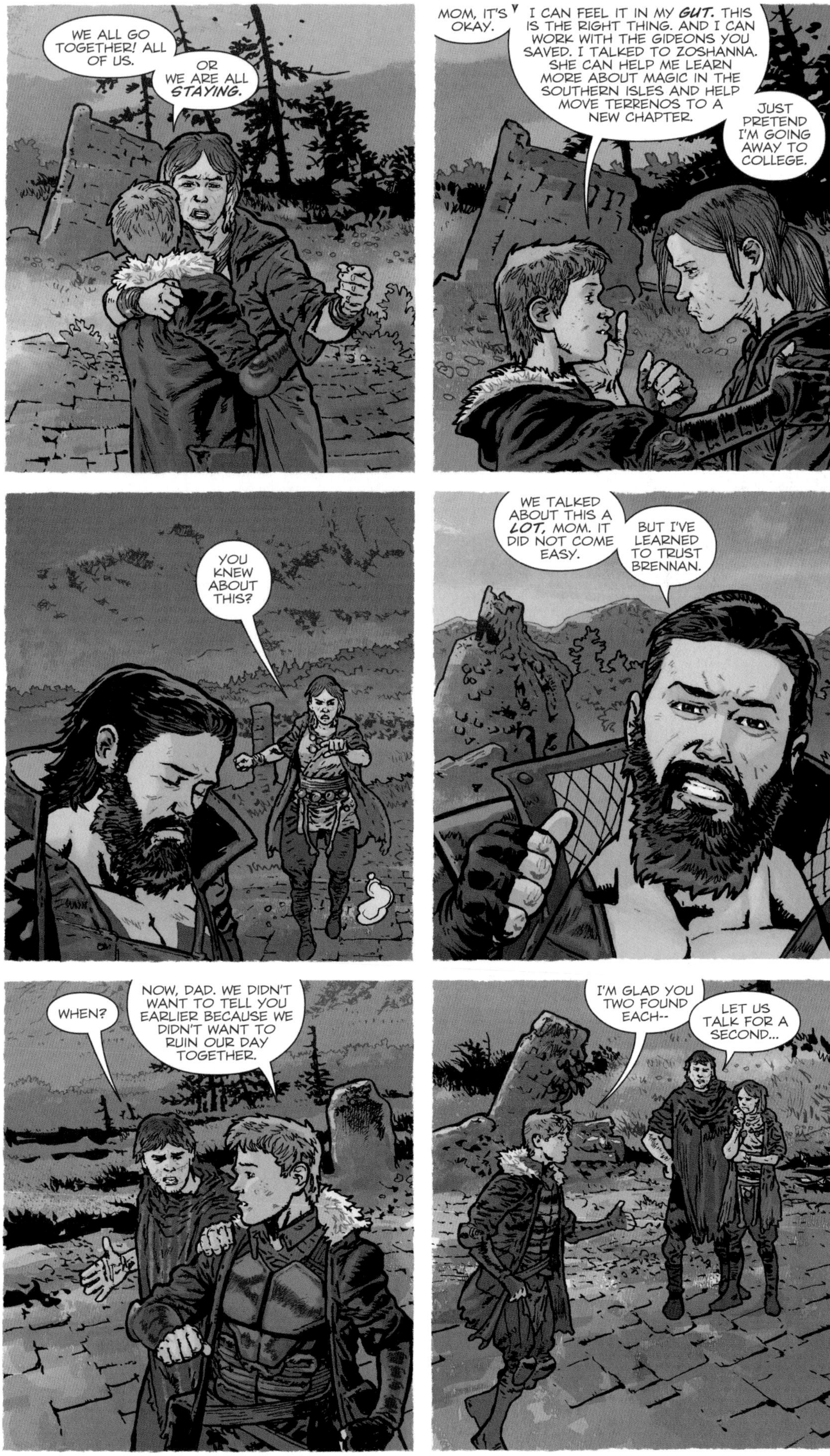
WE ALL GO TOGETHER! ALL OF US.
OR WE ARE ALL STAYING.
MOM, IT'S OKAY.
I CAN FEEL IT IN MY GUT. THIS IS THE RIGHT THING. AND I CAN WORK WITH THE GIDEONS YOU SAVED. I TALKED TO ZOSHANNA. SHE CAN HELP ME LEARN MORE ABOUT MAGIC IN THE SOUTHERN ISLES AND HELP MOVE TERRENOS TO A NEW CHAPTER.
JUST PRETEND I'M GOING AWAY TO COLLEGE.
YOU KNEW ABOUT THIS?
WE TALKED ABOUT THIS A LOT, MOM. IT DID NOT COME EASY.
BUT I'VE LEARNED TO TRUST BRENNAN.
WHEN?
NOW, DAD. WE DIDN'T WANT TO TELL YOU EARLIER BECAUSE WE DIDN'T WANT TO RUIN OUR DAY TOGETHER.
I'M GLAD YOU TWO FOUND EACH--
LET US TALK FOR A SECOND...

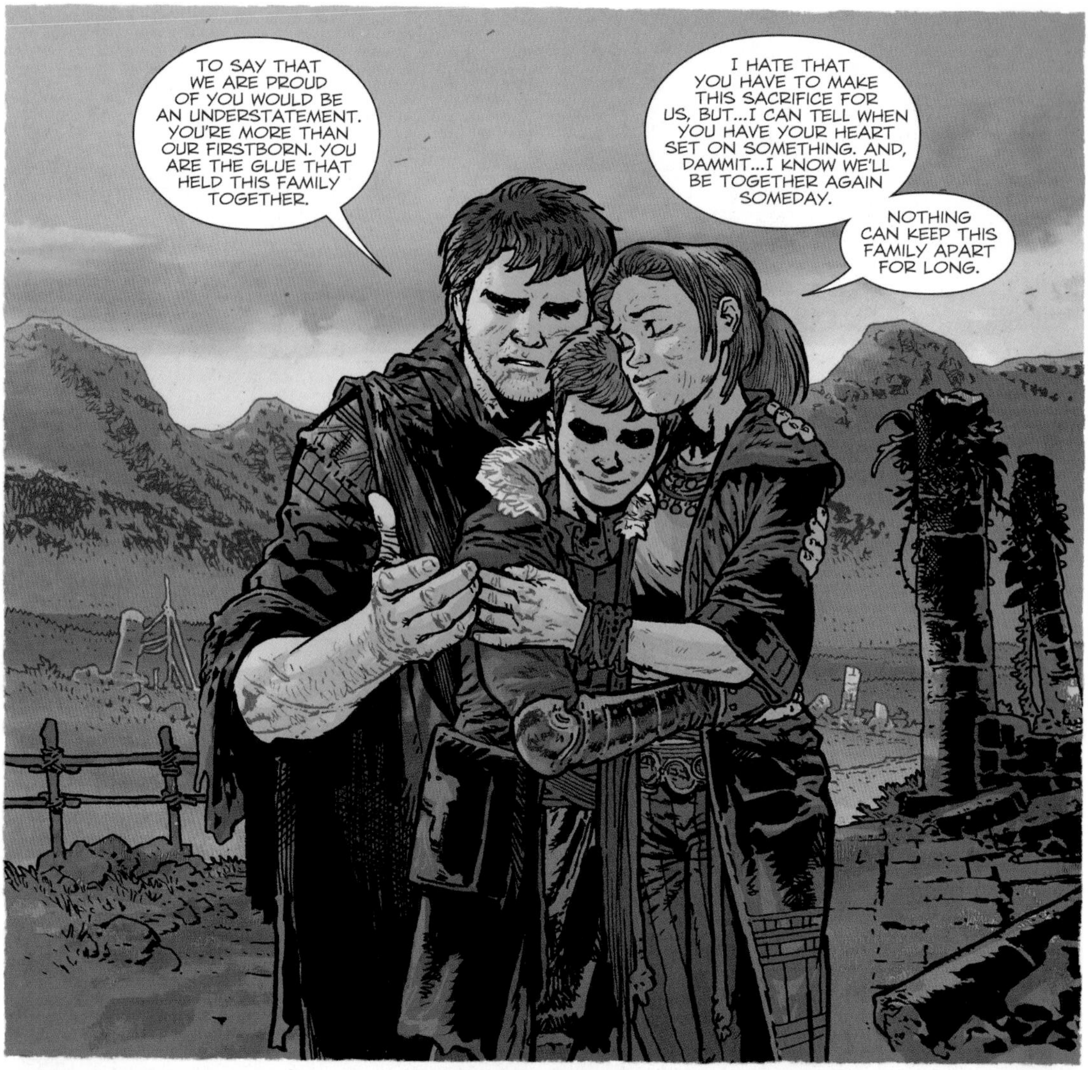
TO SAY THAT WE ARE PROUD OF YOU WOULD BE AN UNDERSTATEMENT. YOU'RE MORE THAN OUR FIRSTBORN. YOU ARE THE GLUE THAT HELD THIS FAMILY TOGETHER.
I HATE THAT YOU HAVE TO MAKE THIS SACRIFICE FOR US, BUT...I CAN TELL WHEN YOU HAVE YOUR HEART SET ON SOMETHING. AND, DAMMIT...I KNOW WE'LL BE TOGETHER AGAIN SOMEDAY.
NOTHING CAN KEEP THIS FAMILY APART FOR LONG.

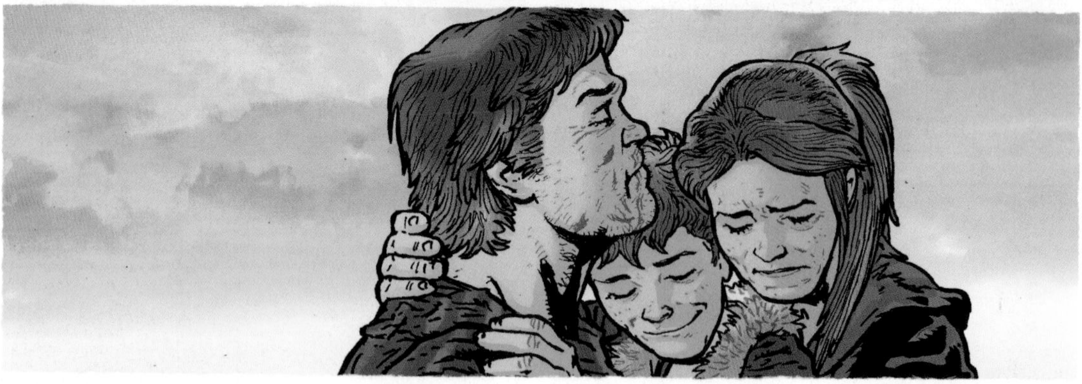

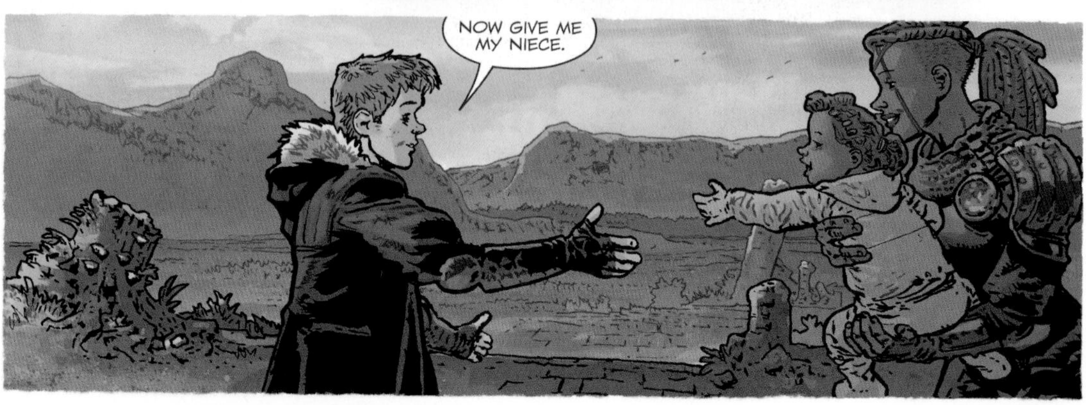
NOW GIVE ME MY NIECE.

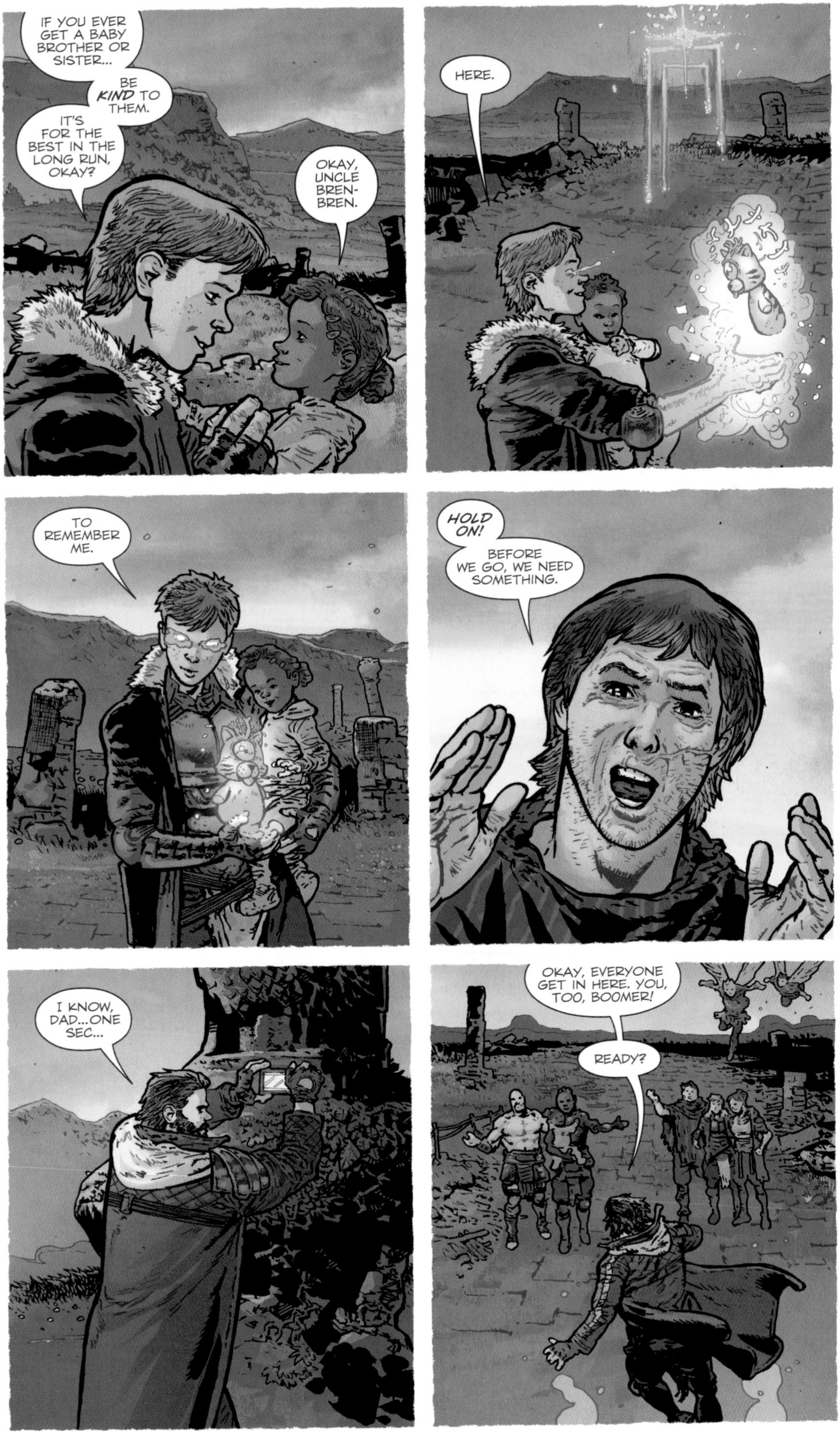
IF YOU EVER GET A BABY BROTHER OR SISTER...
BE KIND TO THEM.
IT'S FOR THE BEST IN THE LONG RUN, OKAY?
OKAY, UNCLE BREN-BREN.
HERE.
TO REMEMBER ME.
HOLD ON!
BEFORE WE GO, WE NEED SOMETHING.
I KNOW, DAD...ONE SEC...
OKAY, EVERYONE GET IN HERE. YOU, TOO, BOOMER!
READY?

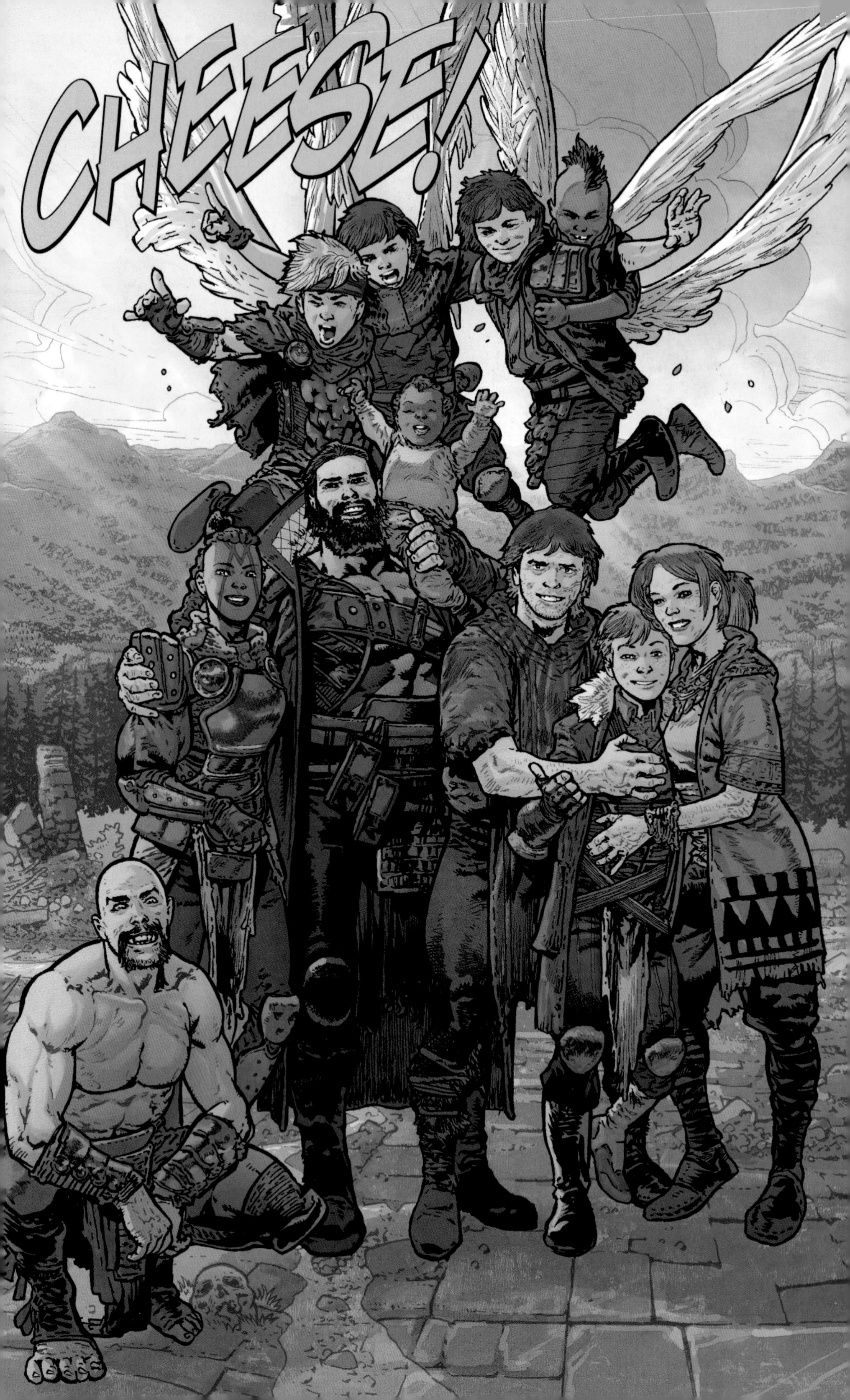
CHEESE!

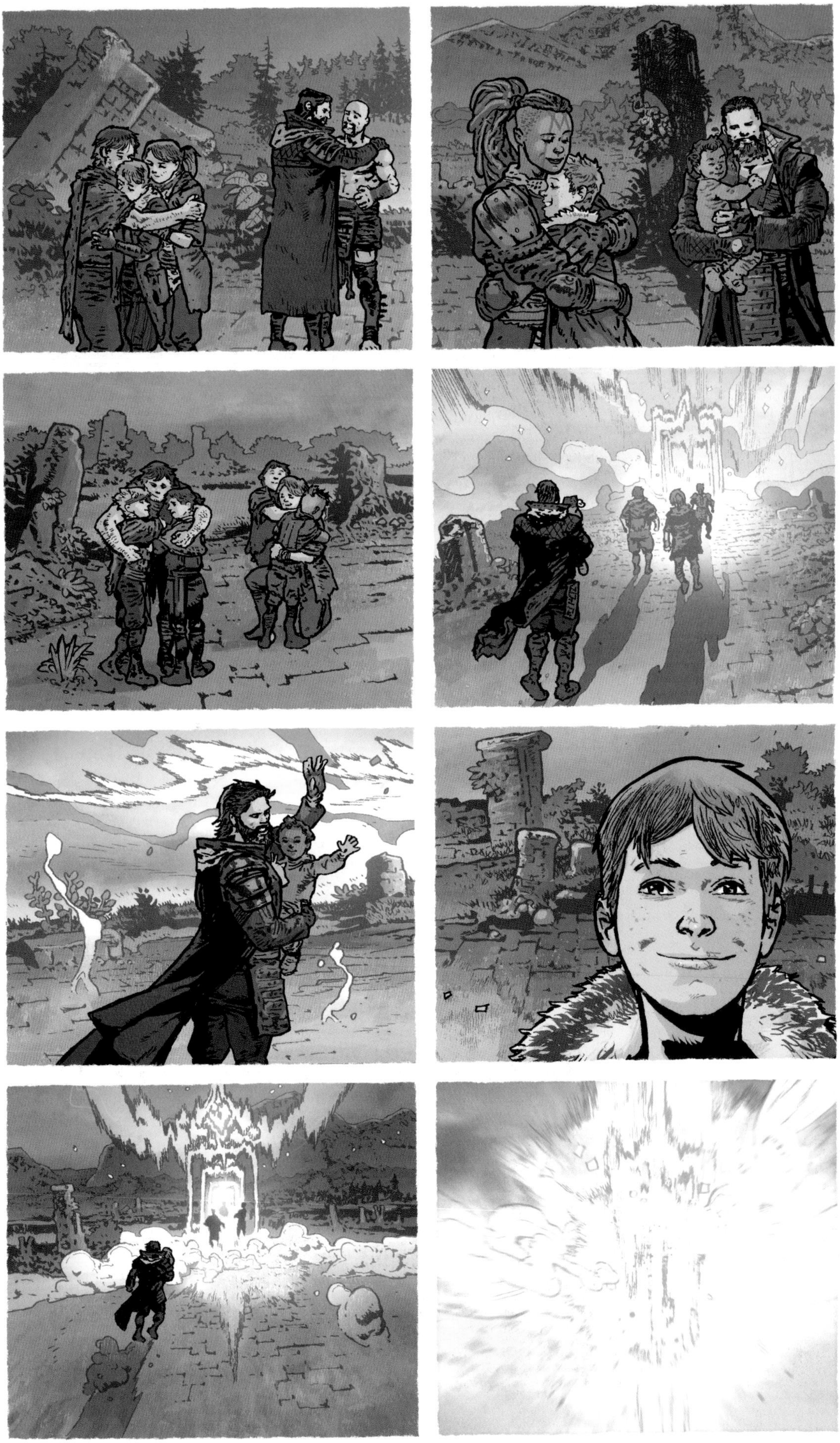

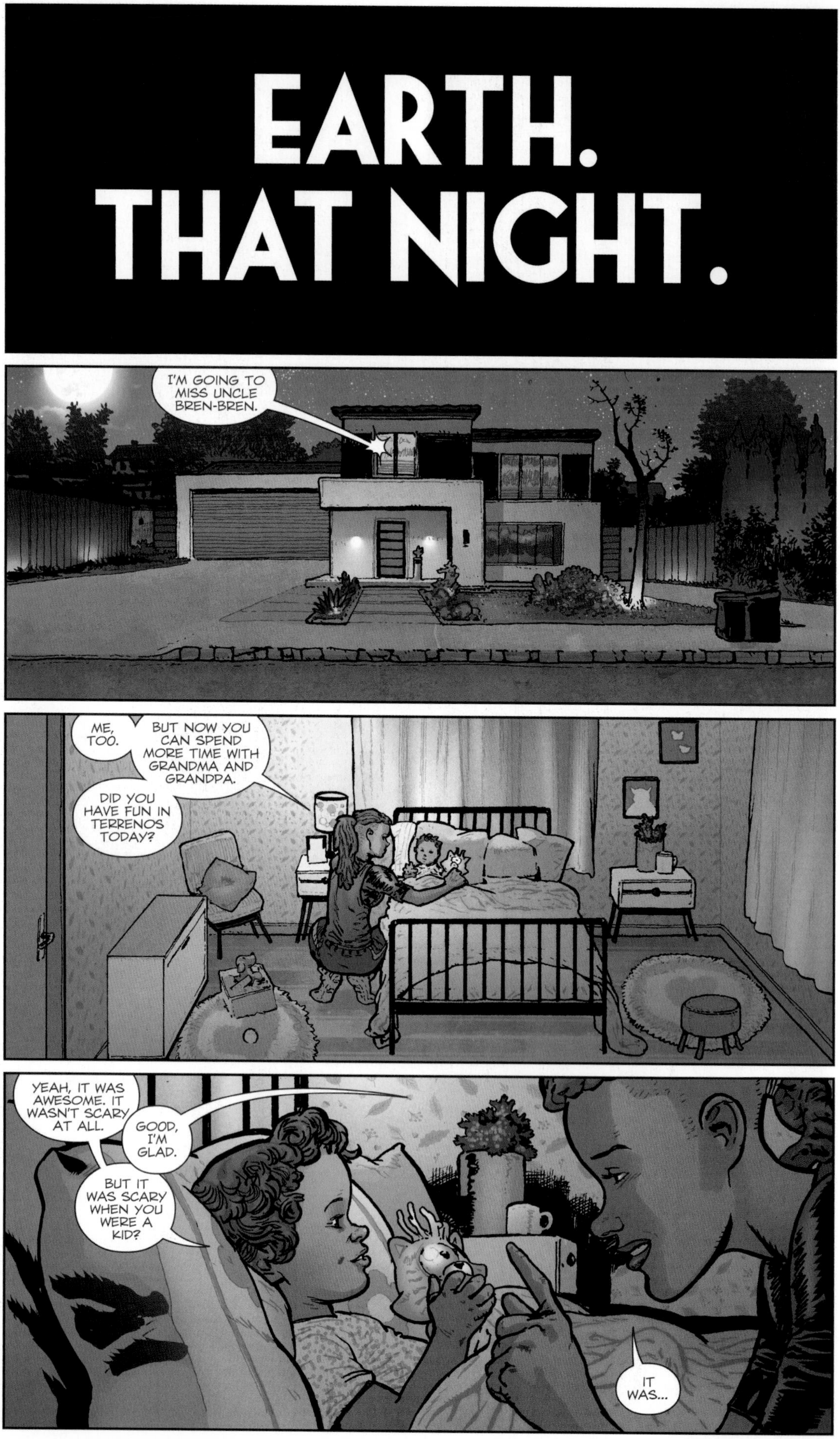
EARTH. THAT NIGHT.
I'M GOING TO MISS UNCLE BREN-BREN.
ME, TOO.
BUT NOW YOU CAN SPEND MORE TIME WITH GRANDMA AND GRANDPA.
DID YOU HAVE FUN IN TERRENOS TODAY?
YEAH, IT WAS AWESOME. IT WASN'T SCARY AT ALL.
GOOD, I'M GLAD.
BUT IT WAS SCARY WHEN YOU WERE A KID?
IT WAS...

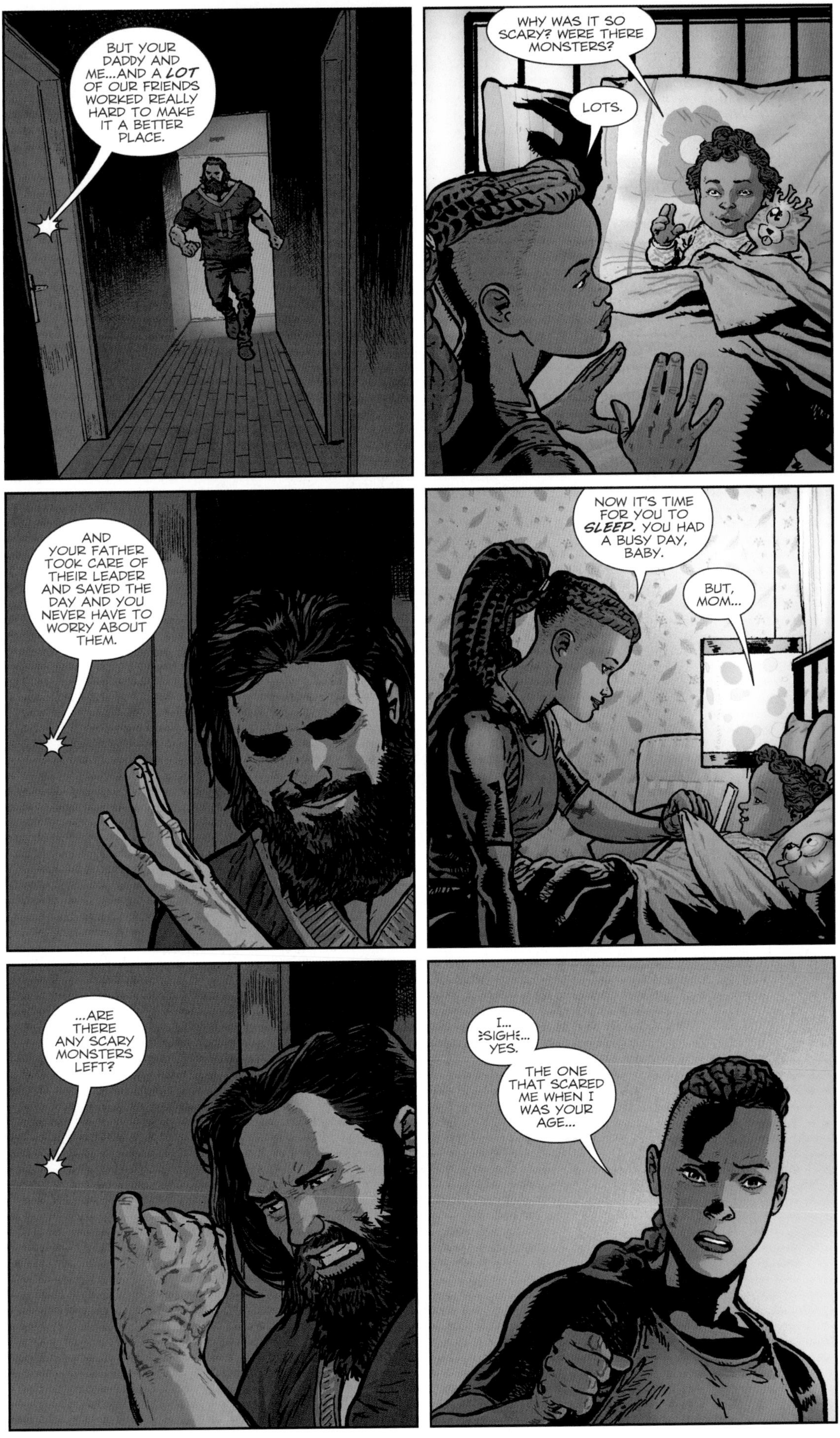
BUT YOUR DADDY AND ME...AND A LOT OF OUR FRIENDS WORKED REALLY HARD TO MAKE IT A BETTER PLACE.
WHY WAS IT SO SCARY? WERE THERE MONSTERS?
LOTS.
AND YOUR FATHER TOOK CARE OF THEIR LEADER AND SAVED THE DAY AND YOU NEVER HAVE TO WORRY ABOUT THEM.
NOW IT'S TIME FOR YOU TO SLEEP. YOU HAD A BUSY DAY, BABY.
BUT, MOM...
...ARE THERE ANY SCARY MONSTERS LEFT?
I... SIGH... YES.
THE ONE THAT SCARED ME WHEN I WAS YOUR AGE...

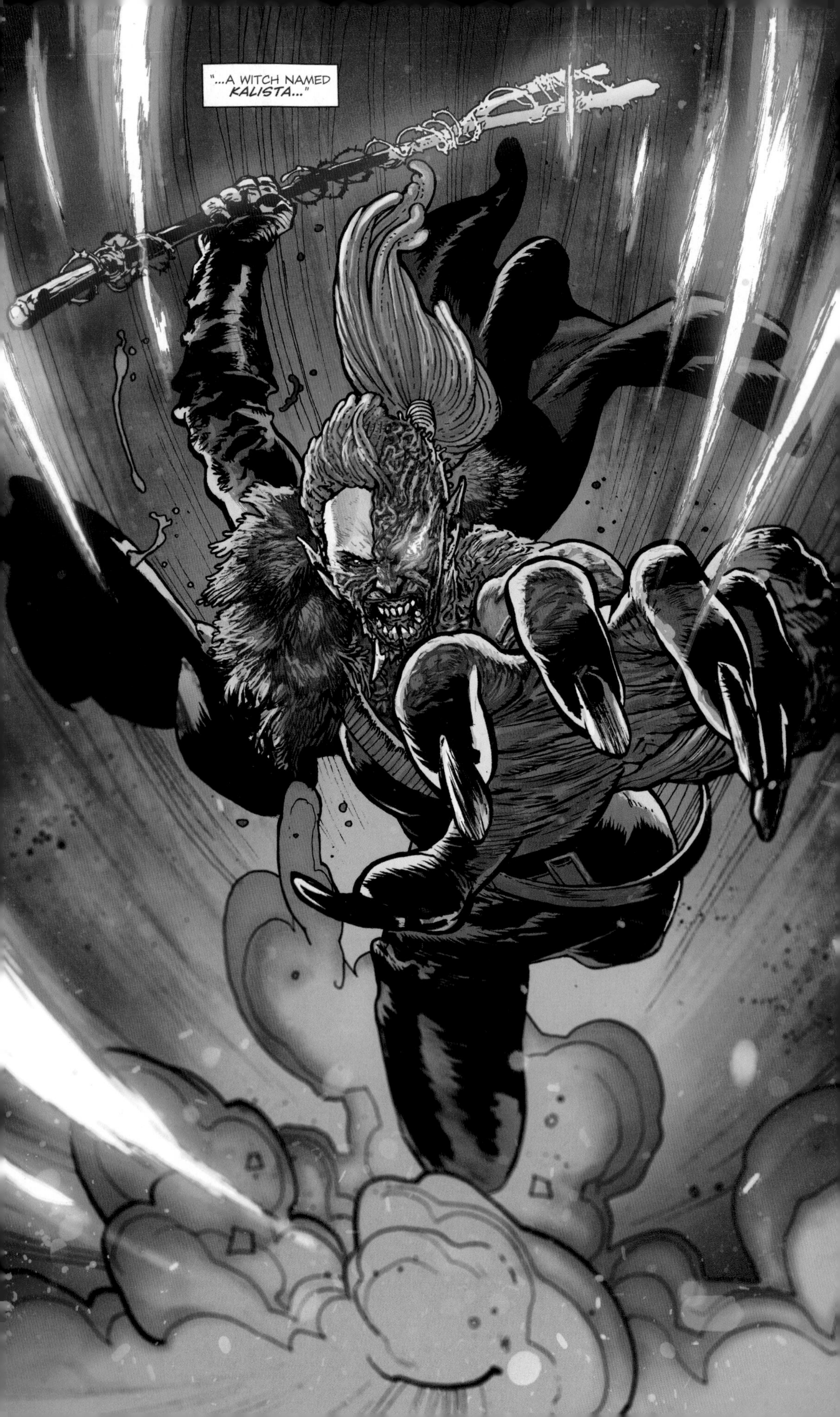
"...A WITCH NAMED KALISTA..."

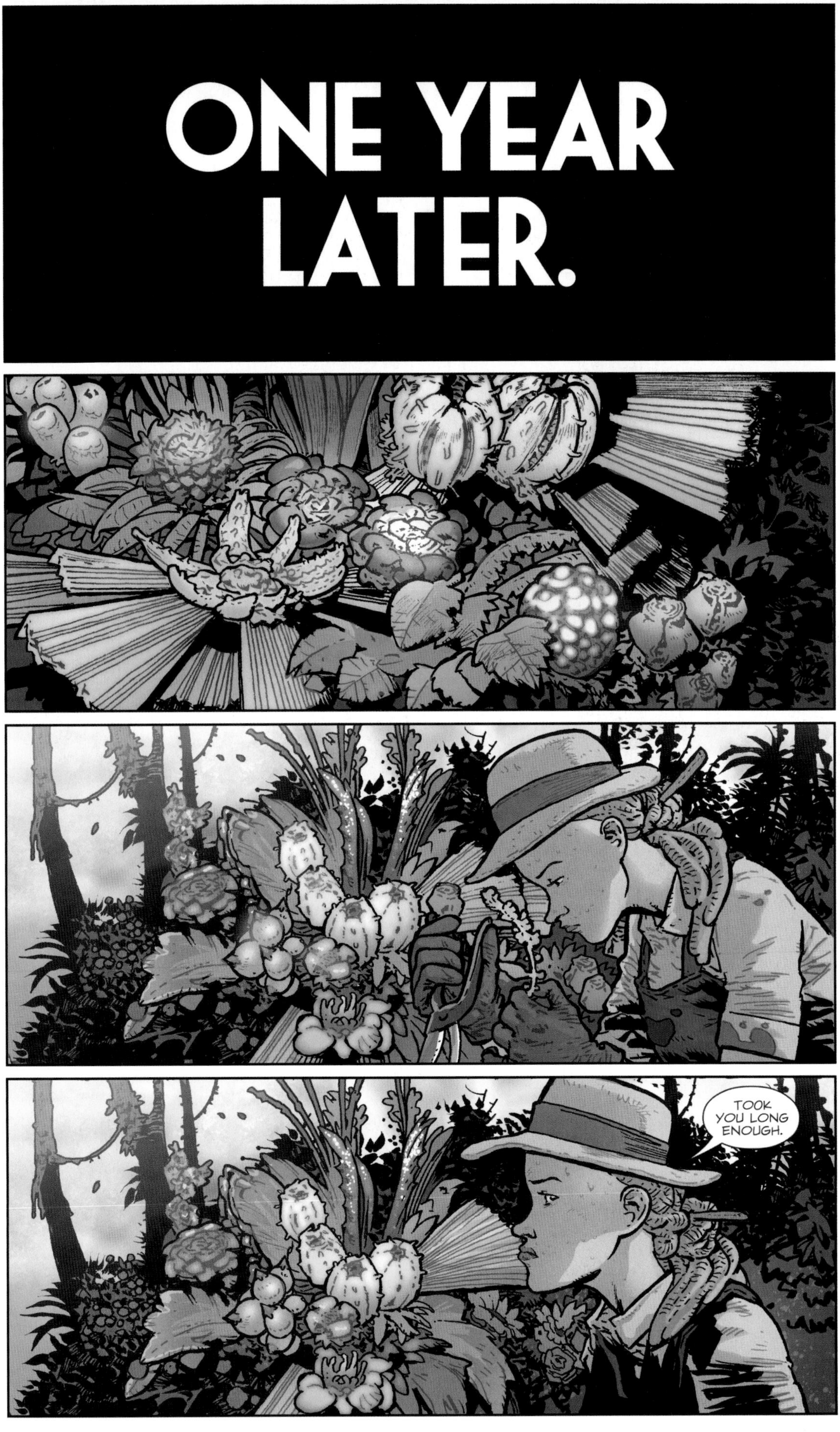
ONE YEAR LATER.
TOOK YOU LONG ENOUGH.

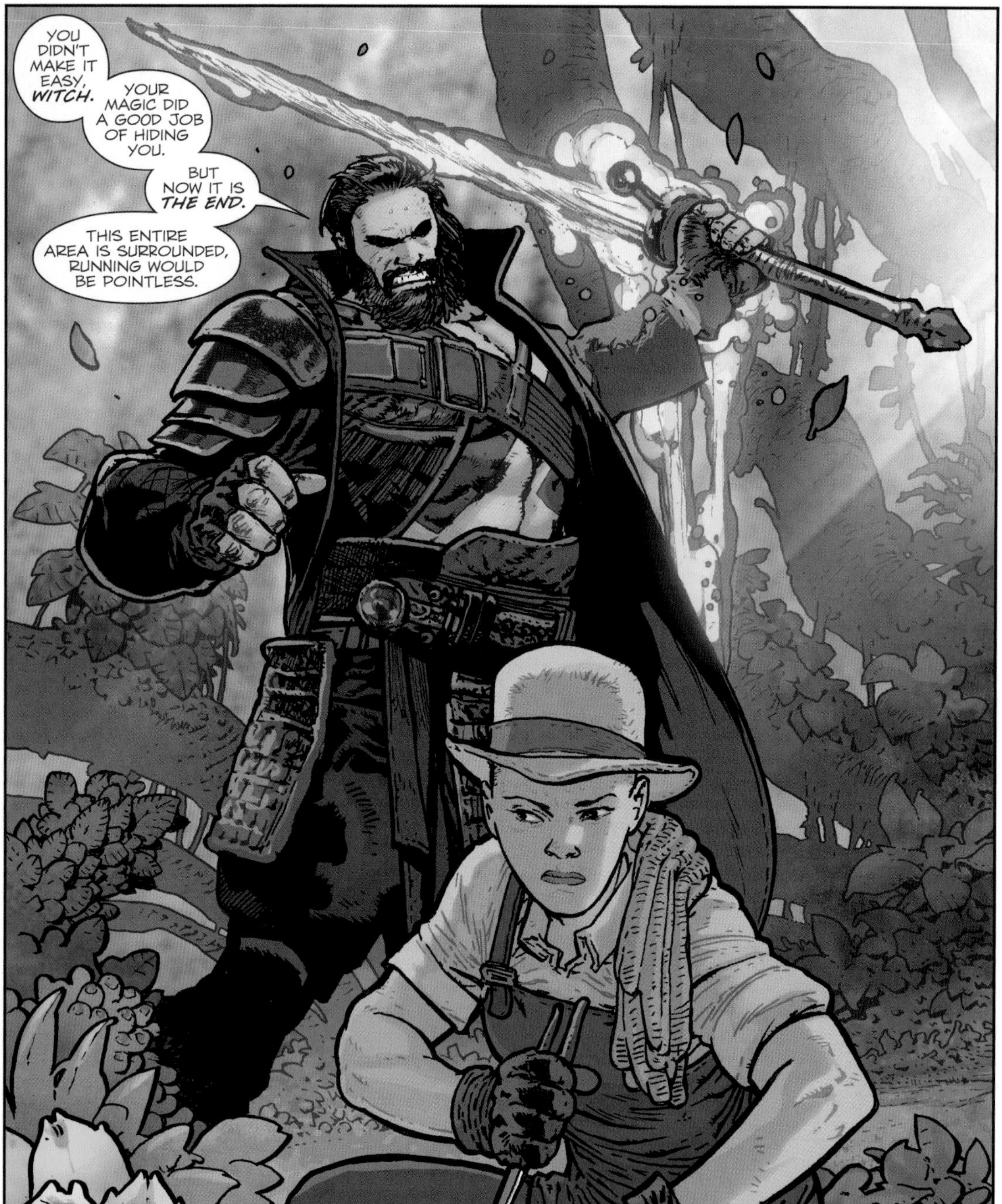
YOU DIDN'T MAKE IT EASY, WITCH.
YOUR MAGIC DID A GOOD JOB OF HIDING YOU.
BUT NOW IT IS THE END.
THIS ENTIRE AREA IS SURROUNDED, RUNNING WOULD BE POINTLESS.
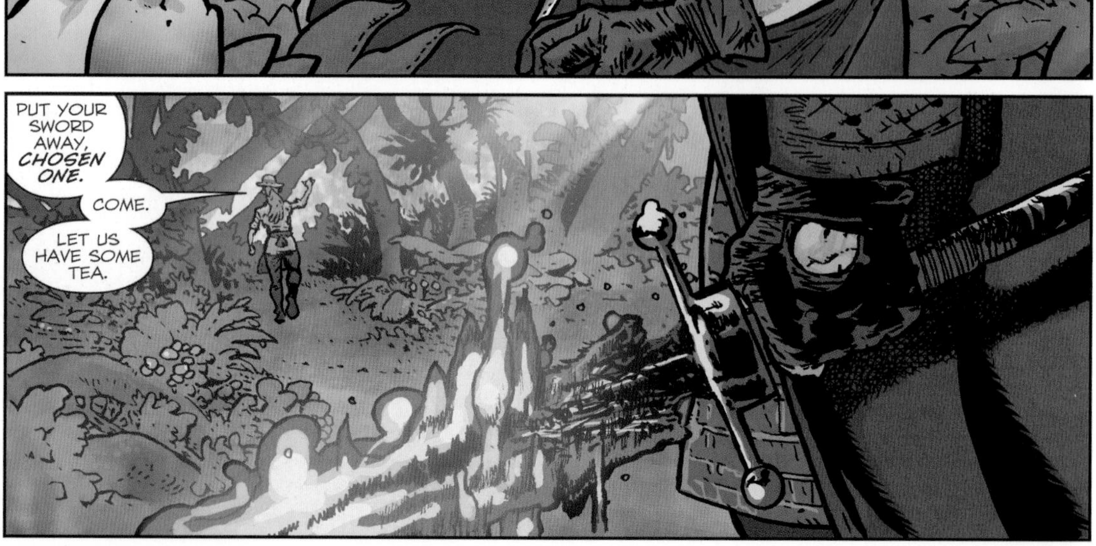
PUT YOUR SWORD AWAY, CHOSEN ONE.
COME.
LET US HAVE SOME TEA.

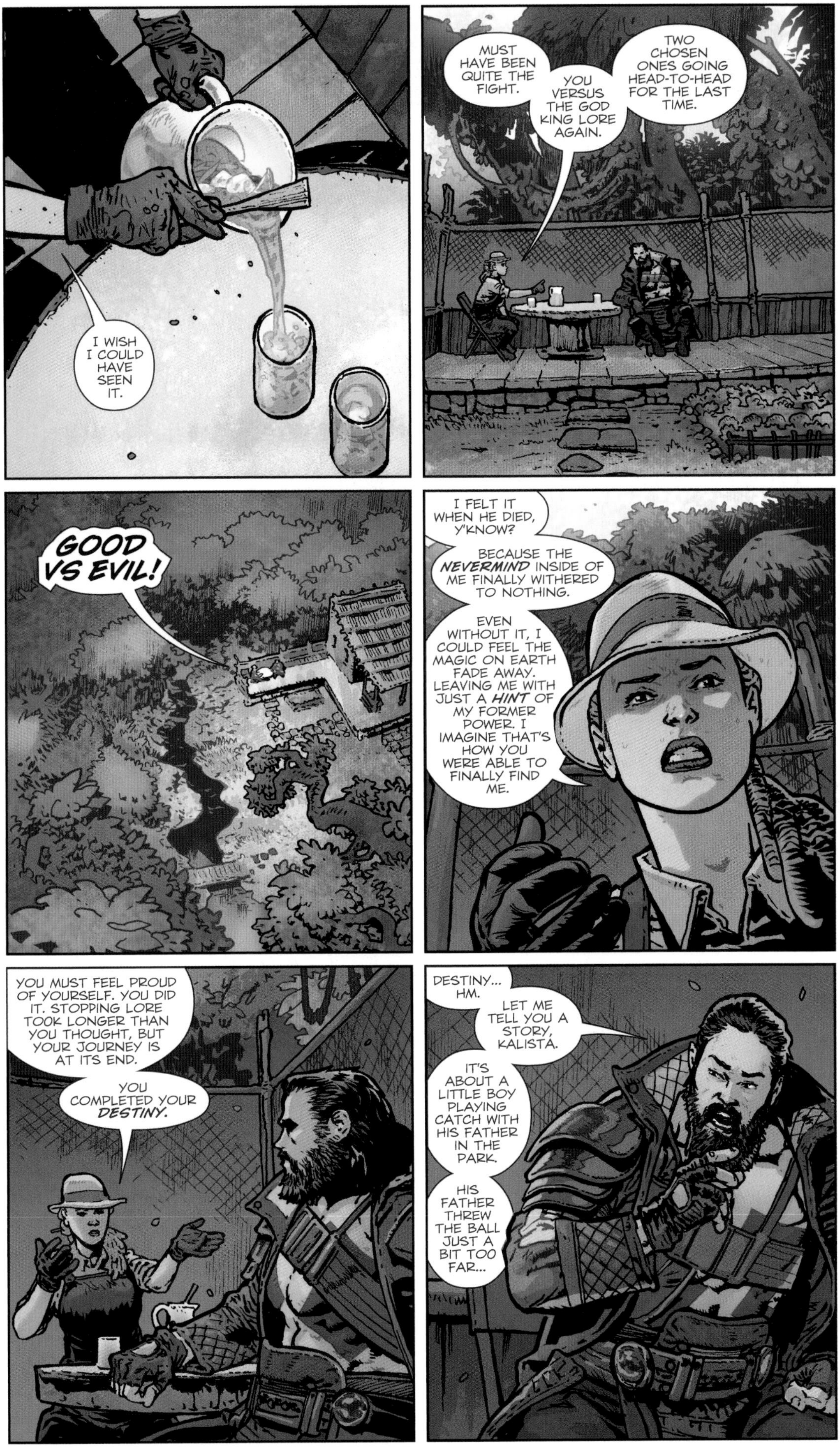
I WISH I COULD HAVE SEEN IT.
MUST HAVE BEEN QUITE THE FIGHT.
YOU VERSUS THE GOD KING LORE AGAIN.
TWO CHOSEN ONES GOING HEAD-TO-HEAD FOR THE LAST TIME.
GOOD VS EVIL!
I FELT IT WHEN HE DIED, Y'KNOW?
BECAUSE THE *NEVERMIND* INSIDE OF ME FINALLY WITHERED TO NOTHING.
EVEN WITHOUT IT, I COULD FEEL THE MAGIC ON EARTH FADE AWAY. LEAVING ME WITH JUST A *HINT* OF MY FORMER POWER. I IMAGINE THAT'S HOW YOU WERE ABLE TO FINALLY FIND ME.
YOU MUST FEEL PROUD OF YOURSELF. YOU DID IT. STOPPING LORE TOOK LONGER THAN YOU THOUGHT, BUT YOUR JOURNEY IS AT ITS END.
YOU COMPLETED YOUR *DESTINY*.
DESTINY... HM.
LET ME TELL YOU A STORY, KALISTA.
IT'S ABOUT A LITTLE BOY PLAYING CATCH WITH HIS FATHER IN THE PARK.
HIS FATHER THREW THE BALL JUST A BIT TOO FAR...

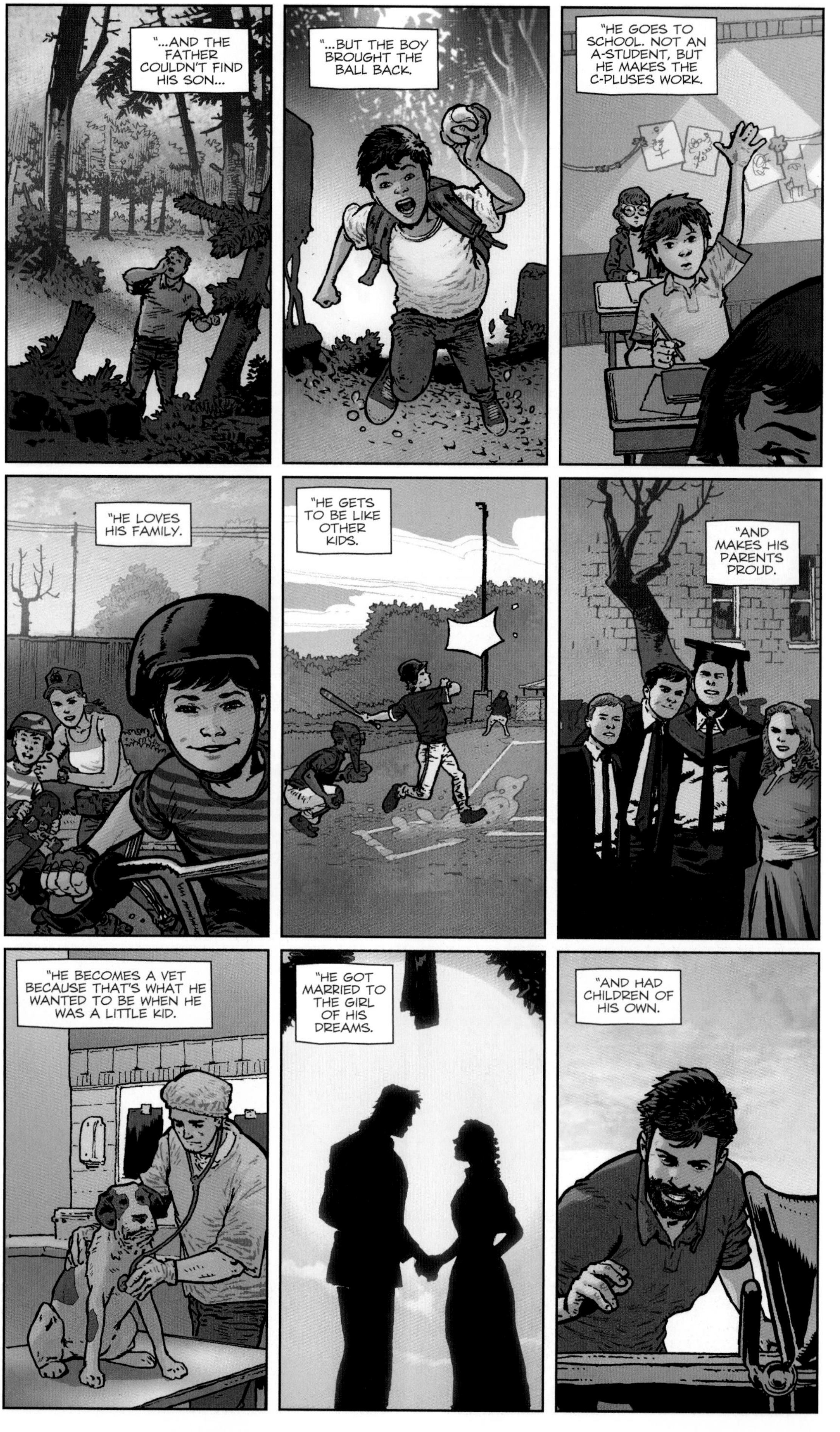
"...AND THE FATHER COULDN'T FIND HIS SON...
"...BUT THE BOY BROUGHT THE BALL BACK.
"HE GOES TO SCHOOL. NOT AN A-STUDENT, BUT HE MAKES THE C-PLUSES WORK.
"HE LOVES HIS FAMILY.
"HE GETS TO BE LIKE OTHER KIDS.
"AND MAKES HIS PARENTS PROUD.
"HE BECOMES A VET BECAUSE THAT'S WHAT HE WANTED TO BE WHEN HE WAS A LITTLE KID.
"HE GOT MARRIED TO THE GIRL OF HIS DREAMS.
"AND HAD CHILDREN OF HIS OWN.

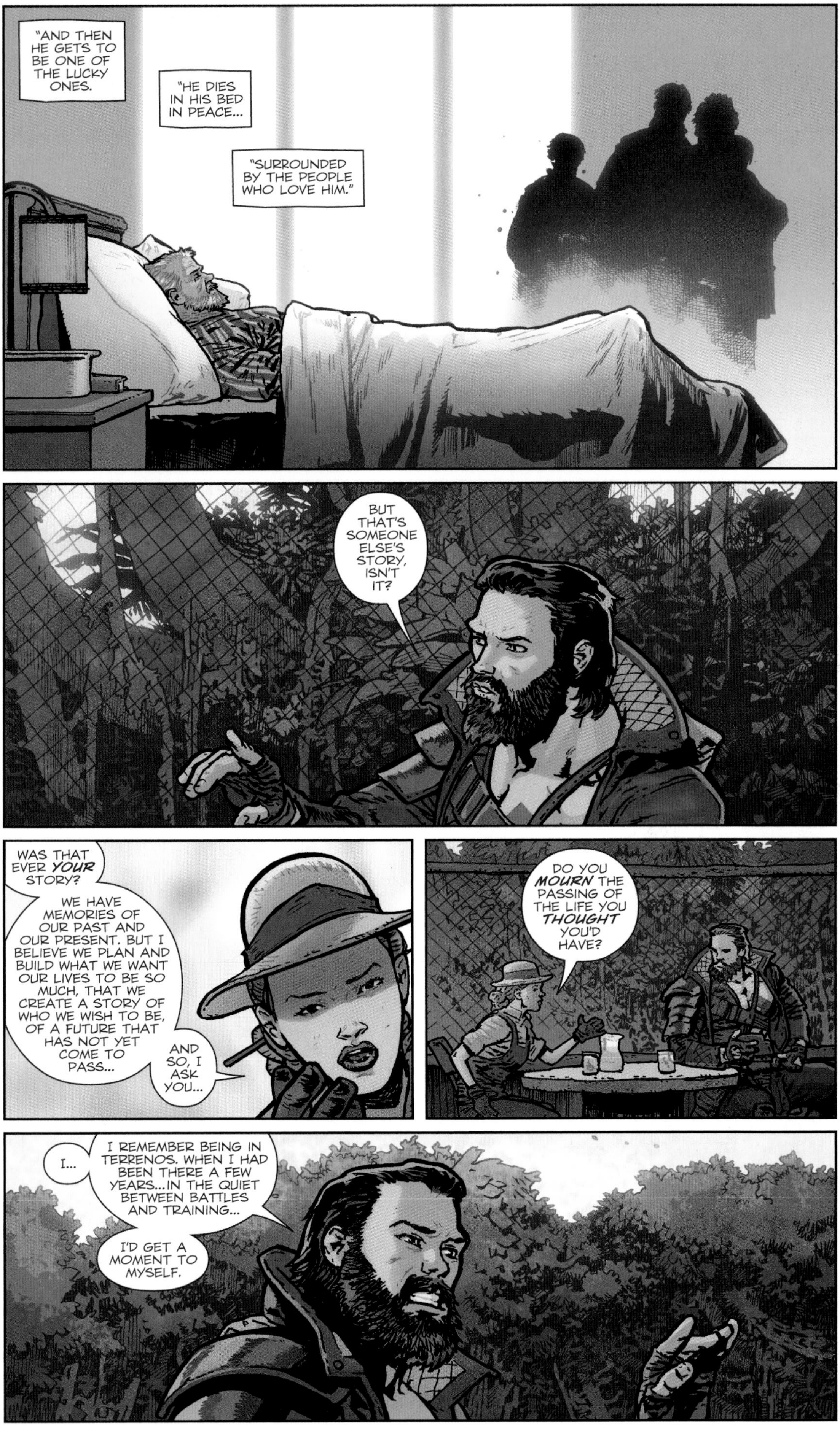
"AND THEN HE GETS TO BE ONE OF THE LUCKY ONES.
"HE DIES IN HIS BED IN PEACE...
"SURROUNDED BY THE PEOPLE WHO LOVE HIM."
BUT THAT'S SOMEONE ELSE'S STORY, ISN'T IT?
WAS THAT EVER *YOUR* STORY?
WE HAVE MEMORIES OF OUR PAST AND OUR PRESENT. BUT I BELIEVE WE PLAN AND BUILD WHAT WE WANT OUR LIVES TO BE SO MUCH, THAT WE CREATE A STORY OF WHO WE WISH TO BE, OF A FUTURE THAT HAS NOT YET COME TO PASS...
AND SO, I ASK YOU...
DO YOU *MOURN* THE PASSING OF THE LIFE YOU *THOUGHT* YOU'D HAVE?
I...
I REMEMBER BEING IN TERRENOS. WHEN I HAD BEEN THERE A FEW YEARS...IN THE QUIET BETWEEN BATTLES AND TRAINING...
I'D GET A MOMENT TO MYSELF.

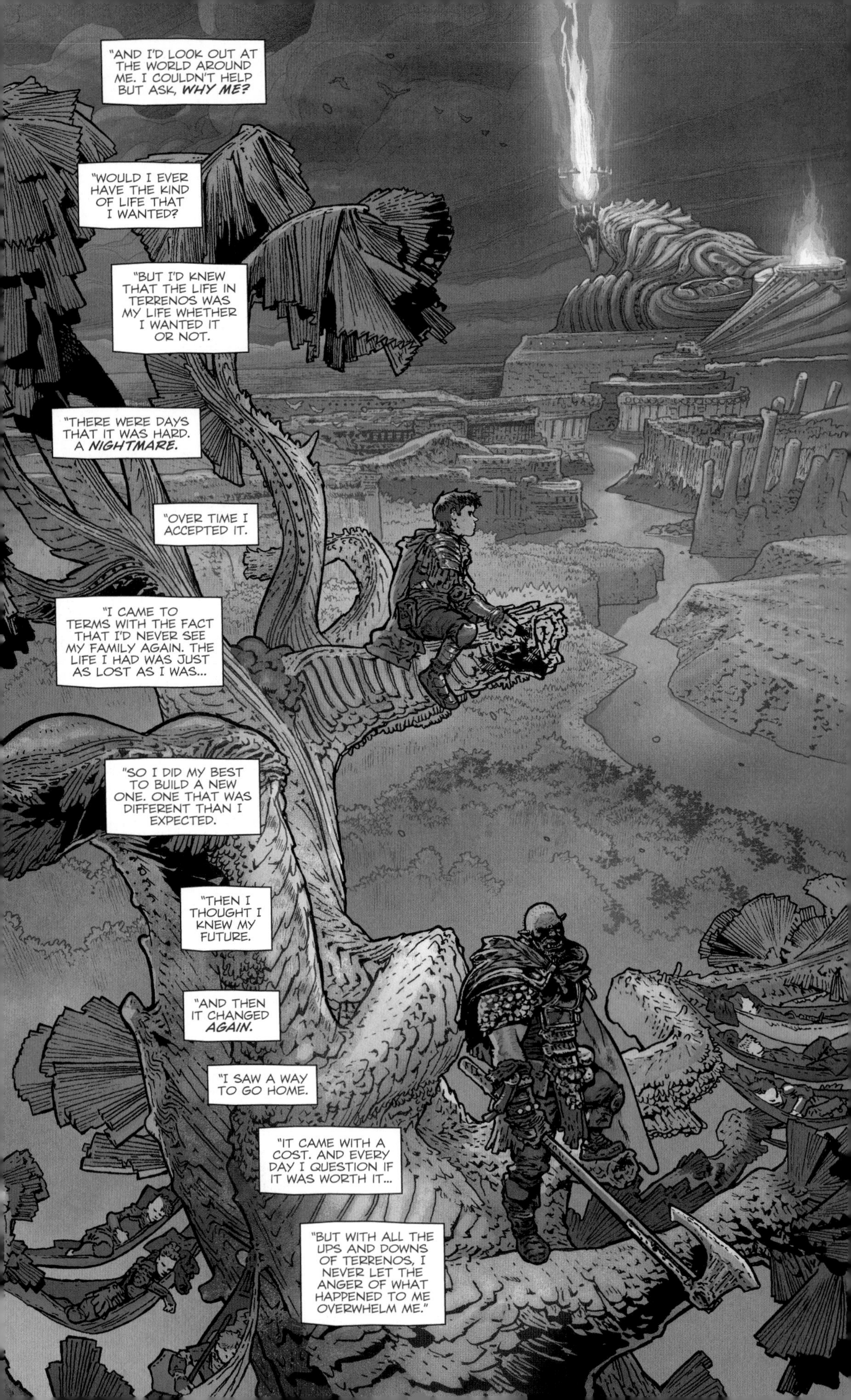
"AND I'D LOOK OUT AT THE WORLD AROUND ME. I COULDN'T HELP BUT ASK, ***WHY ME?***
"WOULD I EVER HAVE THE KIND OF LIFE THAT I WANTED?
"BUT I'D KNEW THAT THE LIFE IN TERRENOS WAS MY LIFE WHETHER I WANTED IT OR NOT.
"THERE WERE DAYS THAT IT WAS HARD. A ***NIGHTMARE.***
"OVER TIME I ACCEPTED IT.
"I CAME TO TERMS WITH THE FACT THAT I'D NEVER SEE MY FAMILY AGAIN. THE LIFE I HAD WAS JUST AS LOST AS I WAS...
"SO I DID MY BEST TO BUILD A NEW ONE. ONE THAT WAS DIFFERENT THAN I EXPECTED.
"THEN I THOUGHT I KNEW MY FUTURE.
"AND THEN IT CHANGED ***AGAIN.***
"I SAW A WAY TO GO HOME.
"IT CAME WITH A COST. AND EVERY DAY I QUESTION IF IT WAS WORTH IT...
"BUT WITH ALL THE UPS AND DOWNS OF TERRENOS, I NEVER LET THE ANGER OF WHAT HAPPENED TO ME OVERWHELM ME."

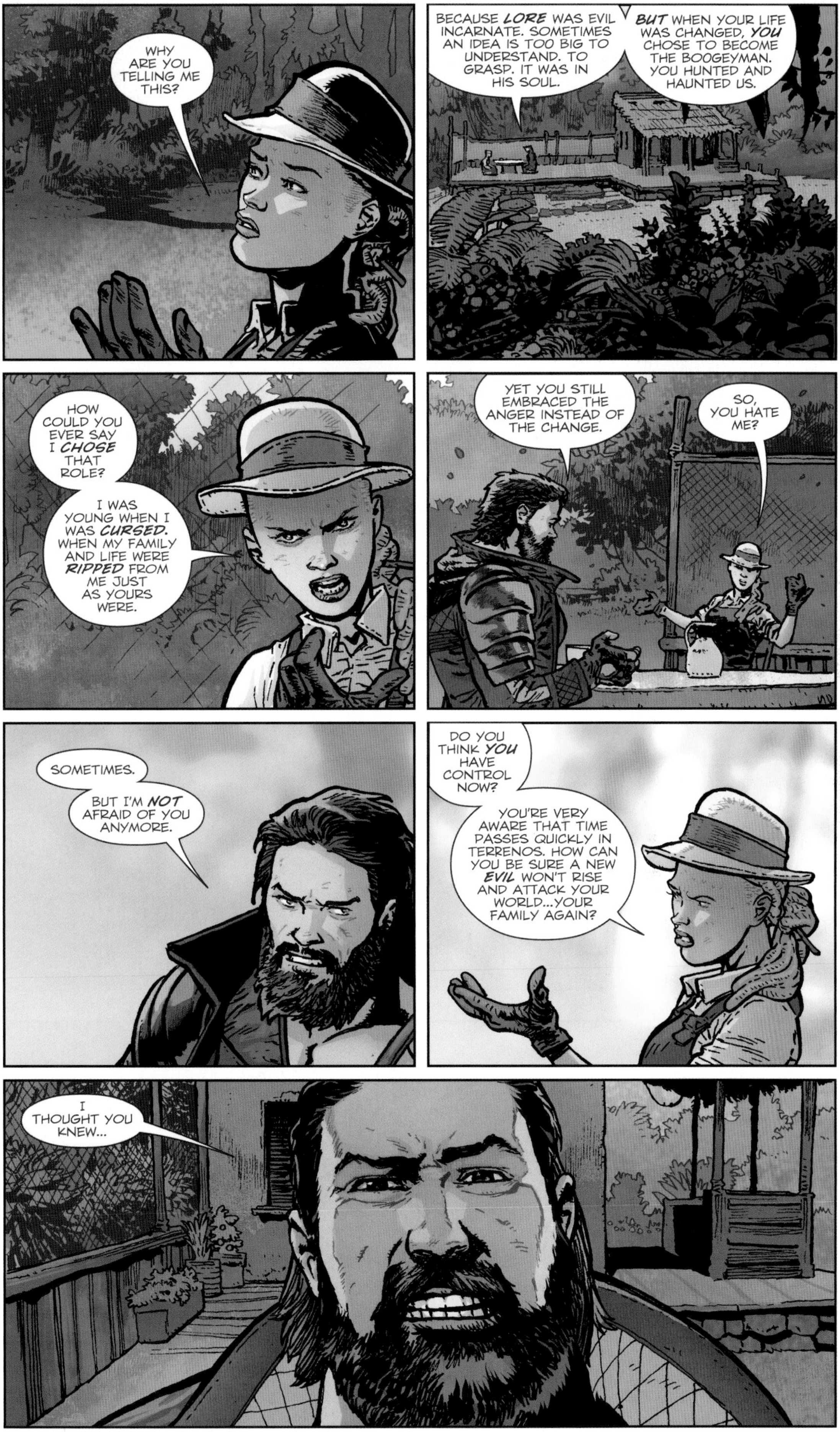
WHY ARE YOU TELLING ME THIS?
BECAUSE LORE WAS EVIL INCARNATE. SOMETIMES AN IDEA IS TOO BIG TO UNDERSTAND. TO GRASP. IT WAS IN HIS SOUL.
BUT WHEN YOUR LIFE WAS CHANGED, YOU CHOSE TO BECOME THE BOOGEYMAN. YOU HUNTED AND HAUNTED US.
HOW COULD YOU EVER SAY I CHOSE THAT ROLE?
I WAS YOUNG WHEN I WAS CURSED. WHEN MY FAMILY AND LIFE WERE RIPPED FROM ME JUST AS YOURS WERE.
YET YOU STILL EMBRACED THE ANGER INSTEAD OF THE CHANGE.
SO, YOU HATE ME?
SOMETIMES.
BUT I'M NOT AFRAID OF YOU ANYMORE.
DO YOU THINK YOU HAVE CONTROL NOW?
YOU'RE VERY AWARE THAT TIME PASSES QUICKLY IN TERRENOS. HOW CAN YOU BE SURE A NEW EVIL WON'T RISE AND ATTACK YOUR WORLD...YOUR FAMILY AGAIN?
I THOUGHT YOU KNEW...

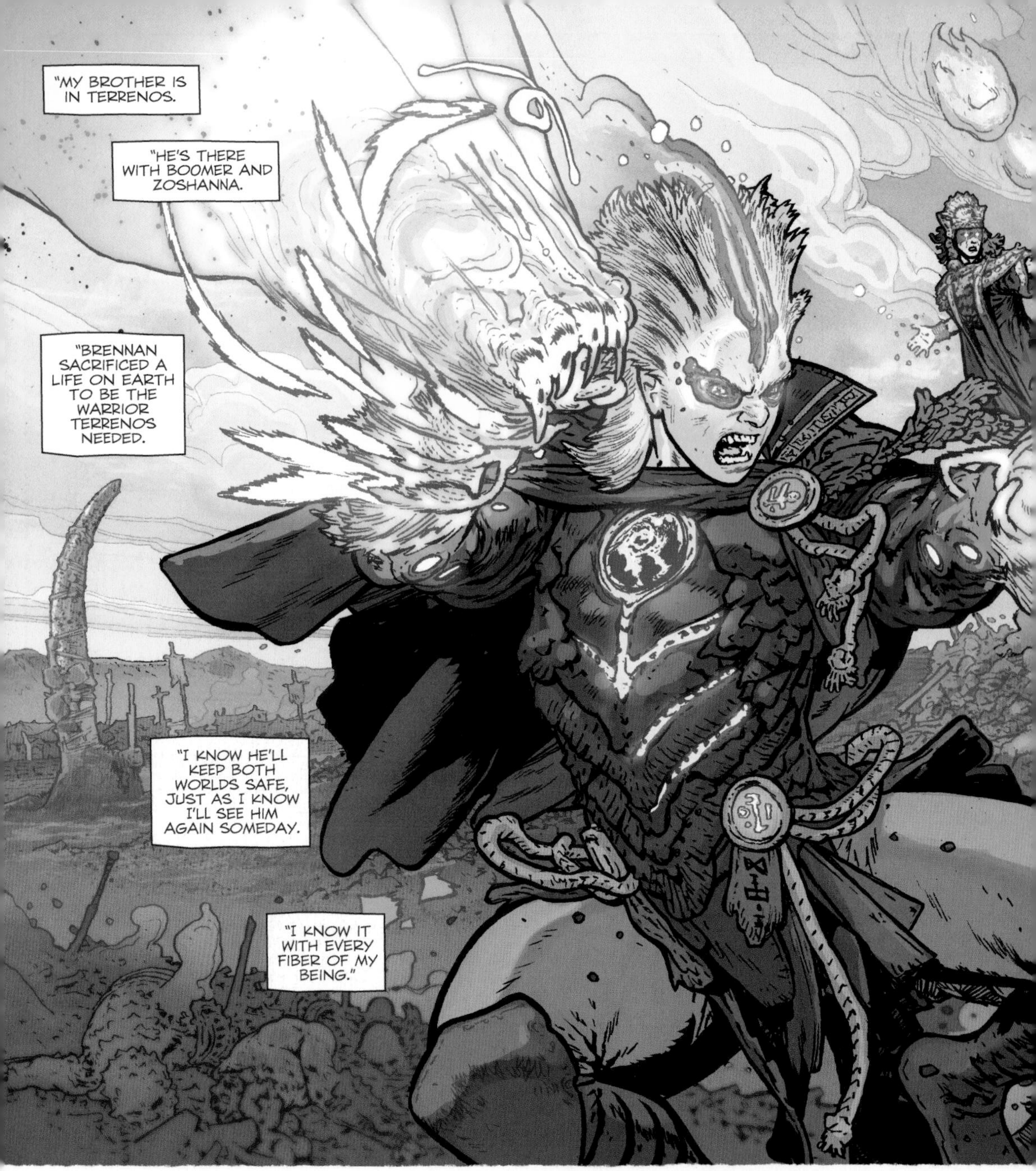
"MY BROTHER IS IN TERRENOS.
"HE'S THERE WITH BOOMER AND ZOSHANNA.
"BRENNAN SACRIFICED A LIFE ON EARTH TO BE THE WARRIOR TERRENOS NEEDED.
"I KNOW HE'LL KEEP BOTH WORLDS SAFE, JUST AS I KNOW I'LL SEE HIM AGAIN SOMEDAY.
"I KNOW IT WITH EVERY FIBER OF MY BEING."

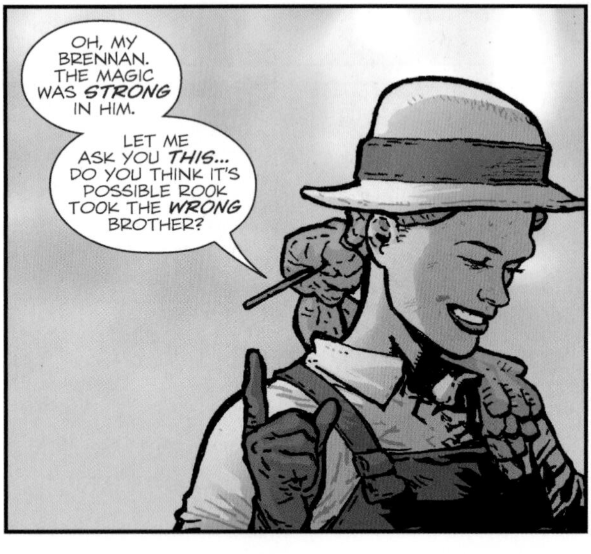
OH, MY BRENNAN. THE MAGIC WAS STRONG IN HIM.
LET ME ASK YOU THIS... DO YOU THINK IT'S POSSIBLE ROOK TOOK THE WRONG BROTHER?

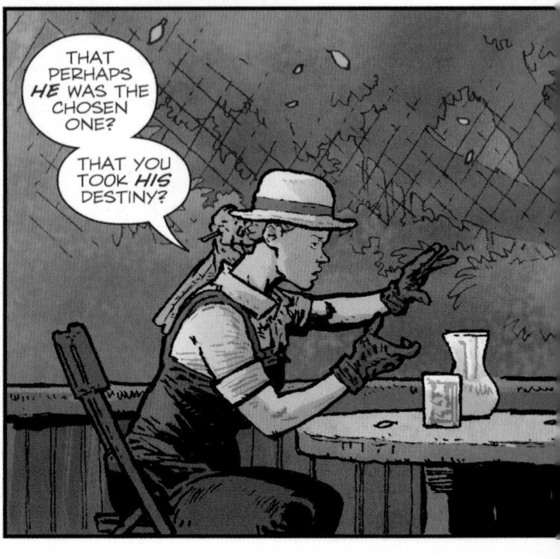
THAT PERHAPS HE WAS THE CHOSEN ONE?
THAT YOU TOOK HIS DESTINY?

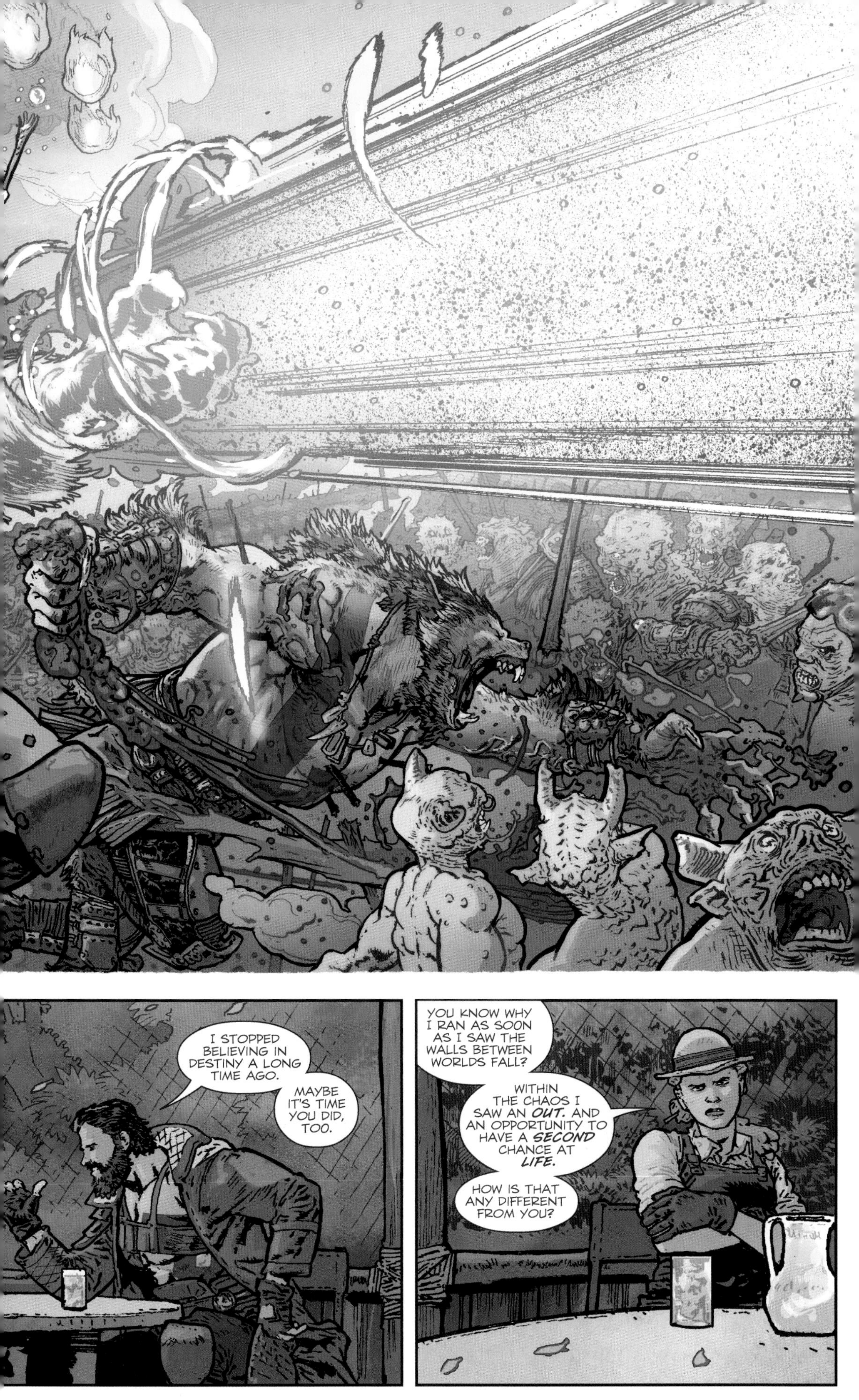
I STOPPED BELIEVING IN DESTINY A LONG TIME AGO.
MAYBE IT'S TIME YOU DID, TOO.
YOU KNOW WHY I RAN AS SOON AS I SAW THE WALLS BETWEEN WORLDS FALL?
WITHIN THE CHAOS I SAW AN *OUT.* AND AN OPPORTUNITY TO HAVE A *SECOND* CHANCE AT *LIFE.*
HOW IS THAT ANY DIFFERENT FROM YOU?

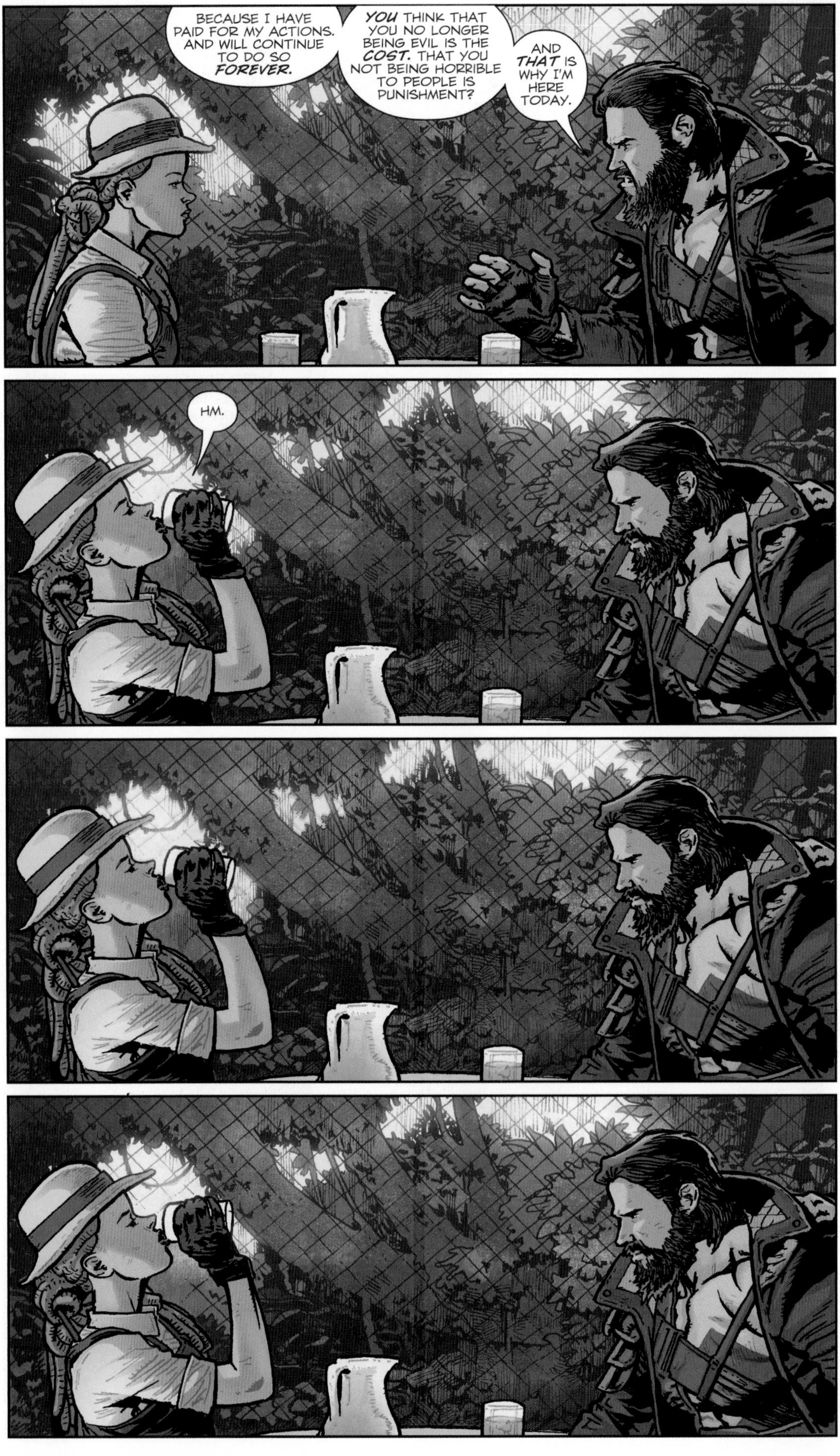
BECAUSE I HAVE PAID FOR MY ACTIONS. AND WILL CONTINUE TO DO SO *FOREVER.*
YOU THINK THAT YOU NO LONGER BEING EVIL IS THE *COST.* THAT YOU NOT BEING HORRIBLE TO PEOPLE IS PUNISHMENT?
AND *THAT* IS WHY I'M HERE TODAY.
HM.

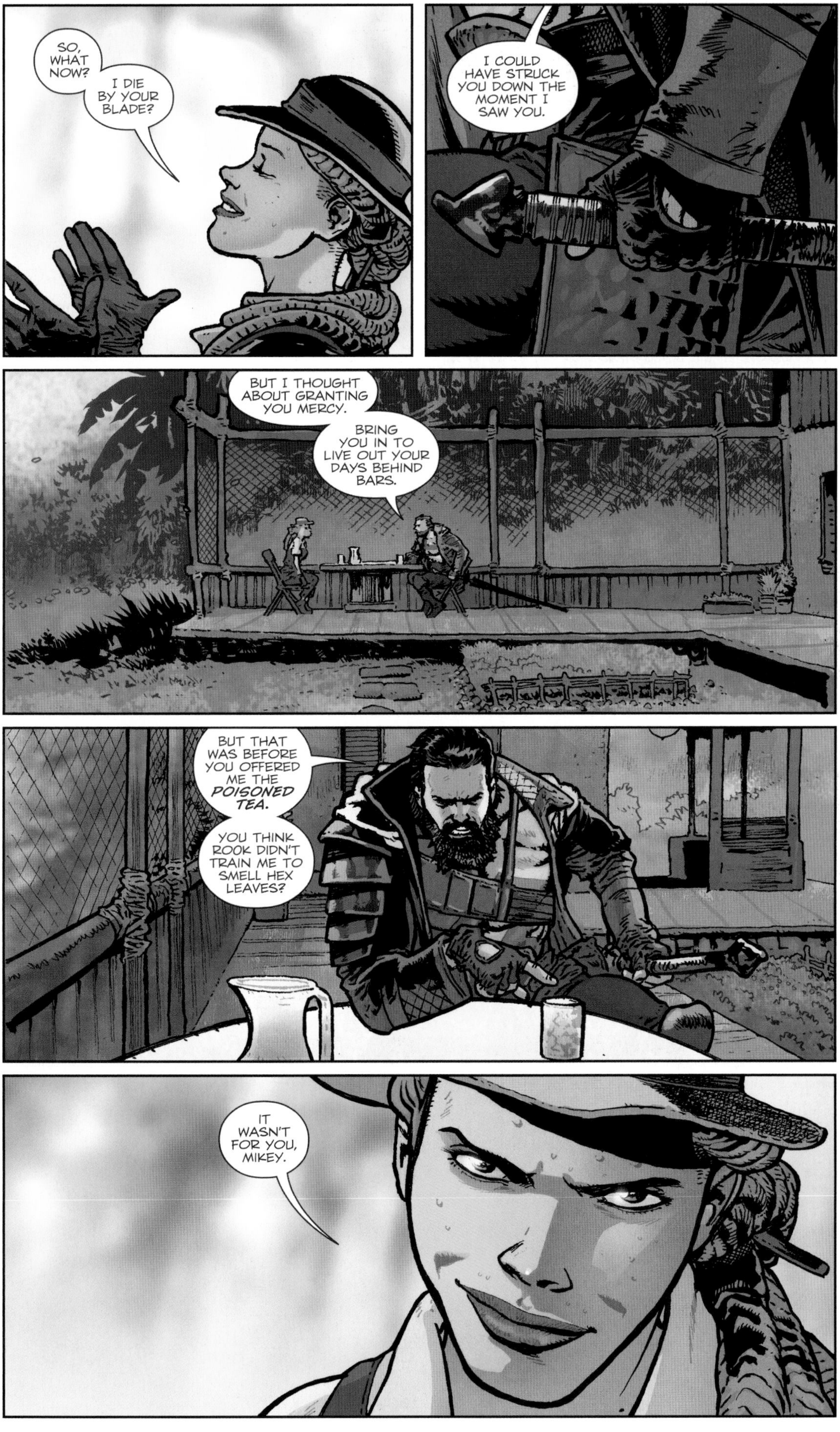
SO, WHAT NOW?
I DIE BY YOUR BLADE?
I COULD HAVE STRUCK YOU DOWN THE MOMENT I SAW YOU.
BUT I THOUGHT ABOUT GRANTING YOU MERCY.
BRING YOU IN TO LIVE OUT YOUR DAYS BEHIND BARS.
BUT THAT WAS BEFORE YOU OFFERED ME THE ***POISONED TEA.***
YOU THINK ROOK DIDN'T TRAIN ME TO SMELL HEX LEAVES?
IT WASN'T FOR YOU, MIKEY.

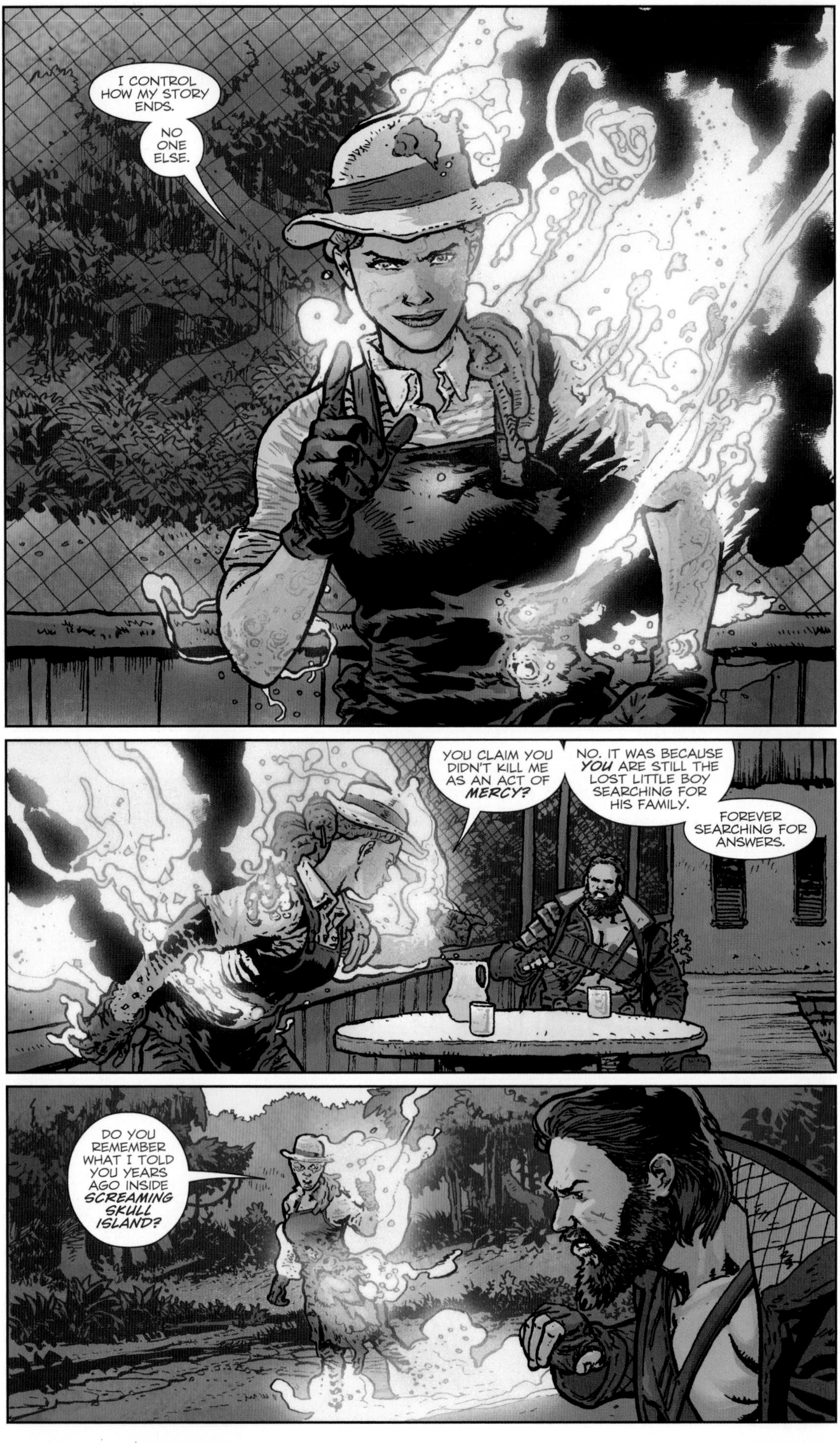
I CONTROL HOW MY STORY ENDS.
NO ONE ELSE.
YOU CLAIM YOU DIDN'T KILL ME AS AN ACT OF MERCY?
NO. IT WAS BECAUSE YOU ARE STILL THE LOST LITTLE BOY SEARCHING FOR HIS FAMILY.
FOREVER SEARCHING FOR ANSWERS.
DO YOU REMEMBER WHAT I TOLD YOU YEARS AGO INSIDE SCREAMING SKULL ISLAND?

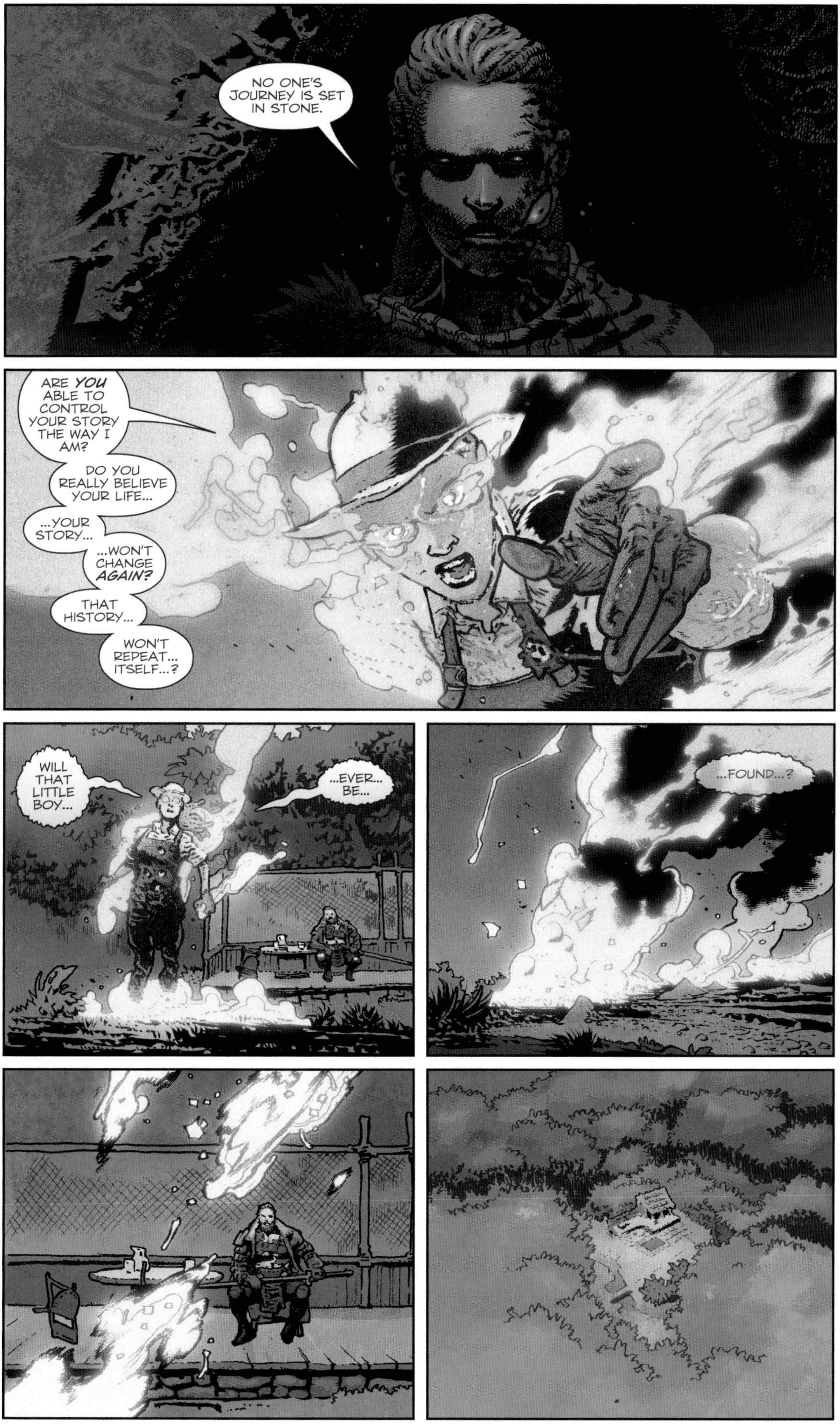
NO ONE'S JOURNEY IS SET IN STONE.
ARE *YOU* ABLE TO CONTROL YOUR STORY THE WAY I AM?
DO YOU REALLY BELIEVE YOUR LIFE...
...YOUR STORY...
...WON'T CHANGE *AGAIN?*
THAT HISTORY...
WON'T REPEAT... ITSELF...?
WILL THAT LITTLE BOY...
...EVER... BE...
...FOUND...?

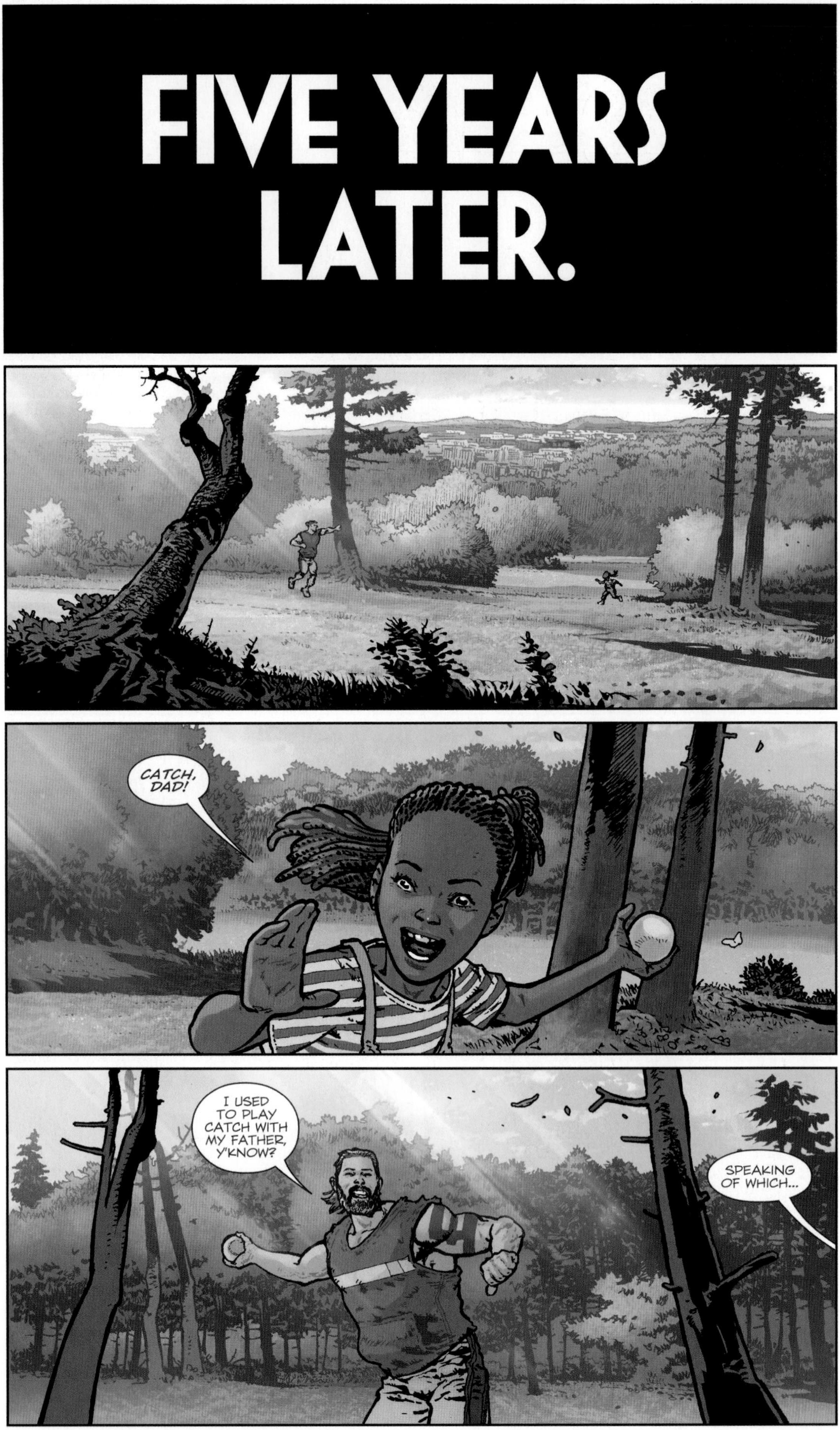
FIVE YEARS LATER.
CATCH, DAD!
I USED TO PLAY CATCH WITH MY FATHER, Y'KNOW?
SPEAKING OF WHICH...

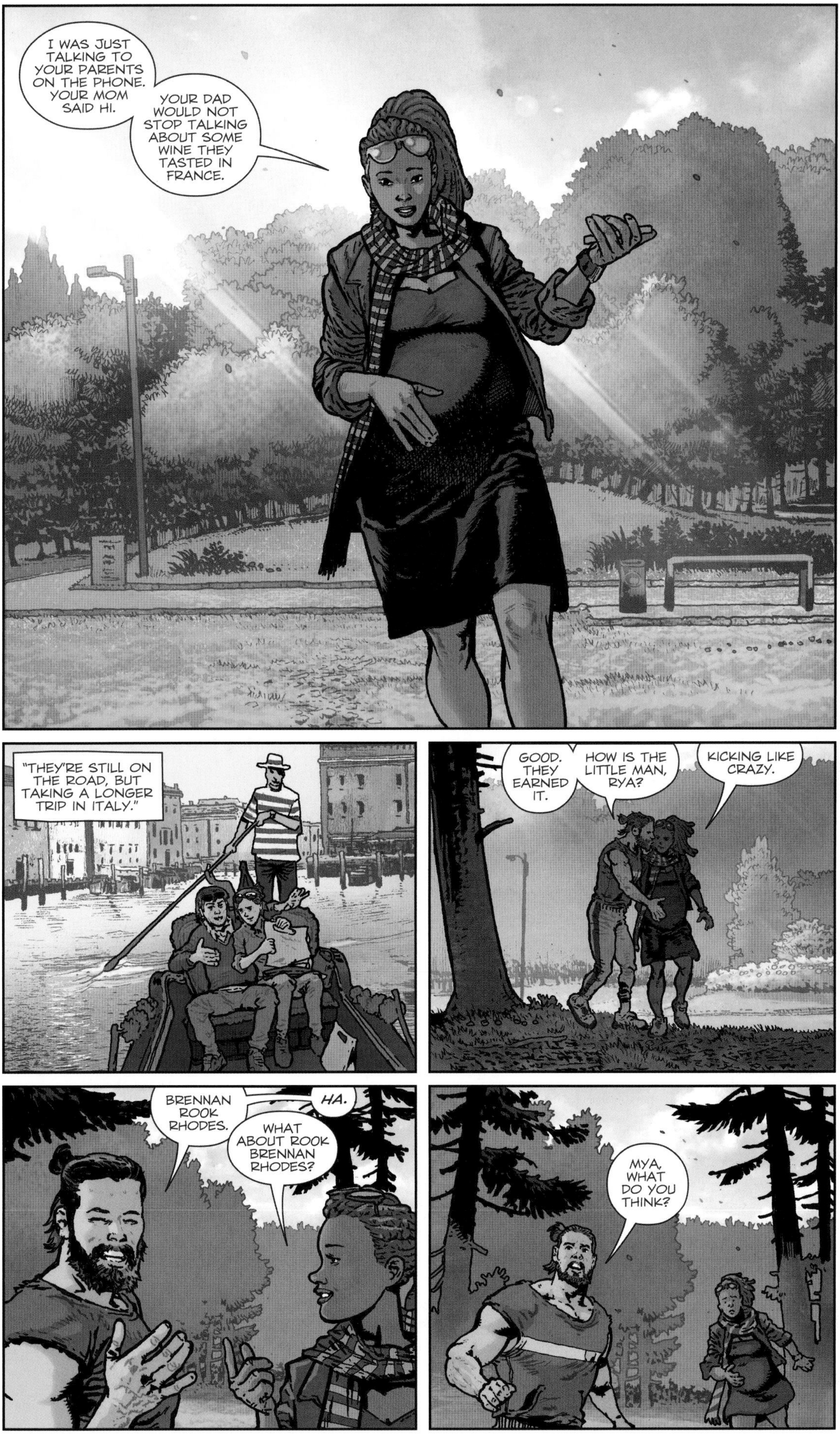
I WAS JUST TALKING TO YOUR PARENTS ON THE PHONE. YOUR MOM SAID HI.
YOUR DAD WOULD NOT STOP TALKING ABOUT SOME WINE THEY TASTED IN FRANCE.
"THEY'RE STILL ON THE ROAD, BUT TAKING A LONGER TRIP IN ITALY."
GOOD. THEY EARNED IT.
HOW IS THE LITTLE MAN, RYA?
KICKING LIKE CRAZY.
BRENNAN ROOK RHODES.
HA.
WHAT ABOUT ROOK BRENNAN RHODES?
MYA, WHAT DO YOU THINK?

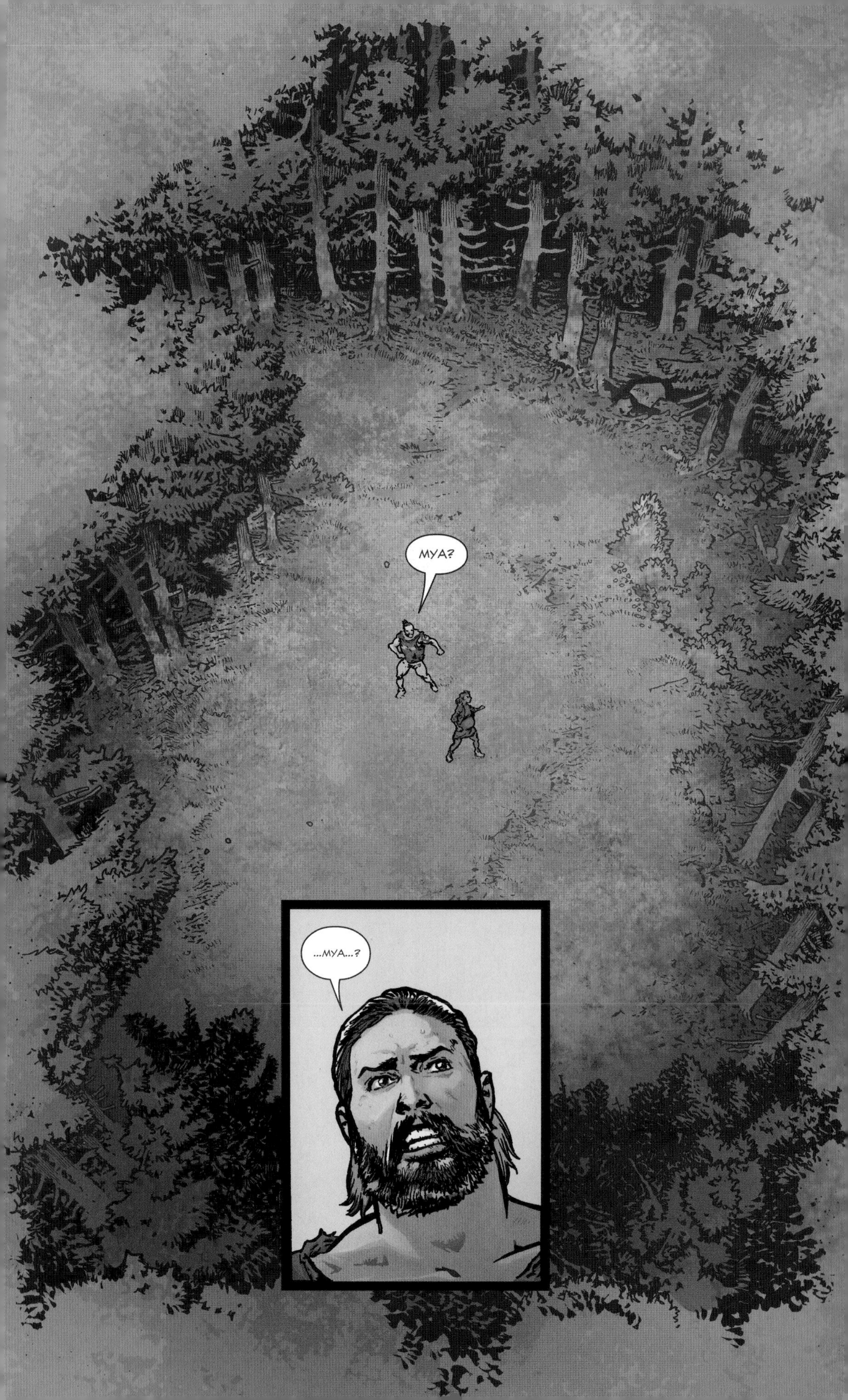
MYA?
...MYA...?

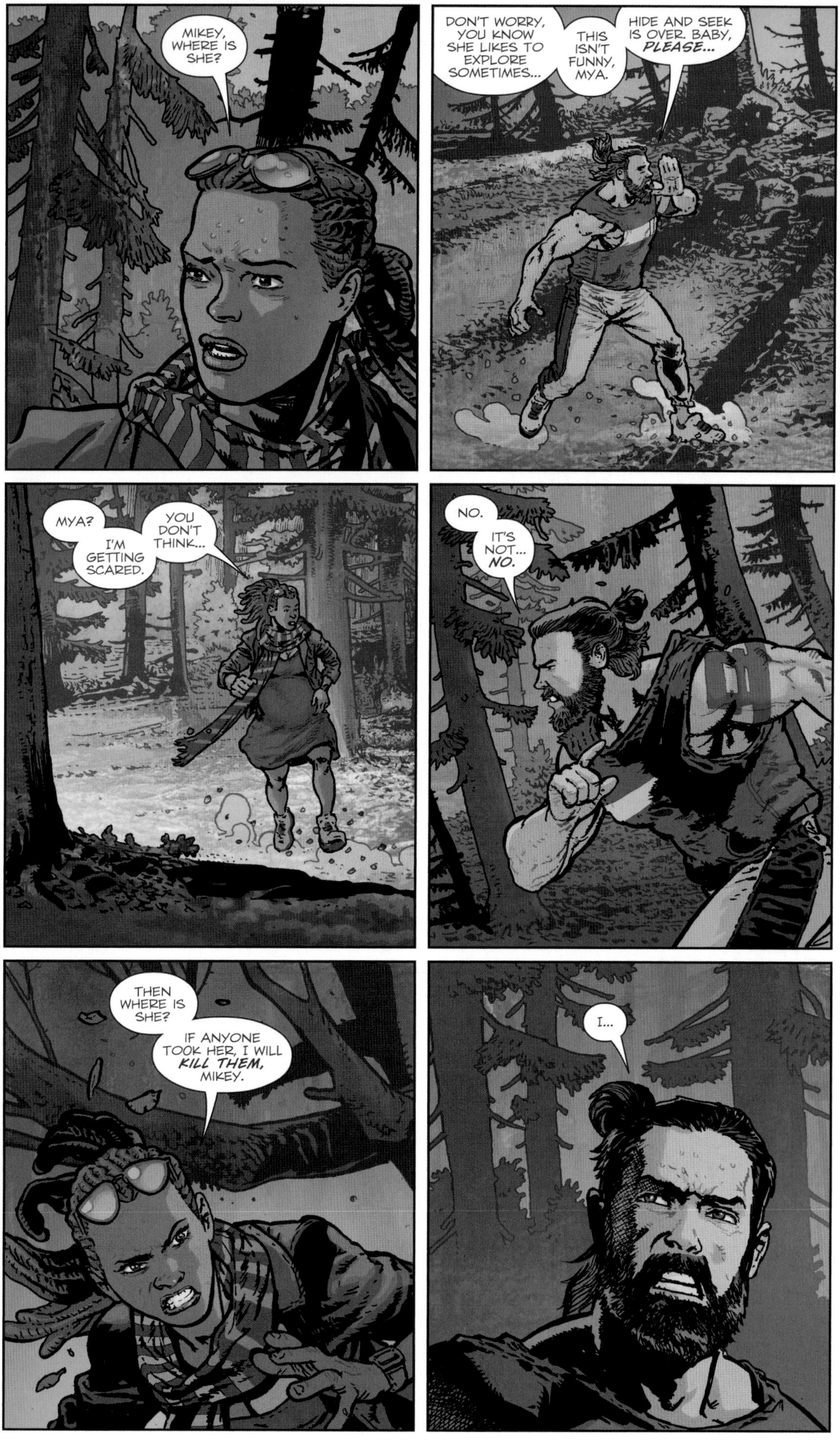
MIKEY, WHERE IS SHE?
DON'T WORRY, YOU KNOW SHE LIKES TO EXPLORE SOMETIMES...
THIS ISN'T FUNNY, MYA.
HIDE AND SEEK IS OVER. BABY, ***PLEASE...***
MYA?
I'M GETTING SCARED.
YOU DON'T THINK...
NO.
IT'S NOT... ***NO.***
THEN WHERE IS SHE?
IF ANYONE TOOK HER, I WILL ***KILL THEM,*** MIKEY.
I...

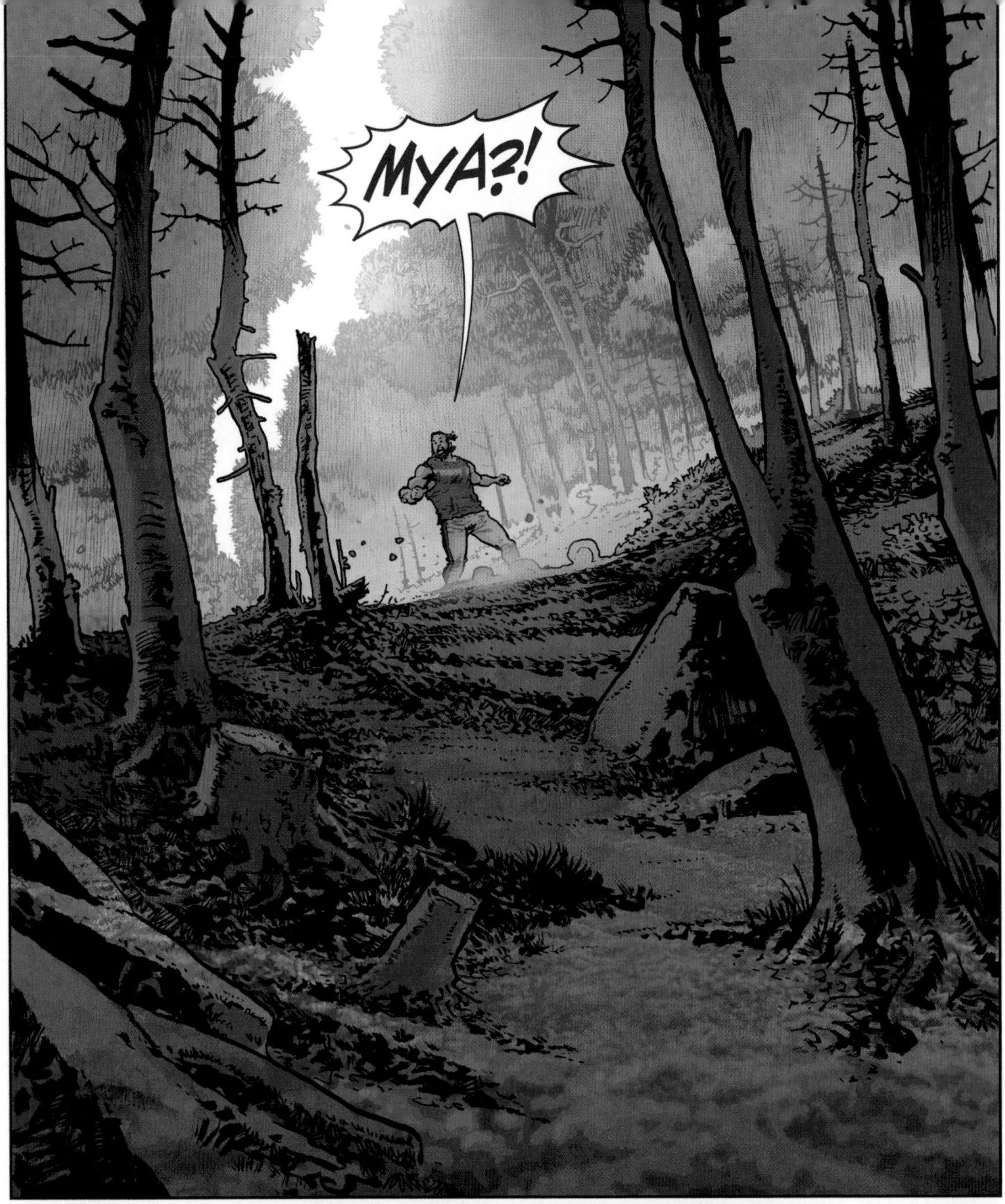
MYA?!

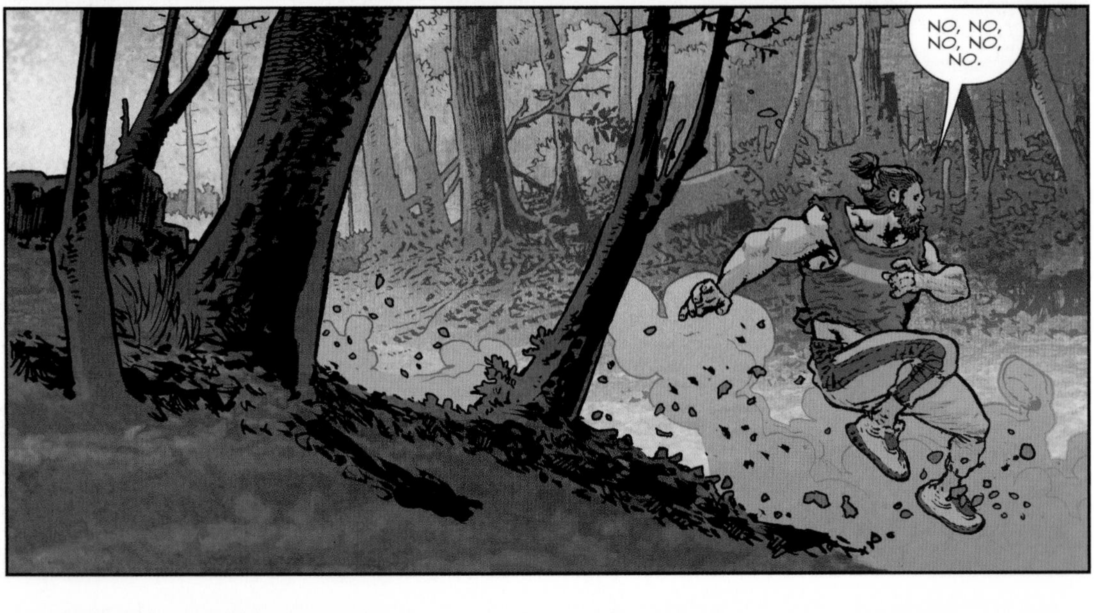
NO, NO, NO, NO, NO.

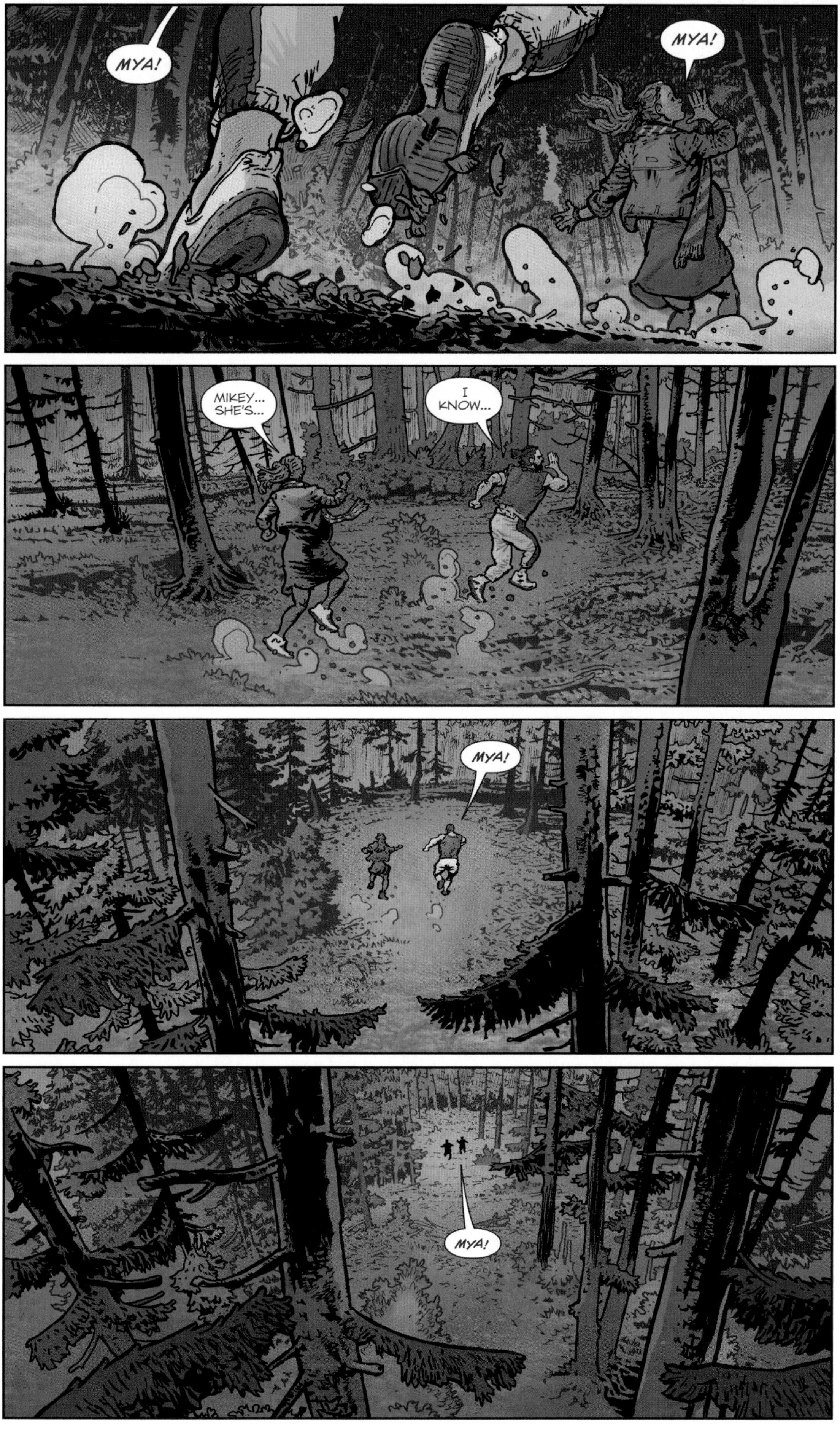
MYA!
MYA!
MIKEY... SHE'S...
I KNOW...
MYA!
MYA!

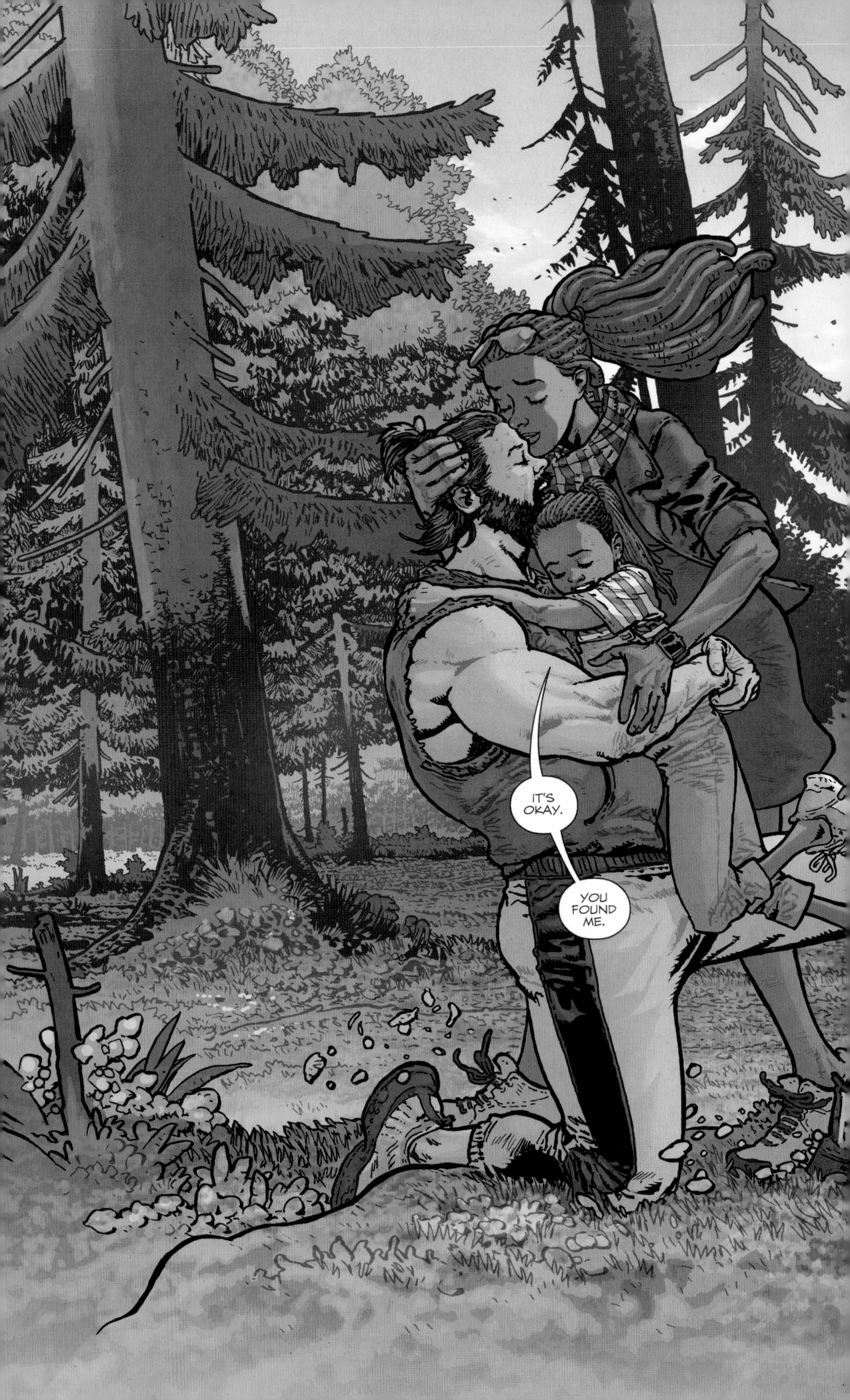
IT'S OKAY.
YOU FOUND ME.

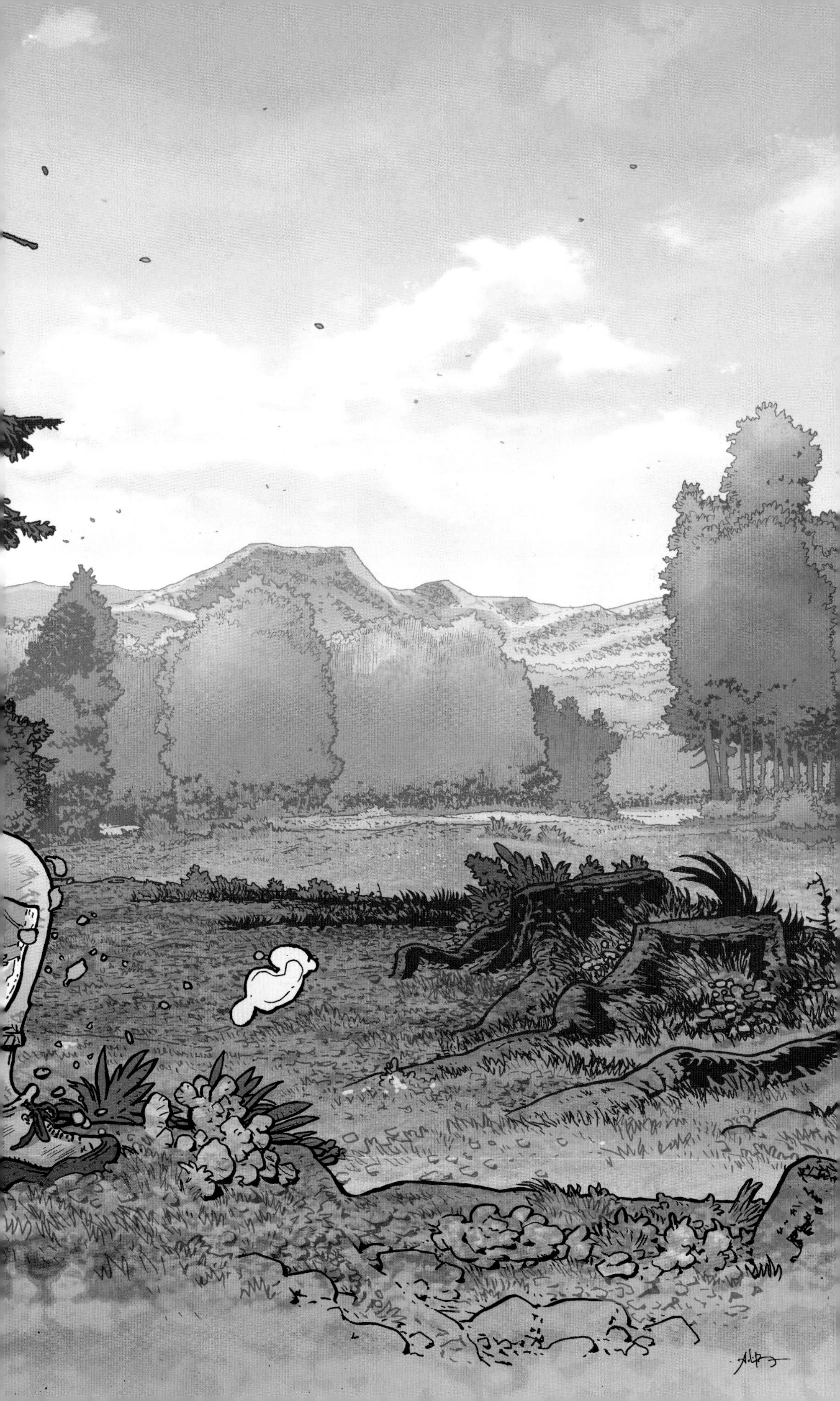

THE

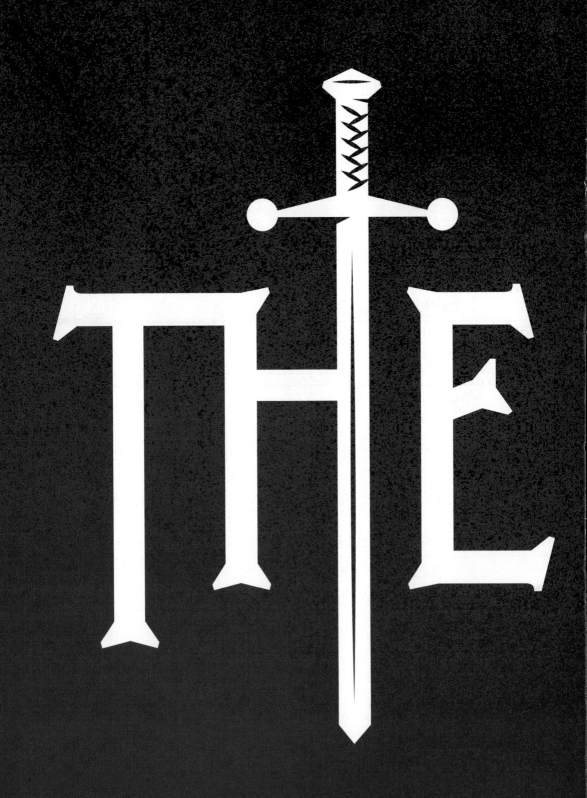

END

Life is funny. And it's funny how much of life is tied to this series.

2007 feels like a long lifetime ago, but that's the year I had the idea for BIRTHRIGHT. I was obsessed with ideas about destiny and faith. But the idea I had then wasn't fully formed. Uncooked. Just thoughts in a notebook that I tried to flesh out, but then I could never land it. It was too dark at times. Just not there. So I put in aside for another day.

Then I got divorced.

The life I had was hit with a curveball. I had to build a new life with a new future. It forced me to rethink a lot of the plans I had. And then it made me take another look at BIRTHRIGHT. I started to think a lot about how much stories and destiny can change. How you think you know what your life is, and then suddenly something will come along that changes everything. Sometimes it's something tragic. Sometimes it's something amazing.

A few years after the divorce, I met someone else. And it was great from Day One. I started to build a new life. It was unexpected and different and better from the life I had before.

And right around this time was when I finally figured out the BIRTHRIGHT story. The pieces that were missing finally came to me, and I found the story I wanted to tell. And then it got picked up by Skybound. It's wild to me to think about how much my life and the changes it's gone through have reflected this series. How Mikey and I both built new lives together. And that's what the series has always been about.

It's been about change. And now change can be scary, but can also lead to your best life. It's about how life can take a sudden turn, and how you have to find your footing again. But it's best to keep moving and work with those changes to find a new life. That's the journey I was on…and so was Mikey and his family. Until they all go on a new journey!

But this series couldn't happen without a few people…

You- The reader. To all of you that stuck with us since #1. Or found the book along the way. You made my dreams come true. I never would have thought I'd get to tell this story. To tell it in this way. A 50-issue fantasy epic about family seems IMPOSSIBLE. It is. But you made that happen. Buying the series and talking about it, writing us letters about it, kept it alive this whole time, and for that I forever grateful to you.

Andrei-The best teammate I could ever ask for. When BIRTHRIGHT was first created, there was no Brennan character. He was added in as we fleshed out the story. And just like Mikey gained a brother in BIRTHRIGHT, so did I. Andrei is my brother, and I'm so thankful we got to go on this journey together. Thank you for always meeting the challenges of this series. To helping me become a better writer. Every time a page would come in from you, I'd learn something about my writing, and it pushed me to find myself. We'll work together again, soon. WINK WINK.

Adriano-There is no one that can color scenic vistas the way Adriano does. The best sunsets in the biz! If Andrei is the heart of the series, Adriano is the soul. His colors wowed me with every issue, and just like Andrei, pushed me to find cooler ideas for him to color. But it was times I'd just stare at his colors and find a kind of calm that helped me keep perspective on the series. Thank you for always doing that.

Pat-Every issue, Pat brought the book to life. Finding room for my wordy ass, and hand-drawing so many great sound effects into the series. Pat made it all look so effortless. Thank you for your amazing work. And for all my last-minute lettering changes.

Sean- Last issue Sean told the part of the story of how I pitched the series at Wonder Con 2013. And how we went to Disneyland to figure out the rest of the story and the ending.

But way back on that Wonder Con floor… Sean and I had only been working together since August 2012 when he took over editing GHOSTED, but it was in that walk around the con floor that I think we became friends. So when I pitched Sean BIRTHRIGHT, I wasn't trying to pitch him as my editor. I was just telling my friend an idea I had for a story. Maybe something about that made it feel more pure or relaxed. More…real? But Sean understood was I was going for. This impossible story that I had to tell. So, a few weeks after that…I was taking a nap. Just passed out on the couch after a big lunch in the middle of the day. Then I got a call. It was Sean telling me he pitched the book to Skybound, and they were excited about it and had an offer. It was nuts. It was everything I wanted. I said yes on the spot and then came to the Skybound offices for a few days to work it all out. Sean had my back from Day One. He supported and championed the series in more ways than one. The bottom line is that the series would not exist if not for him. And I was right…we did become friends! A close friend in the industry that I want to work with forever… or, y'know, just walk around a con floor with.

Robert Kirkman, David Alpert and the rest of Skybound- Thank you for believing in this series and for supporting it the last few years. We went 50 issues! (Holy crap!) And that is because of your belief in it.

Now for the mushy stuff. I want to thank my wife. The woman I met when I started to figure out BIRTHRIGHT. Meeting her changed my life forever. She is my best friend and the love of my life. And now the mother of my two wonderful children. I have the great life I have because of her. She helped shape me as a person, and a writer. Without her, I wouldn't have had the great life I have, but also the end to the happy ending to the BIRTHRIGHT story.

I know I've written a lot here. More than I intended. But maybe it's hard to say goodbye. I've had these characters in my head for years and I don't want to let go yet…But this series taught me how change is good. Just like Mikey can leave behind Terrenos and the life he had before, I can leave BIRTHRIGHT behind me. It will always be a part of my life and who I am as a writer, and a person. So this is not the end.

Thank you for going on this journey with us. Now to the next one!

Joshua Williamson
Portland, OR

Only now did I realize I had a Nevermind myself!

Haha, so true. Even when I wasn't working on BIRTHRIGHT, I was actually working on BIRTHRIGHT. Thinking about characters, references, meaning, and design... I have lived these pages for all of these years.

Seriously, this comic never left my head. I really loved this book from the start! Skybound was all I wanted out of a comic book experience. It feels so much like a dance, each issue having the chance to drive the rhythm of the story and my life. Easily, I am a lucky dude!

I'm still having an "end of the series hangover", but what a blast it is to actually land this ending! 50 issues! And I have to thank all of you who stand here with us, waiting as we cross over from Terrenos's portal for a last time. You people made it possible!

It's been a pleasure, my friends! Now, I can't wait to join my packmates again to embark on the next adventure to come! AHWOOOOOOOOO!

Andrei Bressan
Piracicaba, Brazil

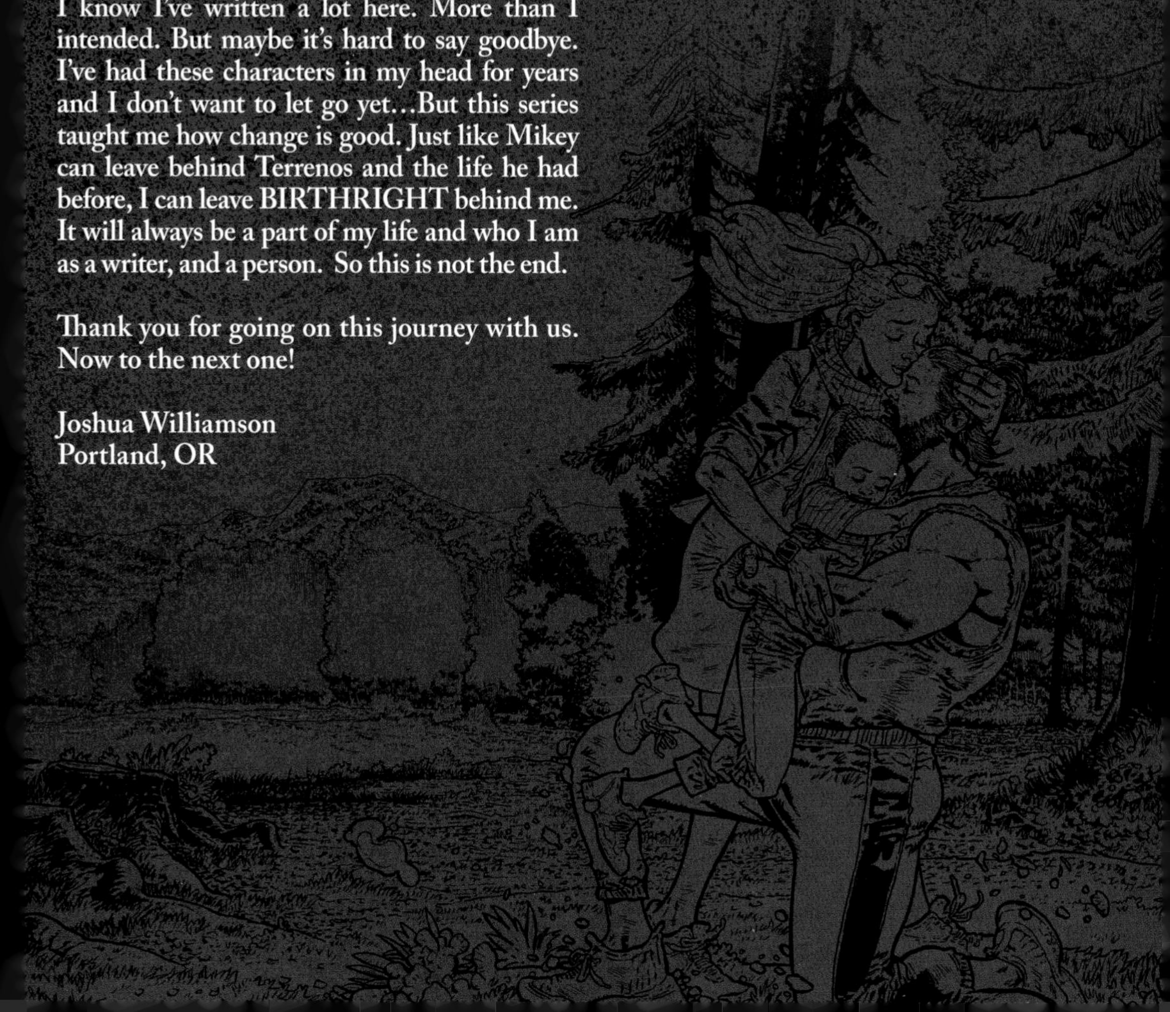

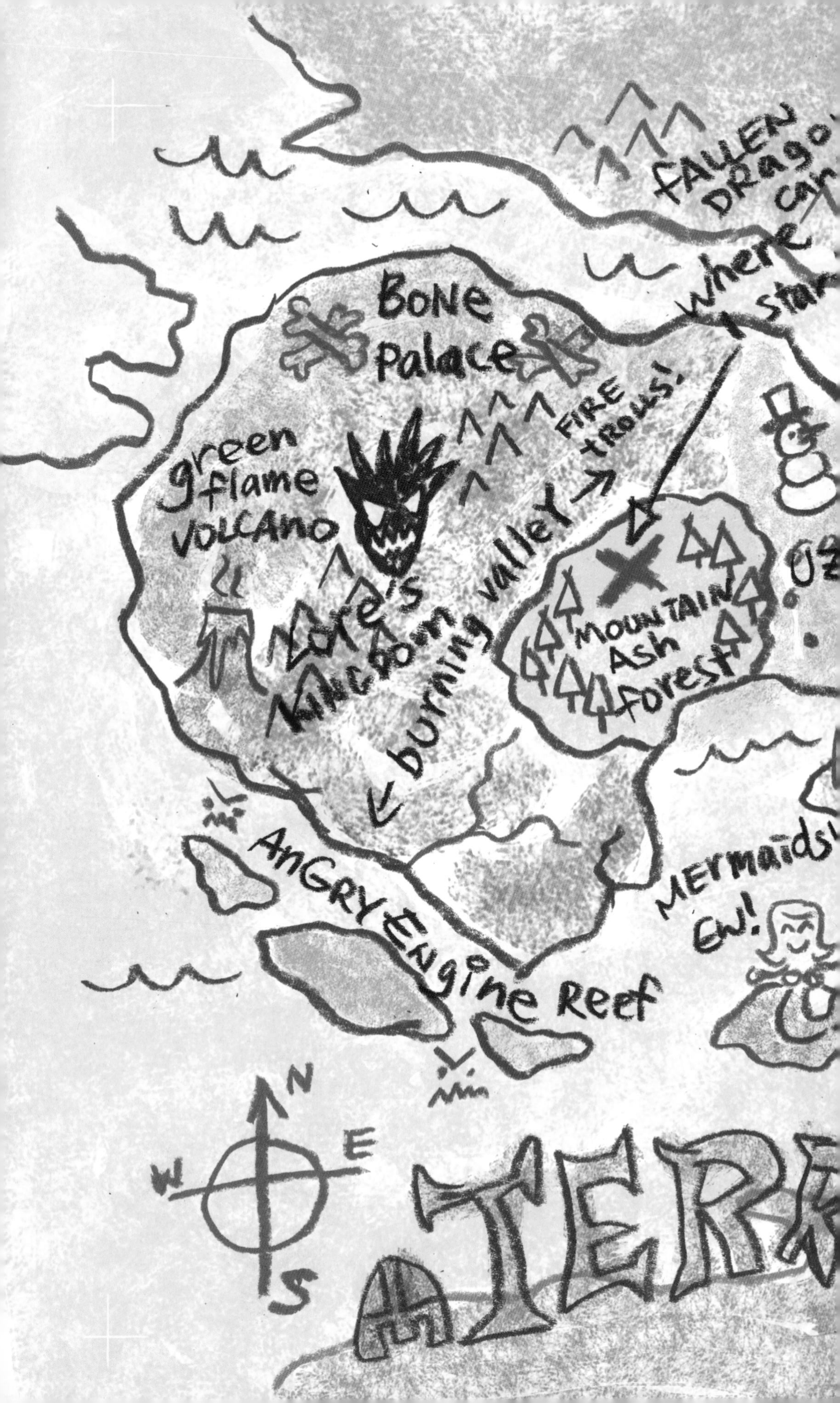

FALLEN
DRAGO
where
car
star
BONE
Palace
FIRE
TROLLS!
green
flame
VOLCANO
Lore's
KINGDOM
burning valley
MOUNTAIN
Ash
forest
OZ
AnGRY Engine Reef
MERMAIDS!
Ew!
N
E
W
S
TERR

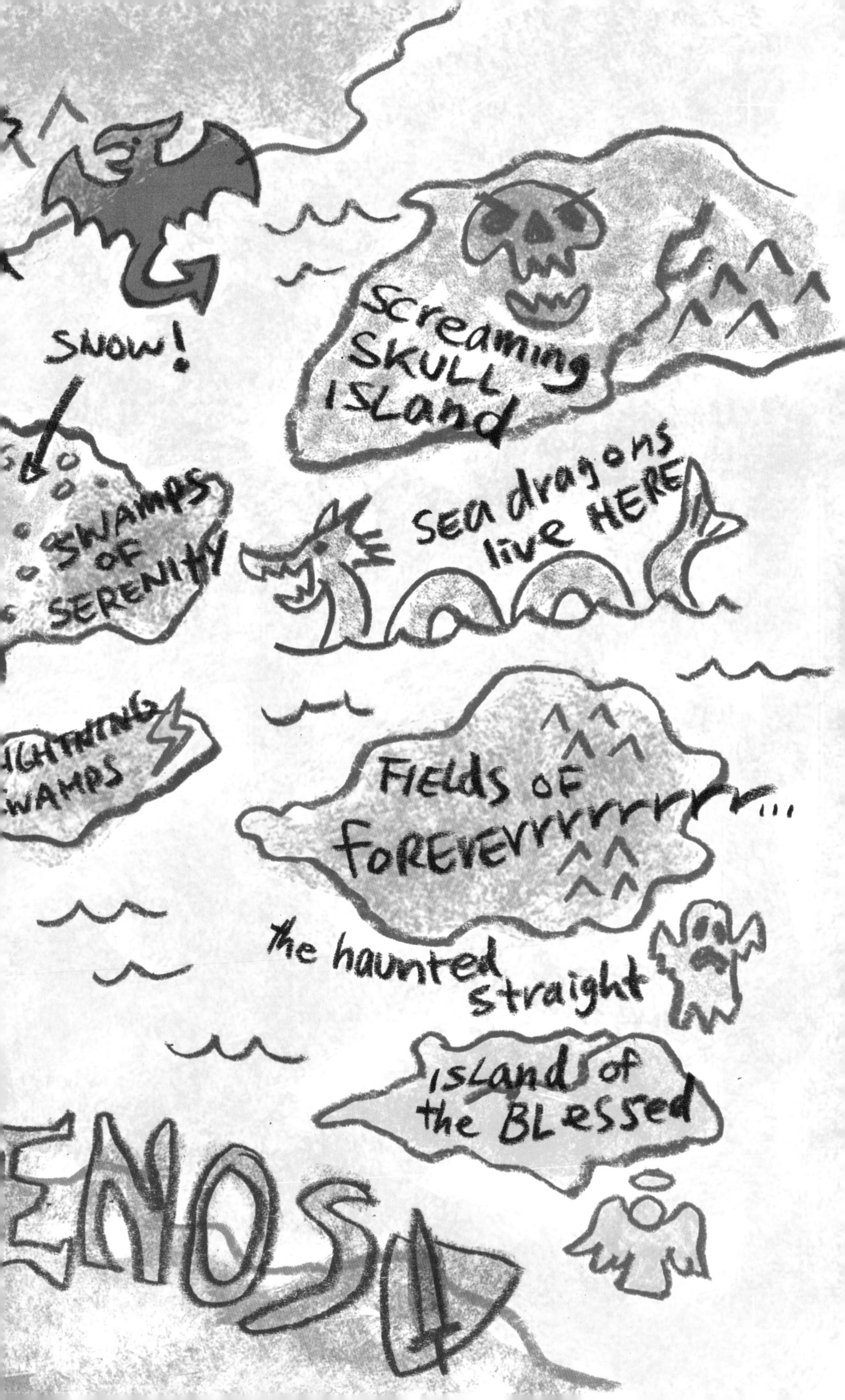

SNOW!
Screaming SKULL ISLand
SWAMPS OF SERENITY
Sea dragons live HERE
LIGHTNING SWAMPS
FIELDS OF foREverrrrrrrr...
the haunted straight
ISLand of the BLessed

For more tales from ROBERT KIRKMAN and SKYBOUND

OUTER DARKNESS
JOHN LAYMAN
AFU CHAN
ROB GUILLORY
CHEW
FUSION CUISINE

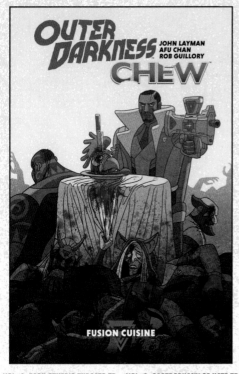

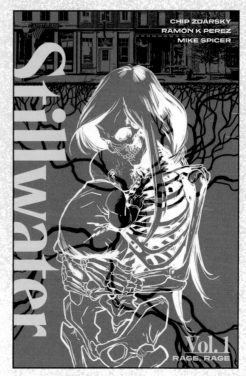

VOL. 1: EACH OTHER'S THROATS TP
ISBN: 978-1-5343-1210-4
$16.99

VOL. 2: CASTROPHANY OF HATE TP
ISBN:978-1-5343-1370-5
$16.99

OUTER DARKNESS/CHEW: FUSION CUISINE TP
ISBN: 978-1-5343-1657-7
$12.99

CHIP ZDARSKY
RAMON K PEREZ
MIKE SPICER
Stillwater
Vol. 1
RAGE, RAGE

VOL. 1: RAGE, RAGE TP
ISBN: 978-1-5343-1837-3
$16.99

BRANDON THOMAS
KHARY RANDOLPH
EMILIO LOPEZ
EXCELLENCE
VOLUME TWO
THE PRESENT TENSE

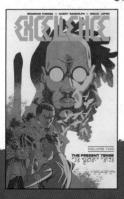

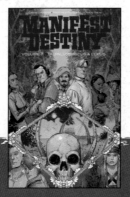

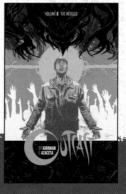

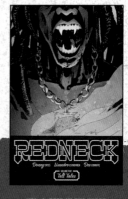

VOL. 1: KILL THE PAST TP
ISBN: 978-1-5343-1362-0
$16.99

VOL. 2: THE PRESENT TENSE TP
ISBN: 978-1-5343-1862-5
$16.99

MANIFEST DESTINY
VOLUME 7 TALPA LUMBRICUS & LEPUS

VOL. 1: FLORA & FAUNA TP
ISBN: 978-1-60706-982-9
$9.99

VOL. 2: AMPHIBIA & INSECTA TP
ISBN: 978-1-63215-052-3
$14.99

VOL. 3: CHIROPTERA & CARNIFORMAVES TP
ISBN: 978-1-63215-397-5
$14.99

VOL. 4: SASQUATCH TP
ISBN: 978-1-63215-890-1
$14.99

VOL. 5: MNEMOPHOBIA & CHRONOPHOBIA TP
ISBN: 978-1-5343-0230-3
$16.99

VOL. 6: FORTIS & INVISIBILIA TP
ISBN: 978-1-5343-0513-7
$16.99

VOL. 7: TALPA LUMBRICUS & LEPUS TP
ISBN: 978-1-5343-1589-1
$16.99

VOLUME 8 THE MERGED
BY KIRKMAN & AZACETA
OUTCAST

VOL. 1: A DARKNESS SURROUNDS HIM TP
ISBN: 978-1-63215-053-0
$9.99

VOL. 2: A VAST AND UNENDING RUIN TP
ISBN: 978-1-63215-448-4
$14.99

VOL. 3: THIS LITTLE LIGHT TP
ISBN: 978-1-63215-693-8
$14.99

VOL. 4: UNDER DEVIL'S WING TP
ISBN: 978-1-5343-0050-7
$14.99

VOL. 5: THE NEW PATH TP
ISBN: 978-1-5343-0249-5
$16.99

VOL. 6: INVASION TP
ISBN: 978-1-5343-0751-3
$16.99

VOL. 7: THE DARKNESS GROWS TP
ISBN: 978-1-5343-1239-5
$16.99

VOL. 8: THE MERGED TP
ISBN: 978-1-5343-1604-1
$16.99

REDNECK
Donny Cates
Lisandro Estherren
Dee Cunniffe
VOLUME FIVE
Tall Tales

VOL. 1: DEEP IN THE HEART
ISBN: 978-1-5343-0331-7
$16.99

VOL. 2: EYES UPON YOU
ISBN: 978-1-5343-0665-3
$16.99

VOL. 3: LONGHORNS
ISBN: 978-1-5343-1050-6
$16.99

VOL. 4: LONE STAR
ISBN: 978-1-5343-1367-5
$16.99

VOL. 5: TALL TALES
ISBN: 978-1-5343-1609-6
$16.99